# The
# Rose Red
# Bride

~

ALSO BY CLAIRE DELACROIX

*The Rogue*
*The Scoundrel*
*The Warrior*
*The Beauty Bride*

# The Rose Red Bride

## CLAIRE DELACROIX

**WARNER BOOKS**

NEW YORK   BOSTON

*Cover design by Tony Russo*
*Book design by Giorgetta Bell McRee*

Warner Books

Time Warner Book Group
1271 Avenue of the Americas
New York, NY 10020
Visit our Web site at www.twbookmark.com

Printed in the United States of America

First Paperback Printing: June 2005

10 9 8 7 6 5 4 3 2 1

*This trilogy is dedicated to my readers,*
*with heartfelt thanks for your loyalty and support.*
*May you enjoy reading about the Jewels of Kinfairlie*
*as much as I have enjoyed recounting their tales.*

# The Rose Red Bride

# Chapter One

*Kinfairlie, on the east coast of Scotland—August 1421*

ALEXANDER CONGRATULATED HIMSELF upon a matter well concluded. Although the marriage of his eldest sister Madeline had not begun auspiciously, his solution had ultimately proven to be a good one. Just as he had predicted, Madeline was wedded and happily so, all the more content for the babe already rounding her belly. Though Alexander had not located Rhys FitzHenry by any conventional means of matchmaking, the man who had bought Madeline's hand at auction had proven to be an excellent spouse.

All had ended well, and Alexander was inclined to grant himself credit for that happy fact. A man had to find encouragement where he could. There was little else that stood to Alexander's credit at Kinfairlie and he often felt overwhelmed by the burden of his hereditary holding.

Alexander stared out the window at Kinfairlie's fields, frowning that they were not more lushly green. The crop was slightly better than his castellan had predicted, but not sufficiently abundant. Though his sister Madeline was wedded, his brother Malcolm was training at Ravensmuir, and his other brother Ross was training at Inverfyre, there remained four unwed sisters for whom Alexander was responsible. The castellan had been firm in his counsel that there must be fewer mouths at the board for the winter.

The fields offered a telling reminder. Alexander would still have to see his sister Vivienne, the next eldest after Madeline, married before the snow flew.

Sadly, Vivienne was not proving to be any easier to wed than her elder sister Madeline had been. Vivienne was willing to wed, but she wished to feel affection for her spouse before her nuptials were celebrated. Indeed, she wished to be in love. Alexander was certain they had visited every man in Christendom to no avail. He might well roar if Vivienne met his gaze and gave that minute shake of her head one more time.

Though Alexander would prefer for Vivienne to be happy, August was already upon them. Soon he would be compelled to take matters into his own hands.

Alexander sighed and buried himself in the accounts of the estate, hoping to discover that matters were slightly better than he knew them to be. He did not have sufficient time to become bored with the tedium of checking tallies before a rap sounded upon the wooden portal.

Anthony, Kinfairlie's elderly castellan, entered the chamber and cleared his throat when Alexander did not immediately respond. "A gentleman to see you, my lord. He begs an audience in privacy at your earliest convenience."

Alexander was intrigued, for guests seldom arrived unbidden at Kinfairlie and even less frequently insisted upon privacy. "Has he a name?"

"Nicholas Sinclair, my lord." Anthony sniffed as Alexander started in surprise at the familiar name. "I am dubious of his character, my lord. No man of merit whispers his name and hides his face within the shadows of his hood."

Alexander sat back in astonishment. "But Nicholas Sinclair was the very man who courted Vivienne some years ago!"

Anthony straightened in disapproval. "I believe as much, sir, though the Sinclair men are rogues indistinguishable each from the other. They are said to be of Viking lineage, my lord, which gives them little credit." He apparently noted Alexander's interest in this new arrival and cleared his throat again. "Although I admit that is solely my own opinion, sir. There are those, often women, I have heard, who find a certain allure in Sinclair men."

What had gone awry between Nicholas and Vivienne? Alexander could not recall. Indeed, he might never have known. He had not paid much attention to Vivienne's loss of a suitor, for in those days, such matters had not been his concern.

"I should be delighted to see Nicholas Sinclair," he said, noting that Anthony was taken aback by his vigor. Alexander smiled, for he had come to enjoy surprising his very proper castellan. "Bring him to me with all haste, if you please, and some ale as well."

"Ale, sir?" Anthony's silver brows rose high. "Are you certain it is wise to make a Sinclair so welcome?"

"Ale, Anthony, to be sure." Alexander spoke with the firmness he had learned to use with his opinionated castellan. "A guest is a guest, no matter his name."

Anthony cast a glance over the accounts, spread over

the table before his liege lord, and his lips pinched yet more tightly. "I would suggest that your affairs not be so displayed, my lord. The Sinclairs have a reputation for coveting what is not their own."

"I have had my fill of the accounts at any rate," Alexander said, then began to put the books away as the castellan left. He rolled scrolls tightly and refastened their ribbons, storing all carefully in a trunk.

The table before him was bare when a tall, cloaked man entered the chamber. The man limped, favoring his left leg, but strode with vigor all the same. As Anthony had noted, the man kept his hood raised, and his face was in shadow.

Alexander turned, his curiosity keen. "Nicholas Sinclair?"

The man nodded curtly. "Good day to you. I thank you for this courtesy." Nicholas offered his hand and Alexander shook it. It was a large hand, tanned and roughened, the hand of a man well familiar with the weight of a blade. Nicholas's grip was no less sure than Alexander might have expected. His manner was purposeful and confident, and Alexander could not help but think that a man resolutely of this world might be a good partner for his sister who loved whimsical tales.

Alexander made to take his seat once more and gestured to the bench opposite. "I confess to a certain curiosity about your arrival here."

The other man pushed back his hood, then sat upon the bench. Alexander struggled to hide his shock. He blinked, he glanced down at his own hands to school his expression. Then he looked his guest squarely in the eyes again.

Nicholas Sinclair watched him shrewdly and Alexander knew that his discomfiture had been noticed. "It was not my intent to startle you," he said, though Alexander suspected this was not perfectly true.

No man could fail to be startled by the scar that ran from temple to chin on the left side of Nicholas's face. It was a puckered angry scar, one so vehement that Alexander was certain he would have remembered if it had been there before, one so angry a red that he suspected it was newly won.

Truth be told, Alexander could not recall Nicholas overwell, though the man looked vaguely familiar beyond the scar. Nicholas was tall enough to tower over Alexander, and was more broad of shoulder. His coloring did hint at some Viking blood in his veins, for his hair was fair and would have fallen straight to his shoulders had it not been tied back with a leather lace. His eyes were a striking, clear blue. He was tanned and muscled, and would have been sufficiently handsome to snare the eye of any maiden, at least before he had gained that scar.

"I apologize, for I am a man of blunt speech," Nicholas said. "I come to make my suit for Vivienne's hand."

Alexander found this man's arrival too convenient to be readily believed. He had learned some caution in arranging the match of Madeline and the hard edge in Nicholas's tone would give any man pause. "I had understood that you and Vivienne had ceased your courtship some years ago."

Nicholas averted his gaze. "Due to my folly alone."

"If you believed as much, then why did you not return sooner?"

"I had no home to offer a bride." If anything, Nicholas looked more grim at this detail.

"I remember this matter now," Alexander said, shaking a finger at his guest as his recollection returned. His father and Vivienne had argued heatedly about the folly of wedding a man who was unlikely to inherit property. Though Nicholas's name had not been mentioned, Vivienne had defied her father with such spirit that all had known the question to be of import to her.

And if memory served Alexander well, the ardent Nicholas had disappeared from Kinfairlie shortly thereafter. He nodded at his guest. "You had an older brother who would inherit afore you, did you not? Erik was his name."

A shadow touched the other man's features. "Erik Sinclair was disavowed. Nicholas stands laird of the Sinclair lands at Blackleith now."

There was no shortage of bitterness in the guest's tone, and though Alexander thought his reference to himself was oddly stated, there was no denying the lilt of the Highlands in his guest's voice. Perhaps the man was less accustomed to speaking English than Gaelic, and in Gaelic, the statement would have passed unnoticed.

Alexander's gaze strayed unwillingly to the other man's scar and he wondered what had passed between the brothers to cause such a disavowal and such bitterness. There was no good way to inquire after such a delicate matter, and what difference truly, if Alexander could ensure that Vivienne wed the man she desired and lived comfortably as well?

If the courtship had ended because of Nicholas's lack of an inheritance, she would certainly be delighted to wed him now that he possessed one.

In fact, a lingering affection for this very man might be the reason that she found no other suitor appealing. Madeline had certainly had a similar reason for finding all suitors lacking, and Alexander was striving to learn as much as he could with regards to understanding and pleasing his sisters.

He had three more to see wed after Vivienne, after all.

Nicholas continued with determination. "It is time I claim a bride and my choice is Vivienne."

Alexander found his reservations melting. This man had faced formidable obstacles, it was clear, and still he was wounded by whatever had riven his family. He could well imagine that Nicholas had never forgotten Vivienne, for though she was his own sister, he was well aware of her abundant charm. Her merry manner and optimism might be just the balm this man needed.

Perhaps his affection for Vivienne had been the one hope that had sustained him in the face of such trials.

The more Alexander considered the match, the more he liked its prospect. He asked after the revenue of Black-leith and its location, as a matter of responsibility, though such details were of less importance than his sister's happiness. He was reassured that Nicholas seemed to know fully the details of his holding, the number of tenants and amount of land, the annual tithes and what was yet to be done. Here was a responsible baron, to be sure.

"You need not doubt the weight of my purse," Nicholas said in conclusion. He removed a sack that jingled as he set it upon the table. He shoved it across the expanse of wood toward Alexander. "And I am prepared to show compense to you for seeing my suit successful in short order."

Alexander stared at the sack of coins, guessing that Kinfairlie's salvation was within it. He lifted the sack, as if less concerned with its contents than he was, and peered inside. His heart leapt at the quantity of silver coin, though he kept his features impassive. This would see them all through the winter, and let him take his leisure in wedding his three younger sisters.

"You seem anxious for haste," he said, noting the sole detail that troubled him. *An honest man has no need to rush,* Alexander's father had often said, and Nicholas's urgency made him suspicious.

"What man would not desire speed when the yearning of his heart is clear?" Nicholas smiled, though his lips seemed so unfamiliar with forming that curve that it looked more like a grimace. "I grow no younger. I have dallied overlong over this matter and would see it resolved. A man must seize the moment when the Fates favor his course."

"You have a scheme." Alexander did not let his hand close over the coin, not yet.

"I would not linger over banns and betrothals."

"What then?"

Nicholas frowned, then leaned forward, bracing his elbows upon the table. His eyes shone a vehement blue, which told Alexander the vigor of his intent. "I would capture my intended in the night, consummate our match, then be wed in the morning."

Alexander put the coin down on the board with force and pushed it back toward the other man. It slid across the polished wood until Nicholas caught it. "It is vulgar to steal a bride! Though others condone kidnapping and rape as expedient, it will not be done at Kinfairlie!"

"This course is a necessary one."

"No man of honor refuses to court his bride."

Nicholas leaned back, touched the wound upon his own face with a fingertip, and said no more.

"The Lammergeier wed," Alexander insisted, fearing

that Nicholas offered some pagan convention instead of marriage. "We exchange our vows honorably and before witnesses."

"I fully intend to wed Vivienne as you suggest. I would merely celebrate the nuptial night before making those vows."

Alexander understood that the other man feared that his injury would repel his intended, but still he was troubled. One heard of such arrangements, though usually the maiden was seduced because her father protested the match. "Why such need for haste?"

Nicholas's lips tightened to a harsh line. "My cousin means to contest my suzerainty of Blackleith on the basis that I have no bride. I have need of a wife and a son, I have need of both soon, and I choose Vivienne." He looked Alexander in the eye. "There is no time to delay, for a babe is not brought to light in a night and a day. I desire to wed Vivienne, and I desire to ensure that she cannot deny my suit because of my wound." He cast the sack of coin back across the table and Alexander caught it.

This time, Alexander let his fingers close over the hard coins. Though he did not like the means, he could find no fault with the end result. And he guessed that if he declined Nicholas's plan, the man would leave Kinfairlie and find another bride.

Alexander could not so disappoint Vivienne. He knew that if ever there was a woman who could look beyond a man's face to his heart, it was his sister Vivienne. And he guessed that the reason she found favor with no other suitor was that this was the man she wished to wed.

"It is Thursday," Alexander said thoughtfully. "And it would be inappropriate for a wedding to be celebrated on a Friday, despite your desire for haste, for that day is meant for penance. Let your meeting with Vivienne be tomorrow night, then, and your nuptial vows be exchanged immediately afterward on Saturday morning. Saturday nuptials are a good omen for future happiness, after all. I will ensure that Vivienne sleeps alone in the highest chamber of the tower."

"How?"

Alexander smiled, knowing precisely the tale he would tell to encourage his sister to do his will of her own volition. "Leave the matter to me. She will be there. I insist only that you grant her every courtesy due to a lady."

His guest inclined his head in agreement. "The wall of your tower faces the sea, and there are windows at the summit."

"Three large windows are there, and they all lead to that chamber. You will have to scale the wall, to be sure, and it was wrought smooth purposely to challenge such a feat," Alexander said. "Surely your desire is sufficient for you to succeed at such a test of valor?"

Nicholas's eyes narrowed as he considered this scheme. He looked suddenly dangerous and disreputable, a man untroubled by the prospect of scaling a wall to seduce his bride.

But then, Vivienne adored old tales. If her true love made such an effort to win her hand, doubtless she would be charmed. Alexander was reassured that Nicholas understood Vivienne so well.

"And the sentries?" Nicholas asked, resolute as he began to rise to his feet.

Alexander mused for a moment, then knew what he would do. "I can ensure that they look away, though their inattention will not last long. Move with haste when the bell on the village church tolls at midnight."

Nicholas nodded and drew his hood over his head once more. He shook Alexander's hand with vigor. "I thank you for your aid in this. You cannot guess its import to me."

"Be warned that I will have your hide if you fail to treat my sister with honor."

The men exchanged a steely glance, then Nicholas turned away, his cloak flaring behind him. By the time Anthony returned with two mugs of ale, Alexander's guest was gone.

VIVIENNE WAS POSSESSED of a new restlessness since her return from Madeline's new abode at Caerwyn. It was more than the rigor of routine after the adventure of pursuing Madeline and Rhys clear across England with several of her siblings. It was more than missing Madeline, though they two had shared more secrets with each other than with their other sisters.

It was the smile that Madeline had gained upon her journey that was at root of Vivienne's dissatisfaction. It was a curious smile, both content and teasing, a smile that Madeline bestowed upon her husband in the most unexpected moments, a smile that claimed Madeline's lips when her hand stole over the curve of her belly, a smile that turned mysterious when Vivienne asked about matters abed.

It was a smile that haunted Vivienne, even after she was no longer in her sister's presence. Madeline knew something—and Vivienne had a fair guess what that something involved—that Vivienne did not. That created a new gulf between the sisters, one wider than the distance that separated them.

Vivienne had never been one to take well to mysteries or matters left undiscussed. She had never been able to keep a secret and usually failed to surprise her siblings, for she could not refrain from sharing the details of any scheme or gift in advance. And she had never had any capacity for patience.

She wanted to know what Madeline knew and she wanted to know immediately, if not sooner.

Vivienne knew that Alexander wished to see her wed, as well, and she was willing to make vows before the altar. She wanted, however, to pledge herself to a man she loved, as maidens and knights loved in her favored tales.

There were not so many women who smiled as Madeline did. Vivienne aimed to be one of them. She had attended every social event of which she heard tell, she had begged Alexander to accompany her to York and to Edinburgh and to Newcastle, she had met every eligible man with optimism.

To no avail. Not a one of them had made her yearn to know more about him. Indeed, Vivienne felt little but desperation. She knew that Alexander would not be patient forever—after all, she had already seen twenty-one summers. Time and the right to choose were slipping away from her, like sand flowing through a glass.

Surely Vivienne, who loved happy tales so well, could not be destined to be live her days unhappily?

Vivienne had a certainty that there were critical moments of choice in each person's life, moments which led irrevocably from the most minute decision to events of great import. The moment her parents had chosen to buy passage upon a specific ship had been a decision of enormous consequence. Once they had boarded the ship and set sail, there had been little or nothing they could have done to avoid the sinking of that ship and the loss of their lives.

The moment in which Madeline had chosen to flee her betrothed, Rhys, had been another of those choices, albeit one which had set a happier sequence of events in motion. Vivienne knew that there must be one such moment in her own life, but as the days passed and no man caught her eye, she began to fear that she had missed her chance.

What if marital happiness could only be found by women like Madeline? As her elder sister, Madeline had always marked an impossible standard for Vivienne to meet. Not only did Madeline do every deed first, but her nature had always been more calm than Vivienne's own. Madeline was less inclined to make impulsive choices than Vivienne, and seldom had any reason to apologize to another member of the family.

Worse, Madeline had always been impeccably groomed. Her hair remained in its braid, her veil never slipped, her hem never tore. Vivienne was plagued by all three flaws, her unruly hair alone prompting sighs from every maid who had ever been compelled to serve her. Madeline had never lost a glove or a shoe or a stocking, while Vivienne had lost so many that the odds often made new pairs. Madeline had been the echo of their mother, composed even as a child, while Vivienne looked unkempt no matter how hard she tried.

Could it be that love was only for those women as composed as Madeline and their mother, Catherine? What if men only found tidy women alluring? The prospect was terrifying to Vivienne.

Hope is a potent elixir, especially for those such as Vivienne, who have drunk heartily from its cup, but even Vivienne's hope began to waver as August evenings took winter's chill.

If only she still had the chance to make her choice!

AS A RESULT OF THIS FRETTING, Vivienne had so little appetite at the board on Friday night that her mood did not escape notice. Even the absence of Ross and Malcolm had not diminished the teasing between the siblings who remained at Kinfairlie, and Vivienne was convinced that her three younger sisters had vision like hawks.

"Do you not want your fish?" Isabella demanded. Already as tall as Vivienne, Isabella had recently begun to grow with vigor, and her appetite showed similar might. "The sauce is quite delicious. I could eat another piece, if you intend to waste it."

Vivienne pushed her trencher toward her sister. "Consider it your own." Isabella attacked the fish with such enthusiasm that she might not have eaten for a week.

"Did you not like it?" quiet Annelise asked, her concern evident. Annelise was the next youngest sister after Vivienne, the two absent brothers between them in age. "I suggested to the cook that she use dill in the sauce, as it would be a change. It was not my intent to displease you."

"The sauce is delicious, as Isabella said," Vivienne said with a smile. "I am not hungry this evening, that is all."

"Are you ill?" Elizabeth, the youngest of them all, asked.

Vivienne fought her frustration as every soul in the hall turned a compassionate gaze upon her. Nothing escaped comment in this household! "I am well enough." She shrugged, knowing they would not look away until she granted a reason for her mood. "I simply miss Madeline."

The sisters sighed as one and stared down at their trenchers. Even Isabella ceased to eat for a moment.

"Perhaps you have need of a tale," Alexander said with such heartiness that Vivienne was immediately suspicious. Their eldest brother, now Laird of Kinfairlie, had played so many pranks upon his sisters over the years that any gesture of goodwill from him prompted wariness.

"He will tell you of the sad fate of a maiden who refused to wed at her brother's dictate," Elizabeth said darkly.

"At least Malcolm and Ross are not here to aid in whatever jest Alexander might plan," Isabella said. The maid that the girls shared clucked her tongue, as Isabella had spoken around a mouthful of fish.

"Ross will be home from Inverfyre at Christmas," Alexander said heartily. "Doubtless he will bring greetings from our uncle's abode."

"Malcolm is too studious to venture the short distance from Ravensmuir, even to visit us," Elizabeth complained.

"Uncle Tynan is a demanding tutor," Alexander said quietly. "You may be certain that Malcolm is too exhausted each night to think of much beyond better pleasing his lord on the morrow."

Vivienne stole a glance at Alexander, for he seldom spoke of his experience in earning his spurs beneath Tynan's hand. He snared her gaze and granted her such a winning smile that she blinked. "What do you desire of me, that you would so court my favor?" she asked abruptly.

Alexander laughed. "I desire only to see you smile again, Vivienne. I am not the only one who has noted your sadness in recent weeks."

"Doubtless though you are the only one who thinks a babe in Vivienne's belly and a ring upon her finger would see the matter resolved," Isabella said. The younger sisters rolled their eyes at this notion, their response only making Vivienne feel more alone.

"He will tell a tale of a maiden made joyous by the arrival of her first child," Elizabeth suggested and the sisters giggled at the absurdity of that.

Vivienne did not laugh. She was, after all, the only one who thought Alexander's scheme had some merit.

"You know how much I love a tale," she said to Alexander, sensing that perhaps their motives were as one. "Though I cannot imagine that you know one I do not."

"Ah, but I do, and it is a tale about Kinfairlie itself."

"What is this? And you never told it afore?" Vivienne cried in mock outrage.

Alexander laughed anew. "I but heard it this week, in the village, and have awaited the right moment to share it." He cleared his throat and pushed away his trencher.

He was a finely wrought man, this brother of theirs, and already Vivienne saw the effect of his recent responsibility upon his manner. Alexander thought now before he spoke, and he spoke with new care, considering his words before he cast them among the company. He treated the servants fairly, and his authority was respected. His courts were reputed to be among the most just in the area, his reputation already rivalling that of their father. He stood taller and was more of a man than he had been merely a year past when their parents had died.

Her younger sisters, however, were less enamored of the change in him. Once Alexander had been the favored playmate of all, and Vivienne knew that her youngest sister Elizabeth, in particular, resented Alexander's new role, no less his demands that they all comport themselves with decorum. It was a remarkable change in the one who had been least concerned with proper behavior of all eight siblings.

But Vivienne knew that it had been no small challenge Alexander had faced since the sudden demise of their parents, and she felt a sudden fierce pride in her brother's achievement. She did not doubt that there was much he had resolved or shouldered without ever sharing the fullness of the truth with his siblings.

"You all know of the chamber at the summit of Kinfairlie's tower," Alexander began, at ease with every eye in the hall upon him. "Though you may not know the reason why it stands empty, save for the cobwebs and the wind."

"The door has always been barred," Vivienne said. "Maman refused to cross its threshold."

"It was Papa who had the portal barred," Alexander agreed. "I have only the barest recollection of ever seeing that door open in my childhood. I fancy, given the details of this tale, that it was secured after Madeline's birth, when I was only two summers of age."

The sisters leaned toward Alexander as one. Elizabeth's eyes were shining, for she loved a tale nigh as well as Vivienne. Isabella, who had made short work of the second piece of fish, wiped her lips upon her napkin and laid the linen aside. Annelise sat with her hands folded in her lap, characteristically still, though her avid gaze revealed her interest. Even the servants hovered in the shadows, heeding Alexander's tale.

Alexander propped his elbows on the table, and surveyed his sisters, his eyes twinkling merrily. "Perhaps I should not share the tale with you. It concerns a threat to innocent maidens . . ."

"You must tell us!" Isabella cried.

"Do not tease us with a part of the tale!" Vivienne said.

"What manner of threat, Alexander?" Elizabeth asked. "Surely it is our right to know?"

Alexander feigned concern, and frowned sternly at them. "Perhaps you demand the tale because you are not all such innocent maidens as I believe . . ."

"Oh!" The sisters shouted in unison and Alexander grinned with the wickedness they all knew so well. Annelise, who sat on one side of him, swatted him repeatedly on one arm. Elizabeth, on his other side, struck him in the shoulder with such force that he winced. Isabella cast a chunk of bread at him, and it hit him in the brow. Alexander cried out for mercy, laughing all the while.

Vivienne could not help but laugh. "You should know better than to cast such aspersions upon us!" She wagged a finger at him. "And you should know better than to tease us with the promise of a tale."

"I cede. I cede!" Alexander shouted. He straightened his tabard and shoved a hand through his hair, then took a restorative sip of wine.

"You linger overlong in beginning," Elizabeth accused.

"Impatient wenches," Alexander teased, then he

began. "You all know that Kinfairlie was razed to the ground in our great-grandmother's youth." He pinched Elizabeth's cheek and that sister blushed crimson. "You were named for our intrepid forebear, Mary Elise of Kinfairlie."

"And the holding was returned by the crown to Ysabella, who had wed Merlyn Lammergeier, Laird of Ravensmuir," Vivienne prompted, for she knew this bit of their history. "Roland, our father, was the son of Merlyn and Ysabella, and the brother of Tynan, their elder son who now rules Ravensmuir where Malcolm labors to earn his spurs. Our grandfather Merlyn rebuilt Kinfairlie from the very ground, so that Roland could become its laird when he was of age." She rolled her eyes. "Tell us some detail we do not know!"

"And so Kinfairlie's seal passed to Alexander, Roland's eldest son, when Roland and his wife, our mother Catherine, abandoned this earth," Annelise added quietly. The siblings and the servants all crossed themselves in silence and more than one soul studied the floor in recollection of their recent grief.

"My tale concerns happier times," Alexander said with forced cheer. "For it seems that when Roland and Catherine came to Kinfairlie newly wedded, there were already tales told about this holding and about that chamber."

"What manner of tales?" Vivienne demanded.

Alexander smiled. "It has long been whispered that Kinfairlie kisses the lip of the realm of fairy."

Elizabeth shivered with delight and nudged Vivienne.

"Nonsense," Isabella muttered, but the sisters elbowed her to silence.

Alexander continued, ignoring them all. "Though Merlyn and Ysabella had not lived overmuch in this hall, there were servants within the walls and a castellan who saw to its administration in their absence.

"And so it was that the castellan had a daughter, a lovely maiden who was most curious. Since there were only servants in the keep, since it was resolved that she could not find much mischief in a place so newly wrought, and since—it must be said—she was possessed of no small measure of charm which she used to win her way—unlike any maidens of *my* acquaintance—" The sisters roared protest, but a grinning Alexander held up a finger for silence. "—this damsel was permitted to wander wheresoever she desired within the walls.

"And so it was that she explored the chamber at the top of the tower. There are three windows in that chamber, from what I have been told, and all of them look toward the sea."

"You can see three windows from the sentry post below," Vivienne said.

Alexander nodded. "Though the view is fine, the chamber is cursed cold, for the openings were wrought too large for glass and the wooden shutters pose no barrier to the wind, especially when a storm is rising. That was why no one had spent much time in the room. This maiden, however, had done so and she had noted that one window did not grant the view that it should have done.

"Clouds crossed the sky in that window, but never were framed by the others. Uncommon birds could be spied only in the one window, and the sea never quite seemed to be the same viewed through that window as through the others. The difference was subtle, and a passing glance would not reveal any discrepancy, but the maiden became convinced that this third window was magical. She wondered whether it looked into the past, or into the future, or into the realm of fairy, or into some other place altogether. And so she resolved that she would discover the truth."

"It was the portal to the fairy realm!" Elizabeth said with excitement.

"There is no such place," Isabella said with a roll of her eyes.

"It is but a tale, Isabella," Annelise chided. "Can you not savor it for what it is?"

Vivienne eased forward on the bench, enthralled by Alexander's tale and impatient to hear more. "What happened?"

"No one knows for certain. The maiden slept in the chamber for several nights and when she was asked what she had seen, she only smiled. She insisted that she had seen nothing, but her smile, her smile hinted at a thousand mysteries."

Vivienne's attention was captured utterly then, for she suspected she knew how that maiden had smiled.

Alexander continued. "And on the morning after she had slept in that chamber for three nights, the damsel could not be found."

"What is this?" Isabella asked.

"She did not come to the board." Alexander shrugged. "The castellan's wife was certain that the girl lingered overlong abed, so she marched up the stairs to chastise her daughter. She found the portal to the chamber closed, and when she opened it, the wind was bitterly cold. She feared then that the girl had become too cold, but she was not in the chamber. The mother went to each window in turn and peered down, fearing that her daughter had fallen to her death, but there was no sign of the girl."

"Someone stole her away," Isabella said, ever pragmatic.

Alexander shook his head. "She was never seen again. But on the sill of one window—I suspect I know which one it was—on the morning of the maiden's disappearance, the castellan's wife found a single rose. It appeared to be red, as red as blood, but as soon as she lifted it in her hands, it began to pale. By the time she carried it to the hall, the rose was white, and no sooner had the castellan seen it, than it began to melt. It was wrought of ice, and in a matter of moments, it was no more than a puddle of water upon the floor."

Alexander rose from his seat and strode to the middle of the hall. He pointed to a spot on the floor, a mark that Vivienne had not noted before. It shimmered, as if stained by some substance that none could have named.

"It was here that the water fell," Alexander said softly. "And when an old woman working in the kitchens spied the mark and heard the tale of the rose, she cried out in dismay. It seems that there is an old tale of fairy lovers claiming mortal brides, that the portal between their world and ours is at Kinfairlie. A fairy suitor can peer through the portal, though they all know they should not, and he could fall in love with a mortal maiden he glimpses there."

Alexander smiled at his sisters. "And the bride price a smitten fairy suitor leaves when he claims that bride for his own is a single red, red rose, a rose that is not truly a rose, but a fairy rose wrought of ice." He scuffed the floor with his toe. "Though its form does not endure, the mark of its magic is never truly lost."

Silence reigned in the hall for a moment, the light from the candles making the mark on the floor seem to glimmer more brightly.

Alexander shrugged. "I cannot imagine that Papa believed the tale, but doubtless once he had a daughter, he had no desire to have her traded for a rose wrought of ice."

"Someone should discover the truth," Isabella said with resolve. "Doubtless some village mischief is behind it."

Annelise shivered. "But what if the tale is true? Who knows where the maiden went? Who would take such a risk as to follow her?"

Vivienne clenched her hands together and held her tongue with an effort. She knew who would take such a risk. She knew, with eerie certainty, that this tale had come to light now because it was a message to her.

Here was the moment she had awaited! A fairy spouse would suit her well, of that she had no doubt, no less the adventure of a life in another realm. Fairies, every sensible person knew, were an unruly and less-than-fastidiously groomed lot. She would fit into their ranks perfectly.

So she resolved: Vivienne would sleep in the tower chamber on this night. She only had to figure out how the feat could be done without rousing the suspicions of her siblings.

# Chapter Two

VIVIENNE'S TASK PROVED to be easier than she had feared.

She sat with her sisters that evening, bending over her needlework and fighting to hide her impatience. They worked upon a large tapestry for the hall, each embroidering a single panel. The completed work would never be so fine as those embroideries brought from France and Belgium, but there was a charm in it being made by the family.

Annelise had created the design, for she was the most deft with a piece of charcoal. Mythical creatures frolicked across the surface, each slowly taking shape with thread and color. Vivienne loved the design and enjoyed working upon it more than she usually enjoyed needlework, but this night she found no pleasure in the task. In fact, her threads seemed to tangle and knot with a will of their own.

The time passed with such slowness that Vivienne thought she might scream, and for once, she envied Alexander the need to retire to review Kinfairlie's ledgers. Vivienne's toe seemed to tap of her own volition.

She tucked her feet under her skirts, hoping no one noticed her restlessness.

"You are making more of a mess of matters than usual, Vivienne," Isabella noted, she who was as orderly as Madeline.

"I have no talent for embroidery, it is clear," Vivienne said.

Isabella claimed the knot of wool thread from Vivienne's restless fingers and set calmly to sorting it, strand by strand. "You have no patience for it," she said, without censure. "That is different."

"Still, you are usually more artful than this," Annelise noted, studying Vivienne with some concern. "Are you unwell?"

Vivienne yawned and rubbed her eyes in answer, as if too exhausted to remain awake, then pretended to struggle to focus on her needlework.

"You do look tired, Vivienne," Isabella said, sounding for all the world like their mother.

"It is not like you to tire so early," Annelise commented. "You are usually the last of us to come to bed."

Vivienne shrugged. "I was tired all this day."

"And you did not eat your dinner," a sharp-eyed Elizabeth reminded them all.

"Perhaps sleep would be best for you," Isabella said. "And morning will find you hale again."

Vivienne set aside her work with apparent reluctance. "I admit the notion has an appeal."

"Go!" Annelise urged. "You can work upon your panel another day."

Isabella smiled. "Needlework awaits our attention most patiently." The other sisters laughed and Vivienne did not require further urging to leave their company.

She climbed the stairs slowly as long as they could see her, so slowly that she might have been having difficulty lifting the weight of her own feet. She heard Isabella tut-tut and smiled to herself, then darted across the floor above to fetch and light a candle. The moon was new, so there would be no light in the chambers above.

Kinfairlie's keep was no more and no less than a single square tower wrought of stone. It was tall, so tall that Vivienne's father had once called it a finger pointing to the heavens, so tall that it could be seen from as far away as their uncle's keep of Ravensmuir.

Kinfairlie had not been rebuilt precisely to the former design after it had been razed to the ground. Curtain walls, for example, were now believed to be too difficult to defend, thus Kinfairlie's surrounding walls had not been rebuilt. The remnants of the old walls yet marked the property, though they were tumbled in places, choked with thorns in others, and had vanished in still others.

Despite this, the keep could be readily defended by a few stout men. There was but one entry to the tower, marked by a portcullis, and a wide wooden door studded with iron. The entry was cunningly designed so that an intruder would be tricked into taking what appeared to be the larger way, though that corridor led only to the dungeon. Once there, the intruder would be trapped and at the mercy of the laird. Further, the corridor that proved to lead to the hall itself offered many opportunities to assault any assailant who managed to pass through that heavily-secured portal.

Above this entry, the tower was simple in design. The interior was marked by a staircase, which wound its way upward, making a quarter turn around the perimeter of the tower for each successive floor. There were four floors in total, the highest one characterized by a sloped ceiling defined by the point of the roof. The banner of Kinfairlie, graced with a glowing orb, fluttered from the pinnacle of the tower.

Vivienne knew the tower and its whispers as well as her own hand. She knew—as she suspected did most of her siblings—which stair could be relied upon to squeak, which corner was dark enough to hide an eavesdropper. She paused on the landing of the second floor, the one above the hall proper, listening for her brother's whereabouts. She strode past the one empty chamber on the second floor, which had once been shared by her brothers, and wondered fleetingly how her two younger brothers fared in their respective training at Ravensmuir and Inverfyre. Did they miss their sisters as much as Vivienne missed them? She passed the larger chamber shared by herself and her sisters, then continued up the staircase.

The next floor constituted the laird's quarters, including a large solar and a small chamber in which Alexander kept the ledgers of the estate. Both rooms could be secured from the stairs and adjacent corridor. From his rooms, the laird could look in three directions over his holding. There was not so much as a candle lit in the lord's solar, though a glimmer of light marked the bottom edge of the portal to the smaller chamber. Vivienne guessed that Alexander was yet at work.

She crept past his door, then continued silently to the top floor of the tower. The staircase emerged in the center of that level, with a chamber on either side beneath the pitched roof. A ladder led to the peak of the roof, a trapdoor there allowing access to the flag. The portal to Vivienne's left was slightly ajar, and she knew the room was full of items that had seemed useful and thus had been saved, only to have been forgotten and abandoned to dust.

The portal to the right was barred and locked. Vivienne had just bent to consider the lock when she heard men's voices behind her. She snuffed her candle and slipped into the protective shadows of the second chamber. The light of a lantern became visible on the walls of the staircase so quickly that she feared she might have been spied. Her nose tickled at the dust she had stirred and she fought the impulse to sneeze.

"The old tale has made me think about this chamber," Alexander said, as if explaining his ascent to another. His shadow was thrown on the wall as he approached and Vivienne eased back into the chamber behind her. "I cannot think why we do not use it."

"Perhaps because you have a houseful of maidens," Anthony suggested, clearly somewhat put out to be called for this errand at this hour.

"It is but a tale! A mere whimsy," Alexander scoffed. He paused then, and sniffed audibly. "Do you smell a snuffed candle?"

Anthony sniffed dutifully while Vivienne fought the twitch of her nose. "It must have carried from the hall, for no one has climbed to these chambers in years."

"Hmm," Alexander said. Vivienne held her breath, certain he would fling open the door of the second chamber and reveal her there. "It must be as you say," he said and she breathed a sigh of relief.

"We should not even be here, my lord," Anthony said.

"And what harm is there?" Alexander demanded. "I would like to at least see the chamber beyond. Perhaps it would be a more cheerful place to study the ledgers."

"If you will forgive my forthright speech, my lord, I

suspect you would spend more time watching the sea, were that distraction available."

Alexander laughed. "Perhaps it would not be all bad to have a distraction from those cursed ledgers. 'Item: one pound of butter, three pounds of leeks, two hens, one laying, all due to the laird at Michaelmas by Cornelius Smith for the share price upon his plot. Paid and witnessed. Item: two shillings owed by the alemaster of Kinfairlie for selling short of the measure on the Feast of the Annunciation, not paid due to a lack of coin before midsummer.'" Vivienne heard the laughter in her brother's voice. "Truly, a man could lose his wits verifying the endless stream of such entries."

"And a man who did not take the time and trouble to do so might well see himself robbed blind," the castellan said stiffly. Vivienne could readily imagine him shaking a finger at Alexander as he scolded. "Your father spent every morning at the ledgers, my lord, and was known far and wide as a just man who could not be cheated."

Alexander heaved a sigh. "So you have told me a thousand times, Anthony. I fear you will never find me fitting my father's measure."

"I can but try, my lord."

Vivienne peeked and found the two men with their backs to her: Anthony held the lantern, which illuminated the tight disapproving line of his lips. He also carried several tools. Alexander bent and peered at the lock. He jingled a brass ring of keys and tried to fit one into the lock.

The castellan cleared his throat. "Do you think this wise, my lord?"

Alexander spared the older man a smile. "Are you not at least curious? This chamber has been locked for more than twenty years. As it is within my suzerainty, it is my right and my duty to explore it."

Anthony sighed.

Alexander tried each key in turn, so many of them not fitting that Vivienne began to lose hope. She felt cobwebs against her cheek and dared not wipe them away lest her movement make a noise. The dust seemed to roil around her and she surreptitiously rubbed her itching nose.

To her delight, the second to last key on Alexander's ring made the tumblers fall audibly.

"Ah!" Alexander stepped back and studied the beams of wood hammered across the portal. Vivienne peered through the slit between door and frame to watch him take a doughty tool from the castellan.

"We could have one of the men from the stable open it on the morrow, my lord. It would not be appropriate for you to injure yourself in such a task."

Alexander laughed. "I am not so old and feeble as that!" He pried the end of one beam away, then removed the others with speed. He cast the beams into the corner opposite the stairs, then grinned. In the light of the lantern, he looked mischievous and unpredictable, as once he had always looked. "What do you think we shall find inside, Anthony?"

The castellan's lips tightened impossibly further. "I could not begin to guess, my lord."

"Then we shall look." Alexander depressed the latch and pushed open the door. A cold wind immediately swirled around Vivienne's ankles and she shivered even as she peered into the darkness of the chamber beyond. The urge to sneeze grew even stronger and she fairly held her breath to vex it.

Alexander claimed the lantern and disappeared into the room, his footfalls loud on the floor.

"It is large!" he said, his voice echoing. "These windows are enormous. No wonder the cost of glass was so high. But the view is a marvel. Come and see!"

The castellan held his ground. "I shall wait until the morrow, my lord."

A chuckle resonated in Alexander's voice. "Surely you cannot be afraid? It is innocent maidens who are said to be in peril of the affections of fairy courtiers."

Anthony sniffed. "Of course I am not afraid, my lord. I am simply cautious."

"There is nothing in here, save an old straw pallet. Do you think it is the one the girl slept upon?"

"I could not begin to speculate, my lord." Anthony drew himself taller. "Indeed, I would suggest that you not touch it, my lord, as it may be filled with vermin."

"Ha! They would be intrepid vermin who managed to climb to this chamber and subsist upon no food at all."

Anthony held his ground, clearly persuaded that such bold vermin did exist and did in fact occupy that chamber.

"And which window, I wonder, is the one at root?" Alexander mused. "Not that there is likely any merit in the tale, of course. This is but a large disused chamber." He appeared on its threshold, beaming with pleasure. "We shall have it cleaned on the morrow. Perhaps I will ask my Uncle Tynan if the price of glass has become less than it was."

Anthony cleared his throat. "If I might remind you, my lord, the treasury of Kinfairlie is not as blessed with coin as it might be."

"It fares better now," Alexander said mysteriously. Vivienne saw only the flash of his smile before he looked

back at the chamber. "Indeed, this will suit very well."
Then he granted Anthony the confident smile which usually made the sisters suspect that he had a scheme. Before Vivienne could wonder at its cause, Alexander strode down the stairs, calling to the elderly castellan to hasten himself.

Vivienne was left alone, opposite the chamber that contained a portal to some other realm. Though she was sorely tempted to enter it immediately, instead she slipped down to the hall again. She complained to her sisters of a fierce chill and summoned a shiver most readily. She loosed her sneeze and her three sisters were quick to pronounce her in need of a hot posset.

Once Vivienne had the steaming cup in her hand, she returned to the sisters' chamber and retrieved her favorite boots. They had been a gift from her Aunt Rosamunde and their red leather was lavishly ornamented with embroidery just below her knees. They were also lined with rabbit fur and very warm. Her finest chemise of sheer linen was an obvious choice, as she wished to impress her fairy lover with her finery. It was cut full and gathered at the neck on a drawstring, as was typical, but was distinguished by sleeves fitted from elbow to wrist and secured with dozens of tiny buttons made of shell.

It was no small feat to don the chemise without the aid of one of her sisters or their maid, but Vivienne managed the deed.

She then donned her favorite kirtle, also a gift from Rosamunde, which was wrought of silk woven in two shades of emerald. The sleeves were slit from the shoulders to reveal the chemise and trailed to the ground, while the hem pooled upon the floor. The hem and neckline and sleeve edges were all graced with intricate golden embroidery. The men in her family had called it a most impractical garment, while her sisters openly coveted it. Vivienne then made a bundle upon her pallet, so that her sisters would think she had burrowed deep into her covers.

For luck, she flung her fur-lined cloak over her shoulders, for Madeline had taken that same cloak and worn it on her adventure. Madeline's journey had ended well, and Vivienne liked the notion of the cloak bringing good fortune to its wearer.

It was always thus in old tales.

As prepared for a quest in the realm of fairy as she could be, Vivienne took her posset and a lantern and climbed the stairs.

The key shone in the lock of the portal where Alexander had left it. The massive door opened with the barest touch of Vivienne's hand; the hinges did not so much as squeal. The chill fingers of the wind swept around her, and the night sky was visible through the three large windows on the opposite wall. Vivienne blew out the flame on her lantern, letting the stars light her path. She had a flint and would save the oil in case she had dire need of the light. She claimed the key from the lock and it seemed colder than cold in her damp palm.

As if the key itself was wrought of the same fairy ice as the rose.

Vivienne took a deep breath and stepped over the threshold. She closed the door behind herself and leaned back against the door. She could hear the sea and smell its salt on the wind, and might have been alone on a precipice. The familiar sounds and smells of the keep were lost behind her, as if she were far above the concerns and realm of mortals. She could easily believe that this was a place between two realms, that this hushed chamber was a threshold to adventure.

Though she considered each of the three windows lingeringly in turn, she could not discern which one was different. In truth, part of the issue was that she could not bring herself to draw near any one of them. Vivienne had never had any tolerance for heights, she had never been able to leap from the tallest step, or jump into the sea with her siblings. She knew the height of this tower too well to risk so much as a single downward glance from its windows.

Vivienne sat down on the pallet, sipped her posset and studied the windows more intently, even as she willed the erratic pace of her heart to slow.

IT WAS A MOONLESS NIGHT, the perfect night for a nefarious deed. The hidden man shifted his weight off his damaged leg by force of habit, ensuring it would be as rested as possible when the moment came to move, and remained still and silent. His scheme was perfectly wrought.

Despite his resolve, guilt pricked at him as he waited. It was not in his nature to deceive, or even to wreak vengeance, though circumstance had driven him to do both.

He had told Alexander the truth, though he had not confessed all of it by any means, and the truth was not all his own. And indeed, not all he had said *was* the truth. He had no ambitious cousin, for example, though his brother was ambitious enough for an entire family. He had no intent of wedding Vivienne before a priest and witnesses on the following morning.

He did, however, have need of a son.

The bells of the chapel in Kinfairlie village rang, then tolled the hour. Midnight. He tensed as he listened, fearful that all might not be as Alexander had pledged.

But it was. A hue and a cry was raised on the far side of the keep, and he heard the sentries race to that point.

With nary a moment to lose, he stepped out of the darkness and flung his grappling hook skyward with practiced ease. It caught and held on the parapet on the first try, and the scratch of its movement across the roof was lost in the din of Alexander's distraction.

He took a deep breath and swung himself into the air, wincing as his left boot collided with the wall. He grit his teeth, ignored the pain, and climbed, his heart thudding with trepidation.

For truly, the most difficult part of his task lay ahead of him. He had seduced no woman but his late wife, and Beatrice had been willing.

Vivienne might not be willing. After all, the man who scaled Kinfairlie's tower, unobserved on that moonless night, was not Nicholas Sinclair.

And the woman he meant to bed and kidnap this night was the only person in Kinfairlie who knew the truth.

THROUGH THE HAZE OF DREAMS, Vivienne heard the bells in Kinfairlie village toll midnight. Her posset had put her to sleep, whether due to its heat or its ingredients, she could not say. She was warm within her cloak and comfortable upon her pallet and she spared only the barest sleepy glance at the windows.

And then he came.

She sensed his presence, like a prickling along her spine. She knew he arrived, knew with a certainty that should have been alarming for its vigor. She turned and opened her eyes and saw his silhouette against the window. He was wreathed in starlight, his fair hair gleaming with an unnatural light.

He had come for her. Vivienne did not dare to breathe.

He paused for a moment, the night sky framing his silhouette within the frame of the window, against the greater darkness of the chamber. She knew his gaze grew accustomed to the shadows; she knew he sought some hint of her location, or even of her presence. He was large, larger than her brothers, larger than any man she had ever met.

She liked that he was tall. Vivienne was tall herself and did not find comfort in standing beside a man shorter than herself. It was petty, to be sure, for a man's measure lay in his spirit, but still she was glad to find her destined partner taller than she. She liked that his shoulders were broad and his hips were lithe. She liked that he was wrought lean but muscular, and she liked the golden glint of his hair.

Nicholas had had blond hair, Nicholas who had so cruelly cast her aside when she refused to surrender her all in exchange for another of his empty promises.

Perhaps she had found Nicholas alluring because she had known her destined lover would have hair like spun flax. Perhaps some knowledge of her fate had led her so close to making a fool of herself.

It did not matter, not any longer.

Vivienne stirred without intending to do so and the straw of the pallet rustled. He pivoted, listening, and she felt the weight of his gaze as keenly as a touch. No doubt he could see clear through to her pounding heart, for fairies were said to have uncommonly keen vision.

No matter, for Vivienne had nothing to hide.

"Vivienne?" he asked, his voice low and rich.

She shivered in delight that he knew her name, that he had anticipated her presence. He must have spied her through the portal between the realms. Her skin tingled with new awareness, her other senses awakened in the darkness that foiled her sight. The night was as velvet against her skin, the fur lining of her cloak was soft against her chin.

"I have awaited you," she whispered, her voice uncommonly hoarse. She reached for the lantern and fairly spilled the oil in her haste, then fumbled with the flint.

He was beside her in the blink of an eye, the warmth of his hand covering her own. "Strike no light on this night," he urged. His hand was strong, far larger than her own, so large that her fingers were fairly swallowed in his grip.

Yet his clasp was gentle. His heat loomed beside her, the scent of his skin making Vivienne's pulse quicken. His thumb slid across the back of her hand in a caress and Vivienne was certain her heart could pound no louder.

"It is the flint and the rasp," she guessed, barely able to reason beneath his disarming touch. In every tale she knew, fairies spurned metal. "You cannot bear its presence, of course."

"It is the light," he murmured. "I would discover you with keener senses than mere sight." And he kissed her then, claimed her lips with a demand that startled her with its vigor. Vivienne gasped and her hand fluttered against his chest.

Of course, he had yearned for her. He had watched her from across the threshold, his passion running higher with each glimpse. She was not a stranger to him, as he was to her. Though she was far from experienced in such deeds, Vivienne opened her mouth beneath his even as she trembled.

And then his manner changed. It was as if her uncertainty had softened his desire, as if her cautious response awakened a tenderness within him. Indeed, he then courted her response. She felt it in his kiss, how he waited for her to become accustomed to the press of him against her, how he waited for her to respond before he deepened his kiss again.

Vivienne was charmed. Only a lover true would command his passion so that his lady was not afraid.

His fingers slipped into her hair, cupping her nape so that he could feast upon her lips. He drew her to her feet and the cloak she had only cast over her shoulders fell to the floor. He caught her against him before she could feel the chill of the night and she heard the thunder of his heart so close to her own.

She felt his other hand trail over her, touching her curves with a feather-light touch, as if he found *her* to be the marvel. Her heart raced when his fingertips trailed down her throat, her nipple beaded when his hand swept over her breast, her belly tightened when his hand rested upon her waist. Something hot and unruly awakened within her, something Vivienne had the wits to recognize as desire. There was dampness between her thighs and hunger in her kiss, and she knew precisely what she desired of him.

It mattered little whether they loved first or wed first, for both would be achieved in time. It could be no other way, for they were intended to be together.

When he broke their embrace, she was breathless but anxious for more of this new pleasure. She thought she could see the glint of his eyes and she smiled at him, wondering whether he smiled back. "That was wondrous," she said.

"More wondrous than any had the right to expect," he said, though Vivienne could not understand fully what he meant. Was lovemaking between destined lovers more potent? He cast off his cloak, letting it swirl in an arc before he cast it across her rough pallet with a graceful gesture.

When he reached for her again, joy rose within Vivienne. She could do naught but acquiesce, for this was the grand passion that she desired beyond all else.

It was Vivienne who stretched to her toes to demand more of him, Vivienne who let her hands cup his face to draw him closer. His jaw was smooth, like that of a mortal man who had just sheared his whiskers. Fairies, Vivienne knew, were eternally young. Perhaps their men did not even have whiskers.

Her questing fingertips found the pulse at his throat, and she was shocked to find it racing as quickly as her own.

"Surely you cannot be afraid of me?" she asked.

He paused, as if regarding her, though Vivienne could not discern his face in the darkness. "How could I have expected such a welcome?" His words were so hoarse that Vivienne felt her breath catch in her throat.

"How could I not welcome you fully?" Vivienne touched her lips to his and revelled in his gasp of surprise. She let her hands slide over him, as he had moved his over her, and knew that she had surprised him once again. He caught her close, and Vivienne let her hands slip into the silky thickness of his hair. She arched against him, bold in her newfound passion, and heard his sharp inhalation.

He whispered something, then caught her up in his arms. He held her captive against his chest for a heady moment, and their kiss left Vivienne dizzy and hot. He knelt on one knee then, with her weight cradled in his lap, and his hand slid beneath the hem of her chemise and kirtle.

Vivienne gasped into his kiss when the warmth of his hand landed upon her knee. His tongue danced with hers, fairly sending sparks along her veins, and Vivienne nigh forgot the weight of his hand.

Then his hand slid up her thigh, his fingertips against her bare flesh, though his kiss did not cease. She gasped when his fingers moved in the heat that none other than herself had ever touched, then she moaned at the sensation. He nibbled at her ear, he kissed her earlobe, he traced a burning path of kisses down her throat, and Vivienne was lost.

The sensations that assaulted her were magical, were surely beyond that savored by mere mortals, were the gift from him to her. Vivienne accepted all he granted and yearned for more.

His fingers moved, tempting, teasing, making Vivienne squirm with desire. He untied the lace of her kirtle and chemise with his teeth, he pushed the fabric aside with his nose and his tongue. His hair fell across Vivienne's skin like a soft curtain, and she moaned as his fingers coaxed her to greater heat with every stroke.

He kissed her pert nipple gently, then laved it with his tongue. Vivienne cried out softly and he chuckled. Vivienne smiled at his delight, then moaned when he suckled her. His fingers dove within her heat in the same moment, his thumb moving against her so surely that she clung to his shoulders. Some tumult rose within her, growing in intensity beneath his embrace. Vivienne rode the crest of desire, uncertain where it led.

And suddenly, a thousand lights flashed in her mind's eye, a heat of pleasure raged through her, singing her from temple to toes. Vivienne cried out in pleasure at this new sensation, until he swallowed her shout with his kiss.

Though she was breathing heavily, though she knew her flesh must glisten with perspiration, her lover granted her no respite. He laid her upon the pallet, removed her garb gently as she caught her breath, then cast his own chemise and chausses aside. Vivienne moaned and buried her face in the thick fur of his cloak, when he knelt down and tasted of the deluge he had just created.

Desire stirred again as he caressed her with his tongue. She twisted and turned, but he held her fast, allowing her no escape from the pleasure he was determined to grant. Vivienne writhed, the climax coming more quickly this time; she grasped fistfuls of the cloak, for her lover was out of reach. She knew the moment was come, she bit down into the fur to stifle her shout of release, she knew she locked her knees around him and shook like a leaf in the wind.

This was what had made Madeline smile, she knew it well.

He was stretched out beside her before the erratic pace of her heart had slowed and Vivienne caught him close. She ran her hands over him as possessively as he had touched her, exhausted but wanting him to share in the pleasure he had granted to her. She felt the muscles beneath his smooth flesh, felt again the strength he held in check.

"Lady mine," he murmured, even as he bestowed a kiss within her ear.

Vivienne reached down, knowing full well what she would find, and let her hand close around his erection. She wanted to return his caresses in kind, though she was surprised when he gasped at her bold touch. He eased her grip upon him and she moved her fingers as he indicated, liking that she roused the same tension of desire in him as he had in her. Indeed, she felt her own passion kindling as his breathing changed. It was potent, to be able to grant such pleasure to him as he had lavished upon her, and she revelled in his every caught breath and moan of pleasure.

Vivienne felt him shiver, saw the glimmer of intent in his eyes, felt his muscles tense. His breathing quickened and she laid her cheek upon his chest to hear his racing heart. She touched him with greater surety, learning quickly what he liked best, savoring her effect upon him.

He muttered something and caught her waist in his hands. The strength of his hands nearly encircled her, making her feel small and feminine. He eased her to her back, and then he was atop her. He braced his weight upon his elbows, and the hair upon his chest tickled her breasts. His golden hair touched her cheek and Vivienne inhaled the scent of him, the taste of the wind that clung to his hair. She felt the length of him against her, his flesh so different from her own, and stretched out beneath him, arching against his heat.

He laced his fingers with hers and she thought she saw his smile before his mouth claimed hers once again. His kiss was tender yet possessive, he kissed her thoroughly and with a languid ease. Tears pricked Vivienne's eyes, for she had never expected such sweetness between her and her mate, and surely not so soon.

He settled between her thighs as he kissed her, the heat of him pressing against her. Vivienne parted her legs, knowing full well what had to happen. She squeezed her eyes shut, hoping it was not as painful as rumor hinted, and willed herself to welcome her lover true.

He eased into her with a care that told her he had heard the same rumors. Vivienne caught her breath at the size of him, then gripped his shoulders as she became accustomed to this new sensation. But the pain was only fleeting.

Indeed, as he moved, she was awed by a sudden sense that they two were as one. She learned his rhythm and matched it with her own, even as she felt the heat rising within her once again.

He slipped one hand between them and touched Vivienne once again, his fingertips making her writhe beneath him. Her body responded to his touch so surely that they might have met thus a thousand times, and Vivienne knew this to be the mark of their entangled destiny. A wild joy seized her heart, for she had won the fate she desired more than anything else.

Even while she marvelled at this gift, the heat rose between them to a relentless crescendo. She laid her hand upon his chest and felt his heart thundering in an echo of her own. Two hearts beat as one, two mouths tasted deeply of each other, two bodies felt the spark of the quickening in the same moment, two voices cried out together in ecstatic release.

And when Vivienne fell asleep in the warm embrace of her lover true, she did indeed smile the smile she had yearned to smile.

HE AWAKENED TO THE SOUND of a cock's cry in the village, so suddenly alert and filled with an unfamiliar sense of well-being that, for a moment, he could not name where he was. It was yet dark, though there was a smudge of pink along the eastern horizon. That light was sufficient to reveal the features of the woman who slept beside him, a smile curving the fullness of her lips.

Then he remembered.

Vivienne's russet hair was strewn across the pair of them like a fisherman's net. He stared at her, savoring the chance to study her unobserved. She was wrought tall and amply curved, though he had felt as much the night before. Her lips were full, her eyes thickly lashed, her complexion fair. He could discern a few freckles across the bridge of her nose, and again across her collarbone, which made her look young and vulnerable.

And the blood of her maidenhead stained the linen chemise tangled about her hips. Guilt stabbed him once again, though he dared not indulge it. He rose abruptly, putting distance between them, knowing that truth would do little to ease what must necessarily follow.

Truly, it was his own weakness that plagued him. He had not been wrought to use other people to his own ends, however justified his goals might be. He dressed with curt movements, his gaze fixed upon the woman who curled into the hollow of warmth his body had left, reminding himself of what he was compelled to do.

He was not truly surprised to find himself hating what he had become, though he hoped with all his heart and soul that the reward would be worth the price.

His daughters deserved no less than his all.

*Chapter Three*

~

VIVIENNE AWAKENED, FEELING slightly chilled, and nestled deeper into the fur lining of her cloak. She was well content, for she had learned the import of Madeline's secretive smile. She smiled herself and stretched out a hand for her lover true, more than amenable to feeling his caress once more.

Vivienne's fingers closed upon emptiness, and her eyes flew open. Surely he had not returned to his fairy realm without sparing her a word?

Only the first touch of the dawn lit the sill of the chamber and shadows yet lurked in the corners. The cold of night emanated from the stone walls. Shapes were discernible as shadows against the shadows, including one large male silhouette before the window. Vivienne sighed with relief.

He stood with arms crossed and feet braced against the floor, the sky behind him a rosy luminescent pearl. His hood was drawn over his head and cast his features in deeper shadow, though Vivienne knew he watched her avidly. She might have been fearful of his size and stillness, if he had not introduced her so tenderly to the delights of the marital bed.

But she knew sufficient of this man to feel no such fear. She granted him a smile, though she could not see whether he responded in kind.

She sat up, knowing her hair would have crept free from her braid and her chemise tangled around her waist, knowing she looked like a maiden thoroughly sampled and sated. For once in her life, she did not care that she was not so orderly as Madeline.

"Surely you cannot mean to leave so soon?" she asked. "It is still dark. Surely you can return to my side for a few moments yet." She eased back, making space for him on the pallet, but he did not move.

"It is late enough," he said, his words terse. He spared the barest glance to the window, and his tone did not soften. "Garb yourself. We depart immediately."

Vivienne struggled to make sense of both his words and his manner. "Depart? But we have only spent one night abed."

"And it is sufficient to require our timely departure." He crossed the chamber and lifted her discarded kirtle from the floor, shaking it out with impatience before offering it to her.

Vivienne pushed her hair back from her brow. "But this is not my expectation," she argued. "The tale clearly declared that there would be three nights of courtship, not one, and a red rose as a bride price before the nuptials."

"Your bride price was considerably higher than a single rose," he said sharply and tried to hand her kirtle to her again.

Vivienne stared at him in astonishment and a dreadful

sense assailed her. Had she mistaken a tale for some other truth?

What had Alexander done?

"Hasten yourself. There is no time to delay."

Vivienne rose reluctantly to her feet and took the garment from him, hoping her fears proved groundless. She tried to touch his hand in the transaction, but he pulled his fingers away. Whether it was by accident or design, his gesture made Vivienne's confidence falter further.

"You cannot mean that you have already paid a bride price," she said, her heart fairly in her throat. "Surely you but know its value and intend to pay it two days hence."

"It is paid, and doubtless half spent."

"What price did you pay?" She thought he might not answer her, so continued, her tone firm. "Surely I have a right to know my own supposed merit?"

"A sack of silver coins, one that your brother was quick to claim for his own."

Vivienne winced at his harsh tone and made to defend her brother. "Alexander did not accept coin for my hand!"

"He most certainly did." Her lover pointed to the floor with impatience. "Your belt lies on that side of the pallet, your boots on this side. I said we had need of haste."

Vivienne tried to discern the features hidden with his hood. "You are not a fairy suitor," she said, though already she knew the answer.

That made him halt and she guessed that he studied her anew. "Of course not. Why would you believe such whimsy?"

Whimsy. Too late, the truth was perfectly clear. Vivienne stared at the kirtle in her hands and felt a fool beyond compare. Alexander's tale had been no more than a ruse to persuade her to sleep in the tower. It had not been coincidence that Alexander unbarred the door last evening.

Her brother had played a jest upon her, as so oft he had done. Vivienne had been deceived, and her choice in this matter had been stolen from her. Worse, her own impulsive nature had betrayed her, for her maidenhead was lost.

Worse again, it had been lost—and she had been sold—to a man whose name she did not know.

"Alexander is a wretch beyond belief!" she declared, not troubling to disguise her anger. It was better than revealing her fear. "How dare he sell my hand? He pledged to Rhys that he would not repeat his error . . ."

"So we know the merit of his word," her lover noted drily. "There is a plague of deceit in our land, it seems."

But Vivienne did not care what he thought of her brother. She thought of her Aunt Rosamunde, who refused to follow the dictates wrought by men, and lifted her chin in defiance.

"I will not indulge Alexander, or you, by ceding to this arrangement," she said firmly. Her lover stilled again, as watchful and wary as a hawk on the hunt. "I was not privy to this arrangement and I will not stand by whatever terms were agreed upon."

"What is this?"

"I will not accompany you." Vivienne glared at the man who had seen fit to purchase her, disliking that he hid his face from her. Was he a stranger in truth, or a man who did not wish her to recognize him before she abandoned herself to his protection?

"You have no choice," he said. "Your brother has sold

you like chattel, and like chattel, you have no choice when or where you go."

Chattel? He could not have chosen a less appealing word!

"Only a fool of a woman would leave her family abode with a stranger who surrenders neither his name nor his destination, a man who does not even reveal his visage."

When he did not move or speak to soothe her doubts, Vivienne hauled her beautiful kirtle over her head and laced the sides with savage gestures. "No matter what price you have paid, I would suggest you depart from Kinfairlie afore I summon sentries against you."

He closed the distance between them with a decisive step and caught her chin in his hand. His touch was not forceful, despite the anger she could feel thrumming through him, and Vivienne felt a dangerous weakening of her will beneath his touch. It was too simple to recall how he had caressed her, how he had coaxed her response, how he had cajoled her participation in their lovemaking.

She realized that only that act or these words must reflect his character, not both. Tenderness and harshness could not both be his nature.

But which was the true measure of the man? Vivienne knew that lies were more readily wrought with words than with deeds, but that was a thin certainty upon which to wager her future.

"Who will aid you, now that your brother has had his due?" he demanded, and there was an unappealing truth in his words. "You are mine, mine since your brother accepted my coin for his own."

She was no possession! "I belong to no man and I never will." Vivienne stared furiously into the shadows of his hood. "You cannot compel me to do your will in this, for there is no bond between us."

His hand closed around her arm and he lifted her slightly off the floor. She could not miss the truth of how much larger he was than she and her confidence faltered.

"Can I not?" he murmured, seemingly aware of her uncertainty. His thumb began to move against her flesh in slow circles, and even through the ruched sleeve of her chemise, Vivienne felt a treacherous desire awaken within her.

But desire alone was not to be trusted.

"I will not make the matter simple for you," she said. "I will not be biddable!"

"And you need not be trussed like a lamb meant for the slaughter," he said with impatience. "It is clear that our paths lie together, and more clear that our course will be easier if you accept the truth of it."

Vivienne pulled her arm from his grip and stepped away, distrusting the power of his touch. "Show me your face. Tell me your name."

He stepped back then, ensuring she could not reach his hood. His determination to hide his face from her only made Vivienne more determined to see him truly.

He could cede that much to her, at least!

"It is better if you accompany me," he said, speaking more gently. "What if you bear my child?"

"After one night? That would be unlikely!" Though Vivienne scoffed, her spirit quailed.

His tone hardened anew. "You have seven siblings, all born of the same woman, and your sister conceived quickly after her nuptials. I heard tell of it in the village. It would not be so uncommon for your womb to bear fruit quickly, particularly in a family so vigorous as your own."

Vivienne folded her arms across her chest. "Then I shall accept that prospect rather than departing with a stranger. The worst price of it would be shame."

"Your fate might be worse than merely shame, though that is harder to bear than you might believe," he said with quiet persistence. "Your brother was quick to sell your hand—why should he not do so again?" He leaned closer, his words persuasive. "What manner of spouse will you win without your maidenhead? And what will such a man believe if your belly rounds too soon? What will he do when you offer him another man's son?"

To Vivienne's horror, he made a dangerous sense. She marched back to the pallet, fastened her belt, knotted her garters and donned her boots. Tears veiled her vision but she would not let him see how he had disappointed her with his hard questions this morn.

She much preferred the magic they had wrought the night before. Had she dreamed the man who had met her abed with such respect and affection? She spared a glance to the silent and hooded man behind her. Vivienne wished she could be certain which was his nature in truth.

Fully garbed with her cloak cast over her shoulder, she pivoted to face him and made an impulsive offer. "If your aims are so noble, wed me then, and I will have no choice but to accompany you."

He shook his head. "There will be no nuptials between us."

Vivienne was shocked that he could consider treating her with such dishonor. "I am no courtesan and I will not become one."

"And I will cross the threshold of no chapel before all

that is mine is mine once more," he said. Vivienne had no chance to ask after his losses, for he offered her his right hand. "I will pledge to you in the old way, for a year and a day. If either of us find fault with the other in that time, we shall be free to part and unbeholden from that point onward."

"And if I bear a child?"

"It will be my son in truth, raised in my household and granted every advantage I can offer."

It was a meager offer compared to marriage, but with her maidenhead gone, Vivienne feared that she had little left with which to wager. She glanced at his hand, its strength gilded by a ray of sunlight. This was not how she had envisioned matching her path to that of a man, and she was not yet prepared to believe it was her sole choice.

Vivienne tentatively put her hand in his, and was awed again by the way his fingers engulfed hers. When he offered his left hand, crossing it over the right one then turning up his palm, Vivienne pretended to reach toward it. Then she reached quickly for his hood, so quickly that he barely seized her hand in time.

"I would see your eyes while you make such a vow," she protested. "No man of merit fears as much."

"You will not look upon me."

"Whyever not?"

"Because I forbid it," he said, his tone allowing no argument.

Vivienne chose to argue despite this. "You might be an outlaw, or a man whose repute I know well," she said. "You might be a man who has assailed me in the past, or a man I loathe."

"I assure you that I am none of these."

"Your word will not suffice. You cannot expect so

much of me in exchange for so little." Vivienne sensed
his hesitation and took advantage of it, pulling her hand
from his and snapping back his hood with haste.

He stared at her, his expression impassive, his eyes an
uncanny blue.

To her relief, he was a stranger, not some fiend whose
advances she had spurned before. She supposed she
should not be so relieved to have his name remain a mystery
to her, but his steady gaze instilled confidence in her.

His scarred face should have done the opposite. His
hood hung around his neck like a cowl, leaving his features
bare. The early sunlight caught the puckered flesh
of a scar. That marring line began at his temple, compelling
the end of his brow to tilt upward, narrowly missing
the corner of his eye, slashed across his cheek, tugged at the
corner of his mouth, then ended in the midst of his chin,
perhaps deepening a dimple that had always been there.

Vivienne was haunted by a feeling that he was vaguely
familiar, as if she had met some of his kin before, but
even that sense was far from strong.

He did not so much as blink as she surveyed this
wound, and she sensed that he expected her to recoil in
horror. Vivienne granted the injury a leisurely perusal,
then met his gaze unswervingly once she had seen the
whole of it. She savored her conviction that he was surprised
by her response.

"You thought that I would reject you on the basis of
this injury alone," she charged softly. "But I have wits
enough to know that a man's face is not the measure of
his worth."

He stared at her for a long moment, either incredulous
or skeptical. His eyes became a more impassioned blue
and Vivienne wondered what he was thinking. She was

keenly aware of his hand closed protectively around her own and swallowed when he captured her other hand once more. His thumb moved across her flesh in a slow caress, though she could not have said whether he did as much apurpose or not. The tower chamber seemed to warm around her.

Even his presence changed the air; even the sound of his breath made Vivienne's flesh tingle. She was aware of him as she had never been aware of another person in all her days. His steady regard softened her resistance to him in a most troubling way.

"Then what is the measure of a man?"

"His deeds," she said softly. "Though yours show little merit this morn."

A shadow touched his eyes and she knew that she did not imagine that his expression darkened for a moment. "Then let this be a better deed." He clasped her hands with gentle resolve, then met her gaze so steadily that she could not look away. "And so I swear to you, Vivienne Lammergeier, that I shall treat you with all honor for a year and a day, that I will defend you and honor you, that any children you bear me will be raised as my own, that at the end of that year and a day we both shall have the choice of whether to remain together or nay."

He loosed her right hand and his fingertips landed upon her cheek. They were warm, his touch as light as that of a butterfly upon a flower. Vivienne found herself turning, so that her lips touched his palm, found herself seduced anew by the reverence in his touch. His fingertips eased over the curve of her cheek, across her bottom lip, then he cupped her chin in his hand. Vivienne looked into his eyes and the last of her defiance dissolved.

The truth was that this man could have raped her the

night before, but he had shown her tenderness. He had ensured she found pleasure on her first taste of lovemaking. Even now, he was concerned for the future of any child she might bear, and noted rightly that Alexander might make a worse match for her now that her maidenhead was gone. Even now, he eased closer, his eyes darkening with his intent to kiss her.

And Vivienne was weak enough to want nothing less.

He was wary, to be sure, but no man could bear such a violent and fresh scar without possessing some fear of his fellows. The wound had been wrought by a blade, it was clear, and she shivered inwardly at what he must have borne.

His lips closed over hers, his kiss resolute as he claimed what he believed to be his due. Vivienne knew that a more sensible maiden would have rejected his embrace, would have stepped back from him until all of his mysteries were revealed. But Vivienne found herself welcoming his embrace, found her arms twining around his neck, found herself revelling in the marvel of his kiss.

She rose to her toes, for though she was tall, he was taller. His hand slid into the tangle of hair at her nape, her hands landed on his shoulders, her breasts collided with his chest. She closed her eyes and there was nothing but his kiss, nothing but him and his desire that she depart with him.

Nothing but the desire he awakened within her. He caught her closer and Vivienne almost forgot all she knew to be true.

But not quite.

~

VIVIENNE TORE HER LIPS FROM HIS and he released her, his steady gaze fixed upon her. She retreated, her thinking becoming less addled with every step she put between them. She looked away from him and fought to find her reason.

Kisses and promises should not be enough, not from a man who would not even surrender his name to her, a man who had tried to hide his face from her.

Vivienne wished she had never seen his scar. She knew too many tales of men served false who sought justice, of a fearsome face masking a heart wrought of gold. She knew too many tales in which a bold woman and her love were the salvation of a man who had lost all. It was too simple to see herself within such a tale, too simple to forget that impulse had oft served her false.

It had been a tale, after all, and her belief in it that had led to this circumstance.

"Make haste," he said softly. "We must depart immediately."

"No. I cannot go." Vivienne's words fell quickly in her determination to make a sensible choice. "I cannot leave with you, not so soon. You must show me more reason to trust you than this. You must meet me here again this night."

"Be not afraid, Vivienne," he said.

Even with the use of her name, he made her conviction fade! She held up three fingers, hating how her hand shook. "Three nights the tale pledged."

He shook his head and took a step closer. "The tale, whatever it was, was not true. We depart immediately."

"I will have three nights courtship and a red rose wrought of ice," Vivienne insisted stubbornly. She knew it was a mad demand, but she needed time away from him to consider her course. She needed to speak to Alexander, to find out why he had made this wager, she needed to think without her lover's compelling blue gaze fixed upon her.

"There is no time," he said.

"There must be time." Vivienne hastened to the portal, intending only to flee. Did she choose aright? She did not know, she could not reason with the taste of him upon her lips. Surely caution was never rewarded poorly? She had so little experience with it that she could not be certain.

She knew, however, that impulse could steer her false.

A cock crowed then in Kinfairlie village, though she ignored both it and her companion's muttered curse. Vivienne did not hear his footstep, did not guess that he had moved until his arm locked around her waist. She cried out, but he cast her over his shoulder with dangerous ease.

"Not yet!" Vivienne struggled against him, but he granted her no chance for escape.

"I have pledged myself to you, you have surrendered yourself to me and your brother has accepted his price," he crossed the chamber, untroubled by her protest. "The wager is wrought, for better or for worse, for a year and a day."

"I said not yet!"

"And I said that you had no true choice," he said, even as he stepped to the sill of the window. "We have wasted too much time this morn already."

Vivienne saw the ground far below them and panicked anew. "No!" she cried, fully aware of what he meant to do.

Undeterred, he seized the rope yet hanging outside the

window and swung them both out into the early morning air with a bold confidence Vivienne could not echo.

Indeed, she buried her face in his tabard, clutched his shoulder, and prayed as her stomach roiled in protest. He planted both feet on the wall with surety.

"Hold fast, for I need both hands for the rope," he commanded.

Vivienne had little choice, for she did not wish to plunge to her death. She seized him, knowing that her fingers dug into him like claws, and did not care. She did not remain silent, though she guessed he would have preferred as much.

"Help!" she screamed. "Awaken, sentries of Kinfairlie! Be of aid to me!"

"Be silent!" growled her captor, but Vivienne was no more inclined to heed his words than he had been to heed hers. She screamed with vigor and was delighted when an answering shout carried from Kinfairlie's bailey.

A sentry bellowed from his post and an arrow flew past them, embedding itself in the wall.

Vivienne's lover cursed, and descended with greater haste.

"Help me!" Vivienne cried. "I am the laird's sister Vivienne and this man means to capture me!"

Her captor halted his descent long enough to swing her around and shove one of his leather gloves into her mouth. "You will waken the entire village," he said, anger making his eyes snap with sapphire fire.

Vivienne protested, but her words were muffled by the glove. She did not dare to loosen her clutch upon him to remove it. She was cast over his shoulder once again, apparently no more troublesome than a sack of grain.

Mercifully, the sentries had already seen her and she had made her circumstance clear.

Her captor would not get far.

But, to Vivienne's surprise, no second arrow followed the first. She dared to look and spied a trio of Kinfairlie's sentries conferring in the mist of the morning. They did nothing to intervene, though they could not have been forty paces away.

Indeed, they leaned on their bows to watch.

What was this?

Her captor reached the ground, swung her around into his arms. He clamped her knees tightly and her elbows fast against her side, and she saw the annoyance in his expression. He strode through the village with purpose and she noted now that he limped. He still set an impressive pace and her struggling did little to deter him. Still the sentries did nothing to aid her.

He glanced down and must have noted her surprise, no less guessed the reason for it.

"You have been bought," he informed her as he marched toward one of the crumbled walls. "And your fate is sealed by that. Your brother ensured that I could scale the tower unobserved and it is clear that his men have been commanded to not intervene. You need no further sign of his endorsement than that."

Vivienne ceased to fight at his words. Indeed, she could think of no other explanation for events. Alexander must have given the sentries directions not to interfere with her capture.

Her grim captor did not say something else which Vivienne also knew must be true: Alexander would not have made such an arrangement without complete confidence in her future with this man.

Alexander must have known something to her captor's credit in order to accept his uncommon suit. She could not imagine that Alexander would wed her to a man who meant to do her injury. Her brother loved a jest, but he was not cruel.

Who was this man?

Her captor was disinclined to confide his secrets in this moment. He cast her across the saddle of a horse hidden beside the crumbled wall. Vivienne managed only to sit up before he swung up behind her, caught her fast against him and gave the steed his spurs.

Vivienne was not so foolish as to leap from the back of a racing horse, though her captor held her so tightly that she had little chance of doing so. Kinfairlie's chickens scattered before them, a pair of goats bleated, and Kinfairlie's sentries leaned upon their blades to watch the destrier's departure with indifference.

"All is well!" one shouted as the church bells rang the first hour, though Vivienne most assuredly would have disagreed. She wished with sudden vigor that she knew whatever Alexander had known. She doubted, however, that the man behind her would tell her much.

ELIZABETH, THE YOUNGEST of the siblings of Kinfairlie, was awakened early by some ruckus in the bailey. She heard the sentries shout that all was well, so settled back into the warmth of her pallet. She tried desperately to return to sleep and failed.

Elizabeth was cursed with the ability to see fairies. Actually, Elizabeth felt herself cursed that she was able to see one particular fairy, a spriggan named Darg, who had a talent for matchmaking and had developed a fondness for Elizabeth since that maiden had saved that spriggan's life.

On this particular morning, Elizabeth did not share that affection, for it was Darg who kept her awake. Darg was excited about some matter and insisted upon dancing on Elizabeth's chest.

In fact, Elizabeth was wondering just what had compelled her to save the spriggan from drowning in a pitcher of ale. On this morn, it seemed that having left well enough alone would have been a better choice.

Surprisingly, that near-demise had not lessened Darg's affection for ale. It was true that Darg had an unholy taste for mortal ale, though it affected her even more strongly than it affected mortals. Perhaps that was the root of her fondness for the brew.

"You should not have finished all of the ale last night," Elizabeth said, her manner grumpy. "It always makes you restless, which means that I get no rest at all."

Darg chortled and danced on Elizabeth's chest. *"Great deeds afoot at Ravensmuir; this day we hasten o'er the moor."*

"We are not going to Ravensmuir today, however much you desire it."

Darg cried out as if in pain. Elizabeth grimaced, not in the least bit grateful that she was the only one in her family who could see or hear the spriggan.

*"O'er hill, o'er dale, o'er rose and thorn, thus do the fortunate find their way by morn."*

Elizabeth thumped her pillow and rolled over, closing her eyes against the spriggan's chatter. After a night of broken sleep, she did not much care what Darg desired or where the fairy wanted to go. The sky was barely pink.

Elizabeth could hear chickens clucking and goats bleating to be milked, but it was altogether too early to rise.

She pulled her linens over her head resolutely and tried to will herself back to sleep even as she ignored the capering spriggan.

Darg danced with greater vigor, driving tiny heels into Elizabeth's flesh like small hammers. *"Fairy is one kind, mortal another; no soul of sense sees one in the other,"* the fairy proclaimed. *"Flesh and blood and death and bone; this mortal man will wed his own."*

Elizabeth was intrigued despite herself. She was twelve summers of age, had been suddenly (and alarmingly) endowed with ample breasts, and found the topic of men more alluring than once she had done.

She peeked over the hem of the covers and whispered, so as to not wake her sisters. "What man?"

Darg chortled in triumph. In truth, Darg was not a very attractive creature and did not always have the kindest motives. Elizabeth regarded her with her usual measure of suspicion.

With a final leap, the fairy dropped to sit cross-legged on Elizabeth's new curves, and whispered gleefully. *"A tale was told, some of it true; a wager made, the price come due. The man's true name, no soul knows; what shall be done when he leaves no rose?"*

Then the spriggan clicked her tongue in disapproval, sounding like an agitated bird.

Darg must mean the tale that Alexander had told the night before! One of Elizabeth's sisters must have been beguiled by it — and Alexander must have been playing one of his pranks. The sister would be claimed not by a fairy lover, as the tale recounted, but by a mortal man.

Elizabeth sat up so hastily that the fairy tumbled head

over heels from maiden to hard floor. Darg cursed long after she came to a halt, upside down on the bare wood, but Elizabeth did not care. She looked around the chamber and was relieved to see the tumbled tresses of Annelise and Isabella, auburn and fiery red in their turn. Vivienne, however, had burrowed beneath her covers and only the mound of her body was visible.

Certain that she would be cursed by Vivienne for her deed, and hoping Darg was wrong, Elizabeth crept toward Vivienne's pallet and abruptly cast back the covers.

Then she gasped in dismay, for the mound in the bed was not Vivienne. It was an old cloak, bundled to look like a body in the bed.

She spun to confront the fairy. "Darg, where is Vivienne? What has happened to her?"

The spriggan arched a brow, then brushed down her garb in obvious and elaborate reference to her rough ousting from Elizabeth's bed. She took great care in straightening her cuffs before she replied, undoubtedly aware that Elizabeth seethed with impatience. *"Ill-mannered mortals would show themselves wise, to look upon messengers with kindly eyes."* Darg put her nose in the air and marched away from Elizabeth.

The girl darted after her, knowing that only fulsome flattery would see her question answered. "Darg, I am sorry to have roused you so roughly. I was fearful for my sister." Elizabeth bowed her head at the fairy's indignant glance. "Though that is no excuse to be rude to one so wise as yourself. I apologize, truly I do."

Darg sniffed, though she paused to preen slightly.

"Please tell me what has happened to Vivienne. Only you are sufficiently clever to know the truth of it, while we mortals stumble in darkness in comparison."

*"No more, no less than what she desired,"* Darg laughed and the sound was a little bit mean. *"Blades are not known until touched to fire."*

Elizabeth was fearful of these tidings, though her discussion with Darg was interrupted by the arrival of Vera, the older maid who roused the sisters each morn.

Vera thumped noisily through the portal, dropped her buckets of steaming water with a curse, then rubbed a heavy hand across her brow. "Awaken, my ladies! The church bells ring and the laird himself insists that you all hasten yourselves to early mass."

Darg spat on the floor, communicating an opinion of early mass quite clearly, then disappeared through a chink in the wall. Elizabeth fairly growled in vexation, then turned to find Vera's bright eye upon her.

"Talking with the fey again, are you, lass?" Vera chuckled at the whimsy of that and Elizabeth felt her cheeks burn. Any inclination she had to confess Vivienne's absence faded before the maid's skeptical manner.

Perhaps Vivienne had a good reason to be gone so early this morn. Perhaps Darg was mistaken. Perhaps Vivienne had a tryst, or a secret courtier, or a mission she wished none to know about. It certainly looked as if Vivienne had meant to deceive others about her presence, which could only mean that she had departed willingly.

"Awaken, my lovely lasses, the laird makes no concession for those of us who must labor to see you all dressed, nay, nay, not he. He raises his voice and makes his command and expects all to be precisely as he has decreed."

"Alexander is laird now, Vera," Elizabeth observed, and won a sour look from the maid for her comment.

"Be that as it may, he is not *king*!"

Isabella groaned and rolled over, burying her face in her pillow. "I will go to midmorning mass instead," she mumbled, for she was not one at her best early in the morn.

A gleam lit in Vera's eye, one that did not bode well for Isabella. "His lairdship insisted," the doughty maid declared with boisterous cheer. She trudged across the chamber and pulled the linens away from Isabella with a victorious sweep of one hand.

Isabella screamed and snatched for the linens. "It is cold!"

Vera smiled as she danced backward. "And leaving you cold is the sole way to rouse you, my lady."

"Give me those linens and give them to me now!"

"The laird decreed that none should linger abed this morn, not even you."

Isabella shivered elaborately. "Vera, you are cruel beyond expectation." She sat up and surveyed the room in what was clearly a poor temper, wrapping her arms around herself as she shivered. "And Alexander is wicked to his very marrow."

Vera chuckled. "While you are lazy in the morn, my lady. Rise, rise and hasten yourself to mass like the good demoiselle you are. We each must have some flaw and this surely is yours." She gave Isabella a mischievous glance. "If you rose and attended mass, you could tell our laird what you think of his edicts."

Isabella snorted. "If I were Lady of Kinfairlie, I should pass an edict banning church services before midday." She made another unsuccessful snatch for her bed linens.

Vera marched away with the linens, triumphant. "But you are not Lady of Kinfairlie, and you never will be. You cannot wed your own brother." She shook a finger at

Isabella, clearly enjoying their daily game. "And the laird himself has demanded your presence. You had best rouse yourself, for you do take longest with your hair."

"Because it is too red!" Isabella wailed and fell back against her pillows in apparent despair. She glared at the ceiling. "It is uncivilized to command another to attend mass so early. Alexander is a barbarian to make such a demand."

"I hardly think it barbaric to be so concerned with the fate of your soul," Annelise said sweetly. She had risen and washed while Isabella had complained.

Isabella grimaced then spoke darkly. "He has no concern for our souls."

"I think he is impossible since becoming laird," Elizabeth added. "To think that once I liked my eldest brother!"

Isabella nodded. "Mark my words, there is some jest behind this command. Alexander makes no haste from his bed in the morning either."

The sisters paused to exchange glances, for Isabella spoke the truth. "Do you think he rouses us only to play a trick upon us?" Annelise asked, her skepticism clear.

"What else?" Isabella said. She pushed herself to her feet with a groan. "We shall have to play a jest upon him in exchange, and it will have to be a good one."

"It seems unlikely that any jest of Alexander's would be played in church," Annelise said, quite sensibly. She had already donned her stockings and now tied the lace of her chemise.

The sisters stilled as one at her comment.

"Church!" Elizabeth whispered and her gaze fell upon Vivienne's empty pallet. "Perhaps that is where Vivienne is gone so early in the morn. Do you think Alexander means to compel her to wed?"

Vera strode across the chamber and pulled back Vivienne's linens with a flick of her wrist. The sisters and maid stared at the pallet in dismay, for they all had clearly thought Vivienne still asleep. "What do you know of this?" Vera demanded of Elizabeth.

"Nothing, save that she is gone."

Annelise licked her lips. "Marital vows are exchanged in church," she said in a much smaller voice.

"If Vivienne guessed his intent, she would be the one of us bold enough to flee such a scheme," Isabella said.

The sisters exchanged glances of horror, recalling with dreadful clarity their eldest brother's determination to see them all wed. Vera froze and watched them with undisguised trepidation.

Isabella pounced on the maid and shook the sleeve of her kirtle. "What have you heard in the kitchens, Vera?"

"Not a word, I swear it to you! Though the laird is said to be well-pleased with himself this morn, and demanding a midday meal worthy of a feast."

"A wedding feast," Isabella said sourly and kicked her pallet. "The cur!"

A tear welled in the older woman's eye. "Oh, surely the laird would not plague dear Vivienne with a notorious spouse as he did Madeline? I heard of that folly of an auction, though I was not as yet here, for it was the talk of all Kinfairlie."

"The talk of Scotland, as like as not," Elizabeth said. "It was a folly beyond compare."

"Alexander did pledge to Rhys that he would not auction the hand of any of us, as he did Madeline's," Annelise noted. Vera knotted her hands together, so concerned that she could not practice her usual tasks.

"But he has never summoned us all to early mass, either," Isabella said sharply.

"And in your best garb!" Vera wailed. "That was what he decreed."

"Surely he cannot mean to wed *all* of us this morning," Isabella said, doubt in her voice. "That would be a feat, even for Alexander."

"Surely he but plays a jest upon us, as once he did," Annelise suggested.

"He has forgotten how to jest," Elizabeth said grimly. "All that has merit to him is respectability."

"But where then, is Vivienne?" Vera demanded. They looked again at the empty pallet.

Elizabeth began to fear that Darg had spoken the truth.

"There is only one way to know for certain," Isabella said with resolve. "We must behave as Alexander anticipates and meet him cheerfully at morning mass."

Elizabeth nodded. "And if he means to wed Vivienne against her will . . ."

"Or any of us!" Annelise interjected.

"Or any of us," Elizabeth continued, "then we must somehow ensure that the vows are not exchanged. It is time enough that he learned that all he decrees shall not be done."

The sisters nodded, resolve gleaming in their eyes, then turned to quickly don their best garb for church.

# *Chapter Four*

~

IN SHORT ORDER, Kinfairlie village faded behind them and Vivienne's captor pulled the glove from her mouth. At its removal, she spat once, cleared her throat, and said nothing. She sat stoic before him, her straight spine telling him more clearly than any words that she was displeased.

Or that she did not wish to touch him overmuch.

He was somewhat disgruntled himself, having wasted a goodly amount of time in trying to persuade her, only to have her insist upon some feminine madness. The three nights of courtship she anticipated was no more than reasonable, but he had expected better of her than a demand for a red red rose wrought of ice.

His pragmatic plan had no margin for a whimsical virgin determined to see romance in all around her. His need to conceive a son of unquestionable paternity required that he find a maiden to claim for his own—though Vivienne's passion abed had been a surprise. There was a sweetness about her that made him feel a cur to offer her less than the fullness of marriage and security.

But he had no such security to offer to her. He had paid

good coin for her, and if her brother had been so willing to sell her, then he was a fool to feel any qualms.

Even if she had not flinched from the sight of him.

"You have nothing more to say, it appears," he said, feeling her silence too keenly.

"There is little point. I do not know your name, your destination, or your intent, and you are disinclined to confess any of them." She gestured to the open coast. "There is no soul here to hear my cry, if indeed they had not already received instruction to surrender me to my fate, whatever it is."

"I had no choice," he said gruffly. "It was time we fled."

She scoffed. "I cannot discern any reason for haste, given that none intended to aid me."

There was little he might say to that. It was the anonymity of darkness he had desired, out of habit and the fact that her brother thought him to be someone other than he was.

He was not prepared to discuss that with the lady as yet. He let the horse set its own pace, for none gave chase to them. The morning was clear, the sky slowly turning a milky silver, and the wind was crisp. The steed that the Earl of Sutherland had lent to him was well rested and moved with characteristic grace.

He was aware of more sensory pleasure than this. Vivienne's hair was a loosed cloud, for she had not braided it this morn, and a marvel of rich auburn tendrils dancing in the wind around him. He did not protest the soft hair, though it blew against his face and furled against his shoulder. Its assault was unabashedly feminine, a soft luxury such as none he had known in recent years, and he admitted to himself how much he enjoyed it.

He could almost forget the discomfort of this southern garb, donned solely to ensure that he could pass with less notice. He sorely disliked the constraints of the chausses.

He was particularly aware of that constraint in this moment that he was besieged by Vivienne's allure. He could smell the sweetness of her skin, could see the creamy curve of her cheek and throat. He felt the ripe curve of her buttocks against him, and savored the long strength of her. He liked that she was tall, he liked that she was lean yet curvaceous enough to tempt his touch.

It was too easy to think of meeting her abed once more. After all, it would take more than one night to ensure that she conceived a son and there was no opportunity for delay.

He resolved then to savor each night in Vivienne's embrace until she knew for certain that she bore his son. So lost was he in anticipation of what they might do together that her curt tone surprised him.

"You ride a destrier, as if you are a knight," she said. "Yet your jerkin is leather, not mail."

He inclined his head, sufficiently intrigued by her show of intellect to let her make her own conclusions.

"Is it truly your own steed or did you steal it?"

"I steal only women," he said, surprised to hear a thread of humor in his tone. It had been long since he had made a jest, but the gentle assault of her hair lightened his mood. "And thus far only one, solely because circumstance demanded as much."

She twisted to meet his gaze, her own green eyes alight with curiosity. He blinked, shocked that she was so unafraid of him, astonished by the clarity of her eyes' hue. "What circumstance could possibly demand my capture?"

He frowned. "It is a long tale."

A smile pulled at the corner of her lips. "You no longer give your steed your spurs. It seems that we have time aplenty."

He studied her, incapable of tearing his gaze away from this merry maiden. What was remarkable was that she did not assume any tale would show him badly. She assumed the best of him, had been unafraid to demand more of him. For a man oft condemned by his face and equally oft denied the benefit of the doubt, that was potent indeed.

But tender feelings had led him astray before. He dared not care for this woman, who rode with him only until—and if—her womb proved potent.

He let his expression turn grim. "I have need of a son, a son whose paternity is beyond doubt. Thus I have need of a woman, a woman who was maiden until meeting me abed, a woman of a family known to be fruitful, a woman who will have no opportunity to lie with another until she bears that son to me."

"You have need of a wife," Vivienne said, with a small smile.

"I have a wife," he said curtly and watched her smile disappear so completely that it might never have been. He knew he should have been pleased to have forced a wedge between them, knew he should have been glad that she turned her back upon him once more and freed him from the spell of those magnificent eyes.

But instead he felt a cur and a knave besides, for he alone had dimmed the sparkle of the lady's smile. It seemed small advantage to have halted the lady's questions.

"Though Beatrice is dead," he added quietly.

Vivienne's posture did not change, nor did her curiosity appear to re-awaken. As they rode in painful silence, he had a difficult time persuading himself that it was better thus, even less that such silence was his choice.

ELIZABETH NOTED THAT THE BEST silver was laid upon the altar at Kinfairlie chapel, and Alexander himself was dressed as regally as a prince. He was wearing his favored tabard, the one of deepest sapphire with gold embroidery, the one which made his eyes more strikingly blue. His boots were polished and the hilt of his sword gleamed. The entire village seemed to be gathered at this unlikely hour, their expressions bright with expectation.

Elizabeth took no encouragement from what she saw when she peered through the portal. She and her sisters retreated as one and exchanged grim glances.

"We have guessed aright," Isabella said. "I know it well."

"You cannot know for certain until we have evidence of it," Annelise said, her manner quite reasonable. "There are no men at the altar save Alexander."

Elizabeth took a peek and grimaced. "Though his preening can be no good portent for any other than himself."

"Oh, my lasses," Vera said, her voice tremulous. "I will pray for all of you, that I will." She clutched the hands of each other in turn. "Remember, though, that a fine match oft begins poorly. A start does not a finish make." The maid looked between the three maidens and seemed disappointed to hear no agreement fall from their lips. She patted Elizabeth's cheek, then turned to enter the church.

"I will never wed a man so foolish as to think he can buy my hand," Isabella declared. She straightened and flicked the edges of her shimmering green veil. "If Alexander means to see me wed this day, he will have no easy time of it."

With that, Isabella hauled open the door, her manner striking for its lack of her usual poise, and stalked down the aisle of the church. Annelise and Elizabeth watched as their sister fixed a stern eye upon their elder brother.

Alexander, with exquisite manners, bent low over Isabella's hand and pressed a chaste kiss upon her knuckles. She glowered at him, but he smiled as innocently as an angel.

"But I am eldest, if Vivienne is gone," Annelise said, the waver in her voice revealing her fear.

"I will hate Alexander forever if he sees you treated poorly," Elizabeth said and squeezed Annelise's hand, wishing she could offer greater encouragement than that.

Annelise squared her shoulders and forced a brave smile to her lips, then entered the church in her turn. Elizabeth held her breath as she watched, but Alexander greeted Annelise as courteously as he had Isabella.

There was no doubting, though, the expectant light in his eyes when he looked back to the portal. Though Elizabeth knew herself to be the most unlikely to be wed next, still her heart fluttered. She felt her cheeks burn as she opened the wooden door to the church and kept her gaze downcast beneath the perusal of every soul in the chapel.

She reached Alexander's side and was so relieved

when he kissed her knuckles then looked again to the portal that her knees nearly gave out.

It was Vivienne, then. The sisters clutched each other's hands as Alexander eyed the door with a mix of impatience and pride.

No other shadow touched the door.

Moments passed and no one came.

Alexander frowned, he spared a glance for the priest who shrugged. Elizabeth interpreted this as no good sign.

"If we await Vivienne, you should know that she was gone this morn," she whispered to him.

Alexander nodded once, and not with surprise. Elizabeth felt her eyes widen that her brother had known that Vivienne would be gone.

Which meant that he probably knew *where* she had gone.

Alexander beckoned to his castellan and the elderly Anthony came quickly to his side. The villagers shuffled their feet, clearly wondering at the delay, and watched with interest as Anthony departed on swift feet.

The priest lit the candles upon the altar in the interminable moments that followed.

Just when Elizabeth thought she could bear it no longer, Anthony returned. He paused just inside the portal and shook his head minutely.

"Not in the chamber?" Alexander cried.

Anthony shook his head again.

"Not in the bailey?" Alexander demanded, his agitation clear when Anthony shook his head. "Not at the inn?" The young laird began to stride down the aisle of the church. "Not approaching the gates?"

"I am sorry, my lord, but there is no sign of the pair."

"The cur!" Alexander spun on his heel. He swore, he

drove his fist into his palm. The priest cried out in recrimination but Alexander was clearly so furious that he did not care.

He raised his fist in the middle of the chapel, his ringing voice carrying to every ear. The silver ring that bore the seal of Kinfairlie gleamed upon his index finger. "There was to be a wedding celebrated this morn in this chapel, but cur to whom my sister's hand was pledged has broken his word to me!"

The villagers whispered to each other in consternation, though Elizabeth could not look away from Alexander's fury. Never had he so resembled their father as he did this day.

"And I pronounce a price upon his head for his treachery. Should any person bring to Kinfairlie one Nicholas Sinclair, be he alive or be he dead, I will pay that person four golden sovereigns!"

The company gasped at the sum and the whispering began immediately. Annelise began to softly recite a prayer, while Isabella glared at Alexander.

Nicholas Sinclair? Elizabeth remembered him well enough, for he had had sufficient sweet words to compliment all the women in Christendom. She had never liked him and had taken enormous pleasure in vexing him while he courted Vivienne years past. That had been before she understood that men had any allure, and Nicholas had endured many practical jokes due to her.

She had not even known that he had returned to Kinfairlie, and could not imagine that he would plead for Vivienne's hand with any sincerity.

Nor did she imagine that Vivienne would have him.

But Alexander dug in his purse, and held the glittering coins before the gasping company. The villagers craned

their necks to see more coin in one man's hand than most
of them would see in sum in all their days and nights.

"My lord, it is inappropriate to make such an offer in
the house of God . . ." the priest began to protest but
Alexander silenced him with a severe glance.

"And any soul who brings word of my sister Vivienne," Alexander continued, "shall have four sovereigns—" the villagers inhaled as one at the prospect of so
much coin "—*eight* if she is returned to Kinfairlie un-
scathed."

He glared at the company, as if willing confessions to
fall from their reluctant lips, then turned to his castellan
when none were forthcoming. "Anthony, see that my
proclamation is sent to all surrounding regions immediately. They cannot have fled far." The older man nodded
and bowed.

With that, Alexander Lammergeier, Laird of Kinfairlie, left the chapel, his brow as dark as thunder, without
participating in the mass he had ordered for so early in
the day. The sisters did not have to glance to each other
to know that their eldest brother was fearful of Vivienne's
fate.

"What has he done?" Isabella whispered, but no one
answered her.

"Let us pray for the lady and her safe return!" the
priest cried and every voice was raised to join his.

Elizabeth, for her part, prayed that she could find Darg
again, for the spriggan might be their best chance of aiding Vivienne.

~

VIVIENNE, TOO, WAS THINKING of how she might win aid, when she was not wrestling with her disappointment. Each detail her captor confided in her made her circumstance seem more dire. He had chosen her solely that she might bear him a son, though that was not an uncommon desire among men.

And he had been wed before. His terse manner indicated that he felt strongly about the matter—doubtless his heart had been possessed so fully by his wife that her death had left him a grim shadow of his former self. Vivienne knew that it was thus in most tales and she felt some sympathy for her captor in his loss.

But these were poor tidings for her own future. Vivienne had thought her captor's insistence upon a handfast had been merely due to his being from the Highlands, where old ways held more sway, and that it was but a precursor to a more enduring match. She had thought that the passion they had kindled abed from their first moment together had been cause for optimism for their entwined future ahead.

But he loved his deceased wife.

If nothing else, Vivienne had hoped to be desired for more than any child her womb might surrender.

Despite all of this, Vivienne was achingly aware of the man behind her; she felt every breath he took, she was aware of the strength of his hands where he held the reins. She fancied that she could hear the beat of his heart and wished that she did not remember the taste of his kiss.

How much of a fool was she?

They rode in silence until the sun was past its zenith, then approached an abandoned structure on the coast. The stone walls were crumbling into the soil and the thick vegetation hinted that few had come this way of late.

Vivienne guessed it had once been a hermit's cell, as it was located far from even this day's temptations. The coast was rocky beneath the point, the wooden roof over the structure itself was rotten, though part of it had been repaired of late.

Her captor gave a command to the horse which halted and stood its ground, ears flicking. He dismounted then and lifted Vivienne to the ground. He led the horse away to a patch of grass where it might graze. He took his time in tending the steed, removing its saddle and brushing it down, evidently confident that she would not flee.

And in truth, there was nowhere she might run and not be caught again first. She had seen how quickly her captor could move, even with his limp, and he was much taller than she. Vivienne was well aware of the high tower of her uncle's keep of Ravensmuir still to their north, but it was sufficiently distant that even the sharpest gaze atop that tower would not spy them here. She thought she could see ravens circling over it, the merest black pricks against the azure summer sky, but dared not glance overlong in that tower's direction lest her interest rouse suspicion.

Vivienne folded her arms across her chest and watched her captor, noting how he pulled up his hood once more, as if accustomed to hiding his marred features. Perhaps he meant to hide his thoughts from her!

Not that his expressions were readily interpreted. He had been impassive most of the time, more impassive when annoyed. Vivienne bit her lip, reminding herself to recall that detail.

He wore undistinguished dark garb, none of it wrought of fine cloth or embellished with so much as a symbol or a thread of embroidery. His chausses were dark, his boots darker, his chemise rough and undyed. He seemed to not care about the hue or state of his garments. Perhaps he was not vain. Perhaps he was but pragmatic. He was not poor if he had granted Alexander a sack of coins in return for her.

Perhaps he did not wish to be robbed while he travelled. Vivienne could not guess which was the truth.

His jerkin was of boiled leather, his dark cloak wrought of thick wool coarsely woven. The garment fell to his knees and was cut full. His belt was thick and heavy, a sheathed sword hanging from one side and a sheathed dagger from the other. The hilts of both blades gleamed with fastidious care, though they were simple of design. So, too, with the horse's trap, which was sturdy but without ornament. He had stuffed his leather gloves into his belt.

The sole ornament he wore was a silver pin that fastened at the throat of his cloak. It was about the size of his palm and shaped like coiled rope, though Vivienne knew better than to ask to see it more closely.

He appeared, after all, to be in a foul mood. He brushed the horse with care, giving every sign that he was unaware of her perusal though Vivienne doubted that was the truth.

She wondered how he had found this refuge so readily. They had ridden without catching so much as a glimpse of another living soul. That was a feat, Vivienne knew, for this corner of Scotland was fairly thick with monks and travelling priests, with peasants and shepherds, and journeying noblemen, and the moors did not offer many places to hide.

Her captor knew this land, she guessed, though she wondered whether he had learned of it lately or whether he had been raised hereabouts. She did not deign to begin a conversation with him to find out. She decided that she would flee, at the first opportunity, and lull him into complacency until that time came.

Let him find another maiden with a fertile womb. There was no future for her with a man who loved his dead wife, a man who had need only of her womb and meant to abandon her after claiming its fruit. She would escape, while her family was yet within reach.

He granted her a piercing glance in that moment and Vivienne wondered whether he could hear her very thoughts. Would he ever grow complacent? She doubted that he fully trusted another living soul.

Save his horse. The beast grazed, clearly accustomed to such care, and truly its chestnut coat gleamed with good health. It was a destrier, a knight's horse, with a white star upon its brow.

Vivienne watched with reluctant interest as her captor located a leather sack hidden within the shadows of the structure she had believed abandoned.

He had been here earlier, then.

"Are you hungry?" he asked. Without waiting for her answer—as if he had guessed that she had no intent of granting him one—he began to lay a simple meal upon the flat stones outside the small enclosure. Vivienne would have liked to have refused whatever he chose to offer her, on principle alone, but her belly growled. She moved closer, drawn by the sharp scent of a ripe cheese, and saw that he had bread and apples, as well.

"The bread grows hard," he said without glancing up at her. "But as it is dark bread, it was not overly soft in the first place. I suspect you have never eaten the like of it."

Vivienne could not resist the chance to surprise this man. "On the contrary, at Kinfairlie we eat brown bread every day but Sunday. My father always preferred to sell the fine flour and he said the coarser bread would not harm us."

Her captor glanced up. "Then coin must always have been scarce at Kinfairlie."

"What do you mean?"

"Few noblemen would choose to eat the bread of peasants. Perhaps you are unsurprised that your brother accepted my coin so readily."

"Perhaps I am. My father was unlike most noblemen and my brother follows his lead." Vivienne decided she had little to lose by provoking him. "Perhaps Alexander accepted your offer readily because he was deceived as to your intent." She bit into the bread and met his gaze, fairly daring him to correct her.

He studied her in silence for a long moment, then looked across the sea without saying more. It was hardly an admission of guilt, but neither was it an argument against her conclusion. Indeed, once he had glanced away, he ignored her so thoroughly that she might not have been present.

Perhaps he had not thought their night together to have been so wondrous.

Perhaps his beloved wife had been more ardent than she.

Vivienne ate, astonished at how hungry she was and how good the simple fare tasted. When she finished, noting that he ate no more, Vivienne rolled the remainder of the cheese into its piece of cloth. He returned the remnants of their meal to the leather satchel in silence, then spared her a bright glance.

"We travel at night and only at night. I would suggest you sleep now." Without waiting for her reply or assent, he pushed to his feet and paced the small area. He glanced to the sky and to the sea, then studied the empty stretch of land between themselves and Kinfairlie.

Vivienne had no desire to sleep, but she would not accomplish much else while he was so watchful. She retreated to the cool shadows of the tumbling structure and gathered her cloak about herself as she sat against a wall with some discontent.

A far cry from fated love this had proven to be! She drew up her own hood and narrowed her eyes, hoping she gave the appearance of slumber.

Indeed, Vivienne intended only to wait until her captor eased his vigil. Then she would steal his horse and flee back to Kinfairlie, and have the truth from Alexander.

IN THE END, Vivienne did doze, because her captor showed no signs of taking a repose himself. He paced and he stood, he leaned against the wall and studied her, he surveyed the sea. He moved silently, with the grace of a warrior, but he was restless indeed. Vivienne stifled the urge to tease him, as she would have teased one of her brothers, that he must be tormented with guilt.

This man might well be. He kept his hood raised and his dark cloak furled around him, as if hiding his marked face from the very birds.

Exhausted from recent events, Vivienne felt her eyes drift closed as the sun rose high. The sound of the waves lulled her toward slumber, though she was yet half aware of her surroundings.

She was startled at the cry of a merry voice close at hand.

"Hoy, lad, there you are!"

Vivienne's eyes flew open and she saw her captor pivot at the shout and draw his blade. The tension in his shoulders eased slightly as he evidently recognized whoever called him, though he still was wary.

Vivienne peered around the wall and saw a stocky older man approaching, leading a dappled palfrey. The horse was shorter than those in her family's stables, and its fur grew long.

"Well met, lad!" the man shouted, raising his hand in salute. His face was as cheerful as his voice. "Though you did grant me a merry chase, to be sure."

"Ruari Macleod," the younger man said. He placed the tip of his blade against the ground and braced his hands upon the hilt. "I never thought to lay eyes upon you again."

The arrival grinned. "Ah, there is no evading me when I am charged with a mission, lad. My errand was to seek you out, and so, you see, I have done it." He bowed with a flamboyant air and Vivienne wondered if this portly man would burst his belt buckle at the effort. She was tempted to smile, so charming was his manner, though her captor spoke coldly.

"How did you find me?"

Ruari snorted. "You leave a trail fairly blazed by your passage, lad. If you mean to journey unnoted, you will have to do better than you have done when I am on your trail. Did you learn naught from me? All those lessons I granted to you about following some soul through the wilderness might have fallen on deaf ears for all the good they have done you." Vivienne heard the lilt of the Highlands in his voice, more pronounced than it was in the words of her captor.

Had he truly pursued the younger man so far?

Why?

To her surprise, her captor seemed discomfited by this. "I was cautious," he insisted.

"Not cautious enough," Ruari declared with a shake of his finger. "Men have eyes in their heads and in these days whatsoever they have witnessed can be loosed from their tongues with the smallest coin imaginable. These are dark times, lad, upon that you may rely, and I rue that we are compelled to endure them."

Ruari stretched out a hand in greeting, which the younger man pointedly ignored. He shrugged then and hooked his thumb into some increment of space behind his belt, squinting at the younger man as he surveyed him. "I cannot say that I would blame you for holding a small grudge against me."

"Any grudge I hold is far from small."

Ruari squinted into the shadows of that drawn hood. "You have grown harsher since last we met."

"Perhaps I have grown wiser."

Vivienne leaned against the stone wall and watched her captor walk away from his guest. He shoved his sword back into its scabbard, that gesture and his pose showing that he trusted the new arrival, despite his harsh words.

Vivienne was intrigued and eavesdropped shamelessly.

"Wiser? Is that your word for your circumstance?" Ruari demanded, skepticism in his tone.

"My circumstance is not my fault alone."

"What of the price upon your head in Kinfairlie village? Is that due to the deed of another?"

The younger man glanced over his shoulder at this, but said nothing. Vivienne's heart thrilled at these tidings. Her family had not abandoned her fully! Even if Alexander had agreed to some wager, their departure this morn had not been part of it.

Ha! She had known that Alexander had her welfare at heart.

Ruari shook a finger at the younger man, as if scolding him, though Vivienne could not imagine a man less likely to be scolded. "Four gold sovereigns is the sum named by the Laird of Kinfairlie himself for your sorry hide."

Vivienne bit her lip. Could Alexander afford such a reward?

Her captor scoffed. "Did you seek me that you might collect your due?"

Ruari snorted with disdain. "You should know better than that, lad, though I will not be the last to follow you here." He raised a meaty finger like a preacher delivering the moral of his sermon. "Dead or alive were the words of the laird. Dead or alive! Any man of sense knows that dead is easier. You tempt fate in lingering so close at hand. Had you the wits your father granted to you, you would be half the way to Ireland by now instead of pacing by the sea."

Vivienne's captor turned to confront the sea once more, the hem of his cloak flicking in the wind. "I thank you for your counsel, Ruari. Godspeed to you."

Ruari continued, undeterred by this dismissal. "And four sovereigns more for the return of the laird's sister," Ruari added quietly. "Eight, if she is returned without injury. What do you know of the disappearance of this lass, Vivienne?"

"Nothing you need know."

"Vivienne Lammergeier is her name, Vivienne Lammergeier of Kinfairlie. I cannot be the only one of we two who has heard that name before."

Vivienne's ears pricked at this. How could either of them have heard her name before? She knew nothing of either of these men.

"Your recollections are of no import here, Ruari."

"Are they not? No good comes of using an innocent maiden as a tool for vengeance. You should know the truth of that!"

"She is innocent no longer, Ruari."

The older man swore. He pivoted and paced a distance, then turned to confront the younger man once more. "And what do you mean to do about that? Have you wed the lass?"

"Nay and I will not."

Vivienne's heart sank to her toes at his conviction. So she was to be no better than a courtesan.

"Is this the root of the laird's claim?" Ruari demanded. "He will have your prick for this crime, upon that you may rely! Some cunning man will drag you back there for the price upon your head, upon that you can rely, and the tool you used to do this deed will be the first sacrifice demanded of you."

"Then I had best not be captured." The younger man turned his back upon Ruari once again.

For the first time, the older man looked on the brink of losing his temper. He took a deep breath, reddened in the face, then bellowed. "It was not whim that made me pursue you now, lad, nor was it the prospect of reward from the Laird of Kinfairlie and his kind! I have no need of your secrets and your confidence, but I am determined to accompany you from this point forward all the same."

"You will not do so."

"Aye, I will, and I will tell you why that is so. Nay, do not argue with me. It is not because you make such a cursed mess of what is left of your days, though that would be reason enough. It is because your father saw the truth at the end, and thus he dispatched me to your side. I am to aid you, lad . . ."

"The time when you and my father might have aided me is long past." Vivienne's captor stood tall and straight, his tone telling her that he did not welcome Ruari's offering.

"Have you never erred and regretted your choice?"

"Of course."

"Then so did your father, and you have no right to hold as much against him. The past cannot be changed, only the future can be wrought in new design," Ruari said sternly. "Thus your father taught me, and thus I know he taught you."

"How unfortunate that he did not similarly instruct my brother."

Ruari spat upon the ground. "You cannot say that your brother did not change his future to suit himself better than his past had done. There were other lessons he did not heed, to be sure, but that one was the making of him."

When the younger man might have spoken, Ruari held up a hand. "We are in agreement, lad, as to the true nature of Nicholas and the weight of his crimes. Though I come late to your aid, my intent is no less strong." He offered his hand once again. "Are we met in peace, then?"

"I have no need of your aid. Begone, Ruari."

"You have need of all the aid you can muster!"

"I have the aid of the Earl of Sutherland, and that will suit me well enough."

"Do you now?" Ruari arched a bushy brow. "And how much do you know of the Earl of Sutherland that you are so keen to trust his word? What will he have of you in exchange? These are treacherous times for those too keen to grant their trust, and we both know that you are within their ranks."

"I know little of the Earl and his intent, but I have no other choice. He at least offered me aid when my own kin denied it to me."

"And for what cost?"

The younger man held his ground and folded his arms across his chest. "Why did you come, then, Ruari? You will not depart without the telling of your tale, so tell it all, then mount your steed and begone."

Ruari looked away, his expression pained, and took a few slow paces. He glanced back, his gaze bright, and took a steadying breath. "For many a year, I served a man, loyal and true. I served him willingly, I served him unswervingly. I followed him into every battle, I granted him my best counsel, I loved him like the father that never I had. He treated me well, better than one so lowly born as myself had any right to expect, and never did he ask me for more than my loyalty and trust." He swallowed visibly. "Until a month past."

"No," Vivienne's captor said, his voice wavering slightly.

Ruari bent his head. "Aye, lad, the end comes for all of us sooner or later, and so it came to the man I had served for most of my life. And when he lay dying, when he confessed his sins and make his reckoning, he saw that he had made one grievous error in his days. And because his time was short, he entreated me to set matters aright in his stead."

Ruari turned and appealed to Vivienne's captor. She listened greedily, savoring each detail. "He begged of me to find his eldest son, he asked of me to see the crimes wrought against that son redressed—" Ruari reached beneath his cloak and offered a sheathed dagger on the flat of his hand. The large sapphire trapped in the pommel of the dagger glittered in the sunlight. Vivienne peered at the blade, then noticed that her captor stared at it like a man transfixed.

Ruari continued with quiet resolve. "He charged me with delivering this talisman to his son, along with his heartfelt apology."

"No!" the younger man shouted and turned away, marching to the lip of the cliff. "It cannot be thus."

Vivienne clutched her own hands tightly together, disliking Ruari's tidings herself. She had lost her own parents less than a year before and knew it was a wound that did not heal readily. She felt a sudden sympathy for her captor as well as an urge to console him. How horrific to have lost his father, to not have been present at his father's end, to have been estranged from his father when that man died. There was a chasm that could never be breached.

"It is thus," Ruari said, his tone leaving no space for doubt. "As surely as I stand before you, William Sinclair has breathed his last. As surely as I offer you the legacy that is your own to claim, William Sinclair decreed that you should possess Blackleith once more for all the days and nights of your life. As surely as my name is Ruari

Macleod, your father charged me with aiding you in this quest, with seeing his disservice undone."

Vivienne's captor did not turn. "I thank you for your trouble and your tidings, Ruari, but you will not remain with me. Godspeed and farewell."

# *Chapter Five*

~

Ruari DROPPED THE REINS, left his steed and took a step toward the younger man. "Your father knew he erred! He knew he owed you better than what you had been granted, he knew in the end that he should never have believed the tales told against you. It would have killed him to know that you had been compelled to beg a favor from the Earl of Sutherland."

"So you say. The shadow of those days is long and a dead man's testament serves me far less than that of a live one." Vivienne's captor turned then to confront Ruari and she wished she could have seen his expression. "If my father repented of his judgement in truth, then he might have done it sooner. His forgiveness serves me little now."

"You have more than grown harsh, lad. You have lost your heart!"

"Whatsoever I have lost has been stolen. Farewell, Ruari." And Vivienne's captor marched to Ruari's steed, gathered the reins and offered them to the other man.

Ruari's lips set grimly. He shoved the sheathed blade into his belt and strode after the other man, eyes flashing and voice rising. "How dare you speak to me thus! I have spent a month seeking your sorry hide, lad! I have been in every hovel and every inn between Blackleith and York, I have slept in places with rats so large the white meat could have been carved from the dark, I have gone days without decent food and spent nights battling fleas as big as my fist. And why, why did I do this deed?"

His voice rose to a roar. "I did this for love of your father, no more and no less! I did this because I could not bear to see him so distraught, because it was so unfitting for a man of his ilk to be begging me—me!—to ensure that he could find eternal peace."

Vivienne's captor did not respond, nor did his stance soften.

Undeterred, Ruari stalked the younger man and seized his arm. "I did this because your father demanded more than my word, more than my promise. He demanded that I pledge my own soul's salvation upon the relic in this blade's hilt, that I cut my finger and shed my own blood upon the blade known to hold every oath ever wrought by any man in your family. *This* blade!"

He shoved the sheathed knife at the younger man again, who reluctantly accepted its burden. Vivienne could see her captor's reverence for the weapon in the way he handled it, and knew the token did not mean so little to him as he would have had Ruari believe.

"I did this because the blood of kings courses through your veins, lad, and I swore that if you were too dispirited to fight for your due, then I would do it for you. And what reward do I receive?"

Ruari smartly snapped the reins of his steed from the younger man's grip. "Not so much as a word of gratitude. Not so much as a greeting. Not so much as a handshake between men. Oh, the world has become a sorry place when men cannot even allow courtesy between each other."

The younger man glanced up. "All well said, Ruari, though I do not recall being offered a great deal of courtesy when all went awry at Blackleith."

Ruari swallowed, then nodded his head slowly. "Fair enough, but you must forgive the past, lad, to see yourself bereft of its burden."

Vivienne's captor closed the distance between the two men with quick steps, his posture menacing, then deliberately flicked back his hood. His scar seemed more cruel in the afternoon sunlight, and the hardness of his expression did little to soften its effect. "I will never be bereft of this mark of the past."

The older man winced, looked away, then met the younger man's gaze again with an obvious effort. "I did not know," he said quietly.

"The past will be forgiven when it has been avenged, Ruari. You need not linger to know it will be so."

Ruari's expression brightened at this grim pronouncement. "You do mean to fight, then? You have not surrendered fully?"

"I never meant to leave injustice be. Such a wound as this, though, must heal, and it was not the sum of my injuries. Praise be the Earl of Sutherland took me into his own abode, or I should be bleeding in a ditch yet with no aid from my own kin."

Vivienne's captor walked away, turning the blade in his hands. The older man's lips tightened grimly as he obviously noted her captor's limp.

Vivienne could not fully believe what she had heard. Her captor had been cheated of his holding somehow and his family had done nothing to aid him! It was outrageous treachery and she could not blame him for being bitter and angry. Indeed, she was prepared to argue with this Ruari on his behalf, for no man should be so poorly served by his own kin.

But wait. Her captor's brother was named Nicholas. Vivienne paused to reconsider what she had heard. And the holding in question was named Blackleith. Why was that name familiar?

Her captor's father had been William Sinclair.

Vivienne gasped in sudden realization of how her captor and Ruari Macleod could have heard her name before. Nicholas Sinclair had had an older brother, an older brother who was to inherit their family holding of Blackleith.

Could her captor be Erik Sinclair?

That man paused and glanced toward the half-fallen structure where she supposedly slumbered, perhaps having heard her gasp of dismay. Vivienne instinctively tried to make herself smaller, but Ruari must have spied her.

"There is someone there," he declared. "Is it the laird's sister in truth?"

Vivienne huddled lower into her cloak, hoping she appeared as if she still slept. She heard the crunch of booted feet approaching, and, knowing as she did who walked with such an uneven pace, her pulse began to flutter. She still feigned sleep, hoping against hope that she would not be caught eavesdropping.

She heard him halt before her, smelled his skin, knew he was but an arm's length away from her. She resolutely kept her eyes closed.

"Vivienne," her captor said, a thread of humor in his

words. "You fool no one when your breath comes so quickly as that."

She opened her eyes to find him offering his gloved hand to her. She could not read the expression in his eyes.

"Vivienne," Ruari breathed. He peered more closely at Vivienne. "It is no marvel that Nicholas was so vexed that she denied him. She is indeed a beauty."

"You are Erik Sinclair," Vivienne said to her captor, and he had the grace to not deny her conclusion. He merely bowed his head in acknowledgement, his gaze bright as he watched her. "Why me? Why ride all the length of Scotland to claim me?" she asked softly. "There must be maidens aplenty betwixt here and Blackleith." To her astonishment, it was Ruari who answered her.

"But you are the sole maiden who ever denied Nicholas Sinclair," that man said. "And oh, it irked him mightily, though I must say that he did not do justice to your fair features in his account of his failure."

"It was a marvel that he even admitted as much," Erik said.

Ruari snorted. "He was neither the first nor the last man to admit more than was prudent after consuming too much ale. I do not doubt that he would have preferred to keep the tale to himself, but the ale loosened his tongue and he made the error of speaking in public company, so the tale travelled far." The older man smiled at Vivienne. "He was soundly mocked for his inability to seduce you, of that you can be certain."

"But still, I do not understand . . ." Vivienne paused and stared at Erik in dawning horror. "You chose me purely to irk your brother, purely to claim what he had been unable to possess? You chose me for *vengeance*?"

A muscle twitched in Erik's jaw and his expression

turned yet more grim. He met her outraged gaze without blinking, however, and nodded but once. "That would be the simple explanation."

"As it is truth, there is no need for another more elaborate!" Vivienne's thoughts flew. "You must have told Alexander that you were Nicholas. Then he would have thought he arranged a match that would please me."

Erik shrugged. "I knew only that Nicholas had courted you and that you had spurned him. When I heard that you were yet unwed, I thought it likely that your family had found greater favor with the match than you had done."

"Nicholas proposed a mating, not a match," Vivienne retorted.

Erik shrugged again.

"But then, you have done no different! And I was fool enough to accept your advances!"

Erik merely watched her, letting her make her own conclusions. His complacence infuriated Vivienne as little else could have done. Erik had chosen her, he would use her, he would cast her aside when he had his son of her, and he did not even have the grace to be ashamed of his deeds.

It was difficult to be certain which brother was the less honorable!

"Then it is true that no good deed goes unpunished," Vivienne said, not troubling to hide her anger. "I did not tell my family of the base manners of Nicholas Sinclair, for I saw no reason to defame a man when he was unlikely to return. And what reward is mine for such courtesy? My brother, out of ignorance of the Sinclair brothers and their dark schemes, believed that Nicholas might come court my hand. Worse, he thought that I might welcome that suit!"

Ruari clicked his tongue in disapproval and ran a hand over his brow. The older man sat down heavily, as if burdened overmuch by what he had learned.

Vivienne glared at Erik. "And what will be my fate in this? You have already despoiled me and kidnapped me. Do you mean to leave me for dead in some forgotten corner of Christendom once I have served your purpose? Will I be left to earn my keep as a harlot in some distant hall once you have had your child of me? Or will you return me to Kinfairlie to collect my brother's offered ransom? It is you who have called me chattel, after all!"

"I have already told you," Erik said curtly. "I mean to conceive a son with you, a son whose paternity cannot be questioned, and I mean to raise that son as my own. The Earl of Sutherland will ensure your safety while you ripen, thus he and I have already agreed. You will be rewarded more richly than any courtesan has ever been paid for her trouble, and whatsoever you do after that is entirely your concern."

He managed to say no more, for Vivienne slapped his face with all her might. "Wretch!" she cried. "No man of honor treats a woman thus!" Her words plus her blow wrought silence between the three of them.

Then Ruari whistled between his teeth. "She is far from biddable, this wench."

"I am no *wench*!" Vivienne cried, then granted Erik her most ferocious glare. "You will have to tie me down to get a child upon me, and murder me to tear it from my arms. I will surrender nothing to the likes of you, no matter what the cost to myself."

Erik's eyes were an unholy blue as he regarded her, his words uttered with soft menace. "If that is what is required, then so be it," he said, then turned upon his heel and left her fuming.

"You will never best a Sinclair, lass, upon that you can rely," Ruari counselled in an undertone. "Better grant him his desire easily and be done with it."

"On the contrary, I have bested a Sinclair before," Vivienne retorted, turning upon the older man. "And I shall do it again, Ruari Macleod, upon that *you* can rely."

ERIK STARED AT THE SWELLING of the sea, fighting his desire to soothe Vivienne. She was enraged, as any reasonable woman would be. It was true that he had chosen her because she had spurned Nicholas, though not for vengeance alone. She had been the sole person he knew who had an immunity to Nicholas's charm. Given all that he had endured at Nicholas's instigation, that had seemed a compelling enough reason to choose her for his own.

The lady, however, might see matters otherwise. It was better to say less, in his opinion, than to cast fuel on the flames of her fury. Beatrice had been able to turn his own words against him so adroitly that he had learned long ago to say less to an angry woman rather than more.

Erik cast a sidelong glance in Vivienne's direction, her posture making it clear that she was still livid. She stood with her chin high and her arms folded across her chest as she stared back toward Kinfairlie. The setting sun danced in her hair, the loose tendrils waving on the rising wind.

"I understand now why you did not wed her," Ruari said from sudden proximity. "You cannot know that she will bring you a son until she does."

"And if so, and if she is willing, then I will wed her, but not before."

"And if not?"

"Then I shall take another maiden to my bed. I have little choice, Ruari, for the Earl of Sutherland has decreed that he will aid me only if there is clear succession for Blackleith."

"He is not the only one who tires of war, then." Ruari shook his head. "But it is a poor way for man and woman to be together, that is for certain."

"I handfasted to her," Erik offered, wanting his father's loyal servant to think somewhat better of him.

"Did you then?" Ruari nodded approval. " 'Tis better than naught and, in the circumstance, a wise choice."

The two men looked as one toward the lady, still standing as straight as a blade and appearing to ignore them utterly.

"A handfasting is a scarce measure for most women these days, though," Ruari acknowledged. "They want the blessing of a priest, as I expect this one does."

"If all is well in a year, then she will have it." Erik spared another glance to Vivienne. He touched his cheek, which yet stung from her blow, and wondered how he would meet her abed this night. "Though it will take a measure of charm I may not possess to coax her abed again."

Ruari chuckled. "You might be surprised, lad. She could not be so angered with you if she did not have some fondness for you." He clapped Erik on the shoulder. "And there are those fond of a woman who speaks her thoughts, no less one so prepared to demand that all meet a high moral code. She might well be a good partner for you in this quest."

Erik was not certain that the older man spoke rightly, but he was slightly encouraged. And there was but one way to create a son, so far as he knew, so he would have to mend matters with Vivienne this very night. If nothing else, he could ensure that they were without an audience for an interval.

He pointed to the north. "If you ride along the coast, Ruari, you will find a copse of trees afore the sun sinks much lower. I will meet you there shortly."

"And what is this?" the older man demanded, clearly indignant that he was being dispatched. "You will not be rid of me so readily as that! I pledged to your own father . . ."

"I do not mean to evade you, Ruari," Erik said, interrupting what would likely become a long tirade. "In fact, I doubt it could be done."

"And there is the truth of it, to be sure! I am honor bound to aid you, lad . . ."

"Then aid me now and ride ahead." Erik took a coil of rope from his saddlebag and spared his companion a steady glance. "There is a deed I must do afore we ride this night, and I would not have a witness."

The older man frowned. "You cannot mean to injure the lass. She may be outspoken but she is not wicked, and she does little in truth to injure you." Ruari squinted at Erik. "Save speaking the truth when it might be unwelcome."

"I have need of a son, and she named the terms herself. My intent is to persuade her by less dire means. By the time darkness falls fully, I will meet you at that copse of trees."

"With the lady, of course."

"Of course, be she willing or nay."

Ruari appeared to be skeptical as he granted Vivienne another glance. Her pose had not eased a whit. "I shall pray for you, lad, that you do not sustain greater injury than already you have."

Erik inclined his head. "I thank you for that."

As Ruari nodded and strode away, Erik pivoted to find that Vivienne now faced him. She watched him with wary eyes, poised like a doe intending to flee, hair tossing in the wind. He hoped she would not make this difficult, then reminded himself not to care.

One son was all he needed to set matters to rights.

And he needed that son soon.

VIVIENNE SWALLOWED as Erik began to stride toward her. His expression was grim and the rope he carried was no good portent of his intent. She took a step backward and realized that she stood upon the point itself, nothing but a tumble of rocks to the sea behind her. His pace toward her was relentless, and she noted with dread that his companion was leaving.

The sorry truth was that Ruari had revealed a number of intriguing details, facts that could have made her more welcoming of Erik's attentions if he had confessed some noble intent with regard to her. She was skeptical that Erik would confide any truth in her this night, given that length of rope.

Erik paused a trio of steps away. He rested his weight upon his good leg, as she had seen him do before, and studied her. "You greeted me with enthusiasm last night," he said quietly. "Will you readily do as much on this one?"

"Last night, I thought you were my destined lover," Vivienne declared. "While now I know you to be a man determined to avenge himself upon his brother at any cost."

She could have sworn a twinkle lit his eye. "A destined lover? Surely not. I thought you too sensible for such folly."

Vivienne's face felt aflame as she nodded, so embarrassed was she by what she had believed. "It was because of Alexander's tale, of course."

"What tale?"

"Do you not know what he said to encourage me to sleep in that chamber?"

Erik shook his head. "He pledged only that you would be there. He did not tell me how or why." They stood in silence for a moment, then he eased his stance. "Tell me of it. How would such a destined lover have found you there, according to the tale?"

Vivienne eyed the rope and decided that recounting this tale was the less troubling possibility for her next few moments. "By spying me through some portal between the realms . . ."

"What realms?"

"The realms of fairies and of mortals." What might have passed for a smile touched his lips and Vivienne took a shaking breath. "The tale Alexander recounted was of a maiden, seduced each of three nights in sequence by a fairy lover smitten with her charms, then captured as his wife for all eternity. One of the windows in that chamber is reputed to open unto the fairy realm, by his accounting, and the maiden, once she departed thus, was never seen again."

"She was stolen then, as you were."

"She was courted by her lover true," Vivienne corrected firmly. "And was claimed for the bride price of a red red rose, a fairy rose which proved to be wrought of ice. The mark of its melting remains upon the floor of Kinfairlie's hall, though the event occurred years past."

"Ah, so this is the root of your demand for a three night courtship and a red red rose."

Vivienne only flushed more deeply.

Erik regarded her with an amusement that softened his features in a most alluring way. Vivienne wished he would look stern again, for it was easier to distrust him fully then. "And you believed this tale, with solely the proof of a glimmer upon the floor?"

"It was true. It is true. I believe it yet." Vivienne met his skeptical gaze. "It is not uncommon in these parts for mortals to find their way to the fairy realm, no less to be taken there. Not a hundred years ago, Thomas of Erceldoune did the very same, though he returned briefly to recount the tale of it."

"Doubtless he but strayed away from home and concocted a finer tale upon his return than the truth."

"He proved where he had been, by predicting future events with alacrity," Vivienne argued. "Fairies can see the future, so he proved his visit there when his portents proved true."

"But there is no fairy realm. There is naught in all creation save what a man can see and hold in his hands."

"I know that to be less than the truth."

"Yet you did not meet a fairy lover, much less a destined one."

And Vivienne could summon no argument against that. All the same, their gazes locked and held for a long moment, a moment in which the wind seemed to still around them and the air grow warm. Vivienne recalled her instinctive desire to welcome this man, no less the magic they had wrought together in the tower chamber so easily. She stared into his eyes and remembered her curious sense that they loved as if they had loved a thousand times before and she wondered then if she had unwittingly uttered a truth.

What if Erik was her destined lover, albeit a mortal one? She wondered whether he thought much the same, for his eyes darkened to an unruly indigo. It was not the first time she had sensed that their thoughts were as one, which surely was a mark of those fated to be together.

The prospect fairly made her dizzy. What if she had been granted the chance to have her every desire fulfilled?

Erik cleared his throat and frowned, tearing his gaze from hers. His hand flexed upon the rope, as if he was keenly aware suddenly of its burden and its import. "So you slept in that chamber, seeking the same fate as this Thomas of Erceldoune or the maiden of Alexander's tale?"

"And you came through the window, and you seduced me sweetly," Vivienne said, for she knew she was no fool even if she had behaved impulsively. "Thus I believed that the same tale came true for me as for the lost maiden."

Erik studied her with narrowed eyes. "The mortal truth of me must be a disappointment indeed for one who expected a fairy prince."

"Your scheme for my future certainly is." Vivienne saw uncertainty in his expression and dared to believe that he had been driven to do what was not in his nature. She took a chance, and met him toe to toe, then tapped a finger upon his chest. "What would your father think of this deed you insist upon? Would he be gladdened to know that you were prepared to truss a woman to get a child upon her?"

Erik's eyes flashed. "My father and his opinions are of no import in this!"

Vivienne persisted despite his manner, for she suspected that he would not injure her. She needed to know which side of him was the truth of his nature. "Would your father be glad to know that you chose a woman simply because she had denied your brother?"

"Likely so! If there is but one person in Christendom who is not seduced by my brother's charm, it is only good sense to ally with that person in wresting back what he has stolen from me."

Vivienne regarded him in surprise. "You did not say as much before."

Erik shoved a hand through his hair and turned away with a frown. "Why I make any decision is not of import to you."

"Is it not, though it shapes my own fate?"

He granted her a piercing glance. "But one thing shapes your fate, and that is your ability to conceive my son." He hefted the rope. "How the deed is achieved is your choice."

"What a fine sentiment that is!" Vivienne retorted, stung again that he saw only one advantage in her presence and doubting more with every moment that he would use the rope. "Your father is dead, you have only just heard the tidings and you do not mourn him. Indeed, you think only of your pleasure."

Anger prompted Vivienne to say more than she should have done, but she doubted that Erik would hurt her and she felt she had little left to lose. "My father has been dead almost a year, and I mourn him every moment of every day. The day the tidings came, I wept like a babe all the day and through the night. What merit is there in bearing the son of a man who does not mourn the loss of his own sire? Perhaps it is better for all if the treacherous Sinclair clan is no more!"

She tossed her hair over her shoulder and glared at him, telling herself not to be shaken by the bleak light that had claimed his eyes. "Do what you will to me," she challenged. "You speak aright. I am your captive. I am no more than your chattel. I have been bought and sold, and I have no choice what my fate might be."

Vivienne jabbed her finger at her own chest. "But I can believe whatsoever I will, and I choose to believe that each soul has a fate, that every soul has a destined lover, that injustice will be righted. And I know that a man who does not mourn the death of his father is of no merit whatsoever in any realm. You will scarce persuade me otherwise. Get your son upon me and you can nurse that viper at your own breast."

Vivienne marched away from her astonished captor, not truly believing that she would get far. It was long before his footsteps echoed behind her, though, even longer before his hand closed over her elbow. His grasp was gentle and she closed her eyes against her own weakness, knowing that if he chose to try to seduce her with his touch, he would succeed.

"You speak fairly," he said, his voice gruff. "Though no person can know what another suffers without seeing into that other's heart."

Vivienne knew she should not turn, knew she should not meet his gaze, but did as much anyway. He was silhouetted against the evening sky, so still and intent of manner that her unruly heart skipped.

The sky was smeared with orange and pink, a few dark clouds marring the splendid color. The stars had emerged above them, though the sun still burned red on the horizon. In the light of the dying sun, Erik's hair looked more ruddy than she knew it to be and his scar was illuminated harshly.

But there was pain in his eyes, pain that she knew was not feigned. "Why a son?" she whispered.

He looked across the water, his expression somber. His words were soft when he spoke, an ache lurking beneath each of them. "Because my daughters are lost unless I can produce a son, mine beyond dispute, to reclaim Blackleith." He looked down at her. "And he must be older than any son my brother begets. These are the conditions of the Earl of Sutherland, that there is a line of succession assured afore he aids me to reclaim Blackleith."

"Daughters?" Vivienne whispered, feeling her anger fade as surely as the sun's light.

"Two," he admitted, bowing his head with a grief that made Vivienne yearn to console him. "I have not seen them in a year, I cannot know their fate. I dare not believe that Nicholas will treat my daughters more kindly than he did my wife."

"He killed her?"

He shook his head and turned away, overwhelmed by the tidings he shared. Indeed, a lone tear made its course down his tanned cheek and though he did not wipe it away, his expression turned fierce.

That single tear did more to challenge Vivienne's conclusions than a torrent could. Indeed, she was reminded of a rock finally cracking beneath some pressure, of a fissure appearing where none had been before.

This was why Erik had sought her and her womb, because his dead wife could not produce the son that would see his daughters saved. And because those two lives hung in the balance, he dared not wed her, lest she could not conceive a son, lest he had to find another maiden to provide the son he so desperately needed.

Vivienne could not deny that his choice could not have been one readily made. She saw how it troubled him to confess to what he had done, and knew it was not in his nature to deceive. She could not fight against the appeal of a man who did what was against his very nature for the sake of his children.

"You should have told me sooner."

His blue gaze fixed upon her. "Would you have taken my wager then? Would your brother have agreed to my terms? I think not. The sole way to pursue my goal was with deception."

"You have risked my alliance in so doing."

He shook his head. "There is far more at stake than that. Understand that I will not fail them, independent of the cost. I may have only one chance, but I will pursue it until my dying breath. Be it you or another, a maiden will bear my son. My daughters' lives rely on no less. I chose you, but if you spurn me I will merely choose another."

He stared down at her, his eyes a vivid blue, and his words softened. "I would prefer that you not do so, though I recognize that is the risk of confessing the truth to you."

He would not have felt compelled to be honest, unless he felt some regard for her, and Vivienne knew it well.

On impulse, she reached up and caught Erik's face in

her hands. She stretched and touched her lips fleetingly to his, wanting only to console him. She tasted his astonishment, then drew back slightly. She found herself wanting to aid him, wanting to aid those two little girls, though she knew she should not have done so without the benefit of a nuptial vow between them.

"What are their names?"

"Mairi," he said gruffly. "And Astrid. Mairi is dark and has seen six summers, while fair Astrid has seen only three." He measured their heights with one hand as he spoke, the harshness of his features seeming to melt when he spoke of them.

It was his undisguised affection that made Vivienne's choice for her. After all, she was a maiden no longer, so that damage was done. But good could come of Vivienne's loss, if she did not turn away from Erik now, if she still tried to conceive that son.

Impulse guided her tongue and even as she spoke, she wondered whether she erred, though truly it seemed that she had no choice.

"I do not know whether I can do what you desire of me," Vivienne whispered, her heart pounding at her own audacity. "I cannot scry the future. But if you treat me with honor, then for the sake of your daughters, I will try to give you that son."

Erik turned and cast the rope away. He met Vivienne's gaze, determination in his eyes along with something else that made her heart leap. "Then we have a wager in truth, lady mine," he said and claimed her lips with a possessive kiss.

And the joy in that kiss told Vivienne much of his measure. She tasted his relief and his fear, she tasted his sorrow and his desperate hope. She met the demand in his caress unflinchingly, knowing that she would offer her all to aid him now. She did not know if she had chosen rightly, she did not know if all would be resolved well, but she could regret nothing when he kissed her with such leisurely passion. She felt part of a great tale, of the righting of an enormous wrong, and surely that would be reward enough.

IT HAD BEEN SO LONG since any soul had made a concession to Erik that Vivienne's offer astounded him. He did not have the luxury of marvelling in it, however, for he dared not grant her time to change her thinking. He had no intent of letting her rescind her offer, no intent of giving her cause for regret.

This mating must be as wondrous as the last had been.

He caught her close against him, savoring anew how willingly she met him, how readily she trusted him. The trust of another was a forgotten elixir for Erik and he was nigh intoxicated that Vivienne gave of it so generously.

Her kiss was both sweet and wild, unlike any he had tasted before, and it awakened an unexpected yearning within him. He wished that he would be the last man to savor her many charms, he wished that the way they had met had been wrought of destiny, not his scheming. He wished that this venture might prove a success for both of them.

For this night, he put his worries aside. For this night, he chose to lose himself in both Vivienne and the enchanting tale she told.

He kissed her deeply, delighted that she was so unafraid. Her hand slid into his hair and she impatiently urged him closer. She arched her back and stretched to her toes, offering more of the feast of her kiss than he had had before. He shed his gloves with a measure of his own impatience, knowing that half measures would not serve either of them this night. He wanted her nude, he wanted to see her fully in the sun's last light, he wanted to witness her pleasure.

His hands fell on the laces at the sides of her kirtle and he loosed them without breaking their kiss. Vivienne gasped, perhaps at the chill of the wind through her chemise, but he slipped his hands through the sides of her kirtle, letting his hands warm her. She was so slender that his hands almost closed around her waist.

Even with the barrier of cloth between them, he felt her pulse beneath his palms and its quick pace reminded him of how new she was to lovemaking. Not wanting to frighten her, he let his hands ease over her ribs to finally capture her breasts. When he touched her pert nipples, Vivienne broke their kiss with a cry.

Erik held her fast before him, one hand clasped in the small of her back, and stared into her eyes as he caressed her nipple again. She swallowed and her eyes widened to emerald pools, but she did not step away. He watched as his thumb eased over her nipple, felt it grow more taut, noted how she inhaled when the roughened edge of his thumb moved across the tender flesh.

She smiled and he was spellbound. "I like that," she whispered and he could not help but smile himself.

"So I have noted."

She flushed at his comment, but did not remove his hand. He repeated the caress, savoring how her eyes darkened. "Sorcery," she whispered.

Erik shook his head. "It is a force far more reliable

than any witchery," he said and she laughed. It was such
a merry sound that he felt the weight of his burdens
lighten.

He chose to forget his responsibilities for these few
moments. He let one hand curve around the ripeness of
her breast, and lifted the other to the clasp of her cloak.
He unfastened it, letting the cloak fall to a pile around her
ankles. She was garbed in a richness unfamiliar to him,
the garments sliding over his hands in a silken caress.

He lifted her kirtle over her head and cast it aside with
care, his hands returning to her breasts. Her chemise was
so sheer a linen that he could see the darkness of her are-
olas through the cloth, and it was so finely woven that her
nipples made peaks in the cloth.

He pulled her close and kissed her again, untying the
lace that held the neck of her chemise closed while he did
so. Even as he deepened his kiss, he let his hand slide
over her flesh, pushing the cloth away from her neck. He
lifted his head, discovered that both of them were breathless and was tempted again to smile.

He realized that he had not been so tempted for years,
though it was not the first time he had felt his lips curving in Vivienne's presence. She was a balm to his unhap-
piness, a sunbeam that shone into the darkest corners.

He looked down at the treasure in his arms and devoured the sight that darkness had denied to him the night
before. She was indeed a beauty, more beauteous than he
had begun to guess. Vivienne's skin was softer than soft,
its hue like that of a white rose's petals. The charming
freckles upon her nose were echoed by an artful scatter-
ing of lighter freckles across her collarbone. Her breasts
were ripe enough to fill his palm, soft enough to tempt his

touch. He lifted her breast in his palm, then bent and kissed the nipple with no small reverence.

The scent of her skin turned his salute to a more burning desire. He found his lips closing around her with urgency, his tongue flicking the nipple, his teeth grazing the peak that his thumb had recently teased.

Vivienne gasped, then seized a fistful of his hair and rose to her toes. She kissed his ear, his throat, his shoulder with a fervor he could well understand. Her passion fueled his own with astonishing ease. He pushed her chemise away, cursing the dozens of buttons that held the sleeves tight. She laughed and they loosed her from the garment's clutch with impatience. He then caught her buttocks in his hand and lifted her against himself, letting her feel the effect that she had upon him. He burned for her, as never he had for another woman.

Vivienne rolled her hips against him in silent demand. He could have claimed her then, but feared to rush her overmuch. He caught her up in his arms, instead, intending to seduce her more slowly within the ruins on the point.

Vivienne, though, shook her head with unexpected vehemence when she saw his direction. "Not there," she said, wrinkling her nose in a most fetching manner. "Here, in the last of the sunlight, is better." Her hand slid down the side of his face, her fingertip sliding across his lips. "I want to see you fully this night. I want no shadows between us."

He was startled that their desires were so similar. Recent years had taught him caution, that matters which seemed too good to be believed were oft untrustworthy. He wondered fleetingly whether he was a fool to believe her unexpected pledge, whether she deceived him deliberately for some mysterious reason of her own.

Then Vivienne kissed him, her tongue dancing so boldly with his own that he could refuse her nothing, especially a deed he wanted so ardently himself. And thus, Erik, once again, surrendered to Vivienne's enchantment.

# Chapter Six

In moments, Erik had created a nest for them out of their two cloaks, the fur-lined one on top, the lady gleaming like ivory as she sat atop it.

He knelt, intending to loose her garters, but Vivienne kicked her feet playfully. "You are yet fully garbed. I would see as much of you as you have seen of me before we continue."

Erik paused, not wanting to dampen her ardor with the truth of his scars. "There is no need . . ."

"There is every need," she argued, rising gracefully to her knees. "And since you are shy, I will aid you." Her hands caught at the buckle of his belt, her gaze steadily meeting his own. Erik caught her hands in his to halt her, then noted the determined set of her lips. Vivienne lifted her chin, her gaze bright with challenge. He saw that she knew he was not shy, that she knew what he feared to show her.

He saw that she was not afraid to see whatever he bared.

Indeed, she had not flinched at the scar on his face. He

lifted his hands away and let her continue what she had begun.

She smiled, well pleased with her triumph, and unbuckled his belt. His weapons were laid aside with the care they should have been shown, then she returned to unlace his boiled leather jerkin. She moved with an efficient haste and he merely watched her, wanting to witness every nuance of her response in the moment he dreaded. His tabard was laid aside, his boots joined it. His chemise fluttered in the wind and her fingers trembled slightly as she reached for the lace at the neck.

She held his gaze as she worked the lace loose of every hole, as she finally pulled it free, as her elegant hands closed upon the hem of the garment and pulled it over his head. He shook free of it with impatience and watched her look.

The left side of his body was marred more than his face, the evidence of the assault against him written in his own flesh. He knew it was not easy to look upon, he knew that it was yet a livid red in places.

Erik should not have expected Vivienne to hesitate, for she did not. She lifted one hand, even as her gaze ran busily over him, and lifted her fingertips to the worst knot of marred flesh. "Nicholas did this?" she asked in a whisper.

"He dispatched those who did."

She surveyed the scars, tracing the worst of them with a gentle fingertip. "He meant to see you dead," she said and it was no query. Erik did not reply, and she granted him a glance as bright as that of a bird. "Does it still hurt?"

He shook his head, his throat tight at the sight of her. He saw the glitter of tears on her lashes, watched them fall like jewels as she shook her head at what he had borne.

"You should let the sun kiss it," she said softly. "For its caress heals much." He swallowed, then watched incredulous as she bent and touched her lips to his scar.

Erik was humbled by her gesture. He had given her so little, he had offered her less, and yet Vivienne granted him another priceless gift.

Any doubts he had of her were folly, to be certain.

Before Erik could speak, Vivienne ran her hands across him with a proprietary ease. She seemed to sense that he was overwhelmed for she spoke pertly. "My brothers are not wrought so broad as you," she said. "Nor have my younger brothers so much hair upon their chests."

He found his lips coaxed again into forming that unfamiliar curve of a smile. "Am I to be encouraged by this?"

She laughed. "I should think so, for I find you far more alluring than my siblings. Is that not better?"

"It is to my thinking."

"And it can be no small thing to so readily agree," she said, even as her fingertips slid to his nipple and teased it to a peak as he had done to hers. Erik inhaled sharply, but Vivienne did not cease her caress.

"Surely I can torment you with pleasure in my turn?" she whispered. There was pure mischief in her eyes as she kissed his nipple, flicking her tongue against the sensitive peak as he had done to her just moments before.

He whispered her name and caught her close. He pulled her face to his and kissed her soundly, feeling the curve of her smile beneath his mouth. She was as merry as a beam of sunlight herself, as undaunted by whatsoever confronted her that one could not help but be gladdened in her presence.

Erik chose to gladden the lady with his. He laid her upon their piled cloaks, and caught her feet in his hands so that she could not squirm away. He bent then and untied her garters with his teeth, kissing the inside of her knees as he did so.

"It tickles!" she complained, even as she laughed and writhed. He gave no pause, but relieved her of stockings, garters and shoes with deliberate slowness. He flicked his tongue into the hollow behind her knees and kissed her shins. He eased her stockings down first one leg, then the other, with the tip of his nose, pausing time and again to nibble and kiss and tease.

Vivienne twisted on the fur cloak so vigorously that her hair was tangled beneath her. She begged for mercy but he granted her none, she laughed until she was breathless, but the merry sparkle of her eyes urged him on. He grazed the soft flesh around her ankle with his teeth, he kissed her arch, he slid his tongue between her toes. He paused only when her stockings were shed, and then only to savor how flushed and dishevelled she had become.

Then he traced kisses up the inside of her legs, burning a path to her sweet heat. When his mouth closed over her, she arched and moaned, then spread her thighs in welcome. He felt her arousal and it heightened his own. He savored how she responded to his caress and felt his own desire redouble. He held her fast and coaxed her to greater heights, halting just before she found her pleasure and beginning anew. She moaned, she writhed, she knotted her hands in his hair.

"Together," she cried, and he could resist her no

longer. He cast aside his chausses and held his weight over her, was captured utterly by her avid embrace. She held his shoulders while he entered her heat, then caught him close and cossetted him within herself. He moved within her and felt there was no other place or time that mattered.

Vivienne opened her eyes and smiled at him, her cheeks flushed and eyes sparkling, her breath coming quickly. She clutched his shoulders and wrapped her legs around him, she matched her movement to his own and he saw his own marvel echoed in her wondrous eyes.

They shared the moment, as never he had shared it with a woman before. Beatrice had always looked away, even before his face had been marred, as if only enduring her marital obligation to him. But Vivienne delighted in their coupling, she was possessed of as great a desire as he, she was unashamed of her passion. He liked her honest embrace of pleasure quite well and he found that her joy abed only heightened his own.

He could trust her passion, for it was not feigned.

Erik could not have expressed his admiration, not as he moved within her and she cast a spell around them more potent than any potion. There was nothing in all his world save Vivienne. They watched each other, each daring the other to endure longer. Erik thought his very flesh might burst into flames, so ardently did they pursue the highest peak. He noted how her flush rose, how her hips bucked, how the tight bead of her tightened against him, but he waited until she cried out in ecstasy.

Only then did he let passion snare him fully, only then did he roar with his own release.

Only when he laid his brow upon Vivienne's shoulder moments later, awed by the magic they had wrought together, did he mourn this situation. Erik wished he could have known what a man and a woman could share, and that he had known it before taking his wife. Erik regretted that he and Beatrice had never found such pleasure together.

Further, Erik wished that he could have met Vivienne unfettered himself, wished that he could have courted her before his life had become what it was.

He wished he had met Vivienne when he had been as young of heart and as merry as she. He wished she could have seen the best of him, not the worst. Beatrice had claimed that prize, though he knew she had never been glad of it as Vivienne welcomed what meager offering he could make to her now.

There were so many matters that could not be undone. Erik had married to suit his father's ambitions, not his own. He had surrendered the best of himself to a woman who cared nothing for him and only now, when it might be too late to mend matters, did he see the fullness of the price he had paid.

Exhausted to his very marrow, content in Vivienne's embrace, Erik let a single word of regret pass his lips, a word that would cost him dearly.

"Beatrice," he murmured, then sighed at the empty promise of his nuptial vows. He fell asleep then, but he was not destined to slumber for long.

BEATRICE!

Vivienne's eyes snapped open and she stared at the man slumbering half atop her. *Beatrice!* How could Erik have mistaken her for any other woman, after they had conjured such pleasure together?

Had he been thinking of Beatrice while they made love?

Had he imagined that she was Beatrice?

The very prospect was revolting beyond belief. How *dare* he?

Erik slumbered now, his brow upon her shoulder, a man untroubled by his deeds. His hair fanned over his shoulders, the hair upon his chest tickled against Vivienne's breasts. She could feel the weight of his legs atop her own, and the tickle of the hair upon them, as well. Though he still braced most of his weight upon his forearms, Vivienne was trapped beneath him.

That was precisely where she did not wish to be.

In normal circumstance, she might have wished to leave him slumber, but Vivienne was not inclined to consider Erik's wishes in this moment. She placed her hands upon his shoulders and pushed, to no discernible effect.

He did not so much as stir.

Vivienne pushed harder and Erik sighed, then rolled to his side with a murmured apology. His leg was still cast across hers, his heat fast by her side. His hand twined in her hair and there was a rare contentment in his expression.

Vivienne refused to be beguiled. He probably dreamed of his beloved dead wife! She snatched her hair from his fingertips and shoved aside his leg. He blinked that she moved so abruptly and stirred finally, his manner that of a man waking from a dream.

"Cur!" Vivienne cried as she leapt to her feet. "Knave, blackguard, and wretch!" Erik blinked at her, apparently confused. "You know well enough what you have done," she said, shaking her finger at him. "Do not pretend otherwise. I will not be swayed by your guile."

She found her chemise and hastily drew it over herself, seeing already a gleam of desire in Erik's eyes. She left the buttons upon the sleeves unfastened, and the sleeves hung comically long as a result. "Dream all the night long of your wife, if you so desire," she bade him. "For you will never lay a hand upon me again."

She turned her back upon his surprise and gathered her scattered clothing. The night sky was indigo now, the stars gleaming in the firmament, and the wind had turned chill. Vivienne's hands shook so in her anger that she had trouble fastening the garters on her stockings. The cursed sleeves of the chemise were in her way, and she wished heartily that one of her sisters *had* stolen it. It helped little that she felt Erik watching her clumsy attempts to dress, helped even less that he seemed confused by her manner.

He could at least have protested his innocence, she fumed in silence. Though she would have known it to be a lie, it would have soothed her that he cared for her annoyance.

"Were you not pleased?" he asked finally and Vivienne cast a shoe at him in vexation.

"How well pleased were you to invoke your wife?" she demanded. "Beatrice!" she mimicked, then spun in a sweep of skirts. "How sweet to know that I am indistinguishable from your wife abed."

Erik got to his feet with a haste uncommon to him. "I did not do as much."

Vivienne propped her hands upon her hips. "You most certainly did. Do not be so fool as to accuse me of being deaf! I know what I heard, and I heard your wife's name slip from your lips."

Erik shoved a hand through his hair and frowned, then donned his own garb with efficient gestures. It appeared he would say no more, the very prospect of that making Vivienne's blood boil. She glared at him, infuriated beyond belief and unwilling to leave the matter be.

Erik seemed to take uncommon care in fastening his belt and ensuring his weapons were as he desired.

"This is a fine reward you grant to one pledged to aiding your quest," Vivienne said when she could keep silent no longer.

He spared her a glance. "You look as alluring as the Valkyrie must do," he said. "Indeed, it is some prize you surrender to me with such a sight alone." An unexpected twinkle lit his eyes, and though Vivienne blinked, it lingered there. "It might be worth vexing you again in future."

"What is that to mean?"

"That you look like a warrior maiden who will not be denied her due." He inclined his head slightly and shook his head. "Though their price is not small."

Vivienne did not know whether to be insulted or flattered. She regarded Erik warily, feeling the lure of a tale she did not know. "I know nothing of these Valkyries," she said, as coldly as she could manage.

"They are the servants of Odin, the great god, and sent by him to lead fallen warriors to their eternal reward at Valhalla." Erik studied Vivienne for a moment. "They gather men's souls, though be warned that I am not keen to surrender mine as yet."

Vivienne shook her head. "I have no desire for your soul."

"Do you not? I thought it the desire of all women to claim men's souls, and you do not appear to be a woman prepared to accept half her due." He cast his cloak over his shoulder with that graceful gesture she so admired, and Vivienne did not know whether he meant to challenge her or flatter her. "Surely you at least desire to infect a man's thinking, persuading him to acknowledge unseen forces, for example, when he knows there to be none." He offered his hand to Vivienne, though she did not yet take it.

"And what manner of force was Beatrice?"

"One you need know little about." Erik glanced to the sky, to his horse, which now stood expectant, then back at Vivienne. "It is time we ride."

Vivienne folded her arms across her chest and did not step toward his outstretched hand. "Why did you say her name?"

Erik looked away. "It is not of import."

"I say it is."

"You shall have no answer from me."

"Then I shall not travel with you."

"We have made a wager," he said, his tone somewhat sharper. "You have no choice."

He had the wits this time to not call her chattel, though Vivienne guessed he thought it.

"There is always a choice," she asserted. "Though some choices are harder than others, and there are always wagers broken. I could prove as much to you, as well as the existence of the unseen realm of fairies, if I chose to recount to you the tale of Thomas of Erceldoune."

"And do you so choose?"

Vivienne glared at him, thinking the query deserved no answer.

Erik frowned at the coast, then impaled her with a bright glance. "Mine was an unwilling utterance."

"How do I know as much?"

"Because I swear it to you." He held her gaze then, his own bright with surety, and Vivienne found her determination faltering. "And I apologize for it, though it was unwittingly done."

"It must not happen again."

"Be assured that it will not." He lowered his voice to the intimacy of a whisper, he looked at her as if she alone existed in all the world for him. His eyes gleamed with intent and something else, something that made Vivienne's traitorous heart leap.

"Ride with me, Vivienne," Erik urged, her name a caress upon his tongue. "Ride with me, bear my son in due time, and meanwhile tell me of this Thomas of Erceldoune."

The chance to recount a favored tale was an invitation Vivienne could not refuse, or so she told herself.

The truth was that Erik Sinclair, with a plea in his eyes, was hard to resist.

Before she considered her choice, she put her hand within Erik's. Her heart skipped at the warmth of his flesh, at the way his fingers closed possessively around her own. He raised her hand to his lips and kissed her knuckles, as eloquent an apology as she could desire, and she knew herself powerless against his allure.

It was dangerous to let him convince her of his innocence, it was dangerous to ride pressed against his strength, it was treacherous indeed to have pledged to bear his son. But she had made that vow and she would keep it.

A thousand tales had taught her that, no matter the consequences of a promise, breaking one's word led to far worse consequences. Those tales had taught her a number of other lessons as well and she dared to hope that Erik might be persuaded in his turn of some of the beliefs she held so dear.

ERIK WAS STILL SHAKEN by the near price of his error. When she had turned upon him with flashing eyes, he had been certain that Vivienne would spurn him, that she would turn her back upon him forevermore. The prospect had struck fear to his very marrow.

He had been prepared to say nigh anything, to make any pledge, to ensure that she rode forward with him. He dared not consider why he was so determined that this woman should think well of him, though he reminded himself sternly to allow himself no tender feelings for her as yet. Fondness for Vivienne would only make any choice he might be compelled to make all the more difficult.

Instead of concern at his own fear of losing her, Erik felt a certain satisfaction at having persuaded Vivienne to continue their journey. He savored the sweet curve of her in his lap and a sense of triumph as well. He reasoned that it had only been the possibility that she had already conceived his son that had prompted his ready words.

There could be no other sensible reason for his desire to reassure her.

Vivienne spared him a glance over her shoulder, her

eyes already sparkling with the prospect of sharing her tale, and he marvelled anew at how readily she could lighten his mood. Though formidable challenges lay ahead of him, he had not felt such a sense of promise in years.

He had never yet felt that his quest had any chance of success, simply that it was a duty he could not evade. He thought now of Mairi and Astrid, of seeing them again, of hearing their laughter once more, and his heart swelled at the prospect.

"It is said that this tale is true, that there was a Thomas of Erceldoune but a hundred years ago," Vivienne said. "He was reputed to have been laird of the holding of Erceldoune, which was then near the meeting of the Leader and the Tweed rivers. Melrose Abbey is in that vicinity, as well."

"I have heard tell of that abbey," Erik acknowledged. Vivienne fastened the buttons of her sleeves with care, her head bowed. He wished that he could see her features and watch the curve of her lips as she recounted the tale. Erik sated himself—for the moment—by fitting his hand into the indent of her waist.

She took no apparent note of his gesture, as if his hand rightly belonged there, which suited him well indeed.

"He was also called Thomas the Rhymer, and True Thomas, for both the rhymes of his tales and the veracity of his prophecies. He saw the future while in the fairy realm, and told of it upon his return to the mortal world. After his second departure and with the passage of time, his prophecies were proven aright. In this, I think, is your proof that matters unseen are true."

A shadow separated itself from the darkness ahead,

sparing Erik the need to debate this assertion. He would not be so readily persuaded of whimsy as that, but neither did he wish to mar the camaraderie between himself and Vivienne.

Erik recognized the stocky silhouette of Ruari. "I did not ride so far as you bade," that man said gruffly, the way he twisted the reins in his hands revealing that he was not entirely certain what response his disobedience would merit. He cleared his throat when Erik said nothing. "You see, I thought it would be better to turn west here, rather than ride past the high tower ahead. I thought to keep the horse fresh by awaiting you here, rather than proceeding and having to ride back."

Erik was not truly surprised to find Ruari so close at hand. He had known even while arguing with the older man that he would not be easily rid of his presence. His father had oft commented on Ruari's steadfast reliability.

"Your counsel is good, Ruari, as so oft it is," he said and watched the older man's tension ease. "One can never be certain what eyes are open."

"Especially at Ravensmuir," Vivienne said.

"Aye, Ravensmuir," Ruari muttered, casting a look over his shoulder to the keep. "It can be no good portent to invoke the name of that keep with such frequency, and less good it is to linger in its proximity. I have heard tell that the Laird of Ravensmuir can hear the fart of a mouse at the other end of Christendom, no less that he could command a peregrine to bring him that very mouse for his dinner, if he should so desire it, and that his will would be done."

"Nonsense, surely," Erik said, biting back a smile.

"Nonsense, indeed," Vivienne agreed. "My uncle has sharp hearing, though not so sharp as that. And the birds beneath his command are ravens, not peregrines. It is at the abode of my other uncle, at Inverfyre, that one finds falcons beneath the laird's command."

Ruari paused in the act of mounting his steed to regard Vivienne with horror. "Inverfyre and Ravensmuir both! Surely you cannot be kin with them all!"

"Surely I am."

"But they are said to be sorcerers with unholy powers, men who can summon the tide and invoke demons to serve their will!"

Vivienne laughed. "What folly!"

Ruari then eased his steed closer. "Erik, lad, upon the grave of your sire, I feel compelled to warn you that this path can only lead to woe . . ."

"All paths lead to woe for me in this moment, Ruari," Erik said, his light tone belying his words. "I but attempt to choose the least dire fate."

"And you make a poor task of it, lad, that much is certain."

"I thank you for your counsel." Erik's words were so unwelcoming that Ruari heaved a sigh. "Are you prepared to ride onward? We shall take the road west upon your advice."

Ruari was clearly not content even to have had his suggestion accepted. The horses matched pace, settling into a steady gallop, but the older man shook his head ruefully. "Stories I have heard of Ravensmuir that are fit to curdle a man's blood and freeze his very marrow. Aye, I have heard tell of the ravens loosed from Ravensmuir's tower, no less that they are sent forth as spies for the laird or to pluck out the eyes of his enemies."

"What folly!" Vivienne said again, laughter brimming

in her voice. "No raven has ever plucked the eyes from a foe, to my knowledge."

"And even greater witchery," Ruari declared with a raised finger. "I have heard that the laird talks to such birds!"

Vivienne chuckled. "How else would he gather tidings from afar?"

"With messengers and envoys, perhaps, as most men of property do," Erik suggested and Vivienne granted him a bright smile.

Her next words chilled his heart though. "It is true that knowledge of the ravens' language is passed from father to son," she said, clearly at ease with this uncommon detail. "And that secrets are exchanged between laird and bird." She looked back at Erik, eyes twinkling. "But surely a man who grants no credit to matters unseen would simply believe this to be a fable, and thus not worrisome in the least."

A glance to the high shadowed tower looming behind them revealed tiny specks against the night sky. They might well be ravens, circling the tower, and their very presence was unsettling.

"Surely so," Erik said with a resolve he did not quite feel.

Vivienne's gaze glinted with merry mischief. "I think you believe more of this tale than you admit you do, and I shall prove it to you."

Erik scoffed. "You cannot do as much."

Vivienne arched a russet brow, then turned her back upon him once more. To his astonishment, she emitted a piercing cry and raised her fist skyward.

"What in the name of God is that?" Ruari demanded, crossing himself with vigor. "You could stop a man's heart with such a scream, lass, upon that you can rely! Do you think we have need of waking every soul hereabouts to our passage?"

Vivienne ignored him, so avidly did she watch the sky. Erik was certain that she merely teased him, but then there came a flutter of wings. An answering cry rang from the heavens above, one so loud that it nigh rent their ears. Erik's horse shied and he turned his attention then to soothing the beast. He stroked Fafnir's side and spoke firmly to the stallion, holding the reins tightly while he calmed the horse.

A shadow darker than the night sky descended with awesome grace and Vivienne cried again, nigh ensuring that the horse bolted in truth. Erik swore softly and held the reins fast, but she was oblivious to their danger. Her face was alight with joy as she furled her cloak over her arm and, against all expectation, stretched it out in fearless invitation.

"Mother of God!" Ruari cried.

The raven landed so heavily that Vivienne's arm dipped low beneath the burden of its weight. Fafnir whinnied in terror at the unfamiliar rustle of feathers so close behind his head, folded his ears back and began to run. Erik locked his arm around Vivienne's waist and bent his attention upon soothing the horse.

The horse was disinclined to heed him.

Half an eternity and several fields later, Fafnir settled more or less to his previous gait. The steed still tossed his head and trotted sideways for a few steps, discontent with the addition to their entourage. Erik knew that the skittishness in the destrier's step meant that if the bird did not remain still, Fafnir would bolt again.

Vivienne released a shaking breath. "Surely your steed is trained?"

"Surely you are mad to have summoned this bird," Erik snapped. "Can you not see that you have endangered all of us with this folly?"

She looked slightly guilty. "It was not my intent to do as much. Every horse I have ever ridden has been well accustomed to birds."

"Because they were likely reared in Ravensmuir and Inverfyre, and raised to endure such an unholy alliance!" Ruari contributed, galloping from behind them.

Vivienne granted him a scornful glance. "Every nobleman in Christendom hunts with hawks, and does so from his horse's saddle. There is nothing uncommon in this, much less any alliance *unholy*."

"Then Fafnir's experience has been limited by my own deeds," Erik said. "For it is not the lot of outlaws to hunt with hawks and hounds."

He glanced at the bird and was astounded at its size, for he had never seen a raven so close. Its plumage gleamed black, except for a tuft of white feathers over its left eye which gave it a querulous air.

He was even more unsettled by its manner, for what might have been intellect gleamed in its dark eyes. The raven tilted its head and regarded Erik with such an eerie stare that it seemed to know his very thoughts. Indeed, the creature did not so much as blink, its eyes shining as it regarded him steadily.

"Madness and folly!" Ruari cried, gesturing to the bird. "Men may hunt with hawks, but a peregrine is a far cry from a raven so willing to land on a woman's fist. Have you taken a sorceress to your bed, lad? What price will she demand of us if she can summon a wild bird?

Doubtless she can whistle up a wind, or strike a man dead with a glance. Woe will come of this choice, of that you can be certain!"

"Such tales of witches are nonsense, Ruari," Erik said, forcing his voice to sound more calm than he felt.

Did he imagine that the bird smirked at him?

"Indeed, Erik is convinced that the only truth is what a man can hold within his own hands," Vivienne said sweetly. "It surely must be coincidence and no more that brought Medusa to my fist when I summoned her."

Perhaps Vivienne meant to provoke him in return for his uttering Beatrice's name. Erik chose to not let her perceive the effectiveness of her ploy. "It is only good sense to be skeptical of such unseen and unproven abilities."

"Good sense!" Ruari snorted his skepticism. "It is no more than folly! Indeed, lad, you leave half the forces of Christendom out of that accounting, and to your own disadvantage at that. What of the miracles wrought by saints and their relics? What of the marvel of the mass itself? Do common bread and wine not turn themselves to the body and blood of Christ? Why, if there was no more in this world than what a man might see for himself, then there would be much left unexplained, to be sure."

Erik was very aware that the raven looked between them, as if listening to their conversation.

As if it might recall and recount that conversation to another, perhaps the lady's uncle at Ravensmuir.

But that was nonsense!

"You are overly certain, Ruari, of these forces for which you have no evidence," Erik said.

Ruari flung out a hand. "No evidence? What of the eyes in your own head, lad? What of your own fate in these moments? Can you deny that wickedness—a force unseen, to be sure—is not responsible?"

"My brother is scarce a force unseen," Erik said, with no small measure of humor. To avoid lingering upon the details of his situation, he indicated the bird and deliberately changed the subject. "This then would be a bird from Ravensmuir?"

"It is Medusa," Vivienne said. The bird seemed to arch that white-feathered brow in silent acknowledgement. "And what will you tell my uncle of this, when next you fly through the high windows of Ravensmuir?" Vivienne asked of the bird. It cocked its head, seemingly considering her question. "And what will he ask of what you have seen this night?"

"Sorcery and madness!" Ruari fumed. "You allow wickedness to ride in your own saddle, lad, and it will be to your own detriment. Do not let her send a missive with the bird!"

"Ruari, it is but a bird. It cannot talk to any man."

"Fool! It is more than that!" Ruari drew his steed closer. He tried to shoo the bird away to no avail.

Vivienne leaned down to whisper to the bird. "I confide in you, Medusa, that our likely destination is Blackleith." The raven tilted its head, as if absorbing this morsel of information, then looked to Erik, appearing to seek confirmation.

Was he so transparent as this? Erik had said nothing of his intent, yet Vivienne had guessed it so readily that he felt exposed.

Then his blood chilled. Who else might have guessed his scheme? Did Nicholas still think him dead? Or had some soul confided the truth in him? Had his daughters met some dire fate in his absence, due to his own folly?

"You cannot know as much!" Ruari protested. "How can you scry the future so readily? I tell you, Erik, the maid is a witch in truth."

"It merely makes good sense," Vivienne replied tartly. "How else would a man regain the holding he had lost, save by returning to it? How else would a man win back his daughters, save by returning to the hall where they could be found?"

"You told her of your daughters?" Ruari demanded in obvious disbelief. "What madness has seized you, lad, that you confide your secrets to every soul who sees fit to cross your path? Do you court failure? I thought you sought triumph! Your own insistence upon trusting others, to your detriment, will see you fail again!"

Erik swore then, swore with vigor as he swung his gloved fist toward the bird. Medusa cried outrage and took flight, the raven's heavy wings beating the air with power.

Fafnir whinnied with no small outrage of his own. Erik had but a heartbeat's warning before the horse shied and bolted hard to the right, away from the flutter of the bird's wings.

And Erik and Vivienne were tossed to the left, right out of the saddle, so abruptly did the horse move. Erik shouted in annoyance as they were thrown, but the horse did not slow. He caught Vivienne in his arms and took the burden of the fall himself.

He landed upon his injured hip and grimaced in pain, even before Vivienne's slight weight landed atop him.

Medusa circled their small party once, screaming in avian disgust as Fafnir's racing hoofbeats faded into the distance. Ruari shouted and gave chase to the horse, a feat that would only make a spooked Fafnir gallop further before he halted. There was little point in shouting after Ruari, though, for he likely would not hear Erik's warning. And truly, the ruckus Ruari raised would have every monk and peasant rising from his bed.

Erik leaned his head back on the hard cold moor, closed his eyes, and sighed. His hip throbbed; he was exhausted. What had seemed a simple plan to ensure his daughters' survival was proving to be neither simple nor successful thus far.

# Chapter Seven

"ARE YOU INJURED?" Vivienne asked. Erik felt her leaning over him. Whether her solicitude was genuine or not, it was welcome. Indeed, the press of her breasts against his chest and the tickle of her hair on his face—no less his body's response to both—persuaded him that he was not as near death as he might have thought.

He opened his eyes and regarded her, noting that she was disheveled and pale. He was immediately concerned. "Are you?"

She shook her head, loosing that cloud of hair over him. "Of course not, for you took the brunt of the fall."

"But?"

"But I was surprised. I have ridden horses all my life and never have I been thrown from the saddle." She grimaced as she sat up, then rubbed one knee. "It is not a new experience to be welcomed."

Erik realized then how fully Vivienne had had a life of privilege and security. She had known no fear, she had faced no danger. She had been cossetted by a large affluent family, one which ensured that she rode no horse that was not utterly tame, one which saw that no peril touched her life.

He wanted fiercely to give the same gift to his daughters. That desire had him sitting up, reinvigorated once more.

"You did not answer me," Vivienne said, glancing over him with a wince that might have been born of guilt or sympathy or both.

"I am no more injured than I have been before," Erik said, hoping it was true. Vivienne eyed him anxiously as he stood and subtly tested whether his leg would support his weight. "It was a surprise, no more than that."

"I did not know that your steed did not like birds."

"Nor, actually, did I."

"I am sorry," Vivienne said, her cheeks staining with becoming color. "I have never known any horse unfamiliar with birds. I see now the folly of assuming all horses would be indifferent to their presence."

Erik liked that Vivienne was unafraid to acknowledge her guilt, that she apologized for her error with such ease. Though she flushed with embarrassment, still she met his gaze steadily. Her sheltered upbringing had given her a confidence that would serve her well in any circumstance.

"How could you have anticipated what you have never known before?" he asked, unwilling to condemn her for a miscalculation, even one that had roused a clamor in his hip. "Your family's abode is hardly typical of what mine was, even in its finest hour."

She nodded, so contrite that he felt a cur for having been irked with her even momentarily. "I never even guessed," she said quietly, then sighed. "And my mother used to tell me that I was keen of wit."

There was little Erik could say to that. Vivienne rose then, and fetched the spilled contents of one saddlebag, which had evidently not been fully fastened. The provisions had been in that bag, though he did not tell her to leave the bread and the cheese in the dust. They might find themselves hungry enough to want it all the same.

He wondered whether Vivienne's ability to accept radical changes in her situation would extend to eating food adorned with dirt. He hoped they did not have to find out.

Erik took advantage of her averted gaze to stretch his leg cautiously. He winced at the vigorous stab of pain which resulted.

"You *are* injured!" Vivienne said, glancing over her shoulder at precisely the wrong moment.

"No more than a bruise."

She looked skeptical in her turn, propping one hand upon her hip as she surveyed him sternly. "Then it will be a large one, I would wager."

"You will find no one to wager the opposite in this company," he muttered.

"You should not have taken the brunt of our fall, not upon that hip."

It had been quite some time since a woman had cared sufficiently about Erik to scold him, and he found himself enjoying their exchange. "In truth, I had no plan to do as much, just as I had no plan to leave the saddle in such a manner," he said and was rewarded by Vivienne's laughter. "That was no jest." He granted her a grim look, and she merely smiled, so undaunted was she by his expression.

"There is no need to glower at me," she said. "You cannot disguise from me that you have noble impulses, much less that gallantry had you ensuring I felt no injury as a result of my own folly. No woman of sense condemns a man for his chivalry, though she might remind such a man that a body can bear only so much." With that, she returned to her task of gathering the scattered goods.

Erik blinked. It had been long indeed since anyone had thought him chivalrous, longer still since he had been credited with noble impulses. He watched Vivienne, discomfited that she had glimpsed secrets he thought hidden, and wary of her expectations all the same.

Mercifully, he heard a horse's hoofbeats approaching in that very moment and was spared the need to consider the matter further. He pivoted to find Fafnir trotting back toward him. The horse had run in a large circle and now returned from the opposite direction, albeit at a much slower pace. The destrier halted half a dozen steps away and regarded Erik with seeming puzzlement, then lowered his head as if in apology as he slowly came closer.

"He looks so surprised!" Vivienne said.

"As if he had naught to do with our not being in the saddle any longer," Erik grumbled.

Fafnir sniffed Erik, seeming confused that he was no longer sprawled upon the ground. Apparently reassured to have found his errant rider, the destrier nibbled on Erik's hair. Fafnir nosed in Erik's collar with shameless enthusiasm, as if Erik were inclined to carry apples in his chemise.

Vivienne laughed. She buffed an apple retrieved from the ground, then came closer to offer it to the horse.

"He needs no reward for throwing us," Erik said.

Vivienne was undeterred by his gruff manner. "He deserves one for returning to us." She rubbed the beast's nose while it devoured the fruit, then turned that sparkling gaze upon Erik again.

Before she could ask him some question, Erik spoke.

"It was but a bird," he told the horse with affectionate disgust, then rubbed its nose in turn. He flexed his leg while he stood there, assessing the damage from the fall. His hip was stiff and sore, it would undoubtedly be black and blue, but he would survive. He bent his leg once or twice and was relieved as it became more agile.

"You must think me no more keen of wit than a child," Vivienne said. She watched him, though he had not realized as much, her eyes narrowed.

"I think you a woman who has lived in privilege," Erik said, not wanting to chastise her when she was clearly judging herself harshly. "I also think your mother named it rightly, and that you are a woman keen of wit, though that does not mean you can know all."

"I am sorry. I never intended that you should be injured."

"Nor did I." Erik felt immediately contrite, for she looked so crestfallen. He reached out and touched her cheek with a fingertip, coaxing her to meet his gaze. "If I confess to believing that you can summon a raven, though it defies reason that such an ability should be so, will you pledge to not do so again?"

Vivienne smiled then, her smile as radiant as the first rays of the dawn. Indeed, the sight warmed Erik to his very toes. "Such a pledge should be sealed with a kiss, do you not think?" she said, then stepped around the horse and rose to kiss him on the mouth.

Her spontaneous embrace was a rare pleasure. Indeed, no man of sense could argue with her reasoning, so Erik returned her kiss.

VIVIENNE MARVELLED that Erik's kiss grew more beguiling with familiarity, not less so. She leaned her hands upon his chest and stretched to the tips of her toes, wanting only to kiss him fully.

And truly, a kiss seemed the most fitting apology for what she had so foolishly done. What had begun as the manner of jest she would have played on one of her siblings had gone awry beyond her expectations. In hindsight, Vivienne felt like a fool.

It had been easy to conclude from her experience that all horses were accustomed to birds, for example, whereas she now realized that all of the horses she had ridden had been trained with care beforehand. Only in hindsight did she see and appreciate the many hands that had ensured she and her siblings had met with no harm.

It was not thus for every woman, nor indeed for every man. Vivienne understood that it certainly had not been thus for Erik. As a result, he had a keener ability to anticipate peril, for he held fewer assumptions than she.

So, even though she had endangered them unwittingly, he had not only ensured that they did not pay a higher price, but he had forgiven her. Once his anger had passed, he had not held her error against her, and Vivienne wished to reward him for his trust.

She kissed him with ardor and felt his response against her belly. She smiled as he pulled her more resolutely against him, savored the passion of his embrace. She wondered whether they might seal this agreement with more than a mere kiss.

Then Ruari exhaled with obvious disgust from close

proximity. Erik muttered a curse as he lifted his lips from hers and Vivienne hid her smile.

Ruari glared at them, hands propped upon his hips. "And here I am, riding the very breadth of Scotland in pursuit of a steed, a steed which has returned to you of its own volition, and the two of you are so consumed with each other alone that you could not trouble to summon me with tidings of that horse's return?"

"I knew, Ruari, that you would not be far behind Fafnir, since you have such a talent for pursuit," Erik said, still holding Vivienne fast against his chest. She leaned her brow upon him and hid her amusement in his cloak.

Ruari harrumphed. He did not dismount, merely peered pointedly at the sky, then back at the embracing pair. "Do you mean to ride further this night? Or shall I make myself absent again while you labor to create a male heir for Blackleith?"

It was clear from his tone that Ruari was yet disgruntled, though he did not grant Erik a chance to protest.

"I should have thought that you would have a desire for haste in this journey," Ruari huffed and puffed. "Seeing as no man knows what occurs beneath Nicholas's hand, but I may have misunderstood your enthusiasm for the pursuit of justice."

"Your counsel is uncommonly wise, Ruari, and indeed I mean to ride north with all haste," Erik said mildly.

Ruari pursed his lips and might have argued further, but Erik moved to depart immediately. He locked his hands around Vivienne's waist and lifted her to Fafnir's saddle.

She noticed that Erik put his good leg in the saddle to swing himself up behind her, no less that he still moved stiffly, and feared that he was more injured than he would have had her believe. He turned the horse, though, and urged the beast to his former speed, as if untroubled.

He appeared so untroubled that Vivienne understood otherwise. She already knew that Erik appeared more impassive when matters were less to his liking.

She was concerned that their riding would injure his hip further, but dared not suggest as much outright in Ruari's presence. She could feel how Erik braced himself, how he periodically caught his breath in pain, and she nibbled her lip in consternation. Not only was she responsible for his injury, but she could do little to ensure that it did not become worse.

"And time enough it is, too," Ruari grumbled, his steed cantering beside Fafnir with easy grace. "The night is half gone and Ravensmuir yet on the horizon. We shall be fortunate indeed if we put enough distance between ourselves and the lady's kin before that cursed bird rouses their suspicions."

"You need not fear as much, Ruari," Vivienne felt the need to admit. "I cannot truly speak to the ravens. I only meant to play a jest upon you both."

Erik made a sound that might have been wrought of amusement, but Vivienne did not turn to see the expression on his face.

"A jest!" Ruari cried. "And what is amusing about striking terror into the innards of an old man? I thought you a fetching lass, but your heart, it seems, is shadowed." Ruari shook a finger at Vivienne. "It is said that there is no wind colder than a fair maiden's heart. Do you mean to prove the truth of it?"

"I erred!" Vivienne protested. "It was not my intent to harm either of you. You and I are in agreement about matters unseen: I meant only to challenge Erik's convictions."

"Ruari, there is no harm done," Erik said firmly.

"No harm," the older man snorted. "Do you think I have no eyes in my head? I saw how you mounted your steed. You may not wish the lady to think you wounded, but I discern the truth of it. You would be best away from this foul land, back in the north where friends and foes are not only known to us but devoid of any unholy powers . . ."

"Ruari, let us leave the matter be and ride," Erik said.

"Ride, indeed we should ride. I counsel that we ride directly for Queensferry, since you hold my advice in such high regard, and that we should not halt until we stand upon a boat and its sails are unfurled and the tide is carrying us away from these lands. Let there be the width of the Firth of Forth between ourselves and Ravensmuir before we sleep is what I say. Let us find ourselves in more familiar—and less travelled—country before we rest our weary selves, the better that we do not have to awaken at every sound. Fife would suit me well enough. Aberdeenshire would be better."

"It is too far to Queensferry," Erik argued, his tone revealing that his patience was strained. "The horses will be pressed overmuch."

"It is two days' ride," Vivienne said, wanting to add weight to Erik's view. "Even if we rode without cease, we could not arrive before Monday morn."

Ruari shook his head, unpersuaded. "The horses are fresh enough, if I may say as much, and they are doughty steeds well capable of a long run when the circumstance demands. If ever circumstance demanded, lad, it does on this night! There is a shiver in my very marrow, which is as reliable a portent of bad fortune as ever a man has known. I felt that shiver the night you were summoned to aid Thomas Gunn and I felt it again the night your father breathed his last. A man must listen to the warnings of his very bones."

"But mine offer no such warning," Erik said.

Ruari shook his head. "We will be ill-advised to remain on this side of the Firth longer than we have need of doing so, upon that you can rely, lad."

"We will not ride during the day, Ruari," Erik said. Vivienne felt him adjust his pose in the saddle. His hip would not be served well by more time in the saddle.

"There will be much activity upon the road to Edinburgh on the morrow for the market," she said, not being certain of any such thing. "We will not make good speed within a crowd."

"All the more reason to let the horses rest," Erik concluded. "For neither of them are accustomed to a busy thoroughfare."

"It is folly, lad!" Ruari flung out his hands. "How can I make the matter clear to you?"

"You cannot," Erik said finally and much to the older man's displeasure. He then leaned toward Vivienne, granting Ruari no chance to further complain. "Were you not going to recount a tale? Ruari is fond of tales, as I recall, and the telling will pass the time more quickly."

"Of course." Vivienne noted that Ruari settled into a disgruntled silence, knowing that his counsel would not be heeded and not satisfied with that in the least. Wanting only to leave dissent behind them, she cleared her throat and began to sing.

*"True Thomas lay on Huntlie bank,*
*When he espied a fairy lady;*
*This lady she was brisk and bold,*
*and she rode to the Eildon Tree.*

*Her skirt was of the grass-green silk;*
*her bridle of gold most fine;*
*and woven into her horse's mane,*
*were fifty silver bells and nine."*

"A tale of a fairy, is it then?" Ruari asked, his expression brightening in his interest. "I like a tale with beauteous women, to be sure." He spared Vivienne a telling glance. "Doubtless she has a heart wrought of ice, though."

*"True Thomas he took off his hat,*
*and bowed him low down till his knee.*
*'All hail, Mary, mighty Queen of Heaven!*
*Your peer on earth I ne'er did see.'*

*" 'Oh no, oh no, True Thomas,' she said,*
*'That name does not belong to me.*
*I am the queen of the fairy realm,*
*Come to hunt with greyhounds three.' "*
*Thomas then spake bold to her,*
*Her fairness unfurled his words:*
*'Lady, you have claimed my heart,*
*Come lie and hear the birds.' "*

"A tale of a fairy bedded by a mortal man!" Ruari chortled. He winked at Vivienne. "You bear more than one surprise, lass, that is to be certain."

Vivienne did not know what to say to that, so she sang.

*" 'Thomas, you know not what you ask;*
*You care only your will.*
*For if I should lie abed with you,*

*My beauty will be spilled.'*
*'Lovely lady, rue on me,*
*Know I will serve you well.*
*Alight with me, lie with me,*
*I will ever with you dwell.' "*

"Persistence is the key," Ruari muttered. "Therein lies the way to success in any endeavor. This Thomas, he refuses to accept that she declines his suit and I predict that he will see reward for his stubborn regard."

"Do not even think of arguing in this moment for riding directly to Queensferry," Erik said. "That matter is resolved, and your persistence will only be irksome."

"It is like casting pearls before swine," Ruari declared to no one in particular. He beat a fist upon his chest. "I conjure counsel from the weight of my experience, I urge wise courses through the goodness of my heart, I do this purely to ensure that those upon whom I am dependent do not err in ignorance."

Ruari gestured as if offering riches to the poor. "And yet, and yet, my sage advice, culled from decades of experience among men foul and fair, is discarded—" he cast out his hands "—like the dung of chickens." He sighed in forbearance, turning his gaze heavenward as if seeking strength to bear his earthly burdens. "Do not hold matters against me, my lord William," he said, apparently appealing to the ghost of Erik's father. "A mortal man can but try to make others see sense."

"You could break your word to my father instead, and abandon me to my folly," Erik suggested, earning a baleful glance from his companion for daring to tease him thus.

"Never!" Ruari declared.

"Then we shall make the ferry by Tuesday."

Ruari visibly grit his teeth.

Vivienne sang.

*" 'Thomas, Thomas, you speak folly,*
*A price be there for this ride.*
*Your lust leads us astray this day,*
*But I see you will not be denied.'*
*Down then came that lady bright,*
*underneath the Eildon Tree.*
*As the story tells full right,*
*Seven times with Thomas she did be."*

"Seven times!" Ruari chuckled at that, the tale clearly distracting him from his disappointment with Erik. "There is a lusty maiden, to be sure, though fairies are said to have unholy appetites. And Thomas!" He whistled through his teeth. "Seven times. Seven! There was a man of persistence and uncommon fortitude, to be sure."

Vivienne found herself blushing. She had forgotten the earthy nature of these first verses, or perhaps she had not fully understood them when she had heard them last. She had learned much these past two nights, to be sure. Worse, she was curious whether she and Erik might be able to couple seven times in rapid succession. She felt an indication against her buttocks that his thoughts might be following a similar course and her heart skipped a beat in anticipation.

Then she recalled the next verse and did not know whether she could sing it in this company or not.

"Is there not more?" Erik asked. "It seems a short tale otherwise, with little evidence that Thomas truly visited the fairy realm, as you insisted it would prove."

"I merely had to recall the words," Vivienne lied, then raised her voice again. She tried to brace herself for Ruari's response, for she expected he would laugh merrily at this verse.

*"She said 'Thomas, you like this play.*
*What lady could sate thee?*
*You would couple all this day,*
*I pray, Thomas, now let me be.' "*

Ruari did indeed roar with laughter. Indeed, he laughed until the tears ran from his eyes, but Vivienne sang on, granting him no chance to make a bawdy comment.

*"Thomas looked then with merry heart,*
*Upon that lady who was so gay;*
*But her hair hung dull about her face,*
*Her flesh had now turned to grey.*

*"Thomas cried out 'Alas, alack!*
*This is a doleful sight!*
*Beauty has faded from your face,*
*That once shone as sun so bright.'*
*The lady stood, her manner dour,*
*'Is this not as I foretold?*
*A price we both must pay for this*
*To your lust my beauty has been sold.' "*

"And is that not oft the truth of it?" Ruari said, then shook his head at the sad way of matters. "The fairest maid looks less fair after her conquest, upon that you can rely. Many a man has awakened after claiming a maiden whose merits left him blinded by lust, only to perceive her flaws the following morn."

Vivienne fell silent, struck by the similarities between this tale and her own. She had thought Erik had come from the realm of fairy and he had persuaded her to meet him abed. He had been curt the following morn. Had he been disappointed with the sight of her? Did he see flaws in her nature now, after her jest had gone so awry? Did her fears that she was not as composed as Madeline have any merit?

There was no denying the similarity between her agreement to accompany him for a year and a day and the wager that Thomas made with his fairy queen.

Feeling some disquietude, Vivienne sang.

" 'Now you must ride with me,' she said;
'True Thomas, you must come with me;
For you must serve me seven years,
through well or woe as chance to be.'
She mounted then her milk-white steed,
and took True Thomas up behind;
With every ring of her bridle,
Her horse ran faster than the wind.

"It was a dark dark night, with no light;
they waded through red blood to the knee:
For all the blood that's shed on earth;
Runs through the rivers of Fairy.
Then she led him to a fair arbor;
Where fruit grew in great plenty.
Pears and apples, ripe they were,
Dates, roses, figs and wineberry.

> *'Dismount now, my Thomas True,*
> *And lay your head upon my knee,*
> *And you will see the fairest sight*
> *That ever a man did see.'* "

Ruari laughed. "Aye, there is a fine sight to be seen whenever a man rests his head upon a lady's knee!"

Vivienne gasped, never having understood that interpretation of the tale. Erik's hand curved around her waist as if in reassurance. "He is merry," he whispered into her ear. "That is all I hoped of in the telling of your tale. Do not take his comments to heart. You must have noted already that he talks overmuch, and is happiest when talking."

Vivienne turned to grant Erik a smile, and found encouragement in his steady gaze. He was smiling slightly himself, and the expression made him look less formidable.

"You should smile more often," she bade him, then turned when he sobered in surprise. This was the part of the tale that she loved and she sang the fairy queen's words with gusto.

> " *'Oh, do you see yon narrow road,*
> *so thick beset with thorns and briars?*
> *That is the path of righteousness,*
> *though after it but few enquires.*
> *And do you see that broad broad road,*
> *that lies across the little leven?*
> *That is the path of wickedness,*
> *though some call it the road to heaven.'* "

"She grants good counsel, does this fairy queen," Ruari declared. "One has no fear of encountering a crowd on the road to righteousness, to be certain."

" 'And do you see that bonnie road,
which winds about the ferny slope?
That is the road to the Fairy court,
where you and I this night will go.
But Thomas, you must hold your tongue,
whatever you may hear or see;
For if a word you should chance to speak,
Never will you return to your own country.

'Whatsoever men say to you,
I pray you answer none but me.
I shall tell that I took a toll,
And I wrest your speech from thee.'
Thomas looked in that place,
And saw his lady once more gay.
She was again so faire and good,
Rich adorned on her palfrey."

"And how might this be?" Ruari demanded. "Was it the return to her own abode that restored her beauty?"

"I asked the same and was told that there is another variant of the tale," Vivienne explained. "And in that tale, the queen was wedded and her husband had cast a spell upon her that any infidelity would cost her beauty."

"Ah, so he could tell the truth of it with a glance." Ruari nodded. "There would be a useful spell for a mortal man with a beauteous wife," he said, without explaining himself further. He cast a glance at Erik, who said nothing.

Vivienne did not understand Ruari's import. If he

spoke of some past marriage of his own, it would be rude for her to demand details, so she sang.

> *"She blew her horn, took the reins,*
> *And to the castle they did ride.*
> *Into the hall rightly she went;*
> *Thomas followed at her side.*
> *Harp and fiddle there they found,*
> *The gittern and the psaltery;*
> *The lute and rebec there did sound,*
> *And all manner of minstrelsy."*

"Puts me in mind of a wedding, that does," Ruari said with a sigh. "Your wedding was a merry celebration, lad, to be certain. I fairly danced holes in my shoes, the minstrels were so fine."

Again, Erik made no reply, though Vivienne was certain she felt him straighten behind her. And why not? Erik yet mourned his wife, it was clear to any soul who paid attention to his manner whenever she was mentioned. Doubtless, he recalled that merry event himself and the sadness of losing his beloved bride afterward.

Indeed, Vivienne thought that Ruari showed a lack of tact in making such ready reference to Erik's wedding. After all, he had to know that Erik mourned his lost wife deeply. It was unkind to remind Erik of happier days, to her thinking, though Ruari clearly uttered any words that rose to his lips. There was no harm in him, but he was not an overly discreet soul.

She sang lest he choose to say more.

> *"One morn, his lady spake to him;*
> *'Thomas, here you may no longer be.*

*Hasten yourself with might and main,*
*I shall take you to the Eildon Tree.'*
*Thomas said with heavy cheer,*
*'Lovely lady, let me take ease,*
*For scarce have I savored this place;*
*Merely seven nights and days.'*

*" 'Forsooth, Thomas, I tell you true:*
*You have danced seven years and more!*
*You must here no longer dwell;*
*I shall take you home therefore.'*
*She brought him to the Eildon Tree,*
*Underneath the green wood spray;*
*But Thomas did not wish her to part:*
*'Grant me some token, lady gay.'*

*'Harp or carp, Thomas, you choose . . .' "*

"Harp or carp? What is this?" Ruari demanded.

"Surely you must know," Erik said, his tone unexpectedly teasing. "You with such a fondness for tales."

"Surely I do not! What choice does she grant him? A harp or a fish?"

Vivienne laughed. "He can choose the ability to play music or the ability to speak. He will excel at whichever he chooses."

"Ah! A silver tongue or silver fingertips. Aye, it is true that fairies oft grant the gift of music, though never have I heard of them offering a gift for telling tales." Ruari nodded. "Seems to me as those they choose to capture oft have that gift already and in plenty, if you understand my meaning."

"Aye, I understand it well," Erik said. "Perhaps you

have such a belief in matters unseen because you too have been captured by the fairies."

Ruari laughed at that prospect and Vivienne understood that neither man believed her tale. She resolutely sang on, knowing that Thomas's prophecies would change their conclusions.

" 'Harp or carp, Thomas, you choose;
*You will have whiche'er you will to be.'*
*'To carp choose I,' said Thomas True.*
*'For tongue is chief of minstrelsie.'*

" *'Then when you speak, from this day hence,*
*And tales you choose to tell,*
*You shall never loose a lie,*
*Whether you walk by wood or fell.'*
*'My tongue is mine own,' True Thomas cried;*
*'A goodly gift you would give to me!*
*With it, neither I could buy or sell,*
*Not at fair or tryst could I be.*

*I could not speak to prince or peer;*
*Nor ask of grace from fair ladies.' "*

Ruari laughed heartily at Thomas's protest, and Vivienne sang.

" *'Now, hold thy peace!' the lady said;*
*'For as I bid you, it must be.*
*Farewell, Thomas, without any guile;*
*You may no longer linger with me.'*
*'Lovely lady, abide a while,*
*And some fair tale tell you to me.' "*

"Ah, and these would be her prophecies," Erik said when Vivienne paused for breath.

"Indeed, they are," Vivienne agreed. "She made many regarding the fate of Scotland, all of which have proven to be true." She might have raised her voice again, but Erik halted her with a fingertip upon her shoulder.

"Then it is a good place to leave the tale until the morrow," he said. He indicated the eastern sky and Vivienne noted with surprise that it was lightening. They had passed Haddington near the beginning of her song and now the dark profile of Edinburgh rose ahead of them. She had been so intent upon singing the tale that she had not noticed the miles slipping away.

"There is a gully to the south of the road here, well hidden from curious eyes," Erik said, and she was struck again by his knowledge of this area. "I would halt there for the day and have you continue your tale this night."

Ruari looked displeased at this prospect. "At least accept my counsel that we not all huddle together. We could be too readily surprised then, no less cornered."

"There will not be pursuit, Ruari," Erik said firmly. "The lady's brother and I have agreed, after all."

Ruari snorted. "Which would explain, of course, why that man placed a price upon your head in Kinfairlie market. I am unpersuaded of the merit of this agreement, lad, just as I am unpersuaded that the lady did not truly summon her family to us, but I shall follow your bidding, dutiful servant that I am. You might at least follow my lead in ensuring that we are not readily discovered."

Erik inclined his head in agreement, and Ruari led them on a tortuous path far north of the copse Erik had indicated. He marched the horses through a stream, emerging from one side and the other repeatedly, then travelling

far downstream before letting the horses climb the banks
again. Vivienne did not doubt that he chose the rocky
bank deliberately. Even so, he brushed the ground behind
them with a clutch of bracken, though Vivienne could see
no evidence of their passing.

Finally, they circled back toward the gorse and Ruari
pointed to a trio of haystacks, which must have been
newly harvested. "I shall keep a vigil from there." With
nary a backward glance, he dismounted and led his horse
away.

"He is vexed with you, despite my tale."

"He worries overmuch," Erik said mildly, then dismounted in his turn. "Though there is no doubting his
loyalty." He made to lift Vivienne down, but she lifted his
hands away from her waist and slipped from the saddle
herself.

"You are more sorely injured than you would admit,"
she scolded quietly. The grass was thick and green here,
and she could hear the trickle where the stream began.
The trees clustered thickly around the bubbling water and
Vivienne imagined that they would be well concealed in
that shady haven.

She watched Erik lead the horse toward the shadows
and winced anew at his limp. She must ensure that he
rested this day in truth—not pacing its duration as he
tended to do—and she had suddenly a good idea of how
that might be achieved.

She hastened after him and caught his sleeve in her
fingertips. "Do you think it true, what Ruari said?"

"Which detail of what Ruari said do you mean? He
says a great deal." Erik removed the saddlebags as he
spoke, then unfastened Fafnir's saddle and lifted it to the

ground. He cast the reins over the steed's head and Fafnir bent to nibble at the thick grass.

Vivienne fetched the brush that he used upon the horse and handed it to him, ensuring that she granted him a caress in the transaction. "That it would be uncommon for a mortal man to mate seven times in quick succession, of course," she said, feeling herself flush even as she made the suggestion. "It seems to me that that might be a good scheme for conceiving a son in haste."

To her delight, a twinkle lit in Erik's blue eyes and that elusive smile touched his lips. "It seems as much to you, does it?"

Vivienne's cheeks heated further as she nodded.

"Then I can only offer my own best effort. No man of merit, after all, leaves a lady's curiosity unsated."

"It is not my curiosity I would have you sate!" Vivienne said mischievously and was rewarded by his fleeting grin.

Then Erik laid a finger across her lips. "I would never say as much, though it might well be true."

Vivienne had no chance to reply for he quickly replaced the warmth of his fingertip with the heat of his kiss, and truly, she had no complaint with that.

# Chapter Eight

~

VIVIENNE AWAKENED at the sound of a barking dog. It was not simply the bark of a local peasant's dog, for numerous dogs barked in unison and with some anxiety. There were hounds on the hunt, Vivienne realized when she heard the thunder of horses' hoofbeats along with the dogs' baying.

Who would hunt so close to Edinburgh?

She spared a glance to the darkening sky and nestled into Erik's embrace once more, reluctant as she was to move. He moved away, to her surprise, his gestures brusque.

"Rise," he bade her. Vivienne might have protested but he turned upon her, his eyes blazing blue. "Immediately!"

Fearful of whatever he anticipated, Vivienne found her boots. She managed to don only one before the bush around them began to snap with vigor. The hounds barked closer at hand; hunting birds cried overhead.

She glanced up in fear. They were surrounded by snarling dogs and stamping horses. A good dozen knights stood with their swords drawn and directed at Erik and Vivienne, their visors closed.

She and Erik were the prey they hunted. The men's gleaming armor and bright swords revealed that they expected a battle.

Vivienne's heart pounded so hard that she thought it might leap from her chest. Erik eased her behind him, pulling his sword as he did so. With his other hand, he slipped something cold into her belt.

It was his father's blade. She felt the cool stone in the hilt and knew it to be so.

But why?

Vivienne was confused, though she pulled her cloak closed so that the weapon could not be seen. She dared to don her other boot. Did Erik expect her to fight by his side? Did he know these men? What had he done when last he had passed this way?

"Leave the lady be and I will not fight your capture of me," Erik said, his voice ringing with authority. "There is no reason for her to be harmed."

He stood proudly then, his blade raised as he confronted the party. He was sorely outnumbered and Vivienne yearned to aid him, but knew she should keep his blade hidden until she could surprise an assailant.

The men's horses, which had obviously run hard, exhaled clouds into the late afternoon shadows. One blade then gleamed as the man bearing it urged his horse closer.

A terrified Vivienne followed the gleaming length of the sword to the man who wielded it. He pushed back his visor, his expression harsh but his features familiar.

"Alexander!" Vivienne was so filled with relief that her knees weakened. Whatever fate Erik had feared had not come to pass.

Her brother, though, neither shared her pleasure nor

acknowledged her words. Erik did not ease his stance and the air fairly crackled between them.

'Twas then that Vivienne recalled that Alexander had put a price upon Erik's head.

"She has doubtless been harmed already!" Alexander said to Erik, his anger clear. "You broke your pledge to me, Nicholas Sinclair, and I will see my sister avenged."

Vivienne blinked in confusion before she remembered that Alexander thought Erik to be his brother Nicholas. Clearly there were many misunderstandings to be resolved! She stepped forward and raised a finger to explain the truth to all involved, for surely that was the best way to diffuse the tension.

Erik shoved her behind him with such vigor that she nearly tripped on her hem. "And you will have to hew me down to reclaim your sister, unless you pledge her safety."

"Put your blade aside," Alexander bade Erik grimly. "The lady is safe with us, and you cannot fight us all. Save yourself from injury and come peacefully."

"There is no need for such hostility, for you see, all has been resolved." Vivienne said cheerfully but the men ignored her. "I can explain, if you will simply sheath your blades anew."

Alexander did no such thing. He dismounted, then moved Erik's sword aside with the tip of his blade. "She is my sister," he said quietly when Erik might have protested. "It is my intent to defend her honor, thus you may be certain that she will be safer in my company than in yours." He then offered Vivienne his own hand, his gaze unswerving from a silent Erik. "Are you injured, Vivienne?"

"No, of course not."

If anything, Alexander looked more dour. His fingers closed tightly around her own. "And have you been to a chapel to exchange your nuptial vows, as Nicholas and I agreed you would?"

Vivienne looked between the two men who regarded each other with stony expressions. "No," she admitted. "But we have pledged a handfast . . ."

"Lammergeiers do not handfast!" Alexander roared, his eyes snapping with anger. "We *wed*, in chapels, with the blessing of priests, and thus our children are legitimate in the eyes of God and men." He jabbed his sword in Erik's direction. "Our agreement was that you and my sister would wed!"

"And so it was," Erik said softly. "The lady and I chose another course."

Alexander drew himself taller, though he was still shorter than Erik, and spoke through gritted teeth. "I granted you the chance you asked of me, I showed you the honor of my trust, and in return, you have betrayed both me and my sister. You have forsaken my hospitality, despoiled my family name, and treated my sister with dishonor."

"I did what I know to be right," Erik said.

"This is not right. You owe compense to Kinfairlie, that is what I know to be right."

It was evident that the two of them would not resolve this matter by themselves. Vivienne stepped between the pair and raised her hands. "Alexander, you do not fully understand and I am certain that once all is explained, you . . ."

"I understand all that I have need of understanding!" Alexander said, and pulled Vivienne roughly to his side.

"But Alexander!" Vivienne was determined to intervene. "There have been injustices wrought . . ."

Alexander turned a cold eye upon her. "The injustice in this case has been wrought against you!" He was still furious, and that he was angered on her behalf did little to reassure Vivienne.

He took a shaking breath, then studied her face. "I care only for your future, Vivienne," he said more quietly and she nodded, knowing this to be true. His voice dropped lower. "There is injustice here that cannot go unpunished, for I will do no part to encourage our land's descent into lawless chaos." He held her gaze. "Unless, against all odds, you are yet a maiden."

Vivienne flushed crimson and found nary a word upon her tongue. Indeed, the entire company seemed to hold their breath, so interested were they in her reply. Despite Alexander's low tone, all seemed to have heard his words. A dozen men, familiar and unfamiliar, watched her with undisguised fascination.

Vivienne turned to meet the vivid gleam of Erik's gaze. He said nothing, his gaze unblinking and without judgement. What did he wish for her to say? She felt the hilt of his father's blade pressing against her ribs and guessed that he did not trust her kin.

And there was good sense in that. The truth would condemn Erik in her brother's eyes, and she feared that Alexander would have his vengeance before his temper cooled.

"What will you do to him?" she asked, not looking away from Erik.

"I would not sully a woman's ears with the details," Alexander said, his manner ruthless. "But no man who despoils a sister of mine will ever soil a maiden again."

Vivienne felt the color drain from her face, for she believed that Alexander would do as he threatened. His reputation as a competent judge and firm upholder of the law was justly earned and she knew he would not waver from the strict letter of the law.

And Erik had broken his pledge.

But unless she had already conceived—which seemed unlikely—Alexander's punishment would ensure that Erik would not be able to conceive the son necessary to win back his daughters and Blackleith.

She held Erik's fate in her hands. And he merely returned her stare, demanding nothing of her, expecting nothing of any of them.

It was, after all, what he had learned to expect from those who surrounded him. Vivienne's heart clenched that she, she who wanted so much to aid him, could be the one to ensure his failure simply by telling the truth.

She could lie. It was against her nature to tell a falsehood and she knew she would do it badly, but Vivienne refused to betray Erik.

"I am yet a maiden," she declared with vigor, feeling her cheeks burn even as she held her head high. "For I have been unclean these past days."

Another man pushed back his visor and Vivienne recognized her Uncle Tynan. "Speak plainly, Vivienne, for much is at stake! Do you mean that your monthly courses have begun?"

Vivienne nodded, willing for Erik's sake to bear the shame of confessing to such a thing before a company of men.

"Swear it," Alexander demanded.

Vivienne swallowed. "I swear that I am yet a maiden."

The men began to whisper immediately, though Erik's

eyes narrowed. Vivienne turned away from the censure in his gaze, guessing that he did not like that she lied.

Surely he understood though that a small deception in this circumstance was less costly than the truth might be.

Alexander was not as readily persuaded as Vivienne had hoped, his doubt more than clear. He studied her, his skepticism apparent, and she knew that he would have liked to have asked her sisters for verification of the timing of her bleeding.

Vivienne feared that he might demand to see the blood, here and now, and spoke hastily to keep him from making such a request. "Only a barbarian would have bedded a woman in such a state, after all."

Erik's lips tightened to a thin line and he averted his gaze. Vivienne hoped that he feigned a greater disgust with her than he felt.

"And what of you? Did you bed the lady?" Alexander demanded of Erik.

Erik seemed to have been struck to stone, so long did he stand in watchful silence. "I stand by the lady's word, of course," he said finally, his words taut.

Still he did not so much as glance at Vivienne. Perhaps he believed her lie, and was disappointed that they had not wrought his son as yet. She yearned to confess the truth to him, that she did not yet abandon their quest, that she did not bleed, that the pledge she had made to him to bear his son was more binding than this lie she had sworn to be truth to her own brother.

She had a terrible sense that he might not believe her.

"Every soul knows that only monsters are wrought during a woman's time," Alexander said.

Erik granted Alexander a scornful glance. "And even

barbarians such as myself have no desire for misshapen children."

Alexander snapped his fingers and moved with decisiveness. "Seize him then!" He grasped Vivienne's elbow and turned to march back to his steed. "We ride for Kinfairlie without delay!"

"But Alexander!" Vivienne struggled against her brother's grip, only managing to shake free when she was trapped between Alexander's destrier and Tynan's black stallion.

Tynan studied her, his gaze as avid as that of one of his ravens, and Vivienne fought the urge to fidget. "If this man has not injured Vivienne, then there is no reason to pursue the matter," he said with care.

"He has broken a pledge to me, and must face the consequence of that," Alexander insisted.

"Unless Vivienne chooses to wed him now," Tynan suggested. "Indeed, such a course might ensure that no malicious tales stain her repute."

Alexander heaved a sigh, then turned his attention to Vivienne. "If you insist upon it, I will not protest this match," he said and her heart leapt. "Though surely you must know that I would counsel you against it. You can wed better, Vivienne, than to a man whose tongue so readily utters a lie, better than to wed Nicholas Sinclair."

Once again, the company turned their attention upon Vivienne.

HERE WAS VIVIENNE'S CHANCE to wed Erik honorably!

But Vivienne did not want a marriage devoid of love, and one glance in Erik's direction was all the evidence she needed that he still loved his late wife Beatrice. He regarded her coldly, almost certainly doubting her ability to provide him with his son.

It was clear that Vivienne had not loosed that woman's grasp upon his heart, though admittedly she had had little time to do so. She supposed she should have been glad that Erik had known such a potent love, one that endured forever as the love in all great tales did, but she was ashamed to find herself disappointed.

Vivienne turned away, fighting the tears that stung her eyes. The fact remained that she could not bear the prospect of her choice costing Erik all he held dear. Erik's reasons for desiring a handfast were wrought of such good sense that she would not, could not, compel him to abandon them.

His daughters deserved better.

But neither would Vivienne abandon her pledge to Erik. She had vowed to try to bear his son and she meant to keep her word. If so doing meant that she could not wed honorably, that seemed to Vivienne to be a small price to pay for the security of two little girls.

Which left her with several tasks. First, she had to ensure that Erik was left whole, so that he could conceive a son, and then she had to ensure that he was free to do so. As much as she hated to deceive her brother and uncle, Vivienne could not condemn Erik's daughters to whatever fate Nicholas might find for them.

The sorry truth was that Vivienne would have to tell her own family another falsehood. Her mother had always said that one lie necessitated another, and it was no consolation to find such advice to be true.

Though truly, Alexander's conviction that Erik was Nicholas might prove most useful.

Vivienne did not so much as glance Erik's way, lest Alexander guess her intent. She shook her head and shrugged. "He has neither injured me nor tried to collect the gold you offered for my safe return. His deeds give him more credit than you do, Alexander."

Her brother flushed. "You speak the truth in that," he admitted gruffly.

"And you are far from innocent in this matter," she continued, earning her uncle's nod of agreement.

"I would suggest it prudent that Vivienne be privy to any future discussions for her marriage," Tynan suggested.

"I thought you loved him," Alexander said in a whisper. "When he came to me and pledged his ardor, I thought the reason you found all other suitors unacceptable was that you yet loved Nicholas Sinclair. It seemed perfect that he now holds Blackleith, and I meant only to ensure your happiness."

"You thought wrongly, Alexander," Vivienne said, relieved that she could reply without actually lying. "I could never love Nicholas Sinclair, for he is cunning and deceptive. I regret only that I did not denounce him for his deeds to all of you when he ceased his courtship." She looked at her brother and uncle, hoping her expression was resolved. "I will not wed Nicholas Sinclair."

Alexander and Tynan nodded approval of this sentiment and Alexander flicked a finger, indicating that his men should collect Erik. "We ride for Kinfairlie with all haste!" he repeated.

"I recommend a halt at Ravensmuir this night," Tynan said with his usual calm manner. "The horses are tired from this day, and it is both closer and better provisioned for feeding the company."

"And I will ride onward," Erik said. His eyes were narrowed, his expression impassive. "You have no need of my presence since all has been resolved so amiably."

Vivienne knew that she did not imagine the weight he granted to that last word. She understood then that he meant to find another maiden to provide his son.

What if she had already conceived? It would be months before she could be certain, unless she bled. She knew that Erik was only prepared to leave her because he believed her own lie. Oh, her falsehood already made trouble beyond compare!

"Surely, you too should rest at Ravensmuir . . ." she began, though Alexander interrupted her.

"It is not resolved at all, not with regards to you," he said curtly, easing his horse toward Erik. "Still you broke your word to me, still you lied to me about your intent, and still you must answer for your transgression in my courts."

Erik eyed him grimly. "Still you have my coin, which should be sufficient to see the matter resolved."

Alexander straightened and Vivienne knew he did not like to be so challenged before his own men. "In my demesne, my will is done," he said with quiet authority. "And I have declared that you will appear in my court to answer the charge against you."

"And as a freeman, I say that I shall not do so."

"I have the right to pursue you and I have the right to ensure that you face justice in my courts."

Erik's lip curled. "And I have the right to deny the whim of a nobleman who would sell his sister for so paltry a price."

Alexander raised a finger in anger, but Erik drew his

blade so quickly that the man beside him was wounded before Alexander uttered a sound.

"Seize him!" Alexander roared.

Erik's blade whistled as he confronted his assailants and Alexander's men closed ranks around him. Blades clashed as the peaceful glade erupted in furious battle. Vivienne gasped when she saw that they spared no effort to defeat Erik.

"He will be injured for no good reason!" she cried and lunged toward the fray. She did not get far, for her uncle caught her around the waist and swung her into the saddle before himself. "I must aid him!" she cried, fighting his grip. "This is unjust indeed!"

"You cannot aid a man who condemns himself," Tynan said grimly, then turned his steed toward Ravensmuir. "A night in Ravensmuir's dungeon will see him cured of his folly."

Vivienne was suddenly very glad that Erik had entrusted her with his father's blade, though she was disheartened at the prospect of freeing him from her uncle's abode. Ravensmuir was a formidable keep, with a full curtain wall, multiple gates, and a fearsome dungeon.

"Alexander made the wager with him," Vivienne argued, fury fueling her words. "And had his payment for his terms. This man has treated me with honor, and you reward him with brutality."

"I will hear no protest." Alexander met her gaze, his own steely. "Fortune has smiled upon you and you should be grateful for your reprieve. Leave the details to me."

Vivienne was outraged as Erik was forcibly subdued. He was bound and cast across a palfrey's back with indignity. The sight of him, battered and bleeding, redoubled her determination to aid him, even in defiance of her entire family if need be.

She should have held her tongue, but she could not refrain from making one comment. "And so you have an innocent man bound like a criminal for no reason beyond your injured pride," she said to Alexander and his satisfied expression immediately disappeared. "Who in this instance is the barbarian?"

"Justice must be meted with a firm hand," Alexander said, though he colored as he defended his own command. "Much of the woe in Scotland in these days is because men do not stand by their word, and because those with responsibility do not uphold justice. I shall not count myself among their numbers." With that, he turned his steed away.

"You must understand, Vivienne," Tynan murmured to her. "Alexander's authority is tenuous over the men serving him at Kinfairlie. They think him young and untested in battle; some of them seek a chance to defy him. He dared not risk leaving your assailant go free, lest he be later challenged by the men in his own ranks. He dare not risk the safety of your other sisters by failing to deal with this matter with resolve. He has had to choose, and he chose to enforce his authority in Kinfairlie's courts. He could have meted justice here and now, at least that of a less reputable kind."

Vivienne chose not to reply, for she had already said too much. She wondered at these tidings, for she had not guessed that Alexander had any troubles with the men in his service, though Tynan's comment made sense.

Alexander, of all of them, had had to make the greatest change after their parents' sudden demise, for he had been compelled to immediately become Laird of Kinfairlie. All the same, she could not countenance that Erik had suffered for Alexander's woes.

Vivienne's brother, Malcolm, urged his horse to trot beside Tynan's steed. He said nothing, evidently having assumed some of Tynan's quiet manner in the days since he had been sworn to that man's hand. He wore a version of Ravensmuir's colors, which marked him as that estate's heir, and rode another of Ravensmuir's black stallions. Malcolm seemed already much older and more stern than she recalled.

It was only as the party rode away from the glade that Vivienne realized that Ruari was not among the company. Alexander's hounds must not have found him, or Alexander had not realized that the lone man travelled with herself and Erik. Ruari's insistence that he sleep apart from them had proven to be good counsel.

As clearly had been his advice to ride to Queensferry without halting. Vivienne regretted that she had not endorsed his plan. She had feared for Erik's welfare, though halting for the day had only resulted ultimately in his sustaining more injury yet. She swallowed as she thought of the chilling gaze he had granted her earlier and hoped fervently that he would be able to forgive her for her family's deeds.

Vivienne also hoped that Ruari would be sufficiently intrepid to follow the party back to Ravensmuir. She, after all, would need all the aid she could muster to see Erik freed.

IT WAS THE CONVICTION of Ruari Macleod that women were naught but trouble, and worse, that beauteous women were trouble beyond belief. He had thought that Erik's scheme to claim Vivienne had been a misbegotten one from his first hearing of it, but the deed had been done by the time he had found the lad. He had also believed that it was folly to discount the talents of any woman kin with those at Ravensmuir, particularly her ability to speak with the ravens of that keep. He was not in the least bit surprised to find his suspicions proven right on all counts.

Nor was he happy about the result. He watched the large party ride back toward that cursed keep, their manner merry now that they had captured their prey. He had crept closer and listened keenly, disliking every morsel that reached his ears. The lad had treated the maiden with honor and she had rewarded him with treachery.

Her sole favor to Erik had been her insistence that her maidenhead was intact. Ruari did not doubt that this claim was for her own advantage alone, for she could still be wed well if none believed she had been sampled already, but her vow might have the benefit of ensuring that Erik would not be unmanned.

Though it was clear that he was to be roughly treated all the same. Perhaps the brother of the maiden had not truly believed her words.

It mattered little. Ruari trailed the company, its triumphant members not in the least bit cautious about the noise they made. A pair of dark birds circled over the front of the group, where the lass rode with her kin, and Ruari could have readily guessed what manner of birds they were.

He kept his hood raised, and loitered so far behind the company that he might have lost them, if he had not known their destination.

Ravensmuir. Dread rose in Ruari's throat like black bile, but he could not abandon the pledge he had made to William Sinclair. The lad was his responsibility and he dared not fail him.

The sun set like a livid red eye over the highlands, the sky grew thick with clouds. The clouds darkened ominously as they rode ever eastward, the darkness enfolding the last rays of the sun as if extinguishing it. A cold wind stung Ruari's face, and he found no good portent in the fact that it came from the sea.

There was trouble ahead, and foul weather as well. Ruari had no taste for either, and he wondered now why he, as a youth, had not been content to remain by his mother's fire at night, herding goats by day. He could yet be there, content and a little plump, perhaps with a wife of his own who could make a pot of ale now and again. It would not have been so bad a life.

Then Ruari remembered William Sinclair, a great man far beyond any he might have encountered in their small village, a man who had taught him much, and he knew why he had left.

All too quickly, Ravensmuir itself loomed ahead, a massive shadow against the roil of sea and sky. Ruari shivered at the very sight of it, even as he halted his steed. He was relieved when those birds disappeared behind the high curtain wall and did not fly skyward again.

There was no village at Ravensmuir, just empty moor for the last half mile or so before the gates. Those gates opened to admit the company, then swallowed them, like a demon devouring men in its greedy maw. Ruari paused down behind the last thorny hedge that offered a meager shadow and considered his course. The first heavy drops of rain began to splatter on and around him.

Ruari wrapped his cloak around himself and straightened his tabard. He squinted at the brooding face of Ravensmuir and shook at what he was compelled to do to keep the pledge he had made.

But he knew William Sinclair well enough to know that his late lord would not be one to accept excuses. William had never been one to flinch before a deed that needed doing, however unsavory the task might have been.

Ruari was not so bold as to guess whether his destination when he left this earth was to be heaven or hell, but he knew that whichever it was, William Sinclair would be awaiting him there. Ruari knew that any omissions he might have made in seeing that man's last demand fulfilled would not be forgotten by him for all eternity.

Ruari lifted his hood, squared his shoulders, and began to ride toward Ravensmuir's gates. He might well die in the attempt to aid the lad this time, but there was no honor in walking away from one's pledge. He kept his head high, though he feared that he stepped squarely into folly.

He might meet William sooner than either of them had anticipated.

After all, Ruari could not juggle and he could not sing. The Laird of Ravensmuir did not appear to be in need of mercenaries, nor would he be desirous of information about his neighbors with a hoard of spying birds to do his bidding. To be sure, Ruari knew no such news, but he could have fabricated some if so doing had offered some prospect of success. Ruari could recount a tale, though he knew only one and it was hardly whimsy.

He could only hope it would suffice.

Doubts assailed him with every step closer to those dark gates, as if a shadow fell ever longer over his heart.

Ruari hoped with sudden vigor that Medusa had neg-
lected to mention his presence when the bird had told the
laird where to find Vivienne and Erik.

Otherwise, his arrival—and his intent—might be
anticipated.

Ruari swallowed but did not slow his pace, even at that
daunting prospect. He might be stepping into a trap—he
would not put as much past the sorcerers of Ravensmuir—but a man who swore a pledge at the deathbed of
another did not truly have any choice.

Ruari hoped that this act would not be his last one.

He also hoped that William Sinclair would grant him
credit for trying to fulfil his pledge, even if he failed in
so doing.

TYNAN CALLED FOR ALE to be poured in Ravensmuir's hall
when the party returned. Their arrival had clearly been
anticipated—perhaps by some earlier command of
Tynan's—for the trestle tables were at ready in the hall
and the tantalizing smell of roast meat carried from the
kitchens.

Vivienne was in no mood to tell Alexander how wondrous he was, though he clearly was proud of his feat. He
seized her hand and held it high, acknowledging the ap-
plause of Tynan's household. "Vivienne is returned, hale
and untouched!" he cried. The entire company, as well as
those in Tynan's household, cheered.

Vivienne smiled, though her thoughts churned with
the problem before her. How would she manage to set
Erik free? Every gate that clanged shut behind them
seemed to make the feat more impossible.

What if it *was* impossible?

What if she could not aid Erik?

Malcolm, who had once been her ally in many a prank, now hovered so close to Tynan and echoed that man's grim manner so well that his alliance could not be in doubt. There would be no aid for Erik from him.

"Let me tend the prisoner," Vivienne said on impulse to her brother. "He was injured by your men and it is the responsiblity of a good laird to see his prisoners tended."

"Then Uncle Tynan will see the deed done by another, you can be certain," Alexander said dismissively. "Come to the board, so all can see that you are hale."

"I would offer to aid him." Vivienne had thought this might grant her a chance to see Erik, but Alexander shook his head.

"You have need of a bath, a hot meal, and a long sleep," he said with affection. "Not more responsibilities."

"But . . ."

"You will not do this, Vivienne," Alexander said with resolve. "I forbid it." Vivienne glared at her brother, who had never spoken to her with such a harsh tone, and he glared back at her, clearly unapologetic.

"It is common," Tynan interjected, "for one who has undergone an ordeal to feel fondness for the party responsible for that ordeal."

"That makes no sense," Alexander said.

"Nonetheless, it is true." Tynan watched Vivienne with his wise eyes and she wondered again how much he saw of her inclinations. He shook his head, then cupped her elbow in his hand. He was so calm, so certain of himself, that it was easy to let him lead her along. "Come to the board, Vivienne, and revive yourself with ale and meat.

You will forget what you have experienced by the morrow."

Such was Vivienne's attitude toward her kin that his words made her wonder whether rumor contained a germ of truth. Had Ruari uttered a truth in naming her uncle as a sorcerer? Would Tynan ensure that she forgot Erik, by slipping some herb into her ale? There could be no greater travesty, to her thinking, for she was possessive of her memories of their time together.

And she would make more such memories.

"I am not hungry, in truth," she protested. "Nor do I have any thirst."

Alexander laughed. "I wager that you will be hungry beyond belief once you let a morsel cross your tongue. The fare at Ravensmuir is most fine, and you look to be pale for lack of food, Vivienne."

"Nonetheless, I have no desire to eat."

"What did you eat this past day?" Alexander asked.

Vivienne glanced downward. "Some cheese and bread. An apple or two. Simple fare but sufficient of it."

Alexander snorted.

"You must sit at the board for a while," Tynan urged smoothly. "The better for all to see that you are well. Without doubt, you have had an ordeal and the merriment will ease your mood."

It seemed that what Vivienne desired was not to be. She followed their lead to the board and lifted a cup to the company with false cheer, hoping against hope that she could escape her brother and uncle soon.

It was the sight of her youngest sister that eased Vivienne's mood. Elizabeth pushed her way through the crowd in the hall, her eyes dancing with pleasure.

"Vivienne!" Elizabeth cried as she made the high

table. Vivienne darted down from the dais, uncaring what her brother had to say about that.

Elizabeth caught her in a tight hug and spun her around joyously. Her greeting was more to Vivienne's liking. "We were all so fearful for you. Are you hale?"

"Hale enough." Vivienne heard Erik's influence in her short reply but she did not have the heart to say more.

"Perhaps she has greater need of a sister's companionship than a meal at the board," Alexander suggested to Tynan, who smiled with affection at the pair. As always, Elizabeth had a talent for persuading Alexander to soften his stance, sometimes not even by trying to do so. For once, though, Vivienne did not find this vexing.

Elizabeth pulled back and studied Vivienne. "You do not seem that hale."

"I am tired, no more than that." Vivienne forced a smile. "Where are Annelise and Isabella? Did they not accompany you here?"

Elizabeth grimaced, then dropped her voice to a whisper. "They were forbidden to accompany us. I was only allowed to come this far because of Darg."

"Darg?"

"That fairy aided our quest for you," Alexander said. He ruffled Elizabeth's hair, though she ducked from beneath the weight of his hand, then rolled her eyes.

"You will tangle my hair!"

"While you would prefer to tempt a suitor?" Alexander teased.

Elizabeth flushed and folded her arms across her chest, failing completely in her attempt to disguise the fullness of her breasts. She had been embarrassed about her new curves since their sudden and recent appearance, though was more uncertain of the attention men now granted to her. She cast a wary glance over her shoulder at the mostly male company, then turned to Vivienne alone.

"Darg said you would be found this night. Indeed, she granted me a verse specifically for Alexander. *'Ride west, ride west with main and might; a maid will be saved this very night. Between the river and the sea, a dozen strides from the chestnut tree; near the vale of Elphinstone, there you will find the one wanted home.'* "

"And you were there in truth!" Alexander said, hoisting his chalice high.

As the company cheered, Elizabeth dropped her voice so that Vivienne alone could hear her. "I did not tell them the rest, for Alexander would have been furious. Do not trust Malcolm with any morsel you wish to keep secret," she advised, casting a disparaging glance at their brother. "He is as Tynan's left hand since coming here."

It could have been argued that there was no small advantage in Malcolm's choice, for he stood to inherit Ravensmuir if he served Tynan well and allowed himself to be so groomed. Two years Vivienne's junior, Malcolm had the wits to know that he had been graced with a rare opportunity. She did not doubt that he would never jeopardize it and would have readily told Elizabeth as much.

But it was impossible for the sisters to speak further. The company erupted into noise at the sight of the prisoner. The company bellowed, stamped, and spat as Erik was carried into the hall. Vivienne turned away, so unable was she to look upon him so beaten and bruised. He was as yet unaware of his circumstance and Vivienne blamed herself for the many injuries he had sustained.

"That is Nicholas Sinclair?" Elizabeth whispered in shock. "And he was once so handsome a man. Look at the scar upon his face!" She cast a sharp glance at Vivienne. "Has his charm diminished as well as his looks?" She wrinkled her nose. "I never liked him, though it might solely have been because he stole your attention away from our games. I always thought he had too much charm, that he was too certain of his own merit."

Erik was taken to the dungeon and the men settled contentedly to their meal. They were excited after their successful capture of the supposed villain and anxious to share their tales. A song began even as Erik was carried away and Tynan repeated his call for ale.

Vivienne did not want to spend time in their company.

"Can we not eat alone in the solar, as we used to?" she asked, granting their brother a glance. "I should love to have a chance to talk with you, Elizabeth, without Alexander listening to our every word."

"I do not listen to every word!" Alexander protested.

"You try to do as much," Elizabeth retorted. "And you are much less amusing about the matter since you have become laird," she informed him with the honesty of youth. "Once you jested with us and were an amiable companion, now you demand this and that more sternly than ever Papa did. No wonder Vivienne did not miss your company."

Vivienne saw how the casually uttered words stung Alexander, for he looked suddenly stricken, but Elizabeth seemed oblivious. She turned a smile upon Tynan, obviously certain that she could win her way from him. "Uncle Tynan, you cannot make Vivienne remain here with all of you men after what she has endured. I shall ensure her welfare, you can be certain of that."

"Then go," Tynan said with amusement. He laid a hand upon Alexander's shoulder. "And may God judge us more kindly than bold maidens do, especially when we have ceased to be amusing."

Alexander smiled at his uncle's comment, but Vivienne saw that no merriment reached his eyes. She felt torn then, for she guessed that her brother had a more difficult time with the burden of Kinfairlie than she had understood.

She and Alexander had always had a certain camaraderie, and it stung that he had not confided the truth in her even as she felt a desire to ask him for it now.

On the other hand, he was disinclined to even listen to her side of matters and that was disappointing indeed. It was clear that whatever bond they had shared was now severed, though Vivienne wondered if she alone was saddened by that.

It mattered little, for she meant to fulfil her pledge to Erik. Thus, she followed Elizabeth from the hall, only half-heeding her sister's merry chatter.

How would she escape this doughty fortress without detection? That Madeline had managed as much should have been more encouraging than it was, but Vivienne knew she could not match her elder sister's merit.

All the same, she would have to try.

# *Chapter Nine*

Eᴌɪᴢᴀʙᴇᴛʜ ᴛᴜɢɢᴇᴅ at Vivienne's hand and led her toward the stairs. "I can do better than this noisy hall, to be
sure. The castellan's wife likes me, because Darg has
taken a fancy to her and she likes to hear Darg's verses. I
could be Lady of Ravensmuir with such influence!"

"I thought that position was yet held for Aunt
Rosamunde."

Elizabeth shook her head vehemently at that, then
glanced back at their uncle in dismay. "Do not so much
as utter her name," she counselled in a whisper. "Uncle
Tynan becomes most angry at the very mention of her."

"Why? He was the one who sent her away," Vivienne
was disinclined to grant understanding to her brother and
uncle in this moment. "I heard the cruel things he said to
her and I do not blame her for leaving."

Elizabeth winced. "I think he loves her yet. And Darg
says that their ribbons are entwined, for the moment at
least."

Vivienne remembered now this curious matter of ribbons. When their elder sister Madeline had been courted
by Rhys, Darg had shown Elizabeth the ribbons that un-

furled from each person in the hall. The ribbons of those souls destined to live and love together, according to Elizabeth, were entwined together.

The spriggan Darg could make a great deal of mischief, again according to Elizabeth, by knotting ribbons or shredding them, a feat which created obstacles for the lovers in question. Elizabeth claimed that Darg had attacked the ribbons of Tynan and Rosamunde with a vengeance, a result of her dislike of Rosamunde, and certainly that mortal pair had argued beyond expectation.

"That sounds ominous," Vivienne said.

Elizabeth nodded. "I do not like how Darg says it. She still holds malice against Rosamunde, of that I am certain."

Vivienne could not keep herself from being skeptical. "Darg could be lying."

Elizabeth shrugged. "I suspect not in this matter. She wants dearly to avenge herself upon Aunt Rosamunde and awaits her return so keenly that I cannot bear to hear more of it. She is most excited to be at Ravensmuir, I can assure you, and her wild antics have kept me from sleeping at all." Elizabeth yawned widely. "Though, of course, it was fear for your welfare that kept me awake in truth."

"I was hale enough."

Elizabeth granted Vivienne a long glance but said nothing more on the matter. "Darg is utterly convinced that Rosamunde will arrive at Ravensmuir at any moment, despite the fact that I have told her that Rosamunde herself swore never to return. We have argued about the matter so much that my head hurts, but still Darg insists."

Vivienne let her sister lead her up the stairs to the chambers above the hall, only half-listening to her chatter.

"Do you know what Darg wished to do last night, in the very dead of the night?" Elizabeth demanded.

Vivienne shook her head, not truly interested.

Elizabeth flung out her hands. "She wanted to descend to the caverns beneath Ravensmuir! Can you imagine greater folly? Alexander would have my head . . ."

Vivienne halted mid-step as inspiration struck. "Darg knows the caverns," she said, realizing the import of that. She had forgotten about the labyrinth that wound beneath Ravensmuir. Could one get from the dungeons to the caverns and thence elsewhere?

Vivienne did not know, but she thought that she might soon find out.

"Of course, Darg does! She has lived there for centuries," Elizabeth said with easy confidence. "She might even know them better than Uncle Tynan, or than our brothers, who played there so much when we were children." Elizabeth shivered. "I do not like them, not in the least, and I refused to accompany her there. I fear, though, that she may go without me, for she is very intent upon the matter."

"Where is she now?"

"Sitting upon your left shoulder, nodding with her usual glee and recounting the rest of her verse."

Vivienne had momentarily forgotten that there was more of it. "What was the rest?"

" *'Ride west, ride west with main and might; a maid will be saved this very night. Between the river and the sea, a dozen strides from the chestnut tree; near the vale of Elphinstone, there you will find the one wanted home.'* "

"That was the part you told Alexander."

"Indeed." Elizabeth smiled. "And this is the part I kept

from him: *'A mirror of herself she will be, though few will have the skill to see. Though loosed from a suitor most unlikely, changed forever will this maiden be.'*"

Vivienne felt her lips part at the truth of this. "What does Darg say about ribbons?"

"It matters little what she says, for I can see yours with my own eyes." Elizabeth stared over Vivienne's shoulder. "It is a shimmering silver, as if wrought with the dust of opals."

"And is there another?"

"A ragged one, as dark a blue as a midnight sky," Elizabeth grimaced. "It is stained and most disreputable of appearance, though the blue is a wondrously vivid hue. It has been a lovely ribbon, though now less alluring than once it was." She smiled at Vivienne, who wagered that the blue ribbon might also be stronger now than it had been. "It is Nicholas's ribbon, is it not?"

Vivienne declined to answer, for her family's misunderstanding of Erik's true identity might prove useful again. "Are they entwined?"

"They were, though the blue one is torn. A mere thread of it continues and I cannot see whether there is more or not." Elizabeth frowned. "How curious. I wonder what that means."

Vivienne guessed that it meant that Erik was in peril, either from Alexander's justice or simply from his injuries. She would have to aid him this very night.

How she wished she could see Darg for herself! The fairy's aid would be invaluable in this. She spared a glance to her shoulder, but saw nothing uncommon.

"She is over there now," Elizabeth said, pointing to the

rafters. "She likes to oust any birds fool enough to settle there."

Vivienne studied each rafter in the general direction Elizabeth pointed but could see no spriggan.

Elizabeth cast herself onto the cushions piled in one corner of the chamber at the top of the stairs, then turned her sparkling gaze upon Vivienne. "So, now that we are alone, you must tell me all. Did you lie with Nicholas in truth? Was it wondrous? Did it hurt as much as Vera insists it does? I think that she only tells us as much to ensure that we are not overly curious. Perhaps Alexander has even commanded her to do so, for if ever a man lost his ability to savor amusement, it is Alexander this past year."

"I am yet a maiden," Vivienne lied again. "My courses began on Friday, so I have been unclean these days and nights."

Elizabeth winced, then sighed. "How regrettable. I knew that you would tell me what it is like if you knew, for you have always been unafraid to tell the truth." Vivienne tried not to flinch at her sister's certainty of that. Then Elizabeth frowned. "But did you not bleed just a few weeks past?"

Vivienne shook her head. "You must have me confused with Annelise."

Elizabeth shook her head. "No, I distinctly recall you complaining, and Annelise never complains. It is most unnatural, do you not think, and makes the rest of us look discontented?"

Vivienne smiled and sat down. "Perhaps you are discontented."

"Without a shadow of doubt," Elizabeth agreed cheerfully. "You must have some detail to confess, though.

Can Nicholas recount a tale? He must have some merit. You could never love a man who did not share your affection for tales."

"He says little," Vivienne admitted. Erik did not tell tales, she realized, but his quest would make a good one.

Especially if he succeeded, with her aid. She saw him in her mind's eye, naming his daughters and measuring their heights, and her gaze misted with tears.

There had to be a way out of Ravensmuir's dungeons!

"I did not recall that Nicholas was silent," Elizabeth mused. "His sole affection seemed to be for stolen kisses and listing his own merits to any soul fool enough to listen."

Vivienne said nothing.

"Oh, but you must be hungry!" Elizabeth rose suddenly to her feet and made haste toward the door. She moved with the same purpose as their late mother and the unexpected resemblance between Elizabeth and Catherine brought a lump to Vivienne's throat. She saw suddenly from whence Elizabeth had inherited her ripe curves, for she stood the same height and the same shape, and her hair was the same hue, as Catherine's had been. The other sisters were wrought more slender, perhaps more like the women on her father's side of the family.

It was never far, this grief for the loss of her parents, though now it assailed Vivienne at the strangest of times. She thought then of Erik and wondered whether he felt the same way about his father's demise.

She would have wagered as much, so certain was she that they must be in agreement about such fundamental matters, though she knew that her conviction was wrought of little beyond instinct.

"I promised Uncle Tynan to see you fed, after all,"

Elizabeth continued. "I will return in but a moment—do not fear, the castellan's wife will ensure that we have a wondrous meal here!"

With that, Elizabeth was gone and the chamber fell quiet.

Vivienne sank unto a pile of cushions, her fingers worrying the rich fabric as she thought. The challenge before her seemed insurmountable indeed. Without Darg's aid, even if Vivienne managed to free Erik and lead him into the labyrinth, they would probably not find their way out before Uncle Tynan found them.

Which meant that Elizabeth would have to aid in Erik's escape. Vivienne nibbled on her lip, knowing that Elizabeth would earn Alexander's ire thus. She did not want to cause trouble between her siblings and would have preferred to leave her sister in innocence and ignorance.

Where did one find a fairy?

Vivienne raised her chin, carefully studying the beams of the ceiling and every nook in the walls. "Darg?" she asked, then repeated the query more loudly. "Darg? Are you yet here? Can you choose which mortals can see you? If so, I beg of you to choose me!"

There was no discernible reply. Vivienne waited and watched, hoping for some glimmer of the fairy's presence, but she saw nothing uncommon. As far as she could tell, she was alone.

She called again, she prowled the perimeter of the room, but to no avail. All she could hear was the merry-making of the men in the hall below, their raucous laughter and their drinking songs.

Either Darg was not here, or Vivienne could not see her.

Vivienne sat down to await her sister's return and decided that she would simply tell Elizabeth the truth, all of the truth, then hope her sister chose to be of assistance.

There was little else she could do.

While she waited, she pulled the dagger out of her belt that Ruari had brought to Erik from his father's deathbed. It was not a long blade, though the scabbard was richly ornamented. The hilt was an elaborate piece of metalwork. The grip was twisted like plies of a rope wound together and the pommel held a blue stone of remarkable size. Four prongs, shaped like claws, held the stone captive, though it caught the light in a most uncommon way.

Vivienne moved closer to the lamp and saw that there was both a word and an image cut into the gem, which was a rectangle as long as the first two digits on her index finger.

"ABRAXAS" was the word inscribed in the gem, as well as Vivienne could tell. It was not a word she knew and she wondered if she read it incorrectly. Perhaps it was initials or a word in another tongue.

Above the letters was a tiny figure that looked to be of a man—until Vivienne looked closer and saw that his head was that of a bird, and his legs were an odd spiraling shape. Were these errors of the engraver, or of some import?

Vivienne could not say. She pulled the blade from its scabbard out of curiosity and was pleased that the steel gleamed even in the low light of this chamber. It had been honed many times and was graced with a few nicks, but the edge was wickedly sharp. This blade had been treasured, to be certain, and she wondered how old it might be, or what powers it was reputed to hold.

Then she wondered how she would persuade Elizabeth

to aid her, frowned and put the blade away. There were more important puzzles before her than any legends linked to the Sinclair hereditary blade.

ERIK AWAKENED IN A DARK, dank cell, and could have guessed in which keep it was located. There was a flickering lamp left on the floor in the far corner and the wild dance of the flame made ominous shadows. His sword and dagger were gone, though that was scarcely surprising, and he ground his teeth at the recollection that he had willingly granted his father's blade to Vivienne.

No good deed was ever left unpunished, to be sure. Vivienne had said as much and in this moment, he could find no fault with her thinking. He supposed that he should have been glad that none of those rough mercenaries had been able to seize his hereditary blade, but knowing it was in the possession of the woman who had deceived him was no consolation.

For Vivienne had deceived him, and done as much so well that Erik had never suspected her motives. He had thought her persuaded of his reasoning when she had accepted a handfast instead of a marriage. He had believed her when she professed a care for his welfare and had agreed with his plan to halt for the night.

In truth, she had only ensured that they did not ride too far, the better that her family could retrieve her.

She had not truly forgiven him, but had merely feigned as much. She had contrived that they halted close enough to Ravensmuir that they would be discovered by her kin. And there could be no doubt of her motives, for she had refused to wed him when granted the chance.

Vivienne's pledge to aid him was a lie, as was her apparent desire for him. Erik Sinclair and his meager charms clearly would not suffice for a lady the like of Vivienne Lammergeier.

Which meant only that he, once again, had been fool enough to grant trust where it was unwarranted.

Erik stared sourly at the lamp and acknowledged that she had undoubtedly suggested the seven couplings not out of lust for him, but to ensure that he slept like a corpse. Her family had been upon them before he had even heard them approach, so exhausted had he been by their lovemaking.

Worst of all, he had been witless enough to believe that a beauteous damsel raised in wealth might find him alluring or his quest worth fighting. Beatrice should have taught him the full measure of his allure to such women, but nay, he was too much of a fool to have already learned his lesson from experience.

His father would have reminded Erik that he had always seen the good in others before he spied the bad, no less that to do as much was a dangerous habit.

That only made him realize that his father was dead, that William's wry voice would never again be heard in Blackleith's hall. And that was a truth that Erik could not face in this moment.

He sat up quickly to avoid his thoughts and the chamber cavorted around him at the sudden move. His head throbbed. There was dampness on his temple, and when he touched it, his fingers were stained red. Indeed, that slight movement had set his head pounding so vigorously that he could almost forget the pain in his hip.

He ignored both, pushed to his feet and crossed the cell to examine the lamp. There was no more than a vestige of oil remaining in the vessel, doubtless to ensure that he could make no mischief of note with it. The flame danced so vigorously because it would gut itself soon.

Erik took advantage of the light now to survey his prison. It was square, the ceiling low enough that he could barely stand, its walls wrought of fitted stone and its floor of pounded earth. There was a drain hole in the floor, as well as the tip of the nose of a rat that peered out at him from that drain.

The rodent seemed to eye him with a measure of assessment.

Erik wondered whether he would be fed some fearsome slop, or whether he would be abandoned in the pending darkness for the rat and its comrades to feast upon. Neither were promising prospects.

He turned his back upon the creature and paced, pausing to try the stout wooden door. The door did not budge, but then he had not expected it to.

The course from this point was clear. Erik would face the laird sooner or later to answer for breaking his word. There was no possible verdict save 'guilty,' for he had not wed Vivienne. No happy compromise could be negotiated, now that the lady had spurned Erik before all.

He glanced at the rat once more, irked that a similar charge had been cast against him—and unjustly—once again. Why was it that women chose to cast doubt upon his potency? He did not doubt that most of the men in Alexander's company would have been glad to sate themselves with Vivienne, whether she had had her courses or not. He did not doubt that they jested in the hall over their ale at the impotence of the man imprisoned beneath their feet.

Indeed, he could hear their merrymaking.

This would not end well, that much was for certain. Erik did not expect Vivienne to defend him, much less to reveal that he was not his brother Nicholas in timely fashion.

He considered his fate with a frown. The punishment could vary. He could be disfigured, marked as an outcast for the rest of his days by the loss of an eye or the tip of his nose or one of his ears. That was not particularly troubling, given what he had already endured, though it would be painful. He stretched his leg and thought he could do with somewhat less pain in his life.

He could be condemned to have a more significant part of his anatomy removed, namely the one at root of the issue. That was not a comforting prospect. If Erik survived that ordeal, he would neither be claiming a maidenhead again nor providing that male heir that the Earl of Sutherland had demanded for his aid.

Of course, Erik might simply be executed. Alexander was sufficiently vexed to demand a harsh punishment. Erik supposed that prospect should have bothered him less, as he was already reputed to be deceased, but it was that chance that made him pound upon the wooden door in frustration.

He was not yet prepared to die.

His daughters still had need of him.

Erik hammered his fists against the wood and shouted, knowing it was to no avail, pounded more loudly and bellowed for justice.

There was no reply. If anything, the festivities overhead seemed to grow louder. He finally halted and leaned his brow against the wood. The rat, he noted, watched with some interest, as if curious as to whether he was weakening.

"It is the girls," Erik told the rat, as there was no one else likely to listen. "There will be no one left to defend them once I am as dust." He grimaced at the portal and gave it one last kick. "Although I have done a poor job of that defense thus far."

The rat seemed to find this argument cogent. It appeared to nod several times, weighing the merit of Erik's words, then it turned and disappeared down the hole. There was a faint sound of scuttling feet before silence pressed against Erik's ears again.

He supposed Ruari must be pleased to have his predictions proven aright. The man could not truly have wanted to be burdened with the task of aiding Erik, and now he would be free to make other choices. So, there was an advantage to Erik's disappearance in that.

Indeed, there were many. Nicholas would keep Blackleith uncontested; the children would forget about their rightful father; Vivienne had probably already found another suitor or three; Alexander would keep Erik's coin and the Earl of Sutherland would not have to undertake a battle for which he had no heart. Truly, there would be none to mourn Erik if the Laird of Kinfairlie felt particularly vengeful on the morrow.

Erik surveyed his prison, his fists clenching and unclenching in frustration. He would not surrender. He would fight for his children until his dying breath, and he would fight more fiercely when that last breath seemed closer.

There was no way out of the cell but the single door which was securely locked against him. The drain was no bigger around than his wrist, so that offered no option for escape. Erik paced, willing his aches and pains to diminish. This might be the most dire circumstance in which he had ever found himself, but he would not abandon hope.

Someone at some time would open that door.

Erik had no weapon and he had no tool. The lantern sputtered and died in that moment. He also had no light. He had nothing but his wits—which were proving to be meager—and his bare hands.

But he had his anger and he had his determination. When some sorry fool opened that door, that man would learn what those few assets were worth. This might be destined to end poorly, but Erik would not accept his fate meekly.

He crouched opposite the door and leaned his back against the wall. He placed his booted foot over the drain, for no rat could lift the weight of him and it would take a while for the creature to chew through his heavy soles. These southern boots had the advantage of being sturdy, at least.

In that pose, he took what rest he could while he awaited his chance.

To his astonishment, Erik's thoughts turned unbidden not to all he had lost over the years, but to the lady who had just betrayed him. He found himself wishing that he had one last chance to explain himself to Vivienne, one last chance to kindle a light in her marvelous eyes, one last chance to plant a son in her womb.

And that only proved his wits useless indeed.

ELIZABETH NEARLY TRIPPED on the hem of her kirtle, so anxious was she to return to Vivienne. She carried a pair of bowls of steaming venison stew, a loaf of bread that was yet warm, and a pitcher of ale. The crockery cup she carried for the two of them to share was stuffed into her belt, along with a pair of carved wooden spoons, and she felt the cup loosing itself with every step. She had not a spare hand to secure it, though, and the castellan's wife had been too busy to grant her more aid than she had done.

Elizabeth hastened through the hall, artfully avoiding the grasp of many a man who assumed her to be a serving wench. Curse these breasts of hers! If ever a man looked her in the eye again—instead of looking rather lower than that—Elizabeth was certain she would wed him on the spot.

Provided that he was handsome, rich, and inclined to seek adventure, of course.

She kicked a man who grabbed at her and he laughed even as he tried to tumble her into his lap. Had her burden been only her own meal, Elizabeth would have abandoned it to strike him, but she knew that Vivienne must be famished indeed. She avoided his outstretched leg and contented herself with a scathing glare in his direction before hastening onward.

Elizabeth reached the bottom of the steps, breathless from her efforts, then eased slowly up them so as not to trip upon the hem of her gown.

Cups were abruptly banged upon the board, urging the men to heed some announcement or another. Elizabeth paused on the steps and glanced back. The man who had tried to trip her leered in her direction, but she ignored him.

Alexander stood and cleared his throat, looking as pompous as he possibly could. Elizabeth fairly ground her teeth at the change in her eldest brother, who had been so much more entertaining before their parents' deaths. He had become a tedious old man, obsessed with honor and justice, before Elizabeth's very eyes. She would never have believed it possible had she not seen it herself.

It was time enough, to her thinking, that one of the sisters played a prank upon him, just as he used to play pranks upon them. He was impossibly smug when he had his way, which irked Elizabeth beyond belief.

"Here is a night in need of a tale, for we will none of us be quick to sleep this night, and here is a teller of tales in need of a cup of ale. I bid welcome to Ruari Macleod, a teller of tales arrived in most timely fashion, a man come to our door in the moment we have greatest need of his talent."

A stocky man stood before the head table, where he had obviously made his offer of a tale for a meal. He bowed to the company with clear trepidation, a large saddlebag at his feet. He was older, his hair an unruly russet thatch, his garb rough and his face growing redder by the moment. He looked around the hall, not nearly so at ease to be the focus of attention as one might expect of a storyteller, and cleared his throat a good dozen times.

A serving woman topped up his cup of ale, clearly thinking that was the issue. He nodded at her, then bowed in gratitude, doing so with such clumsiness that he spilled the ale. The assembly laughed, thinking this a jest, but the man's face only reddened to a deeper hue. His uncertainty grew more apparent as the expectant silence stretched ever longer. He stood mute, looking at them, and shifting his weight from foot to foot.

Elizabeth darted up the stairs to find Vivienne pacing in a most uncharacteristic manner. Vivienne pivoted and must have seen that the cup was about to fall. She quickly lifted the two bowls out of Elizabeth's grip and Elizabeth pulled the cup out of her belt just as it worked itself loose.

"Just in time!" Elizabeth said with triumph.

Vivienne did not share her smile. "Is Darg here?"

"Of course. She prefers smaller chambers to the hall and remained here to dance on the rafters while I was gone. Mark my words, she will descend upon the ale if we do not drink it quickly."

Elizabeth poured the ale, and heard Darg's cry of delight. "Can you not hear that?" she asked, but Vivienne shook her head. She pointed, sensing her sister's disappointment, as Darg swung from the rafters on a doughty cobweb, screaming all the while.

The fairy jumped at the precise moment that would ensure that she landed upon the handle of the pitcher. "*Some ale for you but more for me; a finer taste there cannot be,*" she said, smacking her lips. She leaned down to put her mouth to the ale, intending to drink like a dog and doubtless drink it all.

Elizabeth swatted at the fairy and nearly spilled the ale. Darg dodged the blow, scurried around the lip of the pitcher, then squatted on the rim.

"Pest!" Elizabeth cried, pushing the fairy aside. Darg jumped to her shoulder, clucking and complaining, as Elizabeth managed to pour ale into the cup she and Vivienne would share.

She offered her sister the cup and found Vivienne regarding her with confusion. "I will assume that you have not been struck mad," Vivienne said with a smile. "But that you aim to keep the fairy out of the ale."

"Darg likes mortal ale overmuch, and is a cursed amount of trouble once she has had some." To foil the fairy, Elizabeth knotted a handkerchief over the top of the pitcher. Darg crawled across it, peering through the weave at the ale beneath, then whimpered.

Vivienne was no more cheerful than the fairy. She seemed concerned about some matter, perhaps overly disappointed that she could not see the fairy. Despite the fact that she must be hungry, Elizabeth watched her sister push the stew around the bowl.

"You have not taken a bite. I thought your bowl would be clean by now," she teased, and gained only a tiny smile.

"I am not that hungry," Vivienne said and put the bowl aside. The shadows in her eyes were undeniable, though Elizabeth guessed her sister was not ready to speak of what troubled her. Vivienne had a merry heart, by nature, and was impulsive of tongue. Her inclination to silence this night was one that Elizabeth thought should be respected for its rarity.

They had time aplenty to share tales, for Elizabeth doubted that Vivienne would wed soon. Indeed, she was of an age that might preclude her marrying at all.

"A storyteller has arrived," Elizabeth said, hoping to cheer Vivienne, who so loved tales. "He is not a very good storyteller, at least not thus far, for he seems most troubled about making a beginning. And he is old enough that one would think he would have had years to conquer his fear of a large company. Perhaps he is not truly a storyteller at all." She shrugged and ate some of her stew. "We could sit on the steps, out of sight, and listen."

Vivienne straightened and her eyes brightened. "How old is he?"

Elizabeth considered as she chewed. "Maybe he has

seen fifty summers, or maybe he has seen forty that were challenging. I cannot say. He is old, to be sure."

She managed to speculate no more, for Vivienne darted down the stairs. Elizabeth trailed after her with her meal, and found her sister's face alight as she peered around the corner of the wall.

"You know this man," she guessed.

"His name is Ruari Macleod," Vivienne said with certainty.

"Do you know where to begin, old man?" cried some stout soul in the company. "Your tale is thin soup thus far!"

The men roared and murmurings of discontent grew.

"Once upon a time!" Vivienne shouted.

Elizabeth peeked and she saw the older man's relief at this encouragement. He waved a heavy finger in the direction of the stairs. "Aye, there would be the beginning of the tale. Once upon a time, there was a man and there was a woman . . ."

"We know this tale, old man," a man said in the crowd and a coarse laugh echoed through the hall.

Ruari rounded upon the man with annoyance and jabbed that finger in the heckler's direction. "You do not know this tale, you cannot know this tale, for I am here to tell it to you. It is my tale and my gift, though it was lived by another man."

"Then begin it in truth," cried the unrepentant man.

This Ruari squared his shoulders and his voice grew so loud that it filled the hall. "Once upon a time, there was a man who lost his heart to a woman of Norse lineage, a woman with hair as fair as flax and eyes as blue as the sea. She was not so lovely that wars were fought over her favor, and she was not so finely wrought that she might have been confused with a fairy queen. She was simply a woman, a fine woman with a good heart, a woman with a clear brow and vigor in her limbs, a woman who would bear him sons and love him as fervently as he loved her."

"I am needing such a woman myself," another man jested, though his companions nudged him none-too-gently to silence.

"And so this man confessed his admiration to the lady, and asked her to put her hand into his. And she agreed, despite the fact that he had little to his name save his honor and his blade. He was the youngest of five sons borne to an old Highland family, and his family could grant him only their blessing. The lady loved him well enough to accept his suit and so they were wed."

Elizabeth sank down on the step, quietly eating her stew as she listened. She watched Vivienne, who heeded this Ruari's tale with unexpected interest.

"In time, and with much labor, they wrought a home for themselves, albeit one far more humble than either had known before. And in time, the woman bore a son to her husband, a boy with hair as fair as his mother's own. And because the boy so favored his mother's kin, they gave him a bold Norse name. Erik means 'ruler forever' and invokes the great champion Erik the Red."

Elizabeth watched Vivienne ease forward on her seat, the meal forgotten. Did she know some man named Erik? Elizabeth did not. Where might her sister have met such a man?

Meanwhile, the storyteller continued. "So it was that in time, God granted this couple another son, another boy as golden and healthy as the first. But as God gives with one hand, so does he take away with the other, and the woman died in the birthing of her second son. And the husband knew not how he would raise these boys without his wife by his side and he feared his sons would need greater protection than he could grant them. So, he named the boy Nicholas, in honor of the saint known to have had affection for children, and he entreated that saint to show favor to both of his sons."

But wait. Elizabeth frowned. Alexander had pledged Vivienne's hand to Nicholas Sinclair, who had an elder brother named Erik. The Sinclairs were an old Highland family. Nicholas cooled in the dungeon, captured for breaking his pledge to Alexander.

And most intriguingly, Vivienne had spent two nights and days in the company of Nicholas, unchaperoned. Elizabeth eyed her sister and was not at all convinced that Vivienne did not care for the man in Ravensmuir's dungeon. She was also unpersuaded that her sister truly bled as she insisted.

It had not been Annelise a few weeks past, Elizabeth knew it.

Could the arrival of this storyteller, known to Vivienne against all expectation, be coincidence? Elizabeth thought not. She listened more closely as the storyteller continued.

"Though the father taught the boys as well as he could, both of them felt often that their father was merely biding his time before he too slipped away to join their mother. It seemed that as the boys grew, their vitality was gained at the cost of their father's vigor. By the time they were men, tall and strong and triumphant in battle, he never left his bed.

"The older son, fearing that his father missed the plenty of his youth—for both boys had heard the tale of their parents' simple beginnings time and again—began to expand their humble abode. He fought avaricious neighbors on every side, he secured his borders, he built a stone keep, and he did it all in his father's name. He took no credit for himself, but swore it was his father's plan, his father's training, and his father's inspiration that granted him the fortitude to conjure affluence from nothing at all. He was valiant in battle, his word could be relied upon in treaty, and he was trusted for his honor by all.

"The younger son, meanwhile, had no care for labor. He preferred to savor what he could charm from others, or what he could trick them into granting to him, for he believed that only fools toiled, sweat, and shed blood. He was fair to look upon and used that to his advantage in gaining his desires."

This was consistent with Elizabeth's memory of Nicholas Sinclair. She glanced to Vivienne in time to see her sister nod grim agreement. She tapped her on the shoulder. "Then how can you care for Nicholas?" she whispered.

Vivienne started in surprise. "I do not."

"But he is in the dungeon and you clearly fret for him . . ."

Vivienne shook her head, then heaved a sigh. "It is Erik Sinclair who is in the dungeon," she confessed quietly. "It is Erik Sinclair who captured me."

Elizabeth opened her mouth at this revelation then closed it again. Vivienne turned her attention back to the storyteller. Elizabeth scarcely breathed, for she knew now that she heard the tale of which Vivienne was a part. She put her meal aside and even ignored the splash of Darg leaping joyously into their half-empty cup of ale.

Ruari continued. "The brothers argued on occasion, as

two wrought so differently only could, but they hid their quarrels from their father—the younger one had no desire to appear poorly in his father's eyes, and the older one had no yearning to tax his father's strength. Perhaps the father did not fully understand the nature of Nicholas until it was too late. Perhaps he did not wish to know. I do not know the truth of it, save that it was."

Elizabeth was snared by the injustice of the father's error. Darg belched, then climbed from the empty cup of ale, staggering slightly in her course toward the pitcher. The fairy swung up on the handle of the pitcher, landed atop the handkerchief, and began to gnaw a hole in the cloth.

Elizabeth was too transfixed by the tale to care.

"The elder son wed happily, to a local beauty name of Beatrice, and an alliance was sealed with the love match. Two daughters were born to Beatrice, and Erik was proud as ever a father could be. And so it seemed that all was well, though the younger brother had a fierce jealousy of the elder."

"This tale will turn from bad to worse," Elizabeth whispered in trepidation. Vivienne but nodded once, her attention fully fixed on the older man's voice.

# *Chapter Ten*

"AND SO IT CAME TO PASS that one dark day, Erik was summoned without warning by an ally, one Thomas Gunn, who professed need of his aid. Erik left his wife and his children and his home well defended, though it became clear that he had not prepared for treachery from within. Erik arrived at the abode of Thomas to find those lands at peace, and to learn that his neighbor had sent no summons to him."

"Nicholas deceived him!" hissed someone in the company, and Elizabeth was certain that man had named the culprit aright.

"Aye, Nicholas indeed, though none dared make such a bold accusation then. Once Erik had left his home, Nicholas asserted himself as laird, though most thought the claim a temporary one."

"The cur!" shouted one man in the assembly. "I will wager that he had a scheme to see the change wrought permanent!"

Ruari lifted a hand. "Who can say with certainty, save Nicholas himself? I will tell you, though, that Erik was assaulted upon the road while returning to his own abode, that he was attacked where he least expected such a deed—for, as you will recall, he knew nothing of the changes at his home. He knew only that the message he had received from Thomas Gunn had been an error.

"And so it was that Erik was surprised upon his own road, he was beaten senseless, he was cast from a cliff. He was believed to be lost to this world forevermore and, indeed, they held a funeral mass for him when he did not return to Blackleith and mourned his passing for a fortnight. It was said that his horse returned home without him, and Nicholas let it be known that he searched endlessly for his brother, without success."

"While he had been the one to see to his disappearance," muttered one man to assent from the hall.

"This explains his scars," Elizabeth said quietly, though her sister did not reply.

Ruari paused and Elizabeth eased to the lip of the stair, so anxious was she to hear the next increment of the tale.

Vivienne, she noted, listened just as intently, though she did not seem as horrified by the tale. Did Vivienne know it already?

"He cannot have been dead in truth!" roared a man in encouragement. "That would be the end of your tale."

Ruari shook his head. "Erik was close to dead, to be sure, but Fortune finally smiled upon him. A powerful neighbor gone hunting found Erik some days after that man's own funeral. He recognized Erik and thought to grant him an honorable burial. Imagine his surprise when the supposed corpse began to speak!"

The company laughed, though Vivienne did not. Elizabeth watched her sister fold the fullness of her kirtle repeatedly between her fingers, utterly unaware of her own fretful gesture, and guessed that Vivienne had lost her heart to this wronged Erik.

"And so it was from this neighbor that Erik learned of doings at his abode. He learned that it was said that he had been assailed upon the road by bandits and that a funeral mass had been sung in his honor. Erik, though, could not fully credit the rumor of his brother's deception. In the end, the neighbor—who was the Earl of Sutherland—made Erik a wager which would prove the truth of his claim. The Earl of Sutherland offered to make a visit to Erik's abode and to secret Erik within his company, so that man could see the truth for himself."

Elizabeth stood and took Vivienne's hand in her own. Her sister's fingers were chilly. Vivienne returned Elizabeth's squeeze, though she did not glance in her direction.

"And so it was done, though Erik was certain that the Earl must be mistaken. It had long been said that the Earl of Sutherland was overly suspicious, after all. But just as the Earl had foretold, Nicholas called himself Laird of Blackleith. Nicholas was not, however, content with mere suzerainty over what he had stolen from his brother: he not only claimed authority over the family holding, but insisted that his brother's children were of his very own seed."

"No!" someone in the company roared.

"Aye!" Ruari retorted. "Nicholas said that he had been compelled to render the marital debt to his brother's wife, for Erik had been incapable of so doing. No man would have believed that he was not desirous of union with Beatrice, for the woman was a beauty beyond compare."

"And what did she say of it?" demanded a man.

Ruari shrugged. "No one knew, for of Erik's beauteous and loyal wife, there was no sign. The Earl believed that she had defended her spouse and been killed for that deed. After all, Nicholas claimed he had seduced Beatrice in lieu of her rightful spouse, which must have shamed her. This time, Erik put credence in the Earl's suspicions, though he mourned his loyal wife in truth."

"Such treachery must see its due!" shouted another man. The company began to growl in discontent, so fully were they upon Erik's side.

"But surely the father protested," argued one man.

Ruari shook his head sadly. "Beguiled by Nicholas's silvered tongue, the father denounced Erik. He called his eldest son the shame of his beloved wife's womb. And he retired, shaking, to his bed, leaving Nicholas uncontested as Laird of Blackleith."

"It will be a feat to wring a happy ending to this story," Elizabeth whispered.

"That it will," Vivienne agreed.

"What happened?" prompted one of the men, his words quick with impatience.

Ruari lifted his head and spread his hands as he addressed the company in a bold voice once more. "It took a long time to heal Erik's wounds, though I would wager that some of them never did heal. He always limped. He always was scarred. Once hale, choices were before him. He might have left his homeland forever, he might have earned his way as a mercenary in a far country, but fear for his daughters made him desire to remain close. There was little he could do alone, though, and he had no men he could summon to his side. His brother had fortified Blackleith and few even knew of Erik's survival who might have aided him.

"Just when he despaired utterly of success, fickle Fortune smiled upon him again, as so oft she will. The Earl of Sutherland, who was disinclined to enter his neighbor's squabbles but also hated to see injustice pass unpunished, offered Erik a wager. The Earl had been troubled by that visit to Blackleith, nigh as troubled as Erik had been. The Earl was much concerned with stability and the clear passage of inheritance. Many woes come of daughters, such was oft declared by him, and I believe it was a matter of concern to him that only two daughters were the progeny of the Sinclairs. He saw trouble ahead, did the Earl, and he thought to resolve both that and the trouble at hand.

"And so it was that the Earl of Sutherland pledged to Erik Sinclair that if Erik could conceive a son, a son whose paternity was beyond doubt, then he, the Earl of Sutherland, would not only defend that son, but that he would muster an army to retrieve Erik's holding of Blackleith from his brother Nicholas."

"Erik took the wager," Elizabeth whispered.

"What else might he do?" Vivienne murmured in return. The sisters' hands entwined and locked together, their knuckles white with the vigor of their grip.

"And so it was that Erik sought the one maiden in all of Christendom who had perceived his brother to be the viper he was when first she met him, the one woman who had spied the darkness of Nicholas's heart with a single glance, the one woman whom he believed could grant to him not only the son he needed but grant that son the discernment he would need to survive and to succeed."

Elizabeth watched Vivienne and knew who that woman was.

"What will you do?" she asked.

Vivienne shook her head. "He must escape, this very night, before Alexander condemns him." She flicked a glance at Elizabeth. "I beg you not to betray me to Alexander."

Elizabeth rolled her eyes at the very prospect. "Of course not! But how will you do it?"

Vivienne met Elizabeth's gaze. "I had thought that our sole chance might be through the caverns."

"You mean to leave with him."

Vivienne nodded. "I promised him that son. I pledged to do my best to conceive and we have a handfast for a year and a day, as well. My path lies with him."

Elizabeth hurried to grant her sister a hug, hearing all the unspoken nuances in those few words. This quest might not end well, for great odds were stacked against Erik Sinclair. It frightened her to think of Vivienne in the midst of it, yet she could well imagine her sister making a difference in the end result.

Elizabeth wanted to do her part. "I will persuade Darg to show us through the caverns. We can ensure your escape with her aid."

"You would do this for me?"

"Of course!"

"But Alexander will be angry with you, of that I am certain."

Elizabeth waved away that concern. "Alexander has his own way far too often these days. I shall savor the chance to ruin one of his schemes."

Darg gave a cry then as she fell through the hole she had gnawed in the handkerchief. There was a splash as the spriggan fell into the pitcher of ale. The fairy made a gurgling sound and Elizabeth swore. She plunged her hand through the hole in the cloth and seized the wriggling fairy by her breeches, then gave her a stern shake.

Darg coughed with gusto, then released a belch sweet with the scent of ale.

"Immortality has not sharpened your wits," Elizabeth said, tapping the fairy's back with more vigor than was strictly necessary. "We have need of your aid this night, and you might see fit to be sufficiently sober to grant it."

Darg opened one eye slyly, then sat up instead of making some comment. She sniffed the air, as hungrily as a hound on the hunt, and her smile turned malicious. *"The thief returns on the storm's tide; she thinks her lust cannot be denied."* Darg began to cackle as if her merriment could not be contained. She rolled to her back, laughing and laughing, her feet kicking in the air helplessly.

Elizabeth could make no sense of her chatter and had no patience for it. Clearly the spriggan was drunk and that at a most inconvenient time.

"Enough about Rosamunde," Elizabeth said with disgust. "I have told you time and again that she will not return. I ask you only to guide us through the caverns this night." Darg glanced this way and that, murmuring to herself and granting Elizabeth no reply. Elizabeth looked to Vivienne, who watched her with care. "I am sorry, but I cannot warrant what Darg will do this night."

"Then we shall have to do our best," Vivienne said, turning to watch the company with rare resolve. "There will be no other choice so good as this one and we dare not sacrifice it."

Even if it meant sacrificing herself. Vivienne's resolve could mean nothing less. This was love, Elizabeth thought, and found herself thrilled in its very presence.

It was only right that success be theirs this night.

VIVIENNE INCHED FORWARD to peer around the corner at the foot of the stairs. She watched as Ruari shrugged and paced the hall slowly, apparently deep in thought. The hall was silent as all waited for the next increment of the tale.

"Tell us!" cried a bold man in the crowd. "Tell us how he regained all he had lost!" The men roared and thumped their cups on the tables, many of them stamping their feet with enthusiasm. Alexander and Tynan exchanged a smile, Alexander clearly pleased with himself for seeing fit to hire the storyteller this night.

He might not remain so pleased for long.

Ruari sighed and straightened, letting his gaze trail over the company as if he dreaded what he must say. "I wish I could tell you as much, but the Earl of Sutherland's daring scheme came to naught. The chosen maiden betrayed Erik, as had every soul in all of his life. Erik died, nameless, forgotten and unavenged in a sorry pit of a dungeon. As to the fate of his daughters, I dare not guess."

The men in the hall stared incredulously at the storyteller for a long moment of silence. Vivienne rose to her feet, knowing that this tale had been recounted for her ears, knowing that she alone had the power to change its ending.

Erik had need of her.

"No!" cried one man in the hall. "That is not fair!"

"No!" cried another. "He cannot have died afore his quest was won!"

Alexander stood and raised his hands, clearly hoping

that he could calm the company. "I suggest you find a better ending for your tale, old man," he said, but Ruari stood proudly.

"I have recounted the tale as it was," he said. "This is the sole ending that I know, for it is the truth."

"That is no tale!" a man roared and threw his pottery cup with vigor at Ruari. Ruari ducked, the cup smashed against the high table, and was quickly followed by another.

A tempest erupted in the hall. Crockery shattered against the floor and a roaring tide of discontented men surged toward the unrepentant storyteller. Tynan bellowed for order to no avail, Alexander shouted in dismay, and Vivienne knew what she had to do.

"Now!" she cried to Elizabeth and the two young women plunged into the chaos of Ravensmuir's hall. Vivienne pulled Erik's dagger from its sheath, and hoped against hope that she would not have to use it against her own kin.

"Bring Darg!" she shouted to Elizabeth.

"She runs ahead of us, using the heads and shoulders of the company as stepping stones!" Elizabeth replied.

The sisters dodged the crockery that flew through the air and tried not to slip on the ale spilled across the stone floor. Vivienne lunged for the door to the dungeon and collided heavily with a man.

It was Ruari, a bulging saddlebag cast over his shoulder.

He considered her sternly, then heaved a sigh. "There is no portent more fearsome than the attentions of a beauteous woman, upon that any man of good sense can rely."

"I mean to aid him," Vivienne said, certain he was referring to Beatrice. "My sister can help us escape."

Ruari looked skeptical. His gaze flicked away, then he nudged Vivienne roughly out of the path of a pair of men locked in combat. He apologized, then put out his hand for Erik's blade. "You have wrought quite enough trouble, lass. Let me at least save the lad's life."

"You cannot give him a son."

"And you will never persuade the guard to surrender the key to you," Elizabeth interjected. "You have need of us."

Ruari's eyes narrowed and his mouth worked in rare silence.

"This is my sister, Elizabeth. She can see fairies, including the one that will guide us out of Ravensmuir by a hidden passage." Vivienne heartily hoped that was true.

Ruari thought for a mere moment, his expression troubled. "Sorcerers!" he muttered. "No less an entire family of them." He cast a glance back at the disordered company, then abruptly opened the wooden portal. He bowed with the grace of a courtier. "After you, my ladies," he said, behaving for all the world as if it had been his suggestion that they join him.

Vivienne hastened down the steps, holding her skirts high. She feigned delight when the man granted the duty of guarding Erik glanced up from his post. "Hamish! I am so glad to find you here."

"My lady Vivienne! And my lady Elizabeth. What trouble is at work in the hall?" Hamish was silver of hair and doughty in battle, his face creased with the lines of experience. He was trim and muscular, a formidable opponent despite his years of experience at warfare. His impatience to join the fray was most evident. "We sound besieged."

"We are!" Elizabeth cried. "The battle is dreadful!"

Hamish's eyes brightened at the prospect.

"Uncle Tynan has need of every man to come to the defense of Ravensmuir," Vivienne added.

"Aye, I can hear the ruckus, but I cannot abandon my task." Hamish spared a dark glance to the door of the cell in the dungeon. "No man assails one of the ladies of my laird's family and is left free to escape justice."

"Amen to that," Ruari said gruffly. "I will watch the prisoner in your stead."

"Indeed!" Vivienne declared. "Hamish, your blade is needed in the battle above!"

Hamish flicked a suspicious glance at Ruari. "And who is this?"

"Oh, you must know Ruari." Elizabeth waved dismissively at the older man, to Vivienne's pleasure. Her sister, it was clear, was more adept with a falsehood than she. "He has been in Alexander's employ for at least a fortnight." Elizabeth leaned closer to Hamish to whisper. "But he is more sturdy than bold, what with his age, if you understand my import."

Hamish nodded at this, his gaze unswerving from Ruari.

Vivienne added to the tale. "Alexander has made Ruari my escort and he is stalwart. Trust him with the key to the dungeon and no one living or dead shall loose it from his grip."

Hamish looked lingeringly toward the stairs, but he shook his head. "I should wait for my laird's command."

Ruari laughed shortly. "Even one so ancient as I can ensure that a prisoner remains in his cell in this formidable keep." He glanced upwards. "And the laird will have no chance to grant you direct orders soon, my friend. He has need of every ally!"

A bellow carried from the hall above, followed by a resounding crash. Tynan roared for order with perfect timing.

Hamish hastily untied the key from his belt and offered it to the other man. "Mind you are not tricked."

Ruari nodded. "I am accustomed to the silver tongue of Nicholas Sinclair and the wickedness it can unleash. You can be certain that I shall not be beguiled."

Hamish raced up the stairs, then halted just before the portal. "Swear to me, as well, that you will defend Lady Vivienne and Lady Elizabeth."

Ruari nodded. "Never has a woman come to harm beneath my care." He pulled his own blade, as if to show his preparedness. "The ladies will be safe with me, safer here, by far, than in the hall above. Go, man! Go and aid the laird!"

The men's gazes met and held, then Hamish burst into the hall with a battle cry. The heavy portal closed behind him as blades clashed overhead.

"Finally!" Vivienne made to pluck the key from Ruari's hand, the better to hasten to Erik's aid, but the older man shook his head.

"Let me. All may not be as you anticipate."

Vivienne's hand dropped away in trepidation. "Is Darg here?" she whispered and Elizabeth glanced to a high corner of the chamber, then nodded.

Ruari sheathed his blade silently, then squinted as he fitted the brass key into the lock. There was no sound from behind the portal, a poor portent indeed.

Perhaps Erik had been beaten to a stupor.

Perhaps he was dead. Vivienne clenched her hands together and prayed silently. Elizabeth eased closer, her own eyes wide.

The tumblers rolled and Ruari granted them a solemn glance.

Vivienne nodded that she was prepared for the worst, and the older man began to open the massive door. The hinges creaked in protest.

Then the door slammed back with vigor. Ruari fell backward with a cry as Erik leapt from his prison. In the twinkling of an eye, Ruari was on his back on the floor and Erik knelt atop him, his hands locked around the older man's neck.

"No!" Vivienne shouted, forgetting for the moment that she might be overhead.

"No!" Elizabeth cried.

Apparently deaf to the sisters, Erik squeezed tighter. Ruari reddened and choked.

"Fool!" Vivienne kicked Erik in the leg with all her might. "Do not kill Ruari! We have come to aid you!"

ERIK BLINKED REPEATEDLY, struggling to adjust his vision to the sudden light. He had been able to see little beyond the silhouette in the doorway when he launched from the cell.

He was prepared to fight his way out of Ravensmuir. He had been so certain that the door would only be opened by someone charged with leading him to some foul fate, that he had been prepared to kill that messenger.

He had not been prepared for a woman to shout at him, much less for her to kick him with savage might. She leapt on to his back and locked her arms around his neck. The bone of her forearm pressed across his throat and impeded the passage of air.

He tightened his grip, intent upon completing what he had begun while he could. The chamber dimmed around him and his head began to throb with increased vigor.

Then he heard the name "Ruari" being screamed into his ear.

Indeed, the face reddening within his grasp was familiar.

Erik had not imagined that anyone would help him escape. He had certainly not imagined that Ruari would attempt to even enter Ravensmuir, much less gain an opportunity to release him in a timely fashion. The odds were rather against such fortuitous intervention.

Yet here was Ruari, choking for air within his grip.

"Ruari!" Erik loosed his hands and the older man took a shaking gasp of air. Erik helped the older man sit up and patted his back while that man laboriously caught his breath. Ruari coughed and spat, choked and rubbed his throat. He granted Erik a foul look, which was not undeserved.

It was Vivienne who slipped from Erik's back, against all expectation, Vivienne who had kept him from making a grievous error.

If anything she gave him a darker glance than Ruari had.

It defied belief that Vivienne had ensured his escape, yet Erik's shin ached so mightily where she had kicked him that she could be no figment of his fancy.

And his body responded to her presence most keenly. Her eyes were flashing and her hair was loosing itself from her braid; her cheeks were flushed and she looked ripe enough to ravish. What sorcery could she summon, that merely the sight of her would awaken such a lust within him? He wanted naught other than to cast her over his shoulder and carry her away, to possess her over and over again, to taste every increment of her flesh a hundred times.

But why had she come to his aid now? He cast a suspicious glance about himself, telling himself that she must have come to bring more woe upon his head.

There were only four of them in the anteroom to the dungeon, the fourth being a young dark-haired girl who resembled Vivienne sufficiently to be kin. She did not appear to be a threat to his survival, but one never knew.

He slanted a cautious glance at Vivienne and his heart leapt when he found her gaze locked upon him. Her full lips tightened in disapproval and she took a deep breath that made the curves of her breasts strain against her kirtle.

"What manner of fool are you to assault those come to rescue you?" Vivienne demanded, her manner disparaging. Her voice trembled, though, and he knew she had feared he might have been successful.

Indeed, he had come close to injuring his sole reliable companion.

"How dare you injure the man loyal enough to aid you?" Vivienne continued. "What manner of witless fool tries to ensure that he is not saved?"

There was little Erik could say to that, so he said nothing at all. Indeed, the vigor of his body's response to Vivienne's presence was nigh overwhelming. He took a step away from her and turned his back upon her. He would remain as aware of her presence as ever but she might be insulted by his manner.

"I thank you for that greeting," Ruari said gruffly. "Remind me never to leave you vexed, lad, if that is the welcome I receive when you are glad to see me."

"I am sorry. I thought you came to lead me to my death."

"I know what you thought, lad," Ruari retorted. "But you might have looked afore you leapt." He shuddered and coughed, making more of a spectacle of his recovery than Erik truly thought was deserved.

The other maiden patted Ruari upon the back with sympathy. She was pretty enough, young and curvaceous.

Ruari, the old rogue, fairly blossomed beneath her attentions.

"Oh, you are the heart and soul of kindness, upon that any sorry soul might rely," he crooned. "Could you rub my back a bit, lass? Have you ever been told that you have the touch of a healer? I should know, for I am descended from a long and exalted line of healers, and I tell you that I can feel the gift in your touch . . ."

"A wise man once taught me that time was of the essence in surprising an assailant," Erik muttered, knowing full well that Ruari would recognize William Sinclair's counsel.

Ruari ignored him. "Here, lass. A bit to the left, on this shoulder here. Aye, there cannot be a shred of doubt about it, you have the fingers of an angel." He smiled up at the maiden, who rubbed his back with greater vigor while he sighed contentment. "A veritable angel."

"An apology is as little unless it is accepted," Vivienne said.

Erik felt the back of his neck heat, knowing that the older man deliberately tormented him. "I halted as soon as I recognized you, Ruari. Again I say I am sorry."

Ruari snorted. "Your vision fades before its time, lad. I would have thought you might have recognized me sooner."

"You should see Ruari rewarded for his efforts in seeing you rescued." Vivienne said. "He was most valiant."

Ruari fairly preened beneath this praise.

"I have thanked him," Erik said tersely. "Though he declines the honor I would grant him. Time there will be to argue about the matter once we are freed of Ravensmuir."

"True enough, lad," Ruari said and finally pushed himself to his feet. "This slender advantage may not endure overlong." The men shook hands and exchanged a glance that resolved all.

"What happens in the hall above?" Erik asked. "It sounds to be a fight. Has the laird lost the order of his hall?"

Ruari nodded, but it was Vivienne who spoke first. She came to Erik's side and laid a hand upon his arm, her touch sending a treacherous shiver over his flesh. He should have expected her to touch him, should have expected her to try to draw his eye to her again. She had to know the potency of her caress, the power she held over him.

Indeed, a fire danced through his veins from the point where her fingertips rested upon his flesh. He scarce dared to breathe, he dared not speak directly to her. He dared not so much as glance her way, so volatile was his desire for her.

"It *is* a fight," she said. "One launched by Ruari's reciting of your tale."

His tale? Ruari had told *his* tale? Panic flickered deep within Erik, a terror that was not tempered by Ruari's chagrined expression. "What is this?"

"I had no choice, lad." Now it was Ruari who was contrite. For once in all his days, the man knew he had said too much. "I had need of a tale to gain admission to the laird's hall. I told the sole tale I know."

"You had no right!" Erik said in a low voice, and Ruari knew the portent of that tone well enough to fidget.

"I know, lad, I know, but the greater good is served . . ."

Erik interrupted him angrily. "What greater good is served by baring a man's soul to a company of strangers and mercenaries?"

"It was a wondrous tale," Elizabeth enthused, either oblivious or indifferent to Erik's anger. "Ruari told of you and of Nicholas and of Beatrice, and Nicholas's deception, and of your children and . . ."

Erik needed to hear no more. "What in the name of God were you doing?" he bellowed, almost regretting that he had not finished his earlier assault. "You could have told any tale at all! There was no need to recount this one! You cannot tell my tale to anyone you so choose!"

"But . . ."

"You have no right to tell that tale and you know it as well as I," Erik continued. "It is not your tale!"

Ruari granted the younger man a steady glance. "Aye, it is your tale, true enough, though my telling of it has seen you released from imprisonment and saved from certain death or dismemberment." Ruari huffed and Erik knew his companion was insulted.

But Erik might as well have had his garb torn away, so bare felt he. It was his tale, his alone, his to share or not to share, as he so chose.

He had been robbed of that choice. Now Vivienne and her entire family knew that he had nothing to his name, that he had been fool enough to be called a cuckold and cheated of his inheritance, that his name was worth nothing at all. Not only was he a scarred cripple: Nay, now Vivienne knew that his father had disavowed him, that his children had been stolen, that his very ability to create children had been cast into doubt. It was one thing to have been beguiled by her charms, another to have lost any dignity in her eyes.

Though now he understood the reason why she had come to assist him. It was pity that had brought Vivienne to his aid after her betrayal, no more than that.

But Erik did not desire her aid, not if pity was its root.

EVEN AS ERIK SEETHED, Ruari made a great fuss over smoothing his rumpled tabard. "I thought it a fitting use of the tale, to be certain, though if you disagree, we can readily lock you back into that cell, and we can ensure that this key—" he waved the offending piece of brass beneath Erik's nose "—that this key is never found again. Is that your preference, my lord?" he asked, his tone cloying. "I certainly would not wish to defy your desire to die by risking my own life to save you."

Erik held up a hand, but was not to be granted a chance to speak. Ruari continued his tirade, barely halting for breath. "Far be it from me, a mere servant, to assume that you might prefer to live rather than to die. Far be it from me, a mere paid escort, albeit one pledged to aid you by a promise made to a man who pledged vengeance for all eternity if I failed, far be it from me . . ." His voice rose in volume.

Vivienne stepped between the men, her gaze simmering in a most troubling way. "To summon Hamish back to his duty with too much loud talk," she interrupted crisply.

When Erik and Ruari turned to her, she shook her head as if chiding naughty children. "If you mean to escape undetected and create a distraction to do so, you should have the wits to utilize that distraction."

The timeliness and good sense of her argument stole the thunder of Erik's anger.

"Well, indeed," Ruari said, his color rising anew as he adjusted his belt.

Vivienne crossed to a bench which the guard must have used, and reached for a familiar weapon. "And here is your blade," she said.

To Erik's astonishment, she handed it to him, ensuring that he was armed once again. He wondered at her intent even as he welcomed the familiar weight of the blade into his hand. This deed made no sense, given what she had already done.

Perhaps he had been loosed for sport. One heard tales of the unholy entertainments demanded by nobles in the south, and truly these lands were alien in a thousand small ways. Perhaps there was a greater challenge ahead and even Vivienne did not perceive it to be fair for him to be without a weapon. Though Erik did not grant much weight to rumor, the prospect made him deeply uneasy.

The sisters clearly did not share his trepidation, which was no good sign. The younger one nodded and spoke crisply. "We must enter the caverns before they realize we are gone."

"What caverns?" Ruari and Erik asked in unison.

"The labyrinth that stretches beneath the keep of Ravensmuir," Vivienne explained. "There are many disguised entries to it, and many portals along the coast. It offers the best chance to escape undetected."

"It is not the provenance of women to make such schemes," Ruari said gruffly. It was clear he shared Erik's discomfiture, for he too looked over his shoulder, then up at the ruckus still erupting from the hall overhead. The men exchanged a glance of uncertainty.

Vivienne granted Ruari an arch glance. "And what would be your alternate plan for escape? We can scarce pass through the hall undetected, as Erik is tall and has already been displayed as my uncle's prisoner."

Ruari colored and for once had nothing to say.

"But how shall we find our way, if it is truly a labyrinth?" Erik asked, not troubling to hide his skepticism.

"We shall follow the spriggan, of course," Elizabeth said.

"What is this?" Ruari demanded in a yelp, then crossed himself with vigor.

"A spriggan is a fairy," Vivienne said.

"I know what a spriggan is," Ruari retorted hotly. "Though little good comes of them and their kind, to be certain." He eased closer to Erik. "Spriggans are more mischievous than most fairies, which says little good of them indeed. And they are said to be able to change form on demand, becoming as large as a house and as terrifying as a storm on the sea." He dropped his voice. "Only a fearsome sorcerer would ever claim to command such an unholy creature." And he crossed himself again.

Vivienne was dismissive of this warning. "The spriggan is named Darg and she is not so fearsome as you claim. Only Elizabeth can see Darg, unfortunately, but she has agreed to grant her aid."

"This child commands the spriggan?" Ruari said with undisguised awe and regarded the younger sister with new wariness.

"You were the one to claim she had a healing touch," Erik reminded the older man, who blanched. Erik, for his part, placed no credence in this spriggan's presence.

He tightened his grip upon his blade, fully convinced that he was being led into a trap. He did not care. He could and would fight any man, now that he was freed from the cell and had his sword once more. Erik had but to triumph in this challenge to see himself free of Ravensmuir, that much was clear.

The error the Lammergeier had made was in failing to understand how much he needed that victory.

# Chapter Eleven

~

THE SISTERS SEEMED OBLIVIOUS to the men's concerns. They turned as one and lifted torches from the wall, so at ease with their mention of fairies and labyrinths that Erik was only more convinced that the tale was a lie.

"This way," Elizabeth said, resting her hand upon the hewn stone of the far wall. There was a shadow that had been hidden by the torch she had lifted away, and that shadow tilted beneath her touch. A gap appeared in the stone there, and the sisters fitted their hands into the space, forcing a portal to open.

Vivienne glanced back at Erik, her eyes alight with determination and some other emotion that made his heart skip in a most unruly manner. He told himself that it was only natural that his body responded with such vigor to her, for she was beauteous and he knew already of the depth of her passion.

All the same, he hoped that the price of escape from the labyrinth was not a triumph over this particular beauty.

The light of the flames gilded Vivienne's auburn hair and caressed her cheek, making her look regal and far beyond his aspirations. Her vitality made a lump rise in his throat, and the bold sparkle in her eyes made him yearn to meet her abed once more.

For a dangerous moment as their gazes locked and held, Erik did not care whether she was the spawn of relic traders and thieves, or whether she had condemned him to captivity and torture. He saw only that she stood fearless on the threshold of a terrifying darkness. Her bravery was not due to folly, for he could see the intelligence in her gaze, which only made him admire her audacity all the more.

And for that potent moment when time stood still, Erik Sinclair knew only that he wanted to be with Vivienne again, for as many or as few moments as were possible, for any time in her company would be well worth any price demanded of him.

This he knew was the true threat of Vivienne, this descendant of sorcerers with her unholy allure. She had betrayed him and, without a word of explanation or apology from her, he was prepared to forget what he knew and to trust her anew — or at least to bed her once again. His body defied his own good sense, and desire would trick him into error.

He knew better than to be so readily seduced.

Erik forced his expression to become grim as he steeled himself against Vivienne. He claimed a torch and stepped past her as if she were not awaiting him, as if there was no expectation in her eyes, as if the scent of her flesh did not make his very innards clench. He told himself not to feel a cur when the shadow of disappointment touched her expression.

He did not trust Vivienne; he dared not do so. She had saved him only to lead him to greater peril. At least, she would abandon him in a labyrinth and leave him to wander until he died of starvation and thirst. No fairy which could only be seen by one of the sisters was going to be his salvation.

"It might well be a trap, but I suppose we have little choice, lad," Ruari muttered, unconsciously echoing Erik's thoughts. He cocked his head at a sudden crash from the noisy hall above. "We will not cross that hall unobserved."

Erik nodded and lifted his sword high. "A man can only choose the path that looks less dire and hope for the best," he replied as he stepped over the threshold of stone.

To his surprise, there were steps hewn out of the rock, steps that led downward. A waft of sea air teased his nostrils and he felt a burgeoning hope that he truly would escape Ravensmuir.

It was enough to send him striding into darkness, following the dancing flame of Elizabeth's torch.

LIKE ELIZABETH, Vivienne would have preferred to remain out of the caverns beneath Ravensmuir.

Unlike Elizabeth, Vivienne did not particularly trust the spriggan Darg to lead them out of the labyrinth. She dared not show her trepidation, not when both Ruari and Erik were so clearly skeptical of this course, but her heart skipped in fear when she stepped into the chill of the labyrinth.

It was so dark. The flickering torches did not seem to cast their light far into the endless blackness of this place, nor did the heat from the flames seem to disperse the coldness emanating from the rock.

Vivienne knew that there were a thousand branchings of the path, a thousand false corridors, more than a thousand dead ends. The network had been partly carved by nature, partly expanded by men who sought places to hide. It was like the comb of a hive, and Vivienne had always been convinced that there were caches of bones from those who had entered the caverns and not been able to find their way out.

She hoped they would not join that company.

"You should close the portal," Elizabeth said with authority, pointing back to the opening that gaped wide. As Ruari was the last to step over the threshold, he crossed himself, visibly muttered a prayer, then reached to do her bidding. The dungeon disappeared as the large stone settled audibly in place.

Vivienne swallowed, for the shadows grew even deeper and the air seemed colder than it had just a moment before. Their torches flickered in unison at the change in the air, then settled. She could hear the whistle of the wind and the crash of the sea.

There had been a storm coming, she recalled, though here she felt more at its mercy than within the stronghold of Ravensmuir's high walls.

"There is a draft," Erik said, his words echoing around them. "It smells of the sea."

Indeed, the flames now all appeared to be blowing back toward the dungeon. Vivienne inhaled deeply, relieved by this evidence of an opening somewhere below them.

They had only to find it.

"This way!" Elizabeth said with a confidence Vivienne did not share, and darted down the wide steps of hewn stone. She disappeared quickly, for the descent was tortuously curved, though the light from her torch guided the others onward.

There was no rail, only the stone wall to steady oneself upon, and the steps were neither level nor of the same height. Occasionally, a trickle of water made its way down a stone wall, splashing in some unseen pool far beneath them. The shadows seemed more ominous with each step, their secrets just barely kept at bay by the light of the torches. Each time an opening yawned wide on one side of the path or the other, Vivienne wondered what threats lurked within it.

It would have been easy to stumble, though Vivienne did not ask either man for aid. If anything, they were more concerned than she. Ruari mumbled his *paternoster* over and over again, the sound more reassuring than Vivienne would have cared to admit. Erik was as taut as a drawn bowstring, though he said nothing at all.

They made their way ever downward, the chill of the earth enfolding them. Erik held his blade high as well as his torch, and the men halted at each opening before they passed it by. Both were vigilant in watching their surroundings, as if they too expected an unpleasant surprise. Vivienne felt Erik's distrust, though she did not wish to argue with him before the others.

And she knew that a deed would go further to regain his trust than any pledge she might make. Once he was freed of Ravensmuir with her aid, she could better explain her innocence to him.

"Why, for the love of God, would a man suffer such a warren beneath his keep?" Ruari demanded finally.

"My family traded in religious relics for years," Vivienne said, well aware that that was no honorable credential. "My great grandfather, who built Ravensmuir, began the trade. He claimed this site, it is told, because of its natural caverns, then had them enlarged into a labyrinth."

"Claimed or stole?" Erik asked softly, and Vivienne flushed at the condemnation in his tone. She supposed that no honest man would find merit in her family's history and source of wealth.

"Stole, no doubt," Ruari said. "One has always heard tales of the Lammergeier and their disreputable trade. Such caverns as these would well suit a family needing to hide dark deeds and plunder." He snorted. "No honest man would have need of them."

"Do you call yourself dishonest?" Vivienne asked, well aware that her family had a tainted history but protective of her kin all the same. "For you clearly have need of them on this night."

The men exchanged a glance but said nothing.

Vivienne continued with her tale, for she ached to fill the oppressive silence. "My grandfather had no desire to continue the trade and used his ship to trade in cloth instead. He brought silk and cloth-of-gold from Araby, as well as gems which were coveted at the courts of kings and barons."

"Which explains your family's uncommon affluence," Ruari muttered. "Though it is ill-gotten, at root."

"My grandfather's brother secretly pursued the trade for some years before abandoning it," Vivienne said, ignoring this charge.

"How could he do so secretly?" Ruari asked. They caught up with Elizabeth then, who was deliberating between the two choices offered by a fork in the path. She nodded and strode to the right, which again led downward, her hem flying behind her.

"There were many ways into the labyrinth and Gawain knew them all," Vivienne said, hoping that her sister truly did follow a good course. "He came without his brother's knowledge and took what he desired from the hoard here. There were many relics remaining even after he abandoned the trade, so many that the last of them were only auctioned this very year."

Elizabeth continued the tale. "They were auctioned because our Uncle Tynan, who is Laird of Ravensmuir now, decided to be finally rid of the relics. They were a cause of a dispute between himself and his cousin."

"What manner of dispute?" Ruari asked, clearly as anxious for the conversation to continue as Vivienne.

"I would expect that the cousin wished to have the relics, for they are valuable even in these times," Erik said grimly.

"Indeed, she did," Vivienne agreed.

"She?" the men asked in unison.

"Our Aunt Rosamunde continued the family trade, for she was taught well by her foster father Gawain."

Ruari whistled through his teeth. "A woman, trading in religious relics. She must have been intrepid, indeed."

"That she is." Vivienne frowned. "We have always called her aunt, though in truth she shares no blood with any of us. My grandfather's brother Gawain adopted her when she was abandoned as a babe. He and his wife raised her as his own child."

"The same brother who pursued the trade in relics?" Ruari asked.

Vivienne nodded, feeling the weight of Erik's disapproving silence. She knew theirs was no respectable family history. In contrast, she was very aware of the weight of his family blade, still hidden in her belt, and had no doubt that the Sinclairs had a more illustrious and valiant past. "The very same."

"And it is Rosamunde whom Darg hates beyond all," Elizabeth contributed. "The spriggan," she clarified when Ruari looked confused. "Darg came to think that the abandoned hoard of relics was her own treasure, so when Rosamunde came to take any of it, Darg believed herself to have been robbed. She is determined to avenge herself, though I have told her time and again that Rosamunde will never return to Ravensmuir."

"Because of that dispute with the laird," Ruari said, nodding grimly. "If he auctioned the relics, he would be rid of her thievery for good. I find myself agreeing with your uncle, for a man cannot suffer infamy in his hall so readily as that."

Vivienne bit her tongue. Though there was far more to the tale, it was not hers to share — nor would an admission of the long-standing intimacy between Tynan and Rosamunde improve Erik's view of her family's moral measure.

"Should we not be ascending already?" she asked of Elizabeth instead. "Surely we make for the stables? We cannot go ever downward without reaching the large cavern that grants access to the sea."

"Or the sea itself," Ruari said grimly.

"I told Darg as much," Elizabeth said, then peered upward once again. She took a deep breath. "She keeps such a pace this night! We shall be winded indeed by the time we reach our destination."

"This makes little sense," Erik said, coming to a halt. "If we continue to descend, we shall land in the sea."

"Or be trapped in some corner when the tide rises," Ruari muttered, stopping beside the younger man.

Vivienne looked their way in alarm. "I had not thought of that."

"Perhaps your sister does not truly know the way," Erik said, his gaze filled with accusation.

"She does not," Vivienne admitted. "But the fairy knows the labyrinth well."

Erik arched a brow. "If, indeed, there is a fairy." It was clear that he did not believe as much. He paused and looked about himself, eying the half dozen portals that opened from the corridor in their vicinity. "I suggest that we break into groups to seek a path that returns upward."

"A sound scheme!" Ruari said.

"But we will become lost if separated." Vivienne argued, echoing the reasoning she had been taught all her life. In truth, she was terrified of wandering alone in this labyrinth. "How will we find each other once again?"

"Darg!" Elizabeth cried and, oblivious to Vivienne's concerns, dashed down the stairs in apparent pursuit of the fairy.

Vivienne took half a dozen steps after her sister, halting when she could still see the men. "Elizabeth!" she shouted. "Await us!" But Elizabeth raced onward, the light of her torch diminishing with alarming speed.

"Ruari and I will seek our own way, while you and your sister follow the fairy," Erik said as Vivienne fought the urge to follow her sister.

"We must remain together," she said, even as Ruari peered into an opening to the left. "We must!"

"This one takes an upward course," Ruari said, then beckoned to Erik. "I would wager that wherever it erupts is better than what we have left behind. There is only space for improvement, after all." Ruari strode into the passageway, his boots grinding on the stone and his torch burnishing the stone.

"Ruari, no!" Vivienne cried. "We must remain together."

"Nay, there is no need of that any longer," Erik said quietly.

His tone prompted Vivienne to look at him, and his stony expression fairly tore her heart in two. "You mean to abandon me here," she charged, dismayed when Erik did not deny it. "But we have a handfast! And I promised to try to bear your son."

"And I tire of your deception," he said. "You ensured that we were not only pursued but found by urging an early halt last evening."

"I did no such thing. You were injured! To ride further would have injured you more."

"Then how did your kin find us?"

"It was the fairy, Darg, who granted them direction."

Erik passed a hand over his eyes and looked away. "There is no fairy, Vivienne. Perhaps you did not contrive to be found, perhaps you did not lie to me fully. Perhaps your family only hunted us with hounds. It matters little. We part ways now, before whatever treachery your family has planned is sprung upon us."

"What treachery? I have just aided your escape!"

"To what end?"

Vivienne gasped at the condemnation in his expression. "You cannot imagine that I have aided you to escape only to cast you in greater peril. You cannot believe that I have betrayed you!"

He granted her a cool glance. "Have you not? When

we were surrounded, I was captured and beaten, all because you denied any bond with me . . ."

"No! I lied so that Alexander would not ensure that you could never conceive a son," Vivienne explained, her words tumbling over each other in her haste to be understood. Erik regarded her so dispassionately that she knew she did not persuade him of her innocence. "Alexander might have unmanned you then and there, so angry was he."

"He is vengeful, your brother."

"He is protective." Vivienne took a steadying breath. "I fear the responsibility for four virgins weighs too heavily upon his shoulders."

"He is responsible for merely three virgins, by my reckoning, though your count appears to differ from mine," he said, his tone hard. "For you have insisted to your brother that you are yet a maiden."

"What else could I have done? Would you have preferred that I had let him do his worst?"

Erik regarded her, as if considering whether she spoke the truth. "You profess concern for me, yet you refused to wed me."

The true reason for her refusal rose to Vivienne's lips, but she did not want to speak of love in this moment, when Erik seemed not even to like her. "Because you argued in favor of a handfast," she said instead, forcing herself to sound calm, as if she had been persuaded by logic alone.

In truth, she thought of beauteous Beatrice and how poorly she must compare with that wifely paragon who had defended his rights to her own death.

"Your reasoning for a handfast is sound," she said with care when he said nothing. "For you will have need of another maiden if your seed does not bear fruit in my womb. I would not tempt failure by demanding that you cede to my family's expectations. I would not risk your daughters so readily."

"And what do you gain in this?"

"The chance to aid two young girls."

Erik frowned and turned abruptly away. Vivienne thought he might leave, but he only peered down the passage into which Ruari had disappeared.

Apparently reassured, he turned back to her, his gaze bright. He spoke more slowly now, his condemnation seeming to lose its vigor. "Doubtless I would have faced some more dire fate on the morrow, rather than simple abuse, courtesy of your kin."

"Perhaps so, if I had not ensured your escape."

Erik watched her so keenly, though, that Vivienne imagined that he tried to read her very thoughts. She returned his regard steadily, hoping he would see the honesty of her intent.

"Perhaps this feat is intended to provide some amusement for your family," he suggested softly. "There is much interest in hawks and horses and hounds in this hall, after all. Perhaps I am to be hunted anew." He took a backward step. "Perhaps I but leap from the fat to the fire."

"My family would not do such a horrific deed!" Vivienne cried. "How can you be so certain that I mean you ill?"

"How could I trust you, after all that has occurred?" he demanded in his turn, his voice rising. "All has gone awry since I came to Kinfairlie . . ."

"It went awry long before that."

Erik spoke with determination. "All was to change

with this plan, and yet it does not. Clearly I have erred yet again. Since Fortune offers me a chance to survive, I mean to seize it. I will follow you and your sister no longer. It would be folly to sacrifice what slender advantage I have in this moment."

They stared at each other in silence in the flickering light. Vivienne did not know what to say, just as she knew she could not let him leave her behind. She knew that she could be of aid to him, she knew that she must hold a key to his ultimate success for she had a sense that their partnership was no mere coincidence. She did not know how to persuade him, a man so dubious of the unseen, of such a conviction.

"Come along, lad!" Ruari roared from some distance. "I make ready progress here, and soon will not be able to retrace my steps back to you. I can fairly smell the stables, upon that you can rely!"

Erik held Vivienne's gaze, unswayed. "What has been between us will remain our secret for so long as I draw breath," he vowed with such intensity that she believed him. "You need fear no repercussions from a loose tongue of mine." She made to speak but he held up his hand. "And I shall ensure that Ruari holds his peace, as well. Wed well, trusting that none will reveal that you are maiden no longer. Farewell, Vivienne."

Vivienne stared at him, shocked to her toes that he would truly leave her side, dismayed beyond belief to hear the clamor of her heart. He stood so resolute, so certain that he could triumph alone, so noble that he would die in the attempt to save his daughters.

She knew then that, against all odds, she had lost her heart to Erik Sinclair. She might never be able to claim his affections, but she could not let him walk away. Love,

Vivienne Lammergeier knew, was too uncommon and of too great a value to be discarded.

It was love that would ensure Erik's victory in the end.

But she dared not argue as much, not yet.

So she shook her head and argued otherwise. "Erik, you cannot do this. If you leave us and Darg, you will only become lost. You will imperil yourself and your daughters in truth! I swear to you, I mean you no ill. I swear to you that I knew nothing of my family's pursuit and I only try to set matters aright."

"Vivienne . . ."

"Erik, I would accompany you. I would yet try to bear your son. I would keep every pledge I have made to you."

"But why?"

Vivienne dared not utter the truth, so fresh and fragile to her, so she impulsively offered another more earthy explanation.

She closed the distance between them with a quick step, reached up and touched her lips to his.

Erik did not move. Indeed, he stood so utterly still that she feared he would reject her again. Undaunted, Vivienne slipped her hand into the hair at his nape and slanted her mouth across his. She kissed him with a gentle ardor, coaxing his response.

Erik remained motionless while she kissed him, and she might have thought her efforts futile had she not let her hand slide around his neck. She felt the thunder of his pulse beneath her palm and knew then that he was not so immune to her caress as he would have her believe.

He felt the link between them, as well, though still he denied its potency.

Reassured, Vivienne cast aside her torch then and cupped his face in her hands. She kissed him again and again, urging him to join her. She heard him catch his breath, she felt his erection, she did not cease her kisses. Indeed, she slipped her tongue between his lips and was rewarded with his gasp.

And then, his resistance crumbled with astonishing speed. His arm locked around her waist and he lifted her against his chest, his kiss plundering her mouth with unmistakable fervor, as if he would devour her whole. Vivienne kissed him back with joy, knowing she had swayed his choice, knowing she could win his love.

Erik abruptly broke their kiss and put distance between them, his eyes narrowed as he regarded her. "It is a more common sorcery that you command," he said. "But one that no sensible man would trust, all the same. Turn back and return to all you know. Farewell, Vivienne."

With that, Erik turned to pursue his companion, raising his voice to call to the older man. "Ruari! Shout directions to me that I might find you."

"No!" Vivienne cried and lunged after him. She took a deep breath, knowing that a confession would not improve Erik's view of her but it was the sole way to keep him from abandoning her. "I lied about my courses," she admitted and he froze.

He glanced over his shoulder, his eyes narrowed. "What is this?"

"I had to stop Alexander, so I lied. I do not bleed as yet. I have not bled in over two weeks. You cannot leave me, as your seed might well be taking root within my womb."

Erik swore and his brow darkened. Vivienne held her breath, for she could see that he did not truly believe her, yet was tempted by the possibility.

Before he could reply, Elizabeth screamed from some point far below.

"Darg!" she cried then, apparently in anguish. "No, Darg, no!"

There was a resounding splash that made Vivienne freeze in terror. A woman screamed.

"Elizabeth!" Vivienne cried, though no one answered her.

A mere heartbeat later, Ruari swore with gusto, his exclamation echoing through the passageway he had followed. There was a crash, as if someone had fallen, and a tumbling of stone. A fierce wind surged up the stairway with sudden force, extinguishing Erik's blazing torch as readily as a puff of breath will douse a candle.

Vivienne was cloaked in darkness, utterly uncertain of where she stood, much less where her companions might be found. "Erik?" she whispered, her mouth dry in fear.

She could hear him breathing, but he did not answer, and that was no good portent at all.

THE WOMAN ADDLED HIS WITS. Erik dared not linger long with Vivienne, not when she could so readily persuade him of whatsoever she chose. He had been prepared to abandon her, until she admitted that she had lied about her courses. He did not know what was the truth, whether she bled or not, whether she lied to him or to her brother, though he dared not abandon her when she might carry his son.

At least that was what he told himself. The truth was that he could not turn readily away from this woman. Even when he thought the worst of her, her kiss seared his very soul. He could not tell truth from fabrication, not when she kissed him with such dizzying abandon.

He feared that she lied, only to have him do her bidding.

Erik was utterly aware of the lady behind him, no less so when she whispered his name. The tremble of uncharacteristic fear in her voice had him turning, reaching out his hand to her. She was so bold, this maiden, so resolute, that he suspected she must be deeply afraid to have given any hint of such weakness.

"Vivienne?" he replied, reaching his hand to where he thought she must be.

He heard her take a step toward him, heard the quaking breath she took, then felt her fingers collide with his. "I hate these caverns," she said, trying to cover her fear with a laugh that only made that fear more evident.

Her bravado had Erik lacing his fingers protectively with hers, had him drawing her closer to his side. "It is no different in darkness than in light," he said. "We still stand in a cavern below the keep."

"It seems much worse," she said, then unexpectedly leaned her cheek against his chest. "Please do not leave me, Erik, not alone in such darkness."

Erik's arm was around Vivienne's waist before he could consider the wisdom of his impulse. In the darkness, his other senses were more sharp. He could smell the sweetness that clung to her skin, as well as the tang of her terror. Her hair wound over his arm and through his fingers like fine silk, the curve of her breast was crushed against his chest. He felt her breath against his throat and knew she had tipped her head back, knew her lips would be parted, knew she would not spurn his kiss.

But too much temptation lay that way.

Indeed, this would have been the perfect moment for some scheme against him to be launched. He had even lowered his sword and was no longer listening to his surroundings.

"Nay," he said with resolve, putting the lady an increment from his side. "This changes naught."

"But . . ."

"Ruari!" he bellowed before she could argue the matter.

There was no reply, except a muffled grunt. Had Ruari been attacked? Or had he fallen?

"I missed a step, lad," that man shouted, his voice wavering. "And dropped my cursed torch in so doing. I am as a blind man, nay a blind man with a hobble!"

Erik sighed with relief. "I am coming, Ruari," he shouted, then added a few words to make the older man smile. "Upon that you can rely."

Ruari's snort of laughter echoed down the stone corridor.

"Farewell," Erik said, though he could not discern the lady's presence. He could hear her breathing, though Vivienne did not return to his side. Some other emotion than fear tinged the air, though, and he thought it might have been annoyance.

Despite himself, he could not leave the matter be. "You do not argue my departure any longer," he said. "Does this mean that you agree with my course?"

"No," she said sharply. "It means that I will not waste my breath endeavoring to persuade you of the truth. My mother counselled against ever begging a man for any due."

Had she lost her desire for him so quickly as that? Erik

was dumbfounded by the prospect, and in truth, a bit disappointed.

To his further surprise, Vivienne exhaled with what might have been a laugh. "Do not imagine that you have seen the last of me, Erik Sinclair," she said with uncommon resolve. "You might abandon me here, but I will follow you. I know, after all, your destination and your goal."

Erik wished he could have seen her in this moment, for surely her chin was tilted high and her eyes burned with determination. There would be a flush upon her cheeks and a set to her lips that both defied argument and demanded a kiss. He had called the matter right: she was a veritable Valkyrie and perhaps it was folly to protest her collection of his soul so vehemently.

Or perhaps her vigor was yet another element of her inescapable spell.

Another scream rose from below them, followed by a splash which concealed Erik's muttered curse.

"I am coming, Elizabeth," Vivienne shouted, though Erik heard the tremor in her voice. He heard her hands brush the stone wall and knew she meant to feel her way in pursuit.

Whatever his convictions about the lady's objectives, he could not abandon her to seek her sister alone, not given her fear of the darkness.

He told himself that he merely returned her favor, that he aided her to find Elizabeth as she had aided him to escape Ravensmuir's dungeon. It made good sense, though even he knew it was not the sum of the argument.

He simply did not wish to be parted from Vivienne as yet.

"I will come for you shortly, Ruari," he shouted. He

would find the sister first, then leave Vivienne in the company of her sister and the supposed fairy guide. Then he would seek out Ruari, tend the other man's injuries, and they both could be upon their way.

Erik reached out and claimed Vivienne's hand, hoping he was not falling prey to whatever scheme she might have concocted with her family. "You feel the right wall and I shall feel the left," he bade a silent and likely astonished Vivienne. "We shall seek each step together. Make no haste and we should be able to descend without incident."

It seemed, like so many of Erik's schemes, to be a plan that offered ready success. That, and the presence of Vivienne, should have warned him of potential complications.

VIVIENNE HEARD A SPLASHING in the distant depths ahead, its sound echoing through the caverns with dizzying speed. Behind that sound were whispers that might have been voices.

"Elizabeth?" she called, her own voice echoing wildly.

There was no reply, merely another muffled scream.

Vivienne would never forgive herself if some foul fate befell Elizabeth, especially after she had persuaded Elizabeth to aid her. She hastened onward as well as she could.

To her relief, Erik seemed to feel the same urgency, and within moments, she had to rush to keep pace with his long strides. He took only one step on each stair, while she needed two or three; he strode into the darkness with a confidence she did not share. They reached a confluence of passageways but Erik did not hesitate in making a choice.

They might have been alone in the labyrinth, for there was only the echo of their footsteps and the distant dripping of water. Vivienne could faintly hear the lapping of the sea. Though she knew that the caverns played tricks with sound, and she knew that Elizabeth and Ruari were in the labyrinth as well, the lack of sound from either of them made her grasp Erik's hand more tightly.

To her relief, he did not seem troubled by her anxious grip. He moved with a surety she could only envy, as if he was well accustomed to being lost in dark places.

They reached a second intersection, a salt-tinged breeze wafting through one of the openings. Vivienne smelled a snuffed torch as well, though she could not discern its source.

"This way," Erik said without hesitation and urged Vivienne boldly onward.

"How do you know? What if you are wrong?" she asked, knowing she would have wasted precious moments weighing each choice.

"Only one course descends at each intersection," he said. "Your sister chose always the downward path."

"She followed Darg," Vivienne corrected and heard Erik's snort of disbelief.

"Her scent comes from this way, as does the smell of the snuffed torch," he explained, his tone patient. "Can you not discern it?"

"What scent does she have?"

She felt his shrug. "I cannot explain it. It is the smell of warmth, of a person, and thus different from the scent of the stone and water surrounding us."

Vivienne wondered what sort of scent she had, and

whether he found it as alluring as she found the scent of his skin. She dared not ask when his manner was so grim. "You know how to pursue someone who leaves no trace of their path, then."

"All men and women leave a trace of their path, even when they strive to not do so." Erik said. "Ruari taught me to discern it."

"And he used his skill to find you."

Erik's grip tightened suddenly on her hand and he pulled her to an abrupt halt. He did not have to bid her to be silent, not when he stood so abruptly still. Vivienne remained motionless, wondering what he discerned, for she could tell that he fairly prickled with watchfulness.

She could see nothing.

She could hear nothing.

She tried to smell her sister's scent and failed.

What Vivienne smelled was her Aunt Rosamunde's perfume. She had never smelled that enticing scent save in her aunt's presence. It was exotic and rare, and she felt Erik's start of surprise when he evidently caught a whiff of it.

Vivienne strained her ears and then heard the faint grunt of men at labor, the muffled tread of boots on the stone. There was another scream, one more infuriated than fearful, and she guessed who had emitted it.

All made perfect sense to her in that moment, the sounds from below and Darg's insistence upon descending ever lower.

"Aunt Rosamunde!" she whispered to Erik in excitement. "That is her perfume. She must have returned to Ravensmuir, after all."

"Perhaps it is not your aunt," Erik said quietly.

"It must be," Vivienne insisted. "So few souls know the labyrinth, and even fewer would care to visit it."

"One cannot be certain of that. If the labyrinth has been unused, any curious soul could have explored it."

"But why?"

"To gain access secretly to a wealthy keep would be motivation enough." Erik sounded grim. "Your sister might have been captured, to be ransomed to the laird above."

Vivienne's heart skipped with fear, then she knew he must be mistaken. "But what of the perfume?" She made to tug Erik onward. "It is only Rosamunde. We must be near the large cavern where so many relics were stored. I was there once, with Uncle Tynan. There is an easy path from there to a grotto that opens onto the sea. It is large enough to hide a small boat, so goods can be moved from cavern to ship . . ."

Erik held his ground stubbornly. "Why would this Rosamunde have returned to Ravensmuir if she not only pledged to not do so, but if the relics she covets are gone?"

And that made Vivienne pause.

Once she would have suggested that Rosamunde had returned for her love of Tynan, but not since Tynan's rejection. She had a feeling that Rosamunde had returned, but not to mend the rift between herself and her former lover. She suspected Rosamunde had come for vengeance, though she did not want to give voice to such a dark thought.

Surely he knew enough about the ignoble impulses of her family.

Instead, she let Erik believe he had persuaded her that

it was not her aunt. "Perhaps you are right," she said and hesitated.

"Even so, we must find Elizabeth," Erik said. He lifted his blade and moved onward, though with greater stealth than before. Vivienne followed his course ever downward, heeded his instructions, and hoped against hope that her family did not provide her with another scandalous credential.

She had a sense, however, that her hope was not to be realized.

# Chapter Twelve

~

WITH VIVIENNE FAST BEHIND HIM, Erik eased his way down the stone pathway. A light appeared after they turned one corner and their course became easier as a result. The sounds of activity grew louder as well; the scrape of boots on stone and the low rumble of men's voices became more clear with each step.

A woman still screamed periodically, which was most troubling. Erik rounded a corner and a lit portal gaped wide before them. He flattened Vivienne into the wall behind him and listened.

There were no sounds of pursuit. He glanced back at Vivienne, intending to tell her to wait, but one glance at her determined expression told him that she would not be persuaded to do so. He drew his blade soundlessly, lifting a finger to silence her protest. He sidled closer and peered around the corner.

Whatever Erik had been expecting, he had not expected this.

A large cavern opened from that portal, so many lit torches braced upon its walls that the chamber might have been illuminated by the midday sun. A chasm snaked its way across its floor, its jagged edges making it look like a recent fault. There was a dark glitter of water within the chasm, as well as someone splashing and thrashing within it.

"I cannot swim!" roared that person, whose voice revealed her gender. Here was the woman who had screamed repeatedly.

Vivienne's sister did a strange dance upon the lip of the chasm, alternately reaching to aid the woman and apparently beating off an invisible assailant. "Darg, no!" she cried. She clearly could not reach the woman in the water, though she tried.

The woman in the chasm clutched the lip of the stone ledge, then jumped upward. She grunted as she braced her hands on the stone and pulled herself higher. Her hips had cleared the water, all of her sodden to the bone, when she screamed in sudden pain. She snatched her left hand away from the lip, then plummeted back into the water with a resounding splash.

"It bit me!" she bellowed when she cleared the surface again, then swore with such vigor that Erik's eyes widened. Elizabeth kicked at something which Erik could not see. He might have thought her mad, but her kick was followed by another smaller splash further down the chasm.

"Rosamunde!" Vivienne cried. She ducked under Erik's arm, seemingly untroubled by this strange scenario, ran across the cavern and fell to her knees beside her sister. "You keep Darg away and I will help Aunt Rosamunde."

"I cannot see Darg any longer," Elizabeth complained and Erik refrained from noting that no one could see the rumored spriggan. "She must be under the water yet."

The girl frowned with a concern no one else shared. "Surely she cannot have drowned?"

"I would drown her gladly myself," the aunt muttered, looking as furious as a wet cat when she managed to climb out of the chasm with Vivienne's aid. To Erik's surprise, she was dressed as a man, in chausses, high boots, and a chemise that had been more white than it was in this moment. Her tabard was cut longer than was typical for a man and came almost to her knees.

Her garb looked as if it had been fine, for there was gold embroidery aplenty at the hems and it was wrought of cloth of deepest black. In this moment, it dripped large puddles on the stone floor and the hem hung crookedly. Her boots squeaked when she walked, though the cut and the leather looked to have been fine. Her hair was long and she wore it loose, though it too was wet and dark.

Her eyes flashed with fury and she turned upon the men who labored diligently behind her. Erik saw now that a number of wooden crates were stacked around the perimeter of the chamber: they were old, their wood stained and their corners battered as if they were of no value. All the same, it was clear that they were being removed.

Erik wondered what their contents might be and thought better than to ask.

One third of the chamber was completely cleared: a number of men carried crates through a lit portal on the other side of the chamber but returned empty-handed. They were dressed as men of little repute, with patches on their knees and the cloth well-worn. Their garments were wet on the shoulders and their hair was wet, as well. Erik assumed this meant not only that the rain had begun in earnest, but that these men somehow were reaching the outside.

His heart leapt at the prospect of escape from Ravensmuir's labyrinth being so close at hand.

A burly man with a golden loop hanging from one ear seemed to be directing the effort, for he watched the men keenly and berated those who slowed their pace.

It was to this man that Rosamunde shouted. "You could have been of aid, Padraig, instead of watching with bemusement."

That man smiled. "You are too cursedly fortunate to drown, Rosamunde." His smile broadened to a wicked grin. "And perhaps it would suit me well to be without your direction."

"To claim my ship, no doubt," Rosamunde muttered, wringing out her tabard with clear agitation. "All men are wrought the same, it is clear, for each thinks solely of his own advantage."

Rosamunde eyed Vivienne, who stood her ground but clearly braced herself for questions. "And what are you doing in these caverns? Should you not be safely in your bed in Kinfairlie?" Rosamunde spared a stern glance for Elizabeth. "I would have welcomed your absence, as well, if it had meant that fiend was not here."

Elizabeth fell to her knees, her gaze fixed on the surface of the water. "This is not right. Darg has not appeared."

Rosamunde snorted. "And good riddance, to be sure." She propped her hands upon her hips and gave Vivienne a steely gaze. "Well?"

"We are aiding a prisoner's escape," Vivienne began.

Rosamunde looked pointedly about herself, then

arched a brow. "And you do well enough, for there is no sign of him or her."

Before Vivienne could summon him, Erik stepped out of the shadows. Rosamunde assessed him with a boldness uncommon in women. He had no chance to introduce himself, however, for Elizabeth decided in that moment to wait no longer.

"Darg must be in peril," she said, casting off her cloak and shoes. "I do not think she can swim."

"Darg is immortal!" Vivienne protested.

"The world would be all the more merry with one less vengeful spriggan in it," Rosamunde said sourly.

"She almost drowned in a pitcher of ale once before!" Elizabeth cried with dismay, then jumped into the chasm of water.

Rosamunde swore again, then shouted. Padraig ran across the cavern, though Erik reached the spot where Elizabeth had jumped in first. The girl had not yet come to the surface. Erik dropped his blade and his cloak, then leapt into the water after her.

The water was cold beyond belief and darker than dark. Erik shivered then forced his eyes open. He spied Elizabeth far below him. He rose to the surface, took a deep breath, then plunged in pursuit of her.

Erik saw then that a long tendril of seaweed had found its way into this chasm. The motion of that dark plume and of the water itself indicated that the sea's tides could still be felt here.

Which meant that it was close indeed.

Erik thought at first that Elizabeth was tangled within the seaweed, but she gestured agitatedly to him when he reached her side. She guided his hands to a knot in the weed and to his astonishment, he could feel a small limb trapped within its coils.

He could see naught but the coil of seaweed, but his fingers told no lie.

It must be Darg.

The spriggan must be snared.

That the fairy existed in truth was so startling that it took Erik a moment to realize that he could feel the creature's struggles becoming more weak. Elizabeth tugged, but the plant was doughty and resisted her efforts to tear it. Erik fitted his fingers into the coil and tried to tear it himself, but to no avail.

Elizabeth, though, had been under the water for too long. Concerned for her fate first, Erik pushed her emphatically toward the surface. She fought against him, tapping his hands upon the coiled weed. Erik nodded with vigor, then pushed her upward once again.

With obvious reluctance she went, though he did not doubt that she would be back. He was running out of breath himself, though the coil around Darg was fearsomely tight. The spriggan went limp even as Erik tried to free the vine, and he knew that he would have to loose the fairy immediately. He would never find this coil again, not without Elizabeth's aid, and he wanted her to stay at the surface.

He tugged at the weed, but it seemed to clutch at the spriggan with greater defiance, as if weed and fairy fought their own battle. He struggled with the plant, wishing he had a blade, and felt his chest tighten painfully.

In a last burst of effort before he was compelled to rise to the surface, Erik wrapped the length of seaweed around his fist and pulled with all his strength.

It broke somewhere further below. Erik did not care for the details. With the spriggan in the palm of his hand, he surged upward. He broke the surface, gasping for air.

To his relief, Elizabeth stood shivering and wet on the lip of the chasm. Rosamunde held her firmly, and Erik guessed she had forbidden the maiden to dive down again.

He found himself liking this aunt who was not truly an aunt, this woman who lived her life as a man but protected those chicks beneath her care as fiercely as a hen.

Rosamunde had wrapped a cloak over Elizabeth's shoulders, her expression stern as the girl shivered. "It is madness to risk death for such an ungrateful creature," she said, but Elizabeth was deaf to her aunt's censure.

"Did you retrieve her?" Elizabeth fell to her knees, her face alight as Erik handed up the spriggan.

The strength of her concern reminded him of his eldest daughter's affection for a lamb born too small once at Blackleith. Mairi had been determined to save it, though her will had been no match for the will of nature. He did not doubt that Mairi would have surrendered her own life to save the lamb, and that she would have taken such a risk without a second thought, just as Elizabeth had done for the spriggan. Though four springs had come and gone since that lamb's demise, a lump rose in Erik's throat at the recollection all the same.

"It may be too late," he said.

Elizabeth cupped her hands, cradling the invisible troublemaker, then eased away the vine with care. She pumped something with a fingertip, and a gush of black water appeared on the stone. There was a minute cough, a sound that Erik barely discerned, then more water appeared. Elizabeth smiled with relief.

"Well?" Rosamunde demanded.

"She lives!" Elizabeth said, then turned glowing eyes upon Erik. "With your aid. I thank you truly!"

"What good fortune that the wretch survives to better assault me another day," Rosamunde said drily. She bowed in Erik's direction, her sarcasm more than clear. "I too thank you for your courtesy in this matter."

Padraig meanwhile reached down a meaty hand to help Erik out of the chasm. Erik's expression must have spoken volumes, for the other man muttered to him. "It is not the strangest sight I have seen in the vicinity of this family. You had best be prepared for more of the same if you mean to linger in their company."

Erik braced his hands on the lip of the chasm and pulled himself out of the water without assistance, for he knew not whether this company could be trusted. Padraig sniffed and turned away, either unsurprised or insulted, Erik did not care.

For Vivienne appeared by his elbow then. Her eyes shone with mingled admiration and concern. "Are you injured?"

"I am but wet," he said gruffly, well aware of Rosamunde's condemning gaze upon him. "And that will scarce injure me."

"We all have need of a bath at least once a year," Padraig said.

"Thank you for aiding Darg," Elizabeth said, aglow with a pleasure that made Erik think once again of his daughter.

Indeed, he was sickened by the realization of what he had missed. How many times since his departure from Blackleith had Mairi been delighted with some detail he took for granted? How many such moments had he missed? And what of Astrid? She had barely been speaking when he had left to aid his neighbor. She would be talking and running by now, probably trying to best her older sister at every small feat.

"Though I do not share Elizabeth's pleasure in that deed," Rosamunde said. "I would thank you for aiding Elizabeth herself. I would have had much to answer for had she come to grief in my company."

"It is as naught," Erik said and turned away, distraught anew at what he had lost to his brother's greed. "I must fetch my companion, now that the sisters are in good care."

Rosamunde stayed him with a fingertip upon his arm. "You have not been welcomed at Ravensmuir, I would wager," she said. "Not if you consider my care to be of any merit at all."

"This is Erik Sinclair," Vivienne interjected. "Alexander pledged my hand to him, but since has changed his thinking. He imprisoned Erik, but Erik and I have handfasted and I have agreed to help him to recover his lost holding."

"Ah," Rosamunde said, embuing the single sound with a weight of meaning. Her expression hardened. "And thus I am to believe that he, unlike all other men of my acquaintance, is somehow deserving of my assistance, as well?"

"I have no need of your assistance," Erik said quickly. "I will simply retrieve my companion and be on my way."

Rosamunde seemed skeptical of that claim. "What is your destination?"

"Blackleith, my family abode."

"Seized by his duplicitous brother," Vivienne interjected. "We have to reclaim it and ensure the welfare of Erik's daughters."

"Just like the tale!" Elizabeth said, her eyes round with wonder, then sneezed. Vivienne wrapped the cloak more closely around her sister's shoulders.

Rosamunde pursed her lips, unimpressed by such credentials. "And where is the closest port?"

"I have no need of a port," Erik said. "As we intend to ride."

Rosamunde smiled. "You will have need of a horse to ride so far as that and I note that you have none."

"We will climb to the stables."

"Which you will be fortunate indeed to find, and more fortunate to escape unobserved," Rosamunde said, one hand upon her hip. "The last time I was here, the Laird guarded his prized destriers with rare vigor. There were no less than twenty ostlers in his employ, and only half were permitted to sleep at one time."

Erik frowned at this unwelcome detail.

Rosamunde continued. "I, however, have a ship, and might be inclined to grant you passage to your destination."

"Why?"

Rosamunde's smile was wry. "To be sure, there would be a certain satisfaction to me in thwarting the plans of Alexander, who kneels too close to Tynan's feet for my taste."

"And the Laird of Ravensmuir is your sworn enemy?" Erik asked, looking pointedly at the crates still being moved from the caverns.

Rosamunde laughed. "One might say that there is a certain debt owing from him to me. At least I would say as much. Tell me your destination, for the storm grows no less."

Erik was uncertain whether to trust this offer or not. Rosamunde's gaze was steady, though, and she would scarcely be in alliance with the Laird of Ravensmuir since she was clearly stealing from him.

"Sutherland," Erik began but got no further before Elizabeth sneezed once more.

"Sutherland!" Rosamunde swore softly. "With autumn coming on and this storm upon us, you would have me sail to *Sutherland*? All ships guided with good sense are making their ways south, to Rotterdam, at least, if not to La Rochelle or the Mediterranean itself."

"Sicily," Padraig interjected. "My vote is for Sicily."

"You have no vote," Rosamunde informed him, his mischievous smile telling Erik that Padraig knew as much.

"I yearn only for influence," that sailor said, one hand over his heart.

Rosamunde laughed in her surprise. "You will not have it soon," she said, then tapped a finger upon Vivienne's shoulder. "It is fortunate that you are my favored niece," she said with affection.

"What of me?" Elizabeth demanded, then sneezed again.

"You *were* my favored niece, until you took company with that malicious sprite."

"Darg is a spriggan," Elizabeth insisted, her dignity compromised somewhat by her persistent sneezing. "By her accounting, you are a thief, and she wants vengeance upon you."

"What nonsense," Rosamunde retorted, then yelped and jumped backward, her hand over her face. "Something bit my nose!" Indeed, a red welt rose on the tip of Rosamunde's nose with alarming speed.

"Darg," Elizabeth said, punctuating the information with a resounding sneeze.

"Tell this Darg to leave me be," Rosamunde demanded. "I have as much right to Ravensmuir's hoard as she."

"She does not see the matter that way."

Rosamunde began to dance wildly, as if evading a swarm of angry bees. "It is down my shirt!" she shrieked. "Make it stop! Control your spriggan, Elizabeth!"

Elizabeth tilted her head to listen to something, asked a few questions, then nodded.

Rosamunde stilled as the assault evidently halted, though she looked about herself warily. "Where is it?"

"Upon your shoulder," Elizabeth said. "Darg wishes to make a wager with you."

"Oh no." Rosamunde protested. "The hoard cannot be returned. Everything that ever I have claimed has been sold, and even much of the resulting coin is gone."

"She will make a wager for a single piece, her favored piece."

Rosamunde's eyes narrowed. "Which one?"

"The silver ring you wear upon your left hand."

Rosamunde lifted her hand and Erik saw that a large silver ring did grace her index finger. It was a massive piece of silver, but its value was clearly more than that. Both sisters looked solemn at the mere mention of it and Padraig froze. The consternation of all of them was clear.

It was clearly a sentimental piece, worth far more to Rosamunde than even its considerable value.

Rosamunde's features softened as she regarded the ring. "It was never part of the hoard," she insisted. "There can be no wager for this ring, for your spriggan cannot have favored it."

Elizabeth spoke in an undertone, sneezed, then shook her head. "She desires it because it is precious to you. She calls it fit compense to demand what you value in exchange for what she valued."

Rosamunde laughed, though her merriment sounded forced. "I do not value this trinket!" she said, though she did not remove it from her finger.

Vivienne and Elizabeth regarded her with sympathy. Rosamunde looked between the two of them, but when she spoke, it was of another matter. Erik guessed that the change of topic was no coincidence. "I will undertake the fool's journey to Sutherland, though I cannot guess how long it will take us to find a favorable wind. I suppose you would prefer the port at Wick?" she asked of Erik.

He shrugged. "Helmsdale would suit me better. Though it is smaller, it is also further south."

"I prefer small ports." Rosamunde turned to Padraig, who supervised the workers once again. The cavern had been virtually picked clean while they spoke. "Padraig, you will take Erik and Vivienne to the ship, if you please, and await me there."

"But . . ." Vivienne protested.

"I must fetch my companion," Erik said. "I will not abandon him for he has served me faithfully."

"A man of honor," Rosamunde said with a sigh, her manner mocking. Erik did not know whether she mocked herself or him, so he said nothing. "Why could you not be thirty years older, Erik Sinclair?"

Rosamunde gave him no chance to reply before she strode toward the passageway that Erik and Vivienne had just left. Elizabeth sneezed once again, and Rosamunde seized her by the arm in passing, urging the girl to match her quick pace. "Come along, Elizabeth, you have need of a hot bath. You will not suffer so much as a cold beneath my care."

"But Darg . . ."

"It is customary in all negotiations to leave each party time to consider his or her course," Rosamunde said flatly. "I will find Erik's companion more quickly than any of you might do. What is his name?"

"Ruari Macleod. He is a good thirty years my senior," Erik began, but managed to say no more before Rosamunde laughed aloud.

"And that may be interesting enough. I shall see you shortly. Padraig, make all preparations to depart and ensure that no harm comes to my niece." She seized a torch and marched Elizabeth into the corridor, even as that girl sneezed with vigor once again. The sisters called farewells to each other, then Padraig tapped Erik upon the elbow. He indicated the passageway that the men had followed, and the trio made their way toward the ship.

Vivienne granted him a triumphant glance, as if tempting him to trust her anew. "We shall be at Blackleith more quickly this way," she said. "How fortuitous that Rosamunde was here this night."

"It is not Fortune, but the new moon that brings her to this port," Padraig said. "And the prospect of bounty to be had for the claiming."

"The new moon was four nights past," Erik noted and the sailor granted him a bright glance.

"It is new enough to serve. The wind cannot always be relied upon to do a man's will."

It was not only the wind that could confound a man. Erik cast a wary glance at the lady and recalled her assurance that she did not bleed. If she did not lie, and she did carry his child, her circumstance would change for the worse if she found herself abandoned. Erik knew that he could not trust his urges with regard to Vivienne, so he resolved to remain in her company only until she bled again.

That would show the truth of her circumstance. He would but wait honorably for nature to show what had been done. He would stand by whatsoever he had done thus far, though he would not touch Vivienne again.

He would simply wait, and watch. Erik did not so much as look at the lady as he made his choice, for it would be simpler if she thought him vexed with her.

She said she had bled two weeks past and he knew well enough that another fortnight would see her do so again, unless she bore his child. With luck, the seas would remain unruly and it would take them those two weeks to reach Sutherland. If she did not carry his son, he could leave her in the protective custody of her aunt with no regrets.

Or at least with so few regrets that Vivienne need know naught of them.

WHAT THE TRIO DID NOT REALIZE as they made their way through the caverns to the small boat was that they did not travel alone. A spriggan—in fact, a spriggan who muttered curses against a certain woman—perched on Vivienne's hood. That spriggan shivered and looked about herself balefully as they were rowed to the waiting and darkened ship. She quickly scampered over the decks and down into the hold, snickering as she hid herself in the only cabin to be found.

Darg nestled into a fur-lined hood and cackled to herself in triumph, knowing full well who must occupy this sole cabin of luxury. She could wait for Rosamunde now and have her vengeance at leisure.

Darg knew she would have that silver ring, as well, before all was done.

THE SHIP HAD LONG BEEN LOADED by the time Rosamunde returned to the caverns and the sea was rough as she was rowed to the ship. She raised a hand in triumph and indicated Ruari, whom she had clearly found in the caverns.

Ruari himself was as pale as a bowl of milk by the time he climbed over the side of the ship, though any comment he might have made was snatched away by the wind. He clung to his saddlebag, as if it carried his salvation. Erik aided him to cross the deck, for the older man limped upon his injured ankle.

The pair apparently had no need for Vivienne's attentions.

All three of them were dispatched to the hold on Rosamunde's command as the clouds churned overhead. Rain slashed against the deck with sudden fury even before they reached that sanctuary and the waves lifted the ship like a small toy.

Vivienne doubted that she was the only one to fear that they would be dashed upon the rocky shore. She looked back and saw Ravensmuir silhouetted against the rolling clouds, a dark shadow against the ominous sky.

Then Rosamunde began to shout orders to her men.

The wind was fierce, but the ship began to turn away from the shore as the storm unleashed its power. The sails were unfurled with haste at Rosamunde's command and turned into the wind with considerable effort.

The ship was pulled out to sea, away from the rocks and into greater potential peril to Vivienne's thinking. Indeed, the sea and the wind threatened to tear it asunder, to cast the ship's occupants into the fathomless black waters.

Vivienne wondered whether her parents had endured such a storm before their ship had been sunk. Certainly, they must have known fear such as she felt now.

But there was no one in whom she might share her fears on this night, let alone any soul who might offer her comfort. Erik folded himself into his cloak to sleep, as if oblivious to Vivienne's very presence. Ruari hunkered down fast by Erik's side and similarly buried himself in his cloak. The two men might have been alone together in some inn for all the attention they offered Vivienne, for all the concern they showed for the weather.

Vivienne, meanwhile, sat awake, listened, and felt more alone than ever she had in all her days and nights.

It was long indeed before Rosamunde retired to the hold, for the rudder demanded a stern hand that night.

It was longer still before any soul noted that the silver ring of Darg's desire graced Rosamunde's finger no more.

THE HOUR WAS LATE when the Laird of Ravensmuir climbed to his own chamber. Tynan had no taste for war, and less taste for war coming close to his young kin. He did not like to have mercenaries in his hall, even those in the employ of his nephew's keep of Kinfairlie. He also did not like mercenaries fighting within his hall, even if they merely showed displeasure with a tale.

At least, the storyteller had had the wits to make himself scarce and the hall had gradually quieted in his absence. Tynan would not rest himself until every last mercenary fell asleep. He had sat in the hall, sipping wine from the last keg that had been brought from Bordeaux, and had found himself regretting the loss of Rosamunde.

It was no consolation to him that a storm had been rising, no less that it now beat against the stone walls. He and Rosamunde had loved most fervidly during storms, and as a result, he ached with mingled exhaustion and yearning as he climbed the stairs. He heard the wind whip at his pennant hung over Ravensmuir's high towers, he heard the sea lash the shore.

So potent was Rosamunde's presence that night that Tynan could fairly see her. He easily envisioned the woman who had claimed his heart, a woman with red-gold hair and a bold smile, a woman with daring in her eyes, a woman he knew he would never see again. In his mind's eyes, she kissed her fingertips in silent salute, as if bidding him farewell forevermore, then turned away, the dark cloth of her cloak spinning out behind her as she fled.

He stepped into his chamber with a heavy heart. He set down his lantern, touched a piece of kindling to it and then to the wood stacked in the brazier.

It was then, as the wood hissed and spat, that he smelled the exotic spice of Rosamunde's perfume.

Tynan started, then sniffed. The scent was not conjured from memory. It was real.

Yet it was the dead of the night. Not a sound echoed from within his own keep; save that of the wild whistling between the stones carried to his ears. His chamber was cold, uncommonly cold. His heart thundered, as if he had heard some trespasser within the walls.

There was a cold draft.

The scent rode that chilly current of air. No common scent, that. It was the perfume that haunted his dreams and its summons had Tynan holding a lantern high, crossing the expanse of his chamber.

The hidden door to the labyrinth beneath Ravensmuir hung open on the far side of his chamber. Tynan halted to stare, for he knew he had left it secured. The secret opening yawned wide and dark, the scent of the sea rising from its shadows. Wet footsteps stained the floor, and even though they dried, he knew the size and shape of that boot print well.

Rosamunde had been here. He caught his breath at the tantalizing truth of it, though she was surely already gone. He had lingered below too long and inadvertently missed her.

But Tynan had to know for certain. He was unable to decide whether he was more thrilled or irked by her presence. If nothing else, they would have a rousing argument in the caverns deep beneath Ravensmuir. He had granted six stallions from his own stables to ensure she never crossed his threshold again.

But Rosamunde *had* returned.

In the secret corners of his heart, the Laird of Ravensmuir was glad.

Tynan gripped the lantern and stepped into the darkness. He shivered on the top step, as always he did, then descended with purpose into the hidden caverns. There was a veritable labyrinth beneath his ancestral estate, a labyrinth that had once held a fearsome treasury of religious relics and treasures. The most precious had been auctioned, for Tynan had no desire to continue what had once been his family trade, and he had thought the rest unworthy of attention.

It soon became clear that Rosamunde believed otherwise. Tynan halted and held his lantern high to examine a small chamber. It was empty, and he knew that it had contained at least one ancient crate when last he had come this way.

Tynan hurried down the stairs, his footsteps falling more and more quickly as he discovered more empty chambers. The caverns beneath his keep had been pillaged while his gaze had been turned away.

Tynan reached the largest cavern and halted, aghast. Here there had been a number of crates, their contents unknown and untroubled. They had not been of an appearance to tempt a second look, for they had been old and broken, their wood stained from water and mold. It had been easy to believe Rosamunde's assertion that they were empty or nearly thus, that it was not worth the trouble to be rid of them.

Tynan supposed he should have been more vigorous in ensuring that they were checked, that they contained nothing of value, but Rosamunde—who knew these chambers better than he—had dismissed their contents as worthless rubble.

He had trusted her, and he had been deceived.

He had been robbed.

He had been a fool.

Tynan cursed and kicked a stone. His yearning was replaced by anger. The stone clattered against the wall, then fell through a doorway. He heard it bounce down another staircase, then land with a splash.

If there had been value here, he could have used it to secure Ravensmuir's future in these dark times.

Now it was gone.

Tynan cursed anew. Since the death of George, the earl of March, the year before, many blades had been raised to challenge the regional authority of Archibald Douglas. The death of Tynan's half-brother Roland had not been timely, for it had left his inexperienced nephew Alexander as Laird of Kinfairlie just when their family lands had faced their greatest challenge.

Tynan had expended much coin and effort in keeping war from the gates of both Ravensmuir and Kinfairlie, hoping that they might ride out the storm until stability reigned anew.

But stability had proven elusive and the army in his employ—the one that kept marauding forces from Douglas, Dunbar, and Abernethy from his portcullis—had proven expensive. To his shame, Tynan found himself wishing for the lost revenue of relics, even of relics of dubious provenance.

His treasury was nigh bare and Rosamunde had taken the last chance of replenishing it. Even if she had known that Ravensmuir itself hung in the balance, Tynan doubted that she would have cared. She had always mocked his affection for what she called an old pile of stones, had accused him at the end of caring more for Ravensmuir than for her.

But Ravensmuir was his legacy and his responsibility, the repository of his family's heritage. The holding was something he had been taught to value.

He had sacrificed everything to that responsibility, and

for naught. The treaty that rested unsigned in his treasury, the treaty that made his very blood boil, made a mockery of his sacrifice. It would cost him the remainder of all he held dear.

Tynan had been a thorn in the side of Archibald Douglas too many a time for that man to have any inclination to offer palatable terms. By the treaty's terms, Ravensmuir would be left standing, but the lairdship would be stripped of authority. When Tynan had protested the terms, Douglas had made them worse.

The lairdship would continue if and only if Tynan got a son upon the Douglas bride to be chosen for him.

But Tynan had made his nephew Malcolm his legal heir to secure Ravensmuir's succession. For Ravensmuir, he had been prepared to wed a Douglas bride, but he was not prepared to deny his nephew's legacy for any price. He had surrendered Rosemunde for no gain.

He cursed his own folly and pivoted, marching back to his chamber. He could have used even the smallest measure of coin to mitigate the terms of this agreement, but thanks to Rosamunde, it was gone.

The caverns were silent, the source of the beguiling perfume fading with every moment. Tynan climbed the stairs back to his chamber. He closed the secret portal in his room, leaning back against it as he considered the fire in the brazier, the comfort of this chamber.

It was then that Tynan spied what he had missed earlier. Within the sanctuary of his curtained bed, something glimmered. It looked like a star, spinning captive within the shadows of the bed, but it could be no star.

Suspicious beyond all, Tynan stepped closer. He lifted his lantern higher and the object sparkled, as if tempting him onward. It was silver, it was round, it glimmered against the indigo silk.

It was a ring.

But not just any ring. It was the ring he had given to Rosamunde. It was the ring Tynan's father had put upon his mother's hand, the ring Merlyn had granted to Ysabella as a sign of his protection.

There could not be two rings such as this in existence. It was silver, large enough to fill a woman's knuckle. It was graced with three stars and three names, the names of the three kings who had visited the babe Jesus in Bethlehem.

Rosamunde had worn it on her left index finger.

It was the sole gift Tynan had ever given to her. There had been precious little he could offer to a woman who roamed the seas and claimed the most elegant goods for herself, but he had given her this and he had believed that she had realized the import of his gesture.

Perhaps she had understood, for she had taken no small risk to return it to him thus, to spurn him thus.

Tynan swallowed and reached out to take the ring, letting its considerable weight settle into his palm. He fancied that it was still warm, though that was impossible. Only when he held it did he see that it hung suspended from a single long red-gold hair.

He stood, heart seared. Rosamunde had given back the only gift that he had granted her and in exchange had taken the legacy from the caverns that he had forbidden her to claim. In so doing, she ensured the end of Ravensmuir.

How dare she?

What else had she dared?

Tynan's fist closed tightly around the silver of the ring

as fury erupted within him and he snapped the hair loose of its mooring. He stormed back down the stairs to his dungeon on a suspicion and found his suspicion proven aright.

His prisoner, Erik Sinclair, was gone. Tynan would have wagered that his niece Vivienne was also gone, for Rosamunde could not have lost her ability to make trouble so readily as that. He ground his teeth in frustration. This was beyond revenge, this was beyond retaliation for his harsh words.

This was a taunt that could not pass unchallenged.

Tynan returned the ring to the smallest finger of his left hand, where it had ridden for years until he had granted it to Rosamunde, feeling more alive than he had in weeks.

For all was not yet resolved between himself and Rosamunde. So long as she had the relics, there was a chance that he might retrieve them from her.

Tynan fairly walked into Elizabeth, so unexpected was her presence on the stairs. The maiden halted at the sight of him, flushed, and pivoted to run to the women's chambers.

"Halt!" Tynan roared in a tone that brooked no disobedience. Elizabeth stopped, her expression wary. Tynan beckoned her with a single finger. "You will tell me what happened in the labyrinth this night." She opened her mouth to protest, but Tynan shook his head. "Do not deny that you know of it. You are afoot too late to be in ignorance of Rosamunde's visit."

An increasingly familiar defiance lit the eye of Tynan's youngest and favored niece. "Darg is missing. I have to find her first."

"The spriggan can see to her own welfare for the moment, as she has done for several hundred years." Tynan glared at Elizabeth, knowing the power of his glance. "You, however, will come immediately with me and tell me all that you know."

He turned and strode to the chamber he used to manage Ravensmuir's affairs, knowing full well that his niece would follow. He heard Elizabeth's sigh of annoyance, then halted suddenly when she called after him.

"I will not tell you about Rosamunde," she said.

Tynan pivoted to find his niece looking stubborn. "Whyever not?"

"Because you have been cruel to her, and she has always been kind," Elizabeth said with the blunt manner that was becoming characteristic. "She loves you and you said too much in anger. I do not blame her for vexing you, for she is due an apology."

With that declaration and a toss of her hair, Elizabeth strode into the women's chambers and shut the door fast behind herself.

She had never before defied him.

Tynan stared at the portal in shock as the tumblers fell and a door in his own abode was locked against him by a maiden who had seen only twelve summers.

Worse, he knew that Elizabeth was right.

# Chapter Thirteen

VIVIENNE WAS STILL AWAKE when Rosamunde climbed down into the hold, a fact which the older woman noted immediately. She beckoned to Vivienne, coaxing her up onto the deck.

To Vivienne's surprise, it was morning. She had lost track of the passage of time in the darkened hold. The sky was still overcast, though the clouds had the smooth patina of a pewter platter, and the wind was light. There was a promise of rain, but for the moment there was none. The sea still churned, and she could not see the silhouette of land in any direction.

Rosamunde must have sensed her distress at that. "It is safer to be away from the rocks and shoals of an unfamiliar shore during a storm," she said in a consoling tone, then smiled ruefully. Vivienne could see shadows beneath her aunt's eyes, which were no surprise given the night they had experienced, though the faint lines of age on Rosamunde's face revealed in this light shocked Vivienne.

Rosamunde had always seemed so young and vital, though now Vivienne realized that her aunt must be some thirty summers her senior. Age seemed to have settled suddenly upon Rosamunde's features.

Rosamunde smiled ruefully. "Though I did not expect to be blown quite this far out to sea."

"Where are we?"

"I am not entirely certain," Rosamunde said, more untroubled than Vivienne could possibly be. "The North Sea is vast. We can chart a course after seeing the stars this night."

Vivienne cast a glance at the clouds above. "What if they are obscured?"

"Then we shall wait until we can see them." Rosamunde granted Vivienne a keen glance. "You do understand that it is better to be far from the shore, do you not?"

"I suppose there is sense in that."

Rosamunde slipped an arm around Vivienne's shoulders. "You must have been thinking of your parents last night, and their unfortunate demise. Recognize that I know the seas better than most who ply their trade upon them. I have survived a thousand storms, many far worse than what we endured last night, and I will survive a thousand more." The gleam of determination in Rosamunde's eyes persuaded Vivienne of the truth of that, as little else might have done.

She stood at the rail beside her aunt, soothed despite herself by the rhythm of the sea's undulation. She was exhausted in truth, perhaps more so than Rosamunde might have been.

"I had thought I might find you abed with Tynan's prisoner," Rosamunde mused finally.

Vivienne shrugged. "As perhaps, did I." She did not precisely know why Erik had spurned her. Vivienne suspected that there was a deeper root to his rejection than exhaustion, that he still did not trust her, and that given his choice, he would have left her at Ravensmuir.

So dejected was she by that possibility that she wondered whether her quest was doomed to failure. She had already promised her all to him, she had told him the truth, but apparently to no avail. The man had too many secrets for her to be certain.

On impulse, she pulled Erik's dagger from her belt and offered it to Rosamunde. "What can you tell me of the stone in this blade? It has an inscription upon it."

Rosamunde took the dagger and turned it in her hands, studying the hilt with care before she pulled the blade from the scabbard. The stone in the hilt seemed to command most of her interest, and she turned it in the light with apparent fascination.

"It is his?" she asked, though her tone indicated that she had concluded as much.

"A family heirloom."

"Of course." Rosamunde indicated the gem. "This is an old sapphire, for it has been cut with a remarkable ingenuity that could not be copied in our times. Did you note the inscription?"

"ABRAXAS?"

Rosamunde nodded. "Said to be the name of God, though there are many such names, most notably JHVH for Jehovah. This is a Greek word, claimed to be a charm for protection by many." She glanced up. "The Greek letters that compose the word ABRAXAS have a sum of 365, which is said to be a mark of the potency of the word."

"That is the number of days in a year," Vivienne said, thinking of her handfast.

Rosamunde nodded again. "And the number of eons in God's creation, the number of ranks of angels, the number of bones said to be in the human body." She smiled. "It is said to be a strong number, represented time and again in the world shaped by God's hands." She shrugged. "Or it might merely be a number." She tapped the stone again. "This gem was carved at least a thousand years ago, and has been reset time and again for its value."

"Then it is older than the blade?"

"Of course. His family has had some wealth in their time, if they could afford to not only hold such a gem but to keep it." Rosamunde smiled as she watched the light play in the gem. "But then, a sapphire is rumored to be a noble gem, suitable for kings and queens, one that can reputedly break the stoutest iron fetters."

Her smile broadened when Vivienne said nothing. "How unfortunate that he did not hold it while in Ravensmuir's dungeon, for he would have had no need of your aid then."

Vivienne did not smile at that.

Rosamunde returned her attention to the blade. "And a sapphire is said to give great joy to any who gazes into it, though I would wager that greater joy is felt by one who possesses it." She glanced up, her expression assessing. "I would grant a good price for this weapon."

Vivienne was horrified. "No! I cannot sell it! It is not mine to surrender to another."

"Yet it is in your possession."

"Erik granted it to me in trust. It is rightfully his, all the same, for it is a legacy from his father."

"Ah." Rosamunde studied Vivienne, her gaze perceptive. "You think that you love this man," she said, her amusement evident.

Vivienne bristled. "It would be no jest if I did."

Rosamunde shook her head and gazed across the sea for a moment, then looked back at Vivienne. She returned the dagger. "You are young to be so certain of such matters, but then, perhaps you are certain because you are young."

"What is that to mean?"

Rosamunde did not answer, merely granted Vivienne a piercing glance. "What you must resolve, Vivienne, is whether you love the tale of him or the truth of him. A man's story is not his sum, and we both know well enough that you have a fondness for tales."

"I know the difference between tales and truth," Vivienne said with some pride. Rosamunde did not appear to be convinced, but she did not care. "It is of little import though."

"Whyever not?"

"Because he loves another woman." A slow drizzle of rain began then, enveloping the two women and the ship in a silvery mist. It was chilly, and Vivienne shivered slightly, though she was not yet prepared to leave her aunt's side.

She chose her words with care, for if any soul knew the answer to her woes, it was Rosamunde. "Do you know a means to make a man love a woman, Rosamunde? Surely there is a way to encourage him to see what truth is before his own eyes?"

Rosamunde laughed at the very notion. "There is no philter to make a man love you, Vivienne, at least not one that I know. Do you not see the evidence of my ignorance all around you?" She indicated the ship and its cargo with a disparaging gesture.

"I thought you loved your life at sea."

"I loved a man more, and I surrendered all that I was and all that I desired as evidence of that love." Rosamunde sobered as she spoke. "But my regard was not returned. He felt compelled to choose between me and his property. It was a simple matter for him to choose a pile of stones over whatever merit I might possess. That would be a humbling lesson for any woman, though it was perhaps a harsher one for me." Rosamunde seemed to note Vivienne's disappointment, for she laid a consoling hand upon her niece's shoulder. "If you wish for a man to desire you, however, that is readily achieved."

"How?" Vivienne felt a sudden measure of hope. Surely Erik would have greater regard for her if she did bear his son? "Is there a potion for that?"

Rosamunde smiled sadly. "It is no sorcery, Vivienne. To compel a man to desire you, you have only to desire him." She shrugged. "Whether that will sate you, if it is his love that you desire in truth, is another matter altogether."

Vivienne was dismayed to see her vibrant aunt look so unhappy. "Elizabeth says that mention of your name infuriates Uncle Tynan. She suspects that he loves you."

Rosamunde's smile turned wry. "Then he has an uncommon way of showing as much." She turned away then, her manner purposeful. "You are welcome to use my cabin this day and this night, for I will not sleep until our course is clear. Lock the portal and do whatsoever you will." She cast a piercing glance over her shoulder. "I will plead ignorance of your deeds to Alexander, to be certain. You are old enough and clever enough to make

your own choices, for it is you who will have to live with
the consequences."

Vivienne paid the warning no heed, but merely
thanked her aunt. She was certain that a son would persuade Erik to at least harbor affection for her.

And there was but one way to create that son.

VIVIENNE FOUND ERIK STANDING with Ruari while the
older man heaved his very innards over the side of the
ship. The wind had become colder, the rain grew in intensity, and Ruari looked grim indeed. He still held fast to
his saddlebag, though Vivienne supposed it must hold the
last of his possessions.

She halted beside them just as the older man bent over
the rail once more. Erik spared her no more than a glance.

"How ill is he?" she asked, guessing that she would
have to begin any discussion they had.

"Ill enough to ensure his silence," Erik said with wry
humor, his gaze lingering upon Vivienne when she
smiled slightly.

"Do you feel better or worse, Ruari?" she asked with
concern. "The storm subsides and the sea grows more
steady with every moment."

"Even at its most calm, it is too much for me!" Ruari
wailed, and gripped the rail. He breathed heavily and his
face was yet pale, but he seemed better than he had been
before.

"There is cheese and bread and some ale below," Vivienne suggested. "A piece of bread might improve your
state."

Ruari moaned at the very prospect and coughed anew, although he conjured very little.

"You have not eaten that much of late," Erik said. "Surely you are empty by now."

"I thank you for the jest," Ruari retorted. "Perhaps you might explain the truth of it to my belly."

"It might be better to return to the hold," Erik suggested in his turn. "A bucket would serve you well enough now, and you would have less chance of becoming ill from the cold, as well."

"I favor it here," Ruari said stubbornly.

"And I do not," Erik replied. "Yet I dare not leave you alone. Come below, Ruari. I vow to find you a bucket that suits you well."

Ruari cast him a dark glance. "You make a jest of an old man's discomfort."

"I do no such thing. I but ensure your welfare as best I can. Think of the lady, if naught else. Doubtless she will be determined to remain with you, as well."

Ruari granted Vivienne a baleful stare. "There is no need for you to linger here," he said and she smiled.

"I fret for your welfare," she said with all honesty. To her pleasure, Ruari's features brightened.

"Then perhaps I might be persuaded to come below," he said, with one last glance at the railing. He shook a finger at Erik. "It must be a large bucket, to be sure, for I will not show myself a poor guest, even upon a ship."

"Ah, so you *are* smitten with Rosamunde," Erik teased, to Vivienne's surprise. "I knew you merely had to meet a woman sufficiently bold to capture your affection for all time."

Ruari straightened and his eyes gleamed, as doubtless Erik had intended. "I but hold Rosamunde in respect, the respect due to any soul sufficiently intrepid to brave that weather to aid another."

"I suspect 'tis more than that," Erik said mildly.

"She is a veritable angel!" Ruari huffed, launching into a tirade as if he were fully hale once more. "She came to find me, when you lot were busy amongst yourselves. She risked life and limb to ensure my survival and I am not such a knave that I would insult such generosity by humbling myself in the hold of her ship. Why, this ship is full of fine materials, of gold and silk and relics beyond belief. I would not be so base a knave as to sully such beauty, no less to jeopardize her trade, upon that you can rely."

"If you are sufficiently well to lecture, then you are sufficiently well to come below," Erik replied, though he took the older man's elbow to steady him as they made their way across the slippery deck.

Vivienne took Ruari's other arm. Ruari was somewhat unsteady upon his feet, and he slipped once. Erik's hand was firm beneath his elbow, though, and the older man did not fall. All the same, he seized the lip of the hold with undisguised relief.

Ruari looked suddenly up at Erik through the rain, his eyes bright. "You repay your father's debt to me, against all expectation."

"What nonsense do you speak?" Erik asked, his manner kindly.

"I served him well, served him without complaint for more than forty years, but on his deathbed, William Sinclair noted that he had never had the chance to repay the debt. He noted that I had never fallen sick, that I had never been wounded, that he had never had the chance to offer a courtesy to me."

Ruari heaved a sigh and cast a rueful glance about himself. "I suppose if we had journeyed upon a ship then he might have had his chance, but always he lingered close to Blackleith." The older man stared at Erik and almost smiled. "I thank you, lad, for showing kindness when others might have turned away. You are more than the measure of your father, upon that you can rely."

Ruari descended the ladder then, making slow time in his unsteadiness. Vivienne's hair whipped loose of her braid and the wind stung her face. She watched Erik, seeing that he was touched by the older man's words.

When he gestured that she should descend the ladder next, she laid a hand upon his arm and leaned close to whisper. "Rosamunde offers her cabin, that we may strive to create your son."

Erik looked to be shocked. "You told her of this?"

Vivienne straightened. "My aunt knows what it is to be persuaded of the merit of another's objective, and she knows the import of having given one's word."

Erik looked away, then back to Vivienne. The rain made his hair look a darker hue of blond. His eyes seemed a more vibrant blue than they had before and Vivienne again sensed his vitality.

She did not doubt that he found her suggestion alluring, though she did not understand why he hesitated to accept it.

"Do you not desire that son?"

"I ask you only to consider what you do afore you do it."

"I have already pledged a year and a day to this objective."

He watched her still and she knew he was unpersuaded.

"Why did you bring me with you, if you did not mean to come to my bed?"

"Because your womb might already bear fruit, and you are my responsibility until we know for certain."

It was hardly a sentiment to warm her heart. Vivienne refused to be swayed, all the same, for his gaze was too vivid for him to be as indifferent as his tone implied.

She reached out and laid a hand upon Erik's arm, feeling him tense when she did so. She held his gaze and let her fingertips trace a circle of a caress upon his flesh. She did not know how to seduce a man, but she tried to show her enthusiasm for the deed, and used the slow stroke that he had used to awaken her passion.

Erik swallowed visibly and she thought he grit his teeth. "There is no need for this deed," he said. "We may leave matters as they stand. If you bear a child, I will claim it; if not, you may remain with your aunt."

"I would not rely merely upon what we have already done." Vivienne eased closer to Erik, letting her breast rub against his forearm. Her kirtle was still wet, her skin sufficiently cold that her nipples had beaded. She slid her breasts across the muscled strength of his arm, a move which sent a tingle of desire over her own flesh, and heard him catch his breath.

"Come to my bed, Erik Sinclair," she whispered and noted how a heat kindled in his gaze.

"I should not."

"I am your best chance to create a son with all haste," she murmured. Vivienne ran her fingertip across his lips, her gaze unswerving from his. She felt a tremor slide through him and shivered herself at her own bold manner. She turned then and descended the ladder, hoping against hope that he would accept her offer.

Rosamunde looked up from her place in the hold and nodded once. Vivienne was certain that her aunt would return to the deck to survey sky and sea. Meanwhile, Ruari rubbed a cloth through his wet hair and coddled a stout bucket by his side. A deeply wrought brazier smoked, filling the hold with heat even as its smoke stung Vivienne's eyes. Many of the sailors slumbered or whittled in the hold, taking their leisure while they could.

Padraig rose from where he crouched beside the brazier, then offered Ruari a steaming cup of some concoction. Ruari sniffed tentatively before accepting the brew with a grateful smile.

Vivienne waited at the base of the ladder, fearful of what Erik would do. Would he reject her after she had been so bold? He stepped down beside her and spared only the merest glance to the other men, his gaze lingering upon Ruari. The older man waved as if to reassure him. That Erik did not hasten to Ruari's side was all the encouragement Vivienne needed.

"I desire you," she whispered and saw the fire light in Erik's eyes, just as Rosamunde had foretold. She took his hand in hers, smiling at the disparity of size between the two of them, then tugged him toward Rosamunde's chamber.

To her delight, he followed, his eyes so deep a blue that they fairly smouldered.

ERIK WAS ENCHANTED ANEW and he did not care. Vivienne's hair was stained dark from the rain, and water glistened on her cheeks as dewdrops will on the petals of a flower. She secured the door of the chamber behind herself and leaned against it, eying him through her lashes. He was fascinated that she could look both shy and bold, both innocent and provocative, but she managed the deed with ease.

He had thought himself strong enough to leave her be for this journey, but her desire for him, even if it was feigned, was impossible to deny. Resistance to her charms was futile, when his body was already upon her side of the argument.

And indeed, he reminded himself, the damage was done. Her maidenhead was gone in truth. There was naught more to be lost in accepting her invitation, and only the chance of reward in that son.

Or so Erik told himself.

Rosamunde's chamber was simple in structure, a mere cabin secured from the rest of the hold. The walls were curved and wrought of wood—as was all of the ship—and its entirety rocked in a soothing manner. A pair of lanterns were secured to the wall at the far end, the flames well away from the wall and the receptacle for the oil too small to cause much risk of fire if spilled. Erik could hear the rain drumming steadily on the deck overhead, which only made the room seem like more of a cozy haven.

There was little in the chamber, save a bed built into the frame of the ship. The lip upon it was sufficiently large that one would not be cast out of it in the roughest sea. The bed was large enough to accommodate two persons, though one of Erik's height would have to curl up to fit.

The mattress was thick and clearly filled with down, an indulgence that spoke of Rosamunde's love of luxury. Dozens of pelts were piled on the bed, their silky furs a marvelous jumble of hues. Erik could not identify the animals that must have been once adorned with several of them, for no wolf or squirrel had ever been graced with such stripes and spots.

Bed linens of velvet and silk were folded at one end, drapes of finely woven wool could be drawn to make another barrier against the hold, and pillows of all shapes and sizes spilled from the bed to the floor. They stood in silence and stared at this marvel of a bed, while Erik imagined what they might do upon it. Indeed, the very air seemed to steam with the heat of his desire.

But he would wait for the lady to invite him between her thighs once more. That she hesitated so quickly after her bold invitation made him doubt that she truly did desire him. There would be no charge against him later that he had claimed her against her will.

Erik would wait, if it nigh killed him.

A rap at the door made them both jump, then Vivienne unfastened the latch. Rosamunde stood there, a knowing smile curving her lips. She offered a steaming bucket of water and a large irregularly shaped golden ball. It seemed to be porous.

"A sponge," she said, noting Erik's puzzlement. "And water to bathe. There is attar of roses in the drawer beneath the bed, if you desire scent, and honey, as well, if you desire enticement."

Honey?

Erik took the bucket, looking into the depths of the steaming water as he considered what could be done with honey. Vivienne took the sponge. She plunged it into the water, then squeezed it out, loosing a cascade of water. She laughed then and repeated her deed, clearly as unfamiliar with this marvel as he.

Rosamunde smiled, mischief making her eyes sparkle.

"I shall trouble you only with food," she said, then winked and pulled the portal closed once more.

Vivienne took a deep breath that made her breasts swell, then glanced up at Erik. An echo of Rosamunde's mischief danced in her eyes.

"Honey," she repeated, then smiled wickedly. "Though I should like to bathe before such enticement." Then she turned the latch to lock the door.

Erik eased the bucket into a brace he had spotted on the floor, then faced Vivienne once more. She regarded him with a smile that warmed him to his toes and before he could speak, she raised a hand to the clasp of her cloak.

"You have always led me to passion," she whispered. "Now, I would similarly coax you." She let her cloak drop to the floor, her gaze unswerving. Erik knew that he had no need of coaxing, for his body was fully prepared already, but he let Vivienne set the pace. She planted a fingertip in the middle of his chest. "You have but to stand and watch. I will do the rest."

Erik realized then that Vivienne meant to disrobe before him and his mouth went dry. He had no need of honey, no need of more than the gleam in Vivienne's eyes, the inviting smile that curved her lips.

He stood still with an effort, and watched her shed her garb with frustrating leisure.

She unfastened the lace at one side of her kirtle, taking a cursed amount of time to ease it free. She spared him a smile, then unfastened the one on the opposite side, tugging the lace from each eyelet with tantalizing deliberation. When the kirtle was loosed, she lifted the hem in slow increments, revealing the shadow of her ankles through her chemise, then her finely curved calves.

The woman was fairly wrought to tempt him, of this Erik was certain. He clenched his fists and watched.

After easing the garment ever higher with frustrating slowness, finally Vivienne lifted the green kirtle over her head and cast it aside. Erik could see her rosy nipples through the fine linen of her chemise, as well as their pert peaks, and the auburn shadow of the hair at the top of her thighs. Her curves were no more than tempting shadows spied through the cloth.

Erik made to unlace his own jerkin, but Vivienne seized his hands to halt him. "Let me," she whispered, her eyes dark with a desire that weakened his knees. She kissed his knuckles, each one in turn, lavishing attention upon them with her soft lips. She planted a kiss on each of his palms, her tongue flicking against his skin unexpectedly.

"Vivienne," he fairly growled, but she did not hasten. Indeed, the tip of her tongue darted between his fingers and he caught his breath at the vigor of his response.

Perhaps she did come from a lineage of sorcerers, for his desire for her seemed never to be sated. Indeed, it only grew more potent each time they met abed, only grew stronger with each taste.

Vivienne smiled and stepped away from him, then worked the lace of her chemise loose with that same deliberation. Erik swallowed, transfixed as every increment of soft flesh was revealed. She unfastened the myriad buttons on the sleeves with painful slowness. The chemise finally fell to the floor in its turn, piling around her ankles like a cloud beneath an angel's feet.

Vivienne stepped gracefully out of the cloth, then shook it out, hanging it upon a hook with more care than he thought the matter deserved. She had to reach for that hook, though, stretching out one leg behind herself and pointing one toe. He admired the curve of her buttocks and the graceful line of her back. He thought momentarily about seizing her about her narrow waist and ending this torment, but then she cast him such a smile that he abandoned the notion.

She was savoring this seduction and he was not enough of a cur to deny it to her.

Vivienne retrieved her kirtle and cloak, hanging them in their turn and offering him such a lingering view of her buttocks that Erik guessed that she felt the weight of his gaze upon her. He admired the smooth strength of her legs, as his desire for her was urged to fever pitch.

She granted him a coy smile as she began to loose her hair. She stood before him, clad only in her stockings, garters and boots, and untied the lace at the end of her braid. As usual, the braid held but a third of her hair captive in truth, the rest having escaped its bonds earlier to curl around her face.

He could not help but admire her, and did not try to hide his awe of her beauty. Vivienne's smile broadened, and for once, Erik did not mind that his thoughts could be so readily discerned by another. Vivienne leaned her head back and shook out her hair, her eyes closed, and he watched hungrily.

He leaned forward and planted a kiss in the hollow of her throat. She gasped and he claimed her mouth in a possessive kiss, his hand curving around the back of her waist. When he raised his hand to cup her face, her pulse skipped beneath his hand in a most enticing manner.

He released her and stepped back, well content to have put that flush upon her cheeks and that sparkle in her eyes.

Indeed, these unfamiliar chausses showed themselves to have a marked disadvantage over his customary garb. There was little room within them for his enthusiastic response to Vivienne and he yearned anew for the comfort of his loose chemise and belted length of tartan.

Vivienne reached for the lace of his jerkin then. She spared him a glance through her lashes, her smile provocative. She was flushed, though, more maidenly than she would probably have preferred, though Erik found the contrast most alluring.

She worked the lace loose, one hole at a time, then pulled it free and cast it aside. She slid her hands beneath the boiled leather shell, fanning her fingers as she ran her hands over his chest. He ducked his head, unable to resist the chance to kiss her, but she evaded his lips and kissed the hollow of his throat instead.

The jerkin was followed by his chemise, which was worked loose in teasing increments. She playfully pushed him on to the bed then, and straddled one of his legs as she tugged off his boot. Her buttocks were on his thigh, the ripe curve of her hips tempting his hands. He caught her around the waist and pulled her back into his lap, stealing another thorough kiss before she escaped his embrace once more.

She was breathless when she rapped him on the nose with a scolding fingertip, and her eyes glittered. "You are to be seduced, not to do the seducing," she said.

"But I am seduced already," he argued. "Your quest is complete."

"It has only just begun," she retorted, then squirmed in his lap so that she could not have missed the sign of his enthusiasm. She got to her feet again though, and straddled his other leg, her hands locking on his second boot.

Once again, Erik did not obey instructions. He caught her around the waist, liking that his hands fairly locked around her, and the roll of the ship worked in his favor. Vivienne tumbled into his lap. Erik caught her nape in his hand and kept his other arm locked around her waist as he kissed her fully. She arched against him, her tongue dancing with his, her fingers spearing into his hair as they rolled across the bed together.

He loved that she was not shy, that she did not withhold her passion from him. He loved that she responded so ardently to his caress, that she clearly savored their lovemaking as much as he.

Vivienne's eyes sparkled with laughter when she broke their kiss. She sprawled atop Erik, her hands braced upon his shoulders. "What a soft bed," she murmured. "We shall sleep well here."

"We may not sleep at all," Erik replied, then rolled her beneath him. He kissed her fully once more, and she was quick to respond to his caress. She was flushed and smiling when he lifted his head, though still she shook a finger at him.

"You were not to do anything," she protested.

Erik tugged off one of her boots then claimed her ankle, locking one hand around it. He bent to untie her garters with his teeth. Vivienne gasped when his thumb moved in a slow circle against her ankle bone and she moaned with pleasure when he kissed behind her knees. It took some time to be rid of both of her garters and stockings, though the lady did not complain.

He had only a heartbeat's warning, a mere glimpse of the mischief dancing in her eyes, before she bent to untie the lace of his chausses with her teeth. He feared then that he would tear the cloth, that the chausses from the Earl of

Sutherland would not be able to contain him. That Vivienne caressed him though the cloth, teasing him with her fingertips, nigh drove him mad with desire.

He laid back and grit his teeth, letting her do what she would so that he could surprise her when she was done. She tormented him, echoing his gesture by kissing behind his knees as she eased the chausses away. No sooner were they dispatched to the floor than Erik reached for her, but she was already upon her feet.

She opened the drawer beneath the bed, biting her lip in an endearing expression of concentration as she looked through the drawer's contents. She wrinkled her nose at the label on the first bottle she lifted, put it back and lifted out another. She removed the stopper and the chamber smelled of roses in bloom. Vivienne poured a healthy quantity of the scent into the steaming water and Erik protested.

"I shall smell as if I have been to a brothel!"

"Who shall smell you, save me?"

"Ruari, for one."

"But he of all men will know that you could not have been to a brothel." She plunged the sponge into the water, then wrung it out, granting Erik a fine view of those buttocks once again. "And he of all men knows your need for a son. Will he not think the scent of roses a small price to pay?" She propped a hand on her hip as she regarded him and the light of the lanterns turned her flesh to the hue of a sunrise. "After all, it smells finer than either of us do already."

"That is true enough."

"And do you truly care what Ruari thinks of your deeds this day?"

Erik had to admit that he did not. He had no need to

say as much, for his thoughts were not so secret now that his chausses were shed.

Vivienne's eyes gleamed with purpose, then she returned to kneel on the bed. She ran the sponge down his chest, making a dripping course of warm water, then caressed his erection with it. It was soft and tickled slightly, her fingers were warm, her stroke resolute. Erik pulled away, certain he would spill his seed too soon.

"Do you not wish to be washed?" she asked.

"I could do it more quickly myself," he said, hearing the strain in his voice. She closed her hand around him, even with the sponge, and moved up and down the length of him. Erik was certain he would not be able to endure much of this attention.

Then Vivienne leaned over him, her hair spilling around him, and kissed his jaw. She touched him with increasing surety, kissing him finally on the earlobe. "You pleased me there with your tongue," she whispered into his ear. "Time 'tis for me to return pleasure in kind."

Before he could protest, she had slid down his chest and pressed her lips to his erection. Erik fell back on the bed and groaned aloud as he realized he would be unable to halt her amorous assault.

It was then that Vivienne truly began to torment him with pleasure. Erik did not want to compel her to stop. She met him with a wild abandon new to her, committing herself to their passion with new vigor. He was beguiled, he was enchanted, he was lost in her allure.

He succumbed to the moment, powerless to do otherwise.

～

IT WAS LONG BEFORE THEY SLUMBERED, sated, their limbs entwined. Erik felt a tremendous languor and his eyes drifted closed of their own accord. He pulled the furs over them both, welcoming Vivienne's soft heat against his side.

She nestled closer and placed her lips against Erik's ear. He thought that she meant to kiss him and he smiled despite himself at the prospect.

"I love you," she murmured instead. She spoke so sleepily that she might have been unaware that the words had crossed her lips.

But Erik's eyes flew open and sleep proved impossible for him after that. He looked at her, incredulous, but she drifted into sleep. He frowned at the timbered walls of the cabin, listening to the rain and the echo of those three words in his thoughts.

Did Vivienne lie to further ensnare him?

Or did he owe this lady far more than he had offered her thus far? Erik could not be certain, though the question plagued him all the night long.

With three murmured words, Vivienne had changed all.

# Chapter Fourteen

~

SOMETHING WAS AMISS.

Vivienne did not know what it was, but she awakened alone in that chamber the morning afterward. She climbed to the deck in search of Erik, and found the ship surrounded by dense white fog. The sails hung damply from the masts and the sea was as still as a mirror. A sailor rang a bell at steady intervals, clearly at Rosamunde's command, but there was not so much as a breath of wind, let alone any hint of another soul.

They might have sailed off the edge of the world. Worse, Erik seemed determined to avoid her. Each time she reached his side, he departed with haste, barely sparing her a glance.

Erik appeared to take pains to avoid Vivienne, which was no small feat on a ship of this size. She felt bereft without his touch, without the merest sign of affection from him, and she wondered at the import of his manner.

What had she done?

Vivienne feared that the change in his manner had less to do with her and more to do with the prospect of his returning home. Doubtless the memory of Beatrice was stronger for him. Vivienne imagined that Erik turned away because he refused to taint the love he had pledged to the mother of his two beloved daughters.

This was not the reward granted to the stalwart lover in all the tales that Vivienne knew! They had made a handfast and she, for one, did not intend to forget as much.

Rosamunde shrugged off the weather and the sailors seemed to take it in stride. But by the second day, several of the seamen were muttering, and by the third, there was a distinct hum of discontent.

The weather did not stir, and Erik took to pacing the deck. Doubtless, he was anxious to see matters resolved at Blackleith.

Worse, Rosamunde could not find her lodestone, though she swore that she always kept it in the same locale. None of the men on the ship confessed to moving it, and Rosamunde hunted for it in increasingly foul temper.

She found it, on the fifth day, precisely where it should have been all along.

The lodestone, though, was useless. It seemed charmed. Vivienne watched in amazement as Rosamunde held it aloft and it spun ceaselessly in a circle. The stone was unable to find true north.

The sailors began to whisper of sorcery and, for once, Ruari held his tongue. Erik paced with greater vigor, his uneven stride echoing through the deck long into the night.

No sooner had the lodestone been found than Rosamunde could not find her ledger. Unwilling to rely upon the observations of other seaman, she had made a compilation of her own considerable experience, noting the direction of winds in certain locales and sketching the shape of the land. She had journeyed often between Ravensmuir and Sicily, and the ledger contained the sum of her own observations, the better that she might orient herself after a storm such as the one they had experienced.

But the ledger was not to be found. Again, no man on the crew admitted to touching it, much less moving it from its secured place in Rosamunde's cabin. Ruari helped Rosamunde search the entire ship for it, and that with dogged persistence, but to no avail.

On the eighth day, the ledger appeared in precisely the spot it should have occupied all along.

All notes regarding the North Sea, however, had vanished.

No tempest had ever raged to match Rosamunde's fury at this development. Even Padraig, ever bold in her presence, clearly avoided her for that day. Rosamunde tore through every corner of that ship, she had cartons unpacked and barrels overturned, she dumped the drawers in her cabin, she declared it within her rights to examine every man's possessions. She interrogated every living soul on that ship.

All to no avail.

Vivienne began to fear that they would never see land again.

OF COURSE, Rosamunde missed one small fey individual in her interrogation. The spriggan Darg knew where the ledger pages were, for she had hidden them. She had also charmed the lodestone. That spriggan laughed heartily over the success of her deed.

It was Erik who heard the faint echo of fairy laughter, Erik who knew better than to believe in matters unseen, Erik who could not fathom who was bold enough to snicker at Rosamunde's expense. He heard the echo of merriment in the midst of the night, when all others slumbered, when he alone paced the deck.

He feared that he lost his wits, and in that surrendered the last of his meager assets.

On the tenth morning, a distraught Rosamunde summoned them all to her chamber. Erik ensured that there was distance between himself and Vivienne. She looked at him with confusion, uncertain at his reserved manner.

Erik certainly did not wish to explain himself. Proximity to Vivienne would scatter his thoughts, would ensure lust decimated his ability to fairly consider all that he knew. He dared not risk even a fleeting touch. He wished there was a way to be certain now whether his seed had taken root within her, for then his obligations would be clear — if not the truth.

Vivienne had changed her garb, probably due to a gift from Rosamunde, and Erik did not doubt that it was intended to tempt him. It nigh did so. The ochre kirtle was fitted to accent her considerable curves and perhaps displayed them more boldly than her previous kirtle had done. Its hems and cuffs were rich with embroidery in hues of blue and green, and her new chemise appeared to be a saffron yellow. Her hair was combed out over her shoulders, its auburn curls glinting in the cabin's light.

Desire lit in Erik's belly like a flame and he was compelled to look away. He heard again her sleepy pledge of love and his innards churned.

"I do not know what to do," Rosamunde confessed to the small group gathered in her chamber. "Without my ledger, I cannot be certain of our locale. Without knowing our locale, I cannot chart a course. We cannot remain adrift forever and we dare not alight upon unfriendly shores."

"Are there so many unfriendly ports as that?" Erik asked, and won a hard look for his query.

"I have pursued a dangerous trade for decades," Rosamunde said shortly. "There are thus more unfriendly ports than amiable ones, at least for me." She paced the chamber in agitation. "Never has something like this happened to me," she muttered, her vexation more than clear. "Some fool plays a jest upon me, some fool who will pay dearly for such audacity."

"Could one of your enemies be hidden upon this ship?" Erik asked.

"Where?" Rosamunde flung out her hands. "There is no place to hide!"

But Erik was not so certain of that, given what he had learned of treachery himself. "Could one of your men have been tempted to serve another, with coin or other reward?"

Rosamunde mused. "It is possible, though unlikely. Padraig and I are known to both reward our men well and to ensure that any unpaid debts are rendered in full."

"And then some," Padraig amended, looking grim. "There are few who would dare to deceive us in these days."

Rosamunde and Padraig exchanged a glance and Erik guessed that they had seen a good measure of vengeance served in their time.

He, for one, would not have defied them. Indeed, he knew better than to ask for details and chose to take them at their word.

Vivienne bit her lip, as if knowing her suggestion would be unwelcome. "Perhaps the spriggan Darg accompanied us. She alone holds a grudge against you."

"And an unjust one at that!" Rosamunde's eyes flashed. "I told Elizabeth to command her fairy. I cannot return the hoard to Ravensmuir, not now, so there is no wager to be made."

"But what of your ring?" Erik asked, noting Rosamunde's barren finger. "The silver ring that the spriggan demanded as her due? Surely if you have surrendered it to her, this fairy has no cause for complaint?"

Rosamunde's eyes narrowed but before she could reply, Vivienne turned upon Erik in astonishment. "You acknowledge the existence of the spriggan?"

Erik had felt the spriggan, when she had been tangled in the seaweed, and he was fairly certain of the source of the malicious laughter he had heard since. He was not prepared to admit as much openly, however, so ignored Vivienne's query.

Rosamunde, to his surprise, flushed like a maiden and dropped her gaze. "The ring is gone. I hold it no longer."

"But if you surrendered it to the spriggan, then there should remain no issue," Erik said carefully.

Ruari snorted. "Fairies are a capricious lot. There is naught to say that this Darg would stand by her wager even if it was accepted immediately, let alone days after it was made."

But Erik was intrigued by Rosamunde's discomfiture.

"It was not mine to surrender," she said gruffly, her gaze flicking as if she would look anywhere rather than meet the gazes of the others. "It is returned to its rightful owner, and thus beyond the reach of both myself and this spriggan."

Erik heard a small scream, seemingly wrought of frustration. He considered that Darg might argue the rightful ownership of that ring.

"Which means," he concluded, "that there is no way to sate the spriggan, for her terms cannot be met." A weight landed on his shoulder then and he heard a small cackle close to his ear. It seemed that the spriggan chattered agreement, though he could not fully discern her words.

Perhaps she spoke another language than the ones he knew.

"The ring is at Ravensmuir," Rosamunde admitted. "For it is Ravensmuir's ring and rightly belongs there."

"Why did you leave it there?" Padraig demanded. "We could be lost at sea for all time, if you have not the ring with which to wager!"

Rosamunde's cheeks stayed ruddy and Erik guessed that she told but half the tale. "I thought this spriggan would remain with the ring, and we would be readily rid of her."

Padraig shook his head and rubbed his brow. "But instead we are doomed, doomed to be lost at sea for the sprite cannot have her due." He granted Rosamunde a stern glance. "Unless you can make another wager that will please the demon."

Rosamunde pursed her lips. She paced, she frowned, she folded her arms across her chest. She surveyed the chamber with a bright eye, clearly seeking some sign that the spriggan was amongst them.

Erik felt that slight weight upon his shoulder ease closer to his neck. He dared not move, for he knew not what the creature meant to do. A tiny claw clutched at his earlobe, then words resonated in his ear. They were words not carried on anything so mortal as a breath, but words he heard all the same.

When he realized their import, he repeated them aloud.

"*Debts must be paid or they stay due, the fey have far less patience than you. The ring of kings is my sole demand, and I will have it from any hand. Be Rosamunde dead or alive, still she will render my prize.*'"

"So, you would talk in verse, lad?" Ruari asked in evident surprise. "What madness is this? You have no need for this ring."

Erik felt the back of his neck heat. "It is the spriggan. I can hear her and these words are her own. I but repeat them."

Vivienne's lips parted with awe. "You can even hear the spriggan?"

"Evidently so." Erik felt no small measure of embarrassment to be proven so wrong and before the company as well. The little claw tugged at his earlobe, then the whisper sounded again.

"*Debts can be rendered in many a way, though the price grows higher with each day. Tell her then to make me an offer: I may be fey but I will barter.*"

Erik repeated this as well and the company exchanged glances. Rosamunde sighed and stared at her boots for a long moment before she spoke. "If I return to Ravensmuir, which would be a breach of my own pledge to never cross that threshold again—"

"A pledge you have already willingly broken," Padraig interjected, earning a dark glance for his trouble. Rosamunde folded her arms across her chest, looking fully discontent with what she meant to say.

"If I so do, and if I pledge to try to retrieve the ring

while there, will the spriggan aid us?" she asked, her
manner revealing her own opinion of this course. "There
is no way to claim the ring while we are at sea."

All looked expectantly at Erik, but he could hear no
whisper. The grip upon his ear was gone, as seemingly
was the weight upon his shoulder. He turned, looking
about himself for some hint that the spriggan still remained in their company. He could not see Darg, nor
could he hear any sound from her.

But he saw the ledger, fat with parchment once again.
"Are your observations returned?"

Rosamunde pivoted, gasped, and fairly fell upon the
ledger, her features lighting as she turned the pages
within it. "They are all returned!" she said with amazement. "And as neatly as if they had never been gone."

The bell rang with greater vigor from the deck and the
sailors above gave a shout. "The fog clears!" one
shouted. "It blows away with uncommon speed! Come
and see!"

Padraig hastened out of the chamber, then the ladder
creaked as he climbed to the deck. "Ha!" he shouted, only
half out the hatch. "He speaks the truth! I can see the blue
of the sky."

Rosamunde laughed aloud. She clutched the book in
both hands and raised it high. "We sail for Scotland!" she
cried with evident delight. "We sail this very day, first for
Helmsdale and thence to Ravensmuir."

Padraig ducked his head back into the hold and
granted Rosamunde a grim glance before he met Erik's
gaze. "And you may tell your fairy that I shall ensure that
there is no breach of this pledge."

"You?" Rosamunde asked with a smile. "Your word is
worth precious little."

"I may have a fondness for the sea, but not to the point of being lost upon it," Padraig retorted. "Indeed, I lose my taste for such adventures. I will complete this journey with you, Rosamunde, for I have agreed as much, and this despite the fact that my pledge is worth so little. But then I yearn for the sun of Sicily. I will sail forth from that isle no more."

He climbed fully to the deck then, leaving Rosamunde astonished behind him. She pursued him but a moment later. Ruari turned a merry eye upon Erik, and Vivienne eased closer to his side, her eyes sparkling with laughter.

"So the spriggan has chosen you," Ruari said with no small measure of amusement.

"Darg takes our side in persuading you of matters unseen," Vivienne added.

"It was but a verse or two," Erik said gruffly, as if they made too much of too little, and they laughed at his manner.

Ruari shook a finger at him. "You cannot fight the truth, lad, that much is certain. If you deny what is evident to all, then it shall be made evident to you, in one way or another."

"And you cannot trick a fairy," Vivienne added. "Even Rosamunde has learned as much."

"He probably saw the fairy all along," Ruari teased, then granted Vivienne a knowing glance. "But meant to share your bed for as many nights as possible. After all, you were determined to show him the power of the unseen."

Vivienne opened her mouth, then closed it again, her wondrous eyes filled with shadows when she glanced at Erik once more. Perhaps Ruari did not know that Erik and Vivienne did not meet abed any longer. Erik did not care. With that comment, with the lady's disappointment, the moment had lost its camaraderie for him.

"Only a knave would so inconvenience an entire company for his own pleasure," he said and turned away from Vivienne.

Only a knave despoiled a maiden and did not honorably wed her. It seemed that Erik not only heard the voice of the spriggan but that of his father, as well.

Perhaps it was not so surprising that both fairy and father so vehemently agreed.

DARG APPEARED TO HAVE considerable influence with the weather. The winds changed as soon as Rosamunde struck her wager with the spriggan, and the ship was fairly driven back toward Scotland's coast. They drew near the coast near the Firth of Forth and the entire crew cheered as one.

The ship was turned north with many hands lending their weight to the rudder. They made uncommon speed and Vivienne knew that soon Erik would see his home again. He took to standing at the rail, pointing out this landmark and another to Ruari, his excitement tangible.

Erik did not so much as glance her way, though Vivienne awakened more than once in the night in the ship's hold to find his heat beside her. He did not touch her, much less caress her, but the bite of the wind was cold and Vivienne was glad of his heat.

She hoped she might gain more from him in time. She prayed that she bore his son already.

But when Vivienne learned for certain, it was not the truth she wished to learn. On a night that the moon was just past full and riding high in a clear sky, she awakened in the midst of night to a warm trickle on her thighs. She eased aside the coverlets and let the moonlight fall upon her flesh. The red blood there made her heart plummet to her very toes. There could no longer be any doubt.

She had failed to conceive Erik's son.

Vivienne's tears fell then at her failure, for she had been so certain that their efforts would see the matter quickly resolved.

She cleaned herself with haste and bound a length of linen around herself, then wrapped her cloak more tightly about herself. Erik still breathed with deep regularity and she was loathe to awaken him with such tidings. She eased closer to him, though, feeling the cold more keenly in her disappointment. She willed herself back to sleep, resolving to tell him the truth in the morning.

A resolve grew within her in the darkness. Vivienne was far from prepared to abandon this quest. There were twelve more moons in their handfast, and that meant twelve more chances to conceive a son.

The wager was not lost as yet.

ERIK HAD FELT VIVIENNE stir in the night. He had heard her gasp of surprise and had watched through his lashes as she discovered the blood upon her thigh. He knew the import of that blood and was disappointed that there was no lingering bond between them.

He was touched by her dismay. She thought herself unobserved and further, her response seemed to come from her very core. He understood then that she had truly wished to bear his son, that she felt the failure as keenly as he, that he had been a cur to doubt her. When she nestled beside him again, he felt her tears touch his shoulder.

Vivienne had not lied to him. The truth of it was inescapable. She had lied to her family, against all expectation, and she had done so to aid his quest.

In return, Erik had taken all she offered and granted her naught.

But he had naught to grant, not until he reclaimed Blackleith. No man could offer honorably for a woman in marriage without property beneath his hand, without some means of providing for her and any children they might bear. He had wronged Vivienne with his distrust, but it would only compound his error if he dishonored her now with an empty promise, with a pledge for what he could not guarantee.

Erik wanted to console Vivienne in this moment, he wanted to ease the tears from her cheeks and coax the return of her smile. He wanted to put the sparkle back into her eyes, but he dared not reveal to her that he was awake.

Indeed, it took all within him to keep his arm from tightening around her. He turned as if in sleep and touched his lips to her temple, and she burrowed her face into his chest. Her hair was spread across them, their cloaks were unfurled over them, the softness of her skin touched his own flesh in a thousand places.

And Erik knew that they were entwined in more ways than that. He loved Vivienne, loved her impulsive nature and her confidence, loved that she was unafraid of any peril, that she would pay any price to see a just goal achieved. He loved how she opened like a blossom beneath his caress, loved how they seemed each wrought for the other. No other woman would ever touch his heart as she had done. He loved that she gave of herself unstintingly, fully confident that her gifts would be repaid in greater abundance.

He wanted to be the one to render the balance due to her.

He loved her, but he had not the right to tell her as much.

Not yet.

Erik would confess his love only in triumph. He feared that Vivienne would accept him for the offer of his love alone, even if he remained a failure.

But she deserved better than love alone. She deserved wealth and security, a home and a hearth, a husband and a future filled with promise. Erik could not offer the ending of the tale that she deserved, not on this morning, and if he never could offer it, then Vivienne would know nothing of his love for her.

He knew, however, that he would yearn for her for all his days and nights. He wanted to fulfil her maidenly dreams, he wanted to offer her those three nights of courtship and that red red rose wrought of ice. It might prove to be impossible, but Erik wanted the chance to try.

When Vivienne slept deeply again, Erik eased from her side. Praise be that Ruari had held fast to that saddlebag, for it contained the length of tartan, the yellow chemise and the sturdy leather boots in which Erik was more comfortable. He shunned the southern clothing that the Earl of Sutherland had granted to him, and dressed in his familiar garb. He retrieved his father's blade from the tumble of Vivienne's clothing, for he suspected he might have need of it, and shoved it into the back of his belt.

He stared down at her, watching the moonlight play upon her cheek, and committed her features to memory.

He would never forget Vivienne Lammergeier, and he praised the instinct that had urged him to seek out the one woman who had spurned his brother.

He might have little to offer her in this moment, but he would not leave Vivienne without some token of him. Erik took the silver pin that had been his mother's most prized possession, the silver pin that adorned his own cloak and had drawn Vivienne's eye more than once, and laid it beside his lady's hand.

Her fingers spread across the silver, then closed surely around it. She sighed in her sleep and rolled to her side, pulling the pin to her chest in her closed fist.

Erik took that small gesture as a good portent.

He reached out a fingertip and touched her cheek one last time, his heart aching when she smiled and turned her lips against his palm, her lashes barely fluttering. A tendril of her hair twined around his fingers, as if it would hold him fast by her side forever.

Vivienne sighed, her breath as light as a summer breeze, the stains of her tears yet upon her cheeks. Erik vowed to himself that he would return to her in honor or die trying.

The lady deserved no less than his all.

ERIK SILENTLY ROUSED RUARI, not allowing himself a backward glance. The older man seemed to sense his intent, for he dressed quickly and hastened to the deck behind Erik.

Ruari did not ask about Vivienne.

The coast rose ruggedly to their west within easy proximity and mist swirled in patches over the silvery sea.

The fat moon sank toward the horizon and the few clouds to the east were already touched with pearly light. To Erik's relief, Padraig kept the watch. As he anticipated, that seaman was readily bribed and an arrangement was made both swiftly and quietly.

Erik and Ruari rowed to the shore in the borrowed boat with Padraig huddled between them. None of the men spoke, and they exchanged the barest of nods when Erik and Ruari climbed out of the boat in the shallows. Padraig rowed back toward the ship with powerful strokes.

Erik strode through the water to the shore. He revelled in freedom of movement offered by his tartan, the way that his old boots with their perforations did not hold the water. His feet and his legs would be dry before they had walked a mile, while that southern garb left a man sodden all one day and the next.

Erik liked the feel of the rock beneath his soles, the shimmer of the heather, now in full bloom, across the hills. The River Helmsdale climbed before him, its every turn and leap as familiar as the lines in his own palm. He knew where to cast a lure for salmon, he knew where tiny sea pearls could be found, he knew where every ancient stone stood sentinel. He took a deep breath of the crisp cool air and felt an ease, a contentment, settle in his veins anew.

Erik was home.

He felt a new measure of hope, a new prospect of success. When last he had stood so close to Blackleith he had been certain only of his ultimate and inevitable failure.

Vivienne had taught Erik to see promise where he had perceived there to be none. Vivienne had taught him to

believe that all was possible. And now that his very
sinews were healed and he was as hale as ever he would
be, Erik found himself anticipating his encounter with his
brother, however it might end.

Erik also found himself less persuaded that he approached his own doom. Perhaps it was folly, but that
hope made it easier to turn his back upon Rosamunde's
ship and the lady who would hold his heart for all eternity, made it easier to turn his face toward Blackleith
once more.

"Do you mean to go to the Earl of Sutherland's hall
from here?" Ruari asked, but Erik shook his head.

"We go to Blackleith. The Earl will not grant aid to me
without the son he demanded as his terms."

Ruari hesitated. "There is good and bad in the Earl, to
be certain, but he might be amenable to a request for aid.
Do not be so hasty to discard a potential ally, lad, for it is
difficult indeed to find a man inclined to stand at one's
back."

Erik shook his head again. "This battle is mine alone."

"Nicholas might have men aplenty in his hall, for any
fool can hire mercenaries."

"I shall face him alone, and the better man will win."
Erik granted his companion a glance. "The choice to accompany me is yours, Ruari, for I would not commend
you to a fool's journey. It would be unfair to demand
as much of you, after you served my father with such
loyalty."

Ruari bristled visibly, and glowered at the younger
man. "You will not face this injustice without me, lad,
upon that you can rely. I swore a pledge upon the gem in
that Sinclair blade, and I have wits enough to know that
such a pledge cannot be broken without dire repercus-

sions. Win or lose, I match my steps to yours, to be sure."
The older man's lips set grimly and he tightened his belt.
"I owe your father no less."

It was a sentiment Erik appreciated, though it was not
the best omen for success. The two men exchanged a
glance, then headed into the forest in grim silence.

VIVIENNE AWAKENED ALONE, something cold in her hand.
Erik was gone, she saw immediately, as was Ruari.

As was the saddlebag Ruari had carried.

She opened her hand and gasped to find the silver pin
that Erik had worn on his cloak within her grip. She
guessed then that he had abandoned her, that he had
granted her this beautiful trinket as a gift.

But they had a handfast.

Vivienne dressed in haste and climbed to the deck. It
was early, so early that the sky was just barely touched
with morning's light. It looked as if the weather would be
fair, and the seamen were already stirring. They spoke of
raising the sails, of turning south, of the prospect of a port
soon.

But Vivienne grasped the rail, her gaze snared by two
figures in the shallows. She knew those two male silhou-
ettes, just as she recognized the man rowing the small
boat back toward the ship. She met Padraig at the rope
ladder, knowing what she had to do.

"Padraig, I beg of you, row me to the shore as well."

That man paused on the ladder, the rope from the
small boat in his hand. There was a sheen of perspiration
on his face from rowing against the waves and his expression was not encouraging. "You know better than to

ask as much of me," he said gruffly, then climbed to the deck itself. "Rosamunde would feed me my own liver if I left you alone upon a deserted shore."

"I would not be alone," Vivienne insisted, grasping his sleeve when he would have brushed past her. "Please, Padraig, my path lies with Erik. I have need of your aid."

That man shook his head heavily. "You cannot ask me to endanger you, Vivienne. Such a deed would betray every obligation I owe to your family."

"But Erik and I have pledged a handfast."

"I care nothing for such pledges." He granted her a piercing glance and his tone softened. "He left you behind, Vivienne, do you not see the import of that?" He turned away then, clearly meaning to leave her there.

Vivienne lifted her chin. The import of that was that Erik meant to reclaim Blackleith alone, she knew it well, just as she knew that he had need of her aid to succeed. She was not certain what she could do, but she knew they were destined to be together.

Even if she had to help destiny.

"If you do not aid me, then I will persuade Rosamunde to do so," she said, not certain she could manage any such feat. "And she will take me to Blackleith, perhaps vexing the fairy with her delay in returning to Ravensmuir."

Padraig granted her a dark glance over his shoulder. "You will not so persuade her," he said. "Not when I and the fairy argue the opposing side." He shook his head and his voice softened again. "It is no easy circumstance you face here, Vivienne, though a woman of sense would accept the truth before her." He turned his back upon her once again, striding back toward the middle of the ship.

Vivienne was not prepared to accept this circumstance. She took a deep breath and looked down, seeing then the glint of silver in her hand.

"I will pay you," she cried with sudden vigor.

Padraig paused and turned slightly, a smile of amusement touching his lips. Indeed, his manner was slightly mocking, which only irked Vivienne. "With what? You have no coin with which to tempt me."

"I have better than coin." Vivienne took a deep breath and held out her hand, offering him the silver pin that Erik had just granted to her.

It was clear that Padraig recognized the pin. His eyes narrowed and his gaze flicked between it and Vivienne. He swallowed then and shook his head, taking a backward step as he did so. "You cannot surrender that to me. It is your sole gift from him, of that I am certain. There are items, Vivienne, that have a value beyond their market price. You cannot grant that to me."

"I will," Vivienne insisted, though the words nigh stuck in her throat. "It is but a trinket and as nothing compared to being with him. I need to follow him, Padraig. This price is small."

Padraig swore. He spat upon the deck, he glared at Vivienne, and when he spoke, he fairly growled. "Keep your treasure," he muttered but she did not move.

Vivienne feared he would deny her in truth, but he strode abruptly back past her and seized her elbow. "You had best have every item of which you have need, for we leave immediately. I would not have Rosamunde witness me at this deed."

"Thank you, Padraig!" Vivienne said, jubilant at his agreement. She stretched up and kissed his rough cheek. "All will be well, Padraig, you will see."

"All will be as it will be, that is all that we know for

certain." He wiped at his cheek, then aided her to climb over the rail. "Do not waste time with such foolery as gratitude," he said gruffly when she thanked him again, but the gleam in his eyes told Vivienne that he appreciated her thanks.

She sat in the boat, willing herself to be as light as possible. She fastened the pin upon her cloak and studied the coast as Padraig rowed closer, her heart leaping when she spied the two men climbing the rocks.

"There!" she said and Padraig grunted assent.

# *Chapter Fifteen*

~

"It APPEARS THAT WE WILL HAVE a guest shortly," Ruari said, and Erik looked back over his shoulder in surprise. But his companion spoke aright: Padraig rowed toward the shore once more, a smaller familiar figure in the boat with him.

The glint of the dawn on that tangle of auburn hair only confirmed the identity of the woman who drew ever nearer. Vivienne must have been watching him, for she waved gaily as soon as Erik's gaze landed upon her.

As if he should be gladdened to see her.

As if it had been but an oversight that he had left her behind.

Erik swore with rare vigor.

Ruari laughed, which was little consolation indeed. "There is no trouble so fearsome as that of a beauteous woman," that man said. "Unless, of course, it is a beauteous and stubborn woman."

Erik had no reply for that. He was too vexed with Vivienne for her pursuit. He climbed back down to the water, determined to ensure that Padraig took Vivienne back to

Rosamunde's ship, back to her family and comparative safety.

Vivienne must have anticipated his intent, however, for she climbed out of the boat before he could reach her. She stood in water past her knees and pushed Padraig and his boat back into deeper water with surprising strength.

"Halt!" Erik cried.

Vivienne cast him a defiant glance, then stepped into deeper water to give Padraig and the boat a harder shove.

Erik leapt down the last scree of rock and lunged into the shallows. "You shall not leave her here!" he roared at the cursed seaman.

"Row, Padraig, row!" Vivienne cried, evidently fully prepared to push the small boat further if necessary.

Padraig grinned as he dipped the oars into the water. The golden hoop in his ear glinted and he looked a disreputable rogue indeed. "I wish you well, for this lady has no shortage of determination," he shouted to Erik, then began to row.

"I wish you well, Padraig, in your quest at Ravensmuir!" Vivienne shouted and waved. Padraig said naught, merely labored against the waves with determination.

"Nay!" Erik bellowed. "Come back for the lady, you wretch!"

"He will not," Vivienne declared with fearsome certainty.

Erik knew that she was right. What was he to do? He could not abandon her alone on the shore. He could not swim to Rosamunde's ship with Vivienne on his back, particularly if she did not wish to go there.

There was a dangerous glint in Vivienne's eyes as she lifted her skirts and strode toward him, a glint that told Erik that the lady would accept only one solution to this dilemma. His mother's silver pin shone where she had pinned it upon her cloak, shone as it never had while he had worn it.

"We have a handfast," she began hotly, "and not a month of it is fulfilled as yet. You can return me to Kinfairlie in a year if we choose then to part."

"If we survive that long," Erik retorted. "I thought you a woman of good sense! What folly compelled you to follow me?"

"You have need of me," Vivienne said simply, then halted several steps away from him. Her skirts swirled around her, ebbing and flowing with the waves, the embroidery on the hems shining beneath the water. Tendrils of her hair blew around her shoulders and across her face and it seemed that her freckles had become more numerous these past days. Her bright gaze was steady, her back as straight as a well-honed blade, and there was determination in every line of her being.

She was valiant and breathtaking, a Valkyrie come for his soul and one whose conquest Erik felt little urge to contest.

"I have need of no woman at my side when I walk into such peril as this," he said, feeling he should protest her presence.

Vivienne propped her hands upon her hips and glared at him. "Perhaps you might recount for me again your reasons for seeking my hand? There must be a thousand maidens between here and Kinfairlie, yet you undertook such a journey for me alone. It seems only good sense that you would have had a reason why."

Erik felt the back of his neck heat, for he guessed the path of this argument. "You know the answer well enough."

"Remind me of it," she demanded.

"Because you were the sole other person who had not been deceived by Nicholas," he admitted, fully aware that his cause was already lost. "But you should have remained with your kin. Despite your perceptiveness, still I would not see you endangered."

Vivienne's sudden smile was so radiant that Erik blinked and his heart skipped a beat. "Because you are gallant in truth."

"Not so much that . . ." Erik began before the lady interrupted him again.

"True enough." Her gaze seemed suddenly more intent, so perceptive that Erik feared she could discern his every thought. "You fret for my welfare because you love me."

Erik stared at her. He knew he should protest her claim, knew he should pretend otherwise until he could confess his desire with an honorable pledge to wed her, but the words would not rise to his lips.

Undaunted, Vivienne smiled and laid her hand over the pin he had surrendered to her. "A man's deeds oft say more than his words," she said softly. "You love me as I love you, and thus our destiny is entwined forevermore. You might not have come from the realm of fairies, but you climbed through Kinfairlie's enchanted window to win my heart all the same."

Erik was struck dumb that she should understand him so readily. Her bold declaration should have troubled him more than it did, save that he knew she spoke the truth. He said naught, for he was glad to not be parted from her, even for the weeks it might take to reclaim Blackleith. Her presence would complicate matters but at the same time, the very sparkle of it gave him encouragement.

"You will remain out of all battles," he decreed, ignoring her triumphant laugh. Doubtless she had guessed why he had changed the subject. "And you will not argue with my every choice, but do what you are bidden to do."

Vivienne's smile only broadened. "I will do whatsoever needs to be done," she said with conviction, then spared a mischievous glance to Ruari and did a fair imitation of that man's manner. "Upon that you can rely."

Erik smiled despite himself. She took a step closer to him, majestic and fully persuaded of the merit of her argument. "Tell me what your eyes tell me," she coaxed. "Tell me that you are gladdened by my presence, that you could not imagine days and nights without me at your side." She laid her hand upon his arm and tipped her face up to his, her eyes shining and her ripe lips curved into a bold smile. "Tell me that you would have missed me in truth."

Erik was spared the need to reply. Vivienne made to ease closer but must have slipped on something under the water. She shrieked as her feet suddenly flew out from under her.

Erik caught her just before she landed in the sea. He held her fast against his chest and turned to make for the shore. "Aye, it does a man good to rescue damsels from their own folly," he muttered.

Vivienne laughed and kicked her feet, apparently untroubled by his gruff manner. "You lie, sir," she teased and Erik felt himself smile.

"Perhaps your presence is not so unwelcome as that," he acknowledged. Unable to resist temptation, he bent and kissed the smile from her lips.

He intended only a brief embrace, one that would ensure her silence, but as always, Vivienne's passion was beguiling indeed. She kissed him back with rare fervor, with the same hunger that he felt for her, and he was keenly aware of how long he had been without her wondrous caress. That familiar heat unfolded within him and his grip tightened upon her, his treacherous body more than prepared to return the lady's caress despite his inability to offer for her with honor.

Holding her fast in his arms made Erik realize how finely wrought his lady was, how vulnerable she could be. He recalled Beatrice's fate, feared for his daughters and feared yet more for Vivienne. He deepened his kiss, knowing she would taste his concern and not caring in the least.

"Aye, and that is why we have journeyed so far," Ruari shouted. "The better that you might stand in the sea, lad, and catch some ailment for which there is no cure. It would serve your brother well if you died of the ague afore you even reached his gates. Indeed, why else have we travelled all the length of Scotland, save for you two to rut in the sea?"

With some reluctance, Erik ended his embrace and strode to the shore. He set Vivienne on her feet, then discussed the best course onward with Ruari. Vivienne wrung out the length of her skirts, and appeared intent upon not slowing their pace to Blackleith.

They climbed the rocks once more just as the sun crested the horizon, and began their journey inland. Erik was the only one to glance back at the sea. The sails were unfurling on Rosamunde's ship and billowing in the wind, the vessel already moving to the south.

There was no turning back, no further source for aid. It was between himself and Nicholas, and whomever

Nicholas might have summoned to his side in Erik's absence.

IT GREW DARKER that afternoon, as slate-bellied clouds rolled across the sky and gathered ominously there. The wind came in fits and gusts and was colder than it had been earlier this day. Erik felt that he returned willingly to a nightmare. His scar seemed to burn upon his face, his flesh seemingly recalled the place where it had been so carved, and his limp felt more pronounced.

A shiver rolled over him when they crossed the boundary of Blackleith's lands, though Erik hoped the others did not notice his response.

It was not long before the dark thicket rose high on either side of the road, blocking out the sight of even the roiling sky. Its shadows were dark and deep; Erik's memories of this place were no less dark.

He paused at one end of the hedges that swallowed this increment of road, of this veritable tunnel wrought of vines and thorns, and swallowed.

"It was here then?" Ruari said quietly from beside him, no real question in his query.

Erik took a deep breath, fearful for a moment that he would not be able to pass this place. He recalled Vivienne upon the threshold of the labyrinth, determination gleaming in her eye. He spared her a glance to find her watching him as keenly as a sparrow watches a crumb.

She came to his side, though her touch upon his arm was fleeting. "It is a loathsome stretch of road," she mused, peering ahead into the shadows. "As if the place itself has a recollection of an injustice served here."

Erik knew that she had guessed the history of this place and the reason it troubled him so. He looked down the road again, trying to see it with her eyes, without his memories, and its shadows shrank somewhat. "It is but a stretch of road," he told her tersely, not truly believing as much himself. "It can possess no memory of treachery."

She tilted her head to regard him and he felt a surge of admiration at her resolve. He was convinced that her spirit could never be quailed, that she would stride with confidence into any situation, no matter how dire it appeared.

He fiercely wanted her to give his daughters such confidence.

"Then let us pass through it," she said, as mildly as if they discussed the crossing of a meadow. "For there is nothing to fear upon a stretch of mere road, even if the bushes shade the way."

She was right. Erik stepped into the darkness that consumed this length of road, Ruari upon one side and Vivienne on the other. The older man drew his blade and Erik did the same. The shadows swallowed them in a trio of steps and pressed against them, the vines seemed to whisper innuendo.

The passage seemed longer than Erik knew it to be, each step recalling some blow he had sustained. Indeed, he was besieged by vivid recollections, for he had not passed this way since his assault.

Here his horse had fallen, here the knife had touched his cheek, here he had crawled to the safety of the forest's embrace. Here he had lain bleeding for what had seemed an eternity.

Here he had lost all awareness, certain that he would never wake again.

He relived his worst nightmare upon that stretch of road, though through it all he was keenly aware of Vivienne's presence. She smelled of flowers and sunshine, she was a beacon of light in that treacherous passage so redolent of his past. Her step did not falter and she did not fall back to walk behind him.

There was a patina of sweat over Erik's flesh when they reached the other side of the passage, and the sudden brightness of the sunlight made him blink. He looked back, shuddered to his very toes, and saw only a shadowed course of road behind him.

"A mere stretch of road," Vivienne said, her gaze revealing that she knew it to be otherwise.

On impulse, Erik lifted Vivienne's hand to his lips and kissed her knuckles, knowing that her fortitude had seen him through that darkness.

He could only hope that he could win the chance to have her fortitude beside him for all time.

IT WAS LATE AFTERNOON of the second day in the forest when Vivienne had her first glimpse of Blackleith. They stood a good dozen paces short of the lip of the forest, the underbrush as high as their waists, the trees forming a canopy overhead as glorious as that of any cathedral. Ominous clouds crowded the sun, which had already begun its descent, but its rays touched the leaves overhead, gilding them to a glorious hue.

Blackleith's hall itself was an uncommon combination of Norman construction, local traditions, and a measure of ingenuity. It certainly was not so glorious as the fortresses of the south, neither so massive as Ravensmuir nor as artfully designed as Kinfairlie, but it was doughty and of considerable size.

It had been constructed with a square base. The lower part of the walls were wrought of cut stones fitted so tightly together that the wind probably could not whistle through them. The walls were thick, the better to keep heat within the building. There was only one portal near the ground and no windows below the second story.

The stones continued to the height of two men. The walls above were made of smaller, rounder stones, stacked according to their shape and size, then sealed in place with wattle and daub.

"The large stones were hewn further south," Ruari informed her, "upon the lands of the Earl of Sutherland. They were hauled up the river on barges when the water was low, pulled by ropes hauled by men upon the banks."

"But the stone changes," Vivienne noted.

"That is stone locally gathered, and time it took to collect them, to be sure." Ruari nodded sagely, as if he had gathered the stones himself.

"It would have been finer all wrought of the same stone," Erik said, "but the cost became too much for me."

"You had this built?" she asked, before she recalled that detail of Ruari's tale.

"Such as it is."

Vivienne heard a warning in Erik's tone, as if he would caution her that he was not overly affluent. She did not truly care, and if he did not realize as much, then she would not deign to tell him so.

She was beginning to doubt the merit of her decision to join him. Though he had held fast to her hand in that place where he had been assaulted, though he had kissed her hand with what had seemed to be gratitude, he had then dropped her hand as if her very touch scorched his flesh. Vivienne could make no sense of Erik's manner, though she wondered yet again whether proximity to Blackleith made him recall the great love he had shared with his wife Beatrice.

She ignored his comment and looked upon the holding he meant to regain. The roof of the hall was thick thatch, and the windows had solid wood shutters that could be latched over the openings when the wind was fierce.

Ruari seemed to have appointed himself as a guide of sorts, for he enthusiastically recounted the merits of Blackleith for Vivienne. She could feel Erik behind her, feel his gaze upon her, but she felt it time enough that he granted her a measure of encouragement.

Ruari pointed to the stone structure. "Within the hall, the main floor is used as both great hall and accommodation for guests, and while we abided there, Erik always claimed the upper floor for himself and his family. The second floor is reached by a ladder, though it is sufficiently large to be divided into chambers, to be sure, and the chimney passes through the floor on one side. In this way, the heat of the fire is shared throughout the structure."

"Most clever," Vivienne said.

Ruari nodded. "Indeed. There is a single hole in the roof, where the smoke is emitted. And Blackleith is the first abode in all of Sutherland with a moat dug around the hall, one so deep that the water within it is always dark and cold. Why, the Earl himself thought it such a sound notion that he talked of adding one to Dunrobin after he had seen this keep."

Vivienne noted that the summit of Blackleith's hall lacked a banner, like the heraldic ones that snapped in the wind above her family's keeps. "Is that Blackleith village?" she asked, indicating the cluster of peasant cottages beyond.

"Aye, and there is a small chapel, as well," Ruari noted. "See the abode with the dark door? That is the home of the blacksmith, his skill so considerable that even the Earl sends his favored weapons to this smith for repair. There is also a mill, run by a miller who divides his fee with the laird."

Beyond the village, sheep grazed, white against the purple heather, and a few chickens pecked the earth. Fields spread to the west, along the north bank of the river, though they were falling fallow. Blackleith had the appearance of a holding that had once been more prosperous than it was presently.

Children played on the edge of the fields and Vivienne turned to Erik. "Are your daughters among them?"

He shook his head, for clearly he had already sought their familiar figures, and his expression was somber.

Vivienne forced herself to sound cheerful. "Though they would scarcely play with the children of the peasants. Doubtless they are within the hall."

She saw Erik's gaze slip toward the chapel. She followed his gaze and caught her breath when she saw the small cemetery beside the chapel. Surely, he did not think that Nicholas had killed such young innocents?

"Nicholas is free with coin that is not his to spend, to be sure," Ruari complained, pointing a heavy finger to a structure beyond the keep which might have been new. "Though there is no coin more easily spent than that for which a man owes no accounting, upon that you can rely. Why, I heard tell once of a man in the employ of the Earl who travelled all the way to London for a trio of cloves, the better to make hippogras for the Earl, then demanded that the Earl pay the sum of his expenses, the bills for the stabling of his steed and lodgings for himself, no less every morsel of food that crossed his lips and ale that filled his belly. Now, there was a man with audacity and to spare!"

"It is a stable, and it is new," Erik said. "But what need has Nicholas of a stable? There is only the old grey ploughhorse at Blackleith, and she is well accustomed to the shanty beside the smith's cottage."

They all looked toward the smith's cottage, but no grey horse was tethered there.

"Where *is* the grey ploughhorse?" Ruari demanded with outrage. "What has he done with her? And how are the peasants to till the fields without her?"

"I am not certain that they have," Erik mused.

Upon closer inspection, Vivienne saw his point. The fields might not have been even tilled this year. Certainly it was not a familiar crop to her eyes that grew within them.

"There are not as many sheep as I might have expected, perhaps half as many as in former years," Erik noted with evident displeasure. "And the children look to me to be thin."

The smith's wife stepped out of their cottage to shout at the children and Ruari swore beneath his breath.

"She is but half her former self," he said, concern pulling his lips to a tight line.

Vivienne could have guessed what had happened to the bounty of Blackleith, for she recalled Nicholas's fondness for fine garb.

A trio of squires left the hall then, their silken tabards

glinting in the sunlight. They were plump, these three, and they laughed loudly as they made their way to the new barn.

The smith's wife regarded them with undisguised hostility. She folded her arms across her chest and glared at them, after she summoned the children to her side. They scampered into the cottage, as if fearful of the proud young men.

"Squires?" Ruari demanded with a wrinkled nose. "And what need has the Laird of Blackleith of squires? There are no tournaments hereabouts, upon that any thinking man can rely. Doubtless he has minstrels in his hall each night, and poets at the board! Perhaps there are pearls sewn in rows upon his chausses and gems ground into his ale each night!" Ruari flung out his hands. "While the people who labor beneath him are condemned to starve for lack of a ploughhorse. Doubtless he sold the old mare for a pittance! Your father must be turning within his grave at this, to be sure."

"Hush, Ruari, lest you be overheard."

Ruari snorted and might have said more despite Erik's warning if the squires had not led six splendid steeds out of the barn in that very moment. Instead he exhaled in awe and exasperation, then muttered a curse and shoved a hand through his hair. "It is no marvel that the smith's wife is so displeased. She was always a kindly one, but such abuses with coin as these would drive the sweetness from the ripest apple."

Vivienne watched as hooded falcons were brought on gloved fists, and sumptuous saddles were put upon the horses. The coats of these steeds gleamed, so well did they eat, and their necks arched proudly. They were fine steeds, to be sure, but it was clear how Nicholas had managed to afford them.

The miller's wife stepped out of her cottage, spared a glance for the smith's wife, then regarded the steeds with disdain. "We should demand that the laird grant us one of his horses," she called to the other woman. The squires pretended not to notice her, but Vivienne had no doubt they could hear her words. "Lest our children starve this winter."

"I know not what he thinks we shall eat," the smith's wife retorted. "Since the lambs are taken for the laird's own table and a man will lose a hand for taking so much as a squirrel from the forest. A child does not grow strong and tall upon onions, to be sure."

"I hear horseflesh is fine to eat," the first woman replied. "Though truly, hunger does make the best sauce."

The squires glared at the women and did not deign to reply.

"He would slaughter them all for such a crime," Ruari muttered and Erik did not doubt as much. "It is clear these steeds are prized beyond all else."

"How long will a woman watch her children go hungry?" Vivienne asked. "They may be so desperate that they do not care what his retaliation might be."

A fanfare sounded and a minstrel leapt out of the portal to the keep proper, sounding his horn as he did so. He too was dressed in fine silken garments of bright hues and he bowed low as he glanced back to that portal.

The women sneered, but their expressions became impassive as soon as a party of four nobles stepped through the doorway. Vivienne realized that they were not prepared to fully tempt the laird's wrath.

For it was none other than Nicholas Sinclair, garbed richly from head to toe, who strode across the bridge over the moat. His hair gleamed in the sunlight, the gems upon his fingers flashed. He laughed at some comment made by the other man who strolled with him, the handsome group making their way toward the saddled steeds.

The women wore clothing so ornate as to have cost a king's ransom, their tightly laced vests trimmed with ermine, their sleeves hanging to the very ground, their skirts and sleeves hemmed with deep golden embroidery thick with gems. Both wore gloves of colored leather, both wore their hair curled up beneath elaborate caps adorned with massive feathers. Two maids scampered behind the group, giggling with each other and grimacing at the mud underfoot.

Vivienne turned to her companions, intending to make some comment about the women's rich garb, but the shocked expressions upon the men's faces stole whatever she might have said. Erik seemingly could not look beyond the woman who took his brother's elbow. "What is amiss?" she asked. "You must have expected to see Nicholas here."

Erik swallowed and bowed his head.

Ruari looked to Vivienne with sympathy in his eyes. "The woman who walks with Nicholas."

"She is garbed as richly as a queen and looks most delighted with herself," Vivienne said, not understanding the reason for their dismay. "You must have seen such fine garb in your journey. To be sure, the peasants have contributed the coin and that is shocking, but . . ."

"She is Beatrice," Ruari said grimly.

Vivienne looked between the two men in dismay, but

Erik's features might have been wrought of stone. "Not Erik's wife, Beatrice. She is dead."

Ruari shook his head. "She appears most hale."

And Vivienne understood then the fullness of the challenge before her. No wonder Erik looked like a man struck to stone! His beloved yet lived!

She turned back to watch Erik's wife, tears blurring her vision. She had erred in truth, for not only did Erik love his wife, but his wife still drew breath.

Which meant that Vivienne could never win his regard for her own.

Impulse had steered her false.

BEATRICE WAS ALIVE!

Erik could not believe the evidence of his own eyes. Several matters which had always confused him, however, began to make a dreadful sense.

Why had there been no hint of her presence when he had returned to Blackleith in the Earl's company? Why had no one been willing to tell the Earl outright about her fate? Erik suspected that even Nicholas knew that the Earl of Sutherland would not be hasty to endorse an immediate match with his late brother's wife.

But Beatrice's survival had tremendous import. Erik had committed adultery with Vivienne, albeit unknowingly. He had sinned, and he did not imagine that any judge would grant him clemency for his ignorance. How diligently had he sought Beatrice, after all?

So, he had soiled Vivienne twice: once in the claiming of her maidenhead, then again in committing adultery. There was no question of his embracing her again, not until he could be certain of how matters would be resolved.

Erik urged Ruari and Vivienne further back into the shadows as he considered the best course. The foursome at Blackleith's hall, meanwhile, mounted their steeds and accepted hunting hawks upon their fists. The three squires mounted three fine palfreys and the nine steeds made no haste toward the distant forest.

"Do you think the laird will cast alms from his hall if he takes a hart?" the smith's wife demanded.

The miller's wife shrugged. "He will eat it all, or cast it to his dogs before he grants charity to those beneath his hand, upon that you can rely."

"Aye, you speak the truth in that." The two women exchanged a look of resignation, then returned to their cottages with drooping shoulders.

Erik barely glanced at Vivienne. "You will remain hidden here," he said tersely, unwilling to risk her life. He had already led her to sin and thus endangered her very soul. He could not bring himself to look at her fully, so ridden with guilt was he. "And I will hear no protest on this matter."

"Of course," Vivienne said, so demure that she might have been another woman.

Erik looked at her then and was shaken by her pallor. She stood dejected, as never he had seen her, the bright sparkle of her eyes dimmed to naught. She sighed and sat down, apparently so burdened with patience that she had not the urge to do any deed at all.

Guilt stabbed through him. Clearly, she felt the weight of their sinful deed as fully as he did.

Erik did not know what to say. At the same time, he could not leave without a consoling word, for he knew not whether he would return. He took a step toward her and she averted her face, though still he saw the shimmer of her unshed tears. "I am sorry," he said quietly. "I did not know."

"I know," Vivienne whispered and the first of her tears fell. "I know, just as I know that I have only my foolish trust to blame."

"You may be many things, Vivienne Lammergeier, but you are no fool."

She looked up through her tears and managed a tremulous smile. "I thank you for that courtesy, though I fear you see more merit than I truly possess."

"Impossible," Erik said and their gazes held for a potent moment. He saw her hope, he guessed what she desired of him, and he was sorely tempted to grant it to her.

But he would pledge love when he could not act upon it honorably, not merely to halt a woman's tears.

He inclined his head once in silent salute, then turned away, summoning Ruari with a flick of his fingers. "We will seize the maids' horses, for they do not look to be competent riders," he said. "Then I will pursue Nicholas, wheresoever he might flee."

The older man nodded and grunted, sparing Vivienne a fatherly glance. He stepped to her side and laid a hand upon her shoulder and Erik heard his gruff words. "This tale is not over, lass, upon that you can rely. You know as well as I that the sole folly that can do a soul injury is to lose hope when success is deceptively close at hand. All looks most dire just before matters turn in one's favor, just as the night is most black before the dawn."

"I thank you, Ruari, for your sound counsel," Vivienne said and the older man puffed with pride.

"And a good portent it is that *someone* thinks my opinion worthy of merit, to be sure," he said with forced cheer. He then strode past Erik with marked impatience, as if he had been waiting upon the younger man. He even snapped his fingers. "Come along, lad, the hunt is not begun while one lingers in conversation."

Vivienne and Erik exchanged a glance that warmed Erik's heart before he turned to Ruari. The two men broke into a run then, circling around the meadow while staying within the protective shadows of the forest.

A rumble of thunder echoed in the distance and the sun was swallowed finally by the dark clouds. Those clouds built ever higher and blacker in the sky overhead, and the thunder sounded again, as if it would warn Nicholas Sinclair that his reckoning came due.

Erik knew that no warning could prepare his brother for what was to come.

# *Chapter Sixteen*

I⊤ WAS NOT LIKE ROSAMUNDE to feel trepidation, but she felt it to her very bones as Ravensmuir loomed high on the cliff above her ship. They approached the coast in early evening, as seldom she had before. This time, Rosamunde saw no point in subterfuge.

Indeed, she hoped that Tynan would meet her. She would have to seek him out either way, for she had need of the ring she had returned to him to sate this vengeful spriggan.

The sailors were hushed. They could be superstitious, as Rosamunde knew, and their hesitation to serve a woman would only have been increased by the tidings that she was haunted by a malicious fairy. Padraig stood by her side, like a guardian determined to see an unpleasant duty completed by his ward.

Matters had been strained between them since Rosamunde had learned of Vivienne's departure with Padraig's aid. By the time she had awakened, the ship had been miles south, though, and there had been no real chance of pursuing Erik and Vivienne. Now that her temper had cooled, Rosamunde had to admit that Padraig had meant well.

That did not keep her from fretting about her niece, however.

Clouds scuttled across the sky on this day, which already was touched with rose, and the keep was silhouetted against the painted sky. Rosamunde had to admit to herself that for a pile of ancient stones, Ravensmuir had a certain dignity that prompted one's admiration.

"We cannot even know if the spriggan is yet with us," she complained, as irritable that she was compelled to serve the will of another as for the deed itself.

Padraig snorted. "I doubt it would abandon you now. The creature seems to doubt your intent, though I could not venture a guess as to why."

Rosamunde ignored that comment. Padraig was welcome to end his days in Sicily, to her thinking, for he had grown overly sullen and outspoken of late.

But then, she had possessed less than her usual charm since she and Tynan had argued. The shadow fell over the ship from the cliffs that towered high above and Rosamunde shivered.

"I will go into the caverns alone," she said abruptly. "For I do not know what will happen and would not endanger any of you."

"I will accompany you," Padraig said, his voice dropping in his concern.

"No, not this time." Rosamunde turned to face the man who had sailed in her company the longest of all men. There was silver at Padraig's temples now and lines creased his tan beside his eyes. His eyes had narrowed, though they still were a vibrant hue, and he laughed less than once he had. Rosamunde had a sudden vision of him sailing southward, upon this very ship, without her at the helm. She was oft visited by such visions and knew better than to distrust them.

She laid her hand upon his tanned forearm, knowing that this would be their last parting and feeling a measure of dread at what must lie before her. "Take the ship," she said, her words husky. "See me ashore, then take the ship and sail south to Sicily."

Padraig frowned. "But what of the contents?"

"Sell them, sell them wherever you can fetch a fair price for them, and keep the proceeds for your own." Rosamunde could not look upon him. She was unaccustomed to granting such a large gift, and she feared Padraig would proudly disdain it, although it was his due.

"But . . ."

"I owe you no less for all your years of faithful service."

"But the ship?"

"Sell it as well, or keep it for your own. I do not care, Padraig." Rosamunde heaved a sigh and looked up at shadowed Ravensmuir once more. "I have had wealth and I have had love. Love is better." She forced a smile for him, for he clearly thought her relieved of her wits, and blinked back her tears. "You will fare well enough," she said gruffly. "I have seen it and we know that whatsoever I see, will be true."

Padraig took an unsteady breath himself, his gaze trailing up the cliffs that confronted them. "What do you see for yourself?"

Rosamunde shook her head.

It was Padraig who looked away then, a frown furrowing his brow. "I always said that you saw farther than most, but could not see what was before your own eyes," he said, his manner both rough and affectionate. "Be cautious, Rosamunde, though it is not in your nature. This fairy means you harm, and even if you do surrender the ring to her, her taste for vengeance may not be sated." He lowered his voice. "And even if the fairy spares you, the Laird of Ravensmuir may not."

"It does not matter," Rosamunde said, knowing that to be true. "My fate lies here, as always it did, and the only course forward is through Ravensmuir's caverns." She turned and shook his hand lest she make the parting more difficult than it had need of being. "Farewell, Padraig. May the wind always fill your sails when you have need of it."

To her surprise, he caught her in a tight hug, then released her abruptly. He stared at the deck, and his lips worked for a moment in silence before he found the words. The ones he finally found surprised her, as she was seldom surprised. "We have fought back to back a hundred times, Rosamunde, and always I will consider you to be my friend." He looked at her, his expression fierce, as if daring her to argue with him. "You have been my only friend, but a friend of such merit that I had need of no other."

"No soul ever had a friend more loyal than I found in you," she said.

"I did," he replied.

They both looked away then, Padraig to the sea and Rosamunde to the dark portal of the cavern. Never had they spoken such heartfelt words to each other and Rosamunde knew they would never have done so had they both not feared that this parting would be their last.

"I will wait for the tide," Padraig said, his words hoarse. "It does not turn for a short time yet. If you have need of me, if you have need of this ship, you have but to hail me."

Rosamunde knew she would not hail him, no matter what greeted her in the caverns. She also knew that she would not persuade Padraig of that simple truth. Her destiny awaited her here, whatever it was, and she knew it to her very marrow. She was afraid, as any soul of sense would have been afraid of such a reckoning.

But destiny could not be evaded. It would wait for her, it would turn her steps back to Ravensmuir time and again until she faced her due.

She chose to face it now.

Rosamunde and Padraig parted in hasty silence then, for there was no more to be said. She climbed down the rope ladder under the watchful gazes of the hired seamen and took up the oars in the small boat tethered to the ship. She rowed toward the dark mouth of the cavern with vigor, revelling in her own strength and the splash of the sea water upon her skin. The sea lifted her and seemed to push her forward, the sun made its surface look to be embellished with gems.

Rosamunde felt vitally alive and appreciative of the abundant gifts she had been given. She had always had good health, she had known a potent love, she had always been uncommonly fortunate. She had cheated Death a dozen times at least, she had wrought better terms from Fortune time and again, and she had never lost a man at sea.

It was only when the chill of the cliff's shadow enfolded her that Rosamunde wondered whether her allotment of good luck had all been consumed, if she was left in this moment with no more.

It was then, for the first time, that she fancied she heard the spriggan laugh.

Darg's was not a merry laugh, to be sure.

Rosamunde tethered her boat, not sparing a backward glance to her ship even as she strode off into the cavern. A chasm rent the path from the pool to the large cavern in these days, a chasm with dark water low in it. Rosamunde well remembered its eerie clutch from her last visit here. She lit a torch with a flint she always carried, then lifted it high as she strode further into the labyrinth.

She wondered whether the spriggan accompanied her or not, but had no way of knowing. She could not see the creature and if it matched its steps to hers, it laughed no longer.

Rosamunde moved with quick purpose, following the course she knew as well as the lines of her own hand. She would climb to Tynan's chamber, she decided, for that was where she had left the ring and that was where she was most likely to encounter him alone. If he was not there, if the ring was not there, then she would decide upon an alternate course at that point.

Rosamunde had never been troubled by the labyrinth, though she had known many over the years who found it upsetting. She had always thought of it as corridors, useful corridors filled with useful trinkets, a maze filled with only intriguing surprises. On this day, however, it smelled different to her. On this day, she could feel menace emanating from its walls.

Perhaps it was because the labyrinth was empty as she had never known it to be. Perhaps it was because the relics that had filled the crates stacked here previously had provided a certain mystical protection, a protection which was now gone.

Perhaps Rosamunde was simply afraid.

She walked more quickly, turning a number of corners with a lack of caution that was not characteristic of her, and strode without hesitation into the single large cavern from which most paths branched.

Rosamunde halted so quickly then that she almost stumbled.

Another torch spilled a puddle of light upon the hewn rock floor on the opposite side of the chamber. The man bearing that torch stood with his boots braced against the floor. He did not so much as move, though she felt the weight of his gaze upon her. Despite herself, her heart skipped in a most unruly fashion.

For the man who awaited her was Tynan Lammergeier, Laird of Ravensmuir, love of her life.

VIVIENNE HAD BEEN STEERED FALSE by an impetuous choice a dozen times, but never had she erred so thoroughly as this. She sat dejected in the forest near Blackleith, caring little that heavy raindrops began to fall. She drew her hood over her head, planted her chin on her fist and sighed.

Erik and Ruari had run into the forest and now could not be discerned. Nicholas and his hunting party had disappeared into the distant smudge of forest. The two discontent wives had returned to their cottages, the children had gone home and even the chickens had disappeared.

She had never felt so alone in all her days.

Worse, her fate was her own fault. Matters were muddled in truth. Had she been Madeline, all would have come together perfectly at the end, but Vivienne had never possessed Madeline's ability to note even those details set against her. She oft underestimated the fullness of the challenge she undertook, and in this case, her choice to pursue Erik would affect only her own fate.

Alexander would never find a spouse for her now, of that she was certain. In truth, Vivienne did not much care, for the sole spouse she desired was a man who clearly had a spouse already.

She wished fervently though that her bold choice did not reflect badly upon the natures—and the marital opportunities—of her remaining unwed sisters.

THE MAIDS WERE AS INEPT AS ERIK had suspected. He and Ruari crept up behind the two women with ease, for they were unaware of their surroundings.

Save for the location of their patroness. The pair disparaged her choice of garb and manners with savage glee and ensured that they could not be overheard. The maids lingered on the perimeter of the forest, letting their horses graze as they laughed over their lady's choice of silks.

"That hue of gold makes her look to be dead," chortled the one.

"And the embroidery is more fitting for a wall tapestry than a noblewoman's hems," said the other.

"Yet Lord Henry continues to pay the price of her every whim. Is the man blind or besotted?"

The second maid laughed. "He cares not what the cost is to keep her blind."

"What is that to mean?"

"You will know when he finds you alone in the larder one night."

"You cannot mean that he beds you?" the first gasped.

The other was clearly not prepared to share all of her secrets. "This cursed rain," she muttered. "I seem to always be obliged to relieve myself." She dismounted, leaving the other with her thousand questions, and made her way into the forest.

Fortunately, there was that length of rope in the saddlebag, the one Erik had used to scale Kinfairlie's walls. It would be of use this day, for certain. He eased it from the bag and pursued the maid stealthily. She was just in the midst of lifting her chemise and utterly unaware of any threat when Erik pounced upon her.

She lay trussed on the forest floor, eyes wide in astonishment, in no time at all. She made but one sound of protest before Erik shoved a length of cloth into her mouth.

That sound was sufficient to kindle the other maid's curiosity. "Adele?" she asked, then Erik heard her dismount as well. "Adele? Did you slip?"

She asked no more before Erik granted her the same fate as her companion. The two women wriggled together helplessly on the ground. "I have need of your horses," Erik said to them. "You will be released when all is resolved."

They did not appear to be reassured by this pledge, but he had no time to further placate them. He and Ruari swung into the saddles and rode in pursuit of Nicholas.

VIVIENNE DID NOT KNOW how long she sat despondent, but it was raining in earnest when six horses came galloping wildly across the meadows. So erratic was their pace that

Vivienne rose to her feet, convinced that they were a mark of bad news.

But Nicholas was not among them. It was the other three nobles from the hunting party, the two women and the other man, followed by the three squires. All of them were soaked to the skin, their fine garb looking bedraggled in the rain.

Beatrice fairly flung her hunting hawk at a squire, then marched into the hall. Vivienne bristled that any soul would treat a tethered and hooded—thus helpless—creature so poorly. A peregrine was a noble huntress, worthy of respect for its nature as well as the sheer cost of acquisition and training. Daughter of a family engaged in the training and trade of such birds, Vivienne was outraged.

She might well loose that bird, just to ensure that it did not have to endure such treatment again. It would be a small strike against the woman whose very existence had shattered Vivienne's dream, and perhaps a petty one, but a deed that would aid the bird which could not aid itself.

Vivienne eased closer to the lip of the forest. The other couple remained upon their steeds, though the woman complained bitterly about the weather. The squires made themselves scarce, hastening toward the stable with the hawks. Their palfreys stood with their heads down, clearly discontent to be left in the rain.

Two of the boys then made their way into the hall, pausing en route for a quick word with the man, while the third cast the barest glance toward the hall before he mounted his palfrey and gave the beast his heels. He galloped in the direction the party had just come, and did so with such haste that he might have feared to be caught.

With that squire's departure, Vivienne sensed that

something was afoot. This party must have seen Erik to have come so quickly from the forest, though their plan was far from clear. She would listen, and perhaps she would hear some detail that would be of aid to Erik. The forest curved closest to the new stable and she made her way to that point, clinging cautiously to the shadows though the rain would make it more difficult for them to see her.

"Look," the noblewoman said, her shrill voice carrying easily to Vivienne's ears. "The finest damask that could be had in Paris, the most choice samite from Constantinople, and all of it ruined! What person of sense would abide in this foul clime? If it does not rain, then the rain has halted but moments before, or the rain will begin in moments." She shuddered elaborately. "And the fare is scarce worth the journey. I tell you, Henry, if I am compelled to ingest another hare, no less one with all its bones yet lingering in some thin excuse for a mustard sauce, then I shall scream in fury."

"We leave shortly, my love," the man said calmly. He was clearly accustomed to his wife's manner, though he glanced grimly skyward. "Must we leave this very night?" he asked plaintively. "Surely the rain will halt by the morning?"

"We cannot leave soon enough, in my opinion, though it is vulgar for Beatrice to hasten us from her portal on such an evening as this. I always knew her to be common beneath her fine attire, to be sure. Why do we linger at all? Why do we even wait for Beatrice and her foul children?"

Vivienne's ears pricked at this morsel. She slipped around the stable and strained her ears to hear more.

"Because I have given her my pledge that we shall protect them, of course, my dear."

The wife turned upon her spouse in vexation. "But why? What earthly good are a pair of young girls? If they were boys, they might train in your service, but *girls*? They will have to be wed and they will have to be garbed, and almost certainly they will be as vain as their mother, which will cost you dearly in the end. And for what? They can scarcely be said to be of noble birth, and I doubt they are beauteous enough to make a good match on their own merit alone. Girls are impossible, after all. Look how unreliable those maids have been! They cannot keep themselves in their saddles. I do not care if it takes them all the week to walk back to the hall: Beatrice is welcome to their abilities." She tossed her head. "I do not know what you were thinking in making such an agreement."

"Beatrice's daughters will make a fitting donation to the local convent, of course," the man said softly and his wife stared at him in silent awe.

Vivienne almost gasped aloud, so great was her shock. They could not do this to Erik's daughters! It was one matter to donate one's own child to a life of contemplation, but no man had the right to do as much with another man's child.

How dare they scheme thus?

But clearly, she had not heard incorrectly. The woman smiled. "Oh Henry, you are clever. We shall make a contribution and that without emptying our treasury. Will we not have to make a donation for their care, though?"

"Rely upon me, my dear. I shall make a fair wager for them, one way or the other." Henry laughed shortly. "After all, if the convent does not desire them as they are, then we can sell them into service."

Never! Vivienne forgot the falcons in her newfound determination to aid Erik's daughters.

The woman chortled. "We shall see some advantage from visiting this ghastly abode. I like your scheme well, Henry." She smiled then, as Beatrice tugged two small girls out of the hall of Blackleith. "And here are your beloved angels!" she called in honeyed tones.

The two girls scarce behaved like angels. It was clear to Vivienne that they did not accompany their mother willingly, as if they guessed the fate in store for them. The younger one dragged her feet in sullen discontent, until Beatrice muttered something and caught the child around the waist, lifting her with an effort.

"Come along, my dear Astrid," she said, as if the child was merely slow. A young serving girl, perhaps of fifteen summers, her eyes narrowed, slipped through Blackleith's door to watch. She made no move to aid Beatrice, but folded her arms across her chest and stood her ground.

"They do not seem to wish to leave you, dear Beatrice," the noblewoman said, her words too sweet.

"They were sleeping," Beatrice insisted. "And a child awakened suddenly oft awakens in less than sweet temper." She pressed a kiss to Astrid's temple and the child snarled openly at her. Beatrice feigned a laugh. "Oh, she is so accustomed to her nanny that she scarce recognizes me when she is sleepy!"

The little girl punctuated that comment with a hefty kick to her mother's leg. Beatrice grimaced, then swung the child into her arms, holding her elbows and knees fast against her own chest. Astrid began to kick and struggle with vigor then. Beatrice marched toward the couple, a gleam of determination in her eyes.

"Come, Erin, you could be of aid in this," Beatrice said to the girl standing by the portal.

That girl shook her head and did not move.

"I shall see you whipped for such disobedience," Beatrice said, even as she held fast to the flailing child.

Erin smiled. "You shall have to catch me first," she said, then turned and fled into the forest.

The three nobles looked after the girl, aghast at her disobedience.

"One cannot find a decent nanny in this land, to be certain," Beatrice said, clearly speaking through gritted teeth. "You can imagine the difficulties I face. I am convinced that the girls will be well served by the journey south and you will not regret this small favor to me. Truly, they are usually sweet beyond compare."

The older girl, Mairi, trailed behind her mother sullenly, clearly having no inclination to be sweet.

"Hasten yourself!" Beatrice snapped at the girl, whose expression turned mutinous even as her mother pivoted to smile sunnily at her guests.

With three younger sisters and a house that had not always been tranquil, Vivienne knew the gleam that lit Mairi's eyes. She braced herself for trouble, the kind of trouble a small angry child can make.

Mairi moved with uncommon speed. She leapt forward with vigor and trod determinedly upon her mother's hems. She ground the finely embroidered cloth into the mud with her heel, so vengeful that Vivienne knew there was no affection between mother and this child.

So long and elaborate were Beatrice's hems that that woman managed half a dozen steps, unaware of one child's deeds as she struggled with the other, before the cloth was suddenly taut around her knees. Beatrice only had time to gasp and see the truth before she tripped on her full skirts and fell into the mud. Astrid took advantage of her mother's loosed grasp to leap from her arms. Vivienne saw Mairi's face light with satisfied malice as Beatrice's kirtle audibly tore.

Beatrice spun with startling speed and smacked Mairi full across the face. The little girl sat down in the mud with a splat and began to wail in protest. Beatrice hauled her hems out of the muck with vigor, snatched up Astrid and cast that child into the noblewoman's lap.

The woman recoiled in disgust. "I cannot carry the child!" she cried, raising her hands as if she feared to so much as touch the girl. She looked about herself in dismay. "Surely, they have a maid, or a nanny, or some person who must accompany them. Look how the child soils my kirtle! *Henry!*"

Astrid took one look at the woman's face and began to cry in earnest. Beatrice tried to haul Mairi closer to the couple but that child was sufficiently tall and heavy that she could not be readily moved against her will.

The squires, meanwhile, brought several plump saddlebags from the hall. They moved with purpose as they burdened the pair of palfreys still standing in the rain.

"You must go with Henry and Arabella," Beatrice told the protesting Mairi. "They will give you fine gifts, beautiful garb, and fare so delicious that you will think yourself in paradise."

Mairi glared at her mother. "Do you accompany them?" she demanded with suspicion.

Beatrice smiled for her guests. "I know that you will miss me, Mairi, but I must remain here for the moment. We shall see each other shortly." She bent to kiss the child's cheek, but Mairi pushed her aside, leaving a muddy handprint upon Beatrice's cheek.

The little girl rose from the mud, marched to Henry's stirrup, then lifted her hands toward him. "Up," she commanded, and Henry seemed to not know what to do.

Vivienne imagined that this pair suddenly saw the merit of the two maids they had abandoned in the forest.

And that granted her an idea. She fastened her cloak more fully about herself, the better to hide her fine kirtle. Her cloak was soiled so would not raise suspicions. She hastily moved Erik's pin so that it was hidden beneath her cloak, then stepped out of the shadows, her hood pulled over her hair.

"I would offer my aid," she said and the group spun in their shock to regard her.

"Who are you?" Beatrice demanded.

"I am a serving woman, a freewoman seeking a noble family to serve. I heard tell at the abode of the Earl of Sutherland that there was a fine abode further north, perhaps in need of my skills, and so I came this far."

"What skills have you?" Arabella demanded.

"I have been a wet nurse," Vivienne lied. "And I have been responsible for young girls. I can teach embroidery and matters of etiquette."

"Then what brings you so far?" Beatrice demanded. "Why did you leave your previous abode?"

Vivienne wished she could have conjured a flush. "I feared," she began, striving to think of some plausible detail. Henry granted her an appraising glance, one that did make her blush in truth and granted her an idea. "I feared to become a wet nurse again," she said and the women nodded in unison.

Arabella jabbed Henry with one fingertip. "Fortu-

nately, you will have no such fears in our household —
will she, Henry?"

"Of course not, my dear," that man said with some discomfiture. "But are you certain that we have need of such
a woman? It will be another mouth at our board, after
all."

"Up!" demanded Mairi. Astrid grasped a pearl sewn to
Arabella's kirtle and did so with such vigor that the gem
popped from the cloth. It sprang into the mud and rolled
away. Vivienne hastened to pick it up and offer it to the
noblewoman.

"You must have journeyed far," Arabella said, her
gaze assessing as she accepted the pearl.

"My lord's lust was potent indeed," Vivienne said, her
cheeks stained an even darker hue at this confession.

The woman assessed her openly, then nodded once. "If
you so tempt another nobleman in my abode, I shall see
you flogged."

"Understood, my lady." Vivienne bowed her head as
the servants did at Kinfairlie. "It is my intent to please,
my lady." Vivienne emphasized that by picking Astrid out
of the woman's lap and cuddling her close. The child regarded her with suspicion, but to Vivienne's relief, she
did not scream.

"Baldwin, you shall ride along with Algernon and
grant the other palfrey to the maid," Henry commanded
his squires. "Come, if we ride immediately, we can reach
the hospitality of the Earl's hall before midnight."

It was Mairi that almost foiled Vivienne's scheme, for
once in her lap, the child slipped beneath Vivienne's
cloak. Vivienne thought the girls were cold and let them
ease closer, but Mairi's fingers rose to touch the silver
pin.

Her fingers closed over it and Vivienne's heart nigh stopped. The clutch of the child's fingers and her sudden stillness made Vivienne fear that the child knew the pin.

"Shhhhhh," Vivienne whispered to her, striving to not attract the attention of the noble couple riding just ahead. "There is no need to cry. We shall be in a warm bed soon enough, with fine fare in our bellies."

Mairi continued to finger the pin, her bright gaze—of a vivid blue reminiscent of Erik's own—more knowing than it should have been for her age. She held Vivienne's gaze so solemnly, her grip locked upon the pin, that Vivienne wondered how much this child recalled of her father and his supposed demise.

"I SAW THE SHIP," Tynan said, clearing his throat as if he felt as awkward in this moment as Rosamunde.

She said nothing.

"I saw the ship and I knew you returned. I had hoped that you might come alone."

"Why?" Rosamunde asked, not daring to hope for any kindness from him after his harsh words when last they had parted.

Tynan inclined his head and seemed unduly fascinated with the toes of his boots. "Because I owe you an apology, and I lack grace with such matters."

Rosamunde felt her resistance to him soften, for she knew apologies came no more readily to this proud man's lips than to her own. "You lack grace in no matters."

A fleeting smile curved his mouth then, easing the tension from his face for a bare instant before it disappeared and he frowned anew. "I thank you for that, though I think you too kind." Tynan took a few steps closer and Rosamunde saw new lines of care around his eyes.

Perhaps this interval had been as difficult for him as for her. It was a tantalizing possibility.

Tynan swallowed visibly. "I believed the worst of you when you supported Rhys FitzHenry's suit for Madeline, instead of asking you for the truth of what you knew." He referred to their resounding battle over the welfare of their niece, a fight which had occurred months ago yet still had the power to infuriate Rosamunde. "I assumed he truly was a traitor to have been so charged, but you must have known that they were false charges brought against him."

"I did."

"I apologize that I believed you had cast Madeline into peril for no good cause. I was too troubled to see that it would have been unlike you to have done so, for you have always been protective of your own."

Rosamunde inclined her head in acknowledgement. "You were hardly unjustified in assuming that I consorted with scoundrels. I have been known to do so."

"I was unjust." Tynan cleared his throat again and took another step closer. Rosamunde could see the glint of his eyes now, the quickness of his breath. Could he feel as much trepidation as she did?

"And I apologize," he continued, "for you accused me rightly of treating you unfairly. I knew that you believed I meant to wed you when we chose to auction the relics and yet I did not make the truth of my intent clear. I knew that you would believe our future began when we spent another night abed, but I could not bear to confess the truth to you — nor could I bear to part without loving one last time. And I was wrong, as well, to deny you any legacy from Ravensmuir."

Rosamunde cleared her throat in her turn and took a step closer. "I should not have stolen one," she admitted and was rewarded by the brief flash of Tynan's smile.

"You were provoked."

"I was furious."

He bowed his head. "I was a fool."

Rosamunde almost reached for him but then she realized that he had pledged nothing different. She waited, watching him with care. He lifted his left hand and she saw the glint of the silver ring she had previously worn. It graced his smallest finger, though still it nearly filled the knuckle.

She glanced up and found Tynan watching her. "Wed me, Rosamunde," he whispered hoarsely. "If you can forgive me."

"But what of Ravensmuir?"

He sighed and frowned and looked away. "I fear it lost."

Anger lit within Rosamunde and she lifted her chin. "So you would reconcile with me because you have nothing left to protect? I will be no man's consolation!"

Tynan lifted a hand to halt her tirade and shook his head. "Archibald Douglas would treat with me, but the longer I delay, the more onerous his terms become. He pushes me further each day. I was prepared to wed a woman of his family to seal the treaty, if that would save Ravensmuir, but I am not prepared to disavow my nephew Malcolm."

"They will leave Ravensmuir standing only if you breed an heir with one of their own," Rosamunde guessed and Tynan nodded.

"And Malcolm will be left with nothing, despite my vow to make him my heir." Tynan raised a fist and anger flashed in his eyes. "A pledge made should be a pledge kept, and a man should respect the vows of any man with whom he would treat. Douglas, though, grants no weight to pledges that do not serve his ambition. I will endure his demands no longer, though it means that I will not be able to keep him so readily from my gates."

"Ravensmuir will be besieged by her neighbors," Rosamunde suggested softly.

"We will be assaulted, to be sure." Tynan shrugged, his eyes gleaming. "Perhaps Ravensmuir would have been attacked at any rate. Perhaps the bride they would have chosen for me would have opened the portcullis for them. I cannot know. I do not care." His voice rose. "I have been pushed overmuch and I will be pushed no further." He drew the ring from his finger and offered it to Rosamunde, his gaze intent. "Wed me, Rosamunde, for I love you in truth."

But Rosamunde hesitated. Here was all she had believed she desired, and yet, a dreadful portent stilled her steps. She looked at the ring that once she had worn and trembled at some dark omen it bore. She feared then that Tynan's love for Ravensmuir would come between them once again.

"Wed you because you no longer care what the neighbors think of your bride?" she teased.

Tynan laughed. "They are a deceitful and warmongering lot. No soul of good sense could care what they think." He traced the curve of her cheek with a fingertip then, a glow lighting in his eyes. His voice was husky when he continued. "I have missed you, Rosamunde. Accept my ring and come again to my bed."

"I thought I would not make a suitable Lady of Ravensmuir."

"Only because I was fool enough to insist as much. I was wrong."

"Aye, you were," Rosamunde said. "How fortunate you are that I am a woman with a forgiving nature."

"You are not, which is why your forgiveness would be a gift beyond expectation." Tynan arched a brow.

She was a fool, afraid to accept what she had yearned for when it came within her grasp. There was no shadow ahead, only the unfamiliar prospect of being bound to another soul.

Rosamunde smiled and stepped forward, breaching the last gap between them. "I think our mutual apologies accepted," she said and lifted her hand. Tynan held the circle of the ring between finger and thumb, and Rosamunde smiled as he slipped its weight over her knuckle once more. The silver shimmered, the ring slid down her finger, then an unholy scream filled the cavern.

# Chapter Seventeen

~

Erik and Ruari pursued the hunting party even as fat drops of rain began to plummet from the sky.

"This is to our advantage," Ruari claimed with pleasure. "The women will return to the hall, to be certain. And when the party turns back, we shall be able to catch them for certain."

They gave the palfreys their heels and the beasts galloped onward along the path beaten down in the forest undergrowth. There was a bright point ahead, then the horses leapt out into a clearing. The change was astonishing, no less because a deluge of rain poured suddenly upon them.

Erik sputtered and shook his hair from his eyes. The horse slowed its pace and he saw why.

A riding party emerged from the forest on the far side of the clearing.

The horses nickered at each other. Erik had no time to draw his hood over his head before Nicholas cursed soundly. Beatrice shouted at her horse and smacked its rump, urging it to run to Erik's left. The other horses fled in pursuit, the noble pair in the saddles looking wet and confused.

Nicholas might have followed but Erik roared. He shouted at his steed and gave chase to his treacherous brother. Ruari moved quickly on his left and between the two of them, they ensured that Nicholas could not flee back to the hall.

Nicholas turned his steed abruptly then and raced in the opposing direction, diving back into the cover of the forest. Erik guessed his brother's destination immediately and urged the horse to give chase.

The land curved upward from this point, cresting in a barren hill that Erik knew well. From that point, one could see all the way down to the North Sea. Erik and Nicholas had played there often as boys, for there was an ancient group of standing stones that offered numerous places to hide.

The rain began to fall in cold sheets, but Erik did not care. His pulse quickened and he urged the palfrey to greater speed, though that left Ruari far behind.

He burst onto the hilltop, bald but for the knee-deep bounty of blooming heather. Nicholas turned his horse hard within the circle of stones ahead. The beast reared just as lightning crackled across the sky.

"A reckoning comes, Nicholas," Erik shouted.

His brother laughed. "Surely not one granted by you? Do you trust me no longer, brother mine?"

"You taught me the folly of that long ago," Erik replied. He halted his horse within the circle and confronted his brother in the rain. Nicholas's tabard looked less magnificent as soaked as it was, and his hair was a less glorious hue of gold. He had never been pleased to be seen at less than his best, and he glowered at Erik as if Erik had summoned the rain.

Then he smirked. "Though it was a lesson you took so long to learn that I confess I never thought you would heed it."

"It is less wicked to think well of one's own kin than to think poorly of them," Erik said and lifted his blade in challenge.

Nicholas slashed at him with sudden fury and the blades clanged against each other. Nicholas's blade glanced off of Erik's, so quickly did Erik raise his sword in defense.

"You were ever cursed quick," Nicholas said and thrust his blade again.

This time, though, he struck at Erik's horse. Erik swore and strove to deflect his brother's blade, but it was beyond his reach and struck the beast's neck.

The horse whinnied in fear and Nicholas laughed. The wound was slight, but the horse was frightened and there was a deadly intent in Nicholas's eyes. Erik swung out of the saddle and barely had to touch the palfrey's flanks for the beast to flee.

Nicholas's smile broadened. "Now we are better matched," he said and swung at Erik in turn. Their blades rang as they struck, then stuck again and again. The destrier danced sideways and snorted, even as Nicholas compelled it to run in a circle around Erik. Nicholas stabbed downward, from behind Erik, and cut him across the back of his shoulders.

Erik swung and nearly dismounted his brother with sheer force, which granted him an idea. He dared not swing with all his power lest he injure the horse. He waited until Nicholas slashed at him again, then stabbed upward with sudden vigor.

Nicholas cried out in pain as the sword cut the inside of his upper arm. His eyes flashed in anger and he immediately swung downward with dangerous force. Erik ducked beneath the massive steed and pushed his brother's foot up and out of the stirrup from the opposite side. That, combined with Nicholas's own swing, sent that man tumbling to the ground.

Nicholas swore. He rolled as he fell, coming up on his feet, eyes narrowed. The destrier fled, reins snapping behind it as it raced downhill to safety.

And Erik erred in looking after the beast. In that heartbeat that he glanced away, Nicholas stabbed at him. Erik saw the flash of the blade from the periphery of his vision and leapt backward.

The steel cut across his arm, the wound deep and clean. It bled with fury but he ignored its sting. He held his blade high once again. "You might at least fight one battle honorably," he said.

Nicholas smiled. "My tactics have served me well enough thus far," he said, then arched a brow. "Not a soul missed you in these parts, Erik, to be sure. Your wife is more merry in my bed, your daughters call me Father, and Blackleith has never prospered more. Our own father knew the truth of it when he called you the shame of our mother's womb."

"Did you bury him with honor? Or did it not suit your convenience to do so?"

Their blades met with a resounding ring of steel on steel. The brothers backed away and circled each other warily.

Nicholas chuckled. "The dead tell no tales, Erik, and I

shall not breach that silence. The old man is gone, on my side at the last. At least I finally persuaded him of my merit."

"Did you then?"

"Can you not imagine how vexing it was to always be compared with you? You! You who could not summon a lie to your lips, no less a glib tale, you who could not charm a woman already besotted with you, you who never showed a care for your appearance. Yet always did our father remind me of your merit, no less note my deficiencies. It was tedious, at best." Nicholas smiled. "I loved that he was in thrall to me at the end, that he had to beg my favor to be granted his meals thrice a day."

"You did not so dishonor him!"

Nicholas only smiled.

Then he gasped in horror at the vigor of Erik's assault. Erik swung with all his might, driving Nicholas back against a stone. His blade tucked neatly under his brother's chin and Nicholas caught his breath as a thin trickle of blood mingled with the rainwater on the blade.

"You will rot in hell for such treachery," Erik growled. "You will burn, and rightly so, for so dishonoring the man who granted you life."

Nicholas's gaze hardened. He pursed his lips and then he spat in Erik's eye.

Erik blinked and that was all the opportunity his brother needed to slip from beneath the weight of his blade. They pursued each other around the stones, blades clashing, feet slipping in the mud, then Erik lost track of his brother.

He turned slowly, listening carefully. He heard nothing but the patter of the rain, saw nothing but the heather bowing beneath its assault.

"Ha!" Nicholas cried from his immediate right. Erik spun but too late, Nicholas had hooked his blade beneath the hilt of Erik's sword. Slick with rain, Erik's grip was loose enough that his brother managed to dislodge his blade and sent it scuttling across the ground.

"How sad that you cannot fight honestly, like a man of merit," Erik mused.

"I win, howsoever I can," Nicholas said.

"You win by cheating, for it is the only way you can." Erik met his brother's gaze. "Vivienne Lammergeier said as much, and it is clear that she knows you far better than I."

Nicholas froze. "Vivienne? You have met Vivienne?"

Erik pulled his dagger as he nodded. "Indeed, I have, and you spoke aright. The lady is a marvel."

Nicholas stood, shocked. "You did not bed her?"

Erik only smiled.

Nicholas lunged at him. Sword and dagger met with fury, the clash of blades dangerously close to Erik's face. He fought back, grunting with the effort, and managed to nick Nicholas's cheek.

That man cried out as he leapt backward, his hand rising to his face. "Do not disfigure me!"

"Surely he owes you no less," Ruari interjected, appearing suddenly from behind a stone. Nicholas pivoted and swung his blade at Ruari. His sword was large and weighty, however, and Erik took advantage of the moment. He leapt upon his brother and slashed at his hand.

The sword fell to the ground, Nicholas's blood streaming after it. He backed into a stone, his gaze flicking between Ruari and Erik. "So, this will be the end of it, will it? You will kill your own brother like a dog and leave me unmourned upon this hill?"

Erik hesitated.

"You tried to do the same to your own brother," Ruari noted. "And you had no cause to do so."

"Cease your prattle!" Nicholas spat, then spared a covert glance to the space beyond the circle of stones.

"Your squire is dead," Ruari said, his tone matter-of-fact. "I would have let the boy live, but he was determined to ensure my end. There was little else I could do but guarantee his instead. What manner are you to train a boy so young as that to fight to the death, even when he is outmatched?"

Nicholas's lips tightened, though he did not spare Ruari a reply. He turned an intent gaze upon Erik. "Will you kill me in truth, brother mine? We could reconcile, administer Blackleith as one. Beatrice would return to you with pleasure, at least if I commanded as much, I am certain."

Ruari snorted.

Erik had no urge to kill the last of his own kin, not unless he were certain of Nicholas's intent. The rain beat upon them, the thunder rumbled. Nicholas licked his lips, his breath coming quickly in his fear, and memory stirred.

A horrible truth filled Erik's thoughts, a conviction that allowed no excuses for his sibling. Filled with new resolve, Erik gestured impatiently to Ruari that that man should retreat.

Ruari did his bidding, with obvious reluctance.

Erik passed his dagger to his left hand beneath his brother's avid gaze. He then slowly turned his hand palm up, loosed his fingers and cast the blade away.

Nicholas did not waste a moment. He lunged for Erik, fingers outstretched.

But Erik was prepared. He reached behind himself

with lightning speed. He pulled his father's blade from the back of his belt even as Nicholas's fingers locked around his throat. He raised the blade and drove it down between Nicholas's shoulder blades, watching his brother's eyes widen as the blade sank home.

Nicholas's grip loosened within their deadly embrace, and his eyes glazed with pain.

"It rains this day," Erik whispered. "Just as it rained on the day that I was granted these scars."

Nicholas stared at him, and Erik did not know whether he comprehended his words or not.

Still they had to be uttered.

"In times of peril, a man's senses become more keen. I remember the sound of my last assailant's breath, I remember the sound of his boots upon the road, the rhythm of his step. And I remember his smell." Erik lifted his brother's limp fingers from his neck and for a moment, he held Nicholas's weight in his hands. "I smell it again on this day. Surely you did not imagine that I would forget."

"You were never to know," Nicholas whispered. "You were never to live that you might remember."

Erik let his brother plummet to the ground, let him die mired and alone. He stepped over him, pulled his father's blade from Nicholas's back, and walked out of the stone circle.

Though he knew he had done what was right, Erik felt no pride in his deed. He wiped the ancient Sinclair weapon in the heather, cleaning the blood of a Sinclair from its blade. He felt tears slide down his face, mingling with the rain, and was aware of Ruari close by his side.

He would never climb to this hill again, for he would never forget that he had spilled the blood that stained it.

The older man laid a hand on Erik's shoulder and

heaved a sigh. "It is a man of merit who can complete an unpleasant task, no less one that needs to be done. Your father would be proud of you, Erik Sinclair, upon that you can rely."

"My father would weep with me this day, Ruari," Erik said softly. He granted the Sinclair blade to Ruari's care, unable to look upon it for the moment. "There can be no doubt of that."

IN THAT SAME MOMENT, Rosamunde and Tynan were assaulted by a high-pitched scream in Ravensmuir's caverns.

*"Circle of kings wrought of silver fine; Pledge your troth but that ring is MINE!"*

A wild swirl of orange erupted in the middle of the cavern, so fiery a hue that Rosamunde thought it had come from the torches. It was no flame, though, but an angry cloud.

"What in the name of God is that?" Tynan cried.

"I fear it is the spriggan," Rosamunde had time enough to say before the cloud exploded upward. Stone broke from the high arch of the cavern's ceiling and chunks fell to the ground around them.

*"Treacherous thief who would break a vow; I want my ring, I want it NOW!"*

But there was no time to respond to the spriggan's demands. Tynan swore and pushed the ring all the way onto Rosamunde's finger. She did not know whether he did as much by instinct or choice. He spun and drew his blade. Rosamunde drew her own, though she guessed it was useless against this foe.

Meanwhile, Darg screamed in ear-piercing fury. The cloud that must be her manifestation grew half again as large and fairly boiled against the stone walls. To Rosamunde's dismay, rock began to fall from the tunnel walls with vigor then, crashing around them and falling into the chasm. A veil of dust rose, but still the cloud grew bigger.

The rock began to groan, as if it could not contain the volume of Darg's fury. Cracks appeared and spread wildly across the stone surfacing, gaping wider with every scream the spriggan uttered.

"The caverns will collapse!" Tynan shouted over the din. He seized Rosamunde's hand and they ran together toward the corridor that led upward to Ravensmuir's solar.

The cloud screamed more sharply and a crack gaped wide in the rock above the door. Rosamunde knew they would not make the portal in time, but both she and Tynan ran more quickly all the same. Right in front of their toes, a massive chunk of stone loosed itself and fell squarely into the corridor, blocking the passage and enfolding them in a cloud of dust.

Tynan did not hesitate. He turned to another portal, one that led to the stables. Lightning seemed to flash over their heads as they turned their steps. It snaked through the dust-filled air, striking the stone with a flash. The stone walls roared and vibrated, and another piece of stone fell to block their course.

"We shall be trapped!" Rosamunde said. She pivoted, even as more stones fell into the other portals, then looked up as a fierce snap echoed through the chamber. The very floor shifted with its rumble and Rosamunde feared the worst.

A fissure opened in the high arched ceiling of stone overhead, then gaped wide with alarming speed. Tynan followed her gaze and swore. Far overhead, there was the sound of stone creaking and walls buckling.

It was more than the labyrinth falling in, Rosamunde realized. All of Ravensmuir collapsed around them, the tunnels sealing as the mighty keep was brought to its knees.

And not a single soul knew that she and Tynan were trapped beneath the stone.

"We are lost!" Tynan whispered, making to draw her into his embrace.

Rosamunde was not so prepared to surrender. She knew what the spriggan wanted of her, and the fairy had loosed her ship from the fog. The debt had to be paid. She pulled the ring from her finger that Tynan had just placed there, and cast it into the midst of the angry orange cloud that assaulted them.

"What is this madness that you do?" Tynan cried and dove after the silver ring. "That is my mother's ring!"

"Leave it!" Rosamunde cried over the cracking of stone, but he did not heed her. She saw him fall to his knees, desperately seeking the ring in the rubble. She glanced upward at the crumbling stone, then about herself. "Look there, Tynan!" she cried in sudden relief. "We missed one portal!"

And indeed there was one, gleaming with a strange golden light as if it would beckon them closer.

Tynan glanced up. "That is no passage I know."

"Nonetheless it is there."

"You know not where it leads."

"It scarce matters!"

"I do not like the look of it," he insisted.

"I do not like the look of that!" Rosamunde pointed upward as the ceiling of the grotto began to shift. A hail of small stones scattered over them and she saw blood on Tynan's temple.

"Tynan, hurry!" Rosamunde shouted and lunged for the gleaming portal, assuming he would follow. She just barely made it through the portal, barely had time to note the curious golden light shining ahead of her, before there was another crack.

A deafening roar filled the cavern she had just left as stone fell with gusto. She choked on the dust and saw that she was alone. Rosamunde peered through the portal, glimpsed Tynan's broken body before it was buried beneath stone, and she knew what she had feared to learn here.

Tynan had, once again, chosen Ravensmuir first.

Rosamunde pivoted, her tears rising with uncharacteristic vigor. Another tumble of stone collapsed in Ravensmuir's caverns with such vigor that a vengeful deity might be sealing the labyrinth for all eternity. She lunged into the strange golden light, then a chance chunk of stone struck her brow and Rosamunde Lammergeier knew no more.

VIVIENNE WAS NOT CERTAIN how she would escape with Erik's daughters. The girls were so young that they could not run or fight: Vivienne would have to defend all three of them as well as ensure their escape. She was not certain that they trusted her—why would they, indeed?—or that they would follow her bidding. She also did not know how she would ensure their safety once she left this party.

Perhaps she could wait until they rode closer to Ravensmuir, or Kinfairlie, then abduct the girls and flee to her family's care. Of course, that was predicated upon Henry and Arabella riding as far as Kinfairlie.

It seemed that once again she had believed her abilities to be greater than they might prove to be.

Against her every aspiration, Arabella and Henry had taken to arguing over the merits of pausing at the Earl of Sutherland's abode this night. As the Earl was the sole person of whom Vivienne knew who might recognize Erik's daughters—though truly, he might not have paid any heed to young girls, given his interest in ensuring succession—this decision was of considerable concern to Vivienne.

She eavesdropped shamelessly, and tried to think of a way to affect the choice they ultimately made. Astrid dozed against her chest, thumb securely in her mouth, while Mairi sat behind her sister, facing Vivienne as well. Vivienne thought the older girl dozed, too, though her fingers still caressed the smooth lines of the silver pin.

"I cannot see the merit of halting at so late an hour," Henry repeated for at least the sixth time. "It is unseemly to awaken a host late and demand hospitality."

"Surely you cannot imagine that I will ride in such weather, without so much as a hot meal, a warm bath, and a plump mattress?" Arabella retorted. "The hour is of little import. How are we to affect the distance between abodes? If you had not insisted upon taking these children in our company, we could have been miles further by now."

"If you had not insisted upon visiting Beatrice of Blackleith, we should not even be in these cold lands."

"And what was I to do? Rumor abounded about her and her rich domain in the north, and truly, the tales I heard made it sound to be a veritable paradise. I had no choice but to come, especially after I lost that wager with the Countess. Believe me, Henry, I should have dearly loved to have won. It would have done me good to imagine her in this wretched country instead of me. Doubtless she will make merry at my expense. You must ensure that she hears only good about this journey. Perhaps we should tell her that Beatrice's riches are so great that they cannot be described." Arabella chuckled at the prospect. "Then she will feel compelled to ride here to see for herself."

"Tell her whatsoever you feel the need to tell her, my dear. I need only know what I am supposed to say."

"Henry, you are the most gallant man," Arabella said, drumming her fingers upon his arm. She lowered her voice to a lusty warble. "Perhaps we should stop at the Earl's abode and demand his very best bed for our pleasure."

The squires rolled their eyes and bit back smiles.

"If it would please you, my lady, I believe the children would benefit from a halt this night," Vivienne dared to say.

"Their temperaments can only improve," Arabella said haughtily, then waved her hand. "I have no care for their moods, girl. They are your worry until I have need of them. Children should be ignored until they prove useful."

Henry glanced over his shoulder, his eyes narrowing as he surveyed his small wet party. His gaze lingered overlong upon Vivienne. She thought she put too much weight upon the look in his eyes, but only until he spoke.

"I think the maid makes good sense, Arabella," Henry mused, though Vivienne doubted that his concern was for the children. "A fine plump bed will suit me well this night." And he winked boldly at Vivienne as his wife preened, oblivious to his averted gaze.

The two squires nudged each other, then leered at Vivienne, and she guessed that she had truly underestimated the perils of this circumstance.

VIVIENNE WAS GONE from her hiding place.

Erik was disquieted by this fact, though there was no sign of her. She might have never been at Blackleith, and her absence had Ruari fretful as well. The horses had returned to the stable from the hill and stood shivering in the rain.

Erik left Ruari outside of Blackleith's hall. It was overly quiet in the village and he feared what he would find within the hall itself. Ruari stood guard at the portal, and nodded once before Erik slipped into the smoky shadows of the hall.

Not a single torch burned in the great hall, though there were embers glowing still in the fireplace. It was beyond quiet, as if no one was within these walls. No child sobbed or laughed, there was not so much as a breath of some soul sleeping. Fear seized Erik's heart and he wondered what Beatrice had done with their daughters.

Had she fled south with them, never to be found again?

"I thought you might yet live," she said so unexpectedly that Erik jumped.

He saw her then, seated in the otherwise empty hall, a cup before her on the board. She was as lovely as ever she had been, though her lips pinched as they once had not and her eyes seemed more shrewd.

But perhaps he had not seen the truth before him.

Beatrice smiled, as if there had not been so much time and treachery between them, then took a sip from the cup. "The Earl of Sutherland is not a subtle man, at the best of times, and he has asked some pointed questions of late."

"Where are Mairi and Astrid?"

Beatrice's smile broadened. "I am surprised that you have any concern for them. Does not every man desire a son?"

"They are my children and you have no right," Erik began but Beatrice interrupted him.

"It is the last of the wine." Beatrice rose and strolled toward him, the cup in her hand. She offered it to him. "Do you wish a sip?"

"You greet me solicitously indeed."

She grimaced. "I suspected that you lived. I feared you to have returned when I saw Ruari. It was inevitable you would battle Nicholas for Blackleith, and just as inevitable that you would triumph."

She regarded him and he could not guess her thoughts. "You have always had a cursed talent for survival, and Nicholas, despite his many graces, is less of a swordsman than he might be." She laughed without mirth. "At least with the blade he would raise against you." She saluted Erik with the cup, then sipped of its contents deeply, watching him over the rim. "How much more interesting it would have been if you had battled Nicholas for me."

Erik snorted. "Why would I fight for the regard of a woman who cares only for herself?"

Her eyes flashed and he thought that she might strike him. Instead she studied him and grimaced. "You would strike terror into any maiden's heart, with what has become of your face. Praise be that you will never come to my bed again." Her smile turned bitter. "But then, thanks to you, neither will Nicholas. I assume you have left him dead?"

"Indeed."

She averted her face then and he wondered whether she had cared for another soul, after all.

"Where are Mairi and Astrid?"

"Gone."

"Where?" Erik seized her arm when she did not answer him, forcing her to face him.

Beatrice chuckled. "I do not know. Is that not the beauty of it? I do not know, so I cannot tell you. You may do your worst to me, indeed, you have already taken all that was of merit to me. And I have taken what is of merit to you."

"You cannot have injured them!"

Beatrice only smiled, smiled with such confidence that Erik longed to shake her until her very bones rattled. "Why should you care? I doubt truly that they are even of your own seed."

Erik regarded her in shock. "I thought that was but a rumor . . ."

"A rumor rooted in truth. Surely you did not imagine that you, with your clumsy manner abed and your inability to utter sweet compliments, could sate me? I was a beauty with a hundred suitors at my door! I was sought by barons and princes, I was courted by men from leagues away." She stepped back and regarded him with disdain. "Yet I wed Erik Sinclair, heir to a modest holding, a man who could not praise a woman with poetry to save his life. Did you never wonder why?"

"Every day I was amazed by my fortune," Erik said with care.

Beatrice laughed harshly. "Here is my gift to you, husband. I was no maiden when I came to your bed on our nuptial night. Indeed, I feared that I carried the fruit of a man's seed and I knew better than to vex my own father with such tidings. He would have seen me whipped until I bled, and torn flesh tempts no man. I had to see myself wed and wed in haste, and this was the very moment when you came to my father's gates, seeking alliance. You were of use to me, Erik Sinclair, no more than that."

"And once you knew that you bore no child?" Erik asked, wanting all of the truth, no matter how cruel. She could not speak of Mairi, for that child had not come to them until they had been married for a year.

Beatrice sauntered back to the head table and granted herself another measure of wine. "You do not mind if I pour for myself, surely? There is a cursed lack of servants in this hall, but that, I understand, has always been Blackleith's fate." She spared him an arch glance as she sipped. "When it became clear that I bore no child, I welcomed my lover between my thighs once again. Is it not said that there is but one woman in Christendom who ever denied Nicholas Sinclair? It was simple enough to meet him when we lived in the same abode."

Erik turned away from these unwelcome tidings, delivered with such glee. "So you did couple with him."

"Often," Beatrice said, smacking her lips over both wine and recollection. "It is charming that you are so certain the girls are your own, when I do not share your conviction."

Erik said nothing, for he was surprised at how little ability she had to injure him.

Beatrice shrugged. "And finally, it did not suit me to have to meet both brothers abed any longer."

Erik looked up. "*You* wrought the scheme," he murmured, seeing now who had aided Nicholas to contrive such a plot. Beatrice smiled. "You brought the missive that was supposed to come from Thomas Gunn. You were the one who urged me to aid my neighbor."

She laughed. "And you were too fool to see that I deceived you." She finished her wine, cast the pewter cup in the direction of the board and flung out her hands. "So, now you have reclaimed your deepest desire," she taunted. "Your larder is barren, your treasury is empty, and your peasants are hungry. Your fields lie untended and you have no seed for the spring. All of your kin is dead, your wife despises you, and your children are lost forevermore. How fares your triumphant return to Blackleith, husband?"

Erik sheathed his blade and turned away from her. "It is little different than I expected," he said softly. "For I learned early in my marriage to expect naught of merit from my spouse. You erred in granting me those daughters, Beatrice, for they are the gold in my treasury."

"Do you not hear me? They are likely not of your seed!"

"It does not matter. They are mine in the eyes of the law, and mine because I believe them to be so."

"But they are gone!"

"They cannot be gone far. I shall seek until I find

them, and I shall raise them with honor or die in the attempt."

She lunged after him and seized his shoulder, compelling him to look at her. "I thought you would kill me."

Erik shook his head. "I have no urge to sully my hands with your blood."

"Do you not despise me?"

Erik studied his wife and wondered how he had failed to see her selfishness. He shook his head then and plucked her hand from his shoulder. "Nay. I pity you. Farewell, Beatrice."

With that, he turned to depart Blackleith once again, his wife dismissed from his thoughts. His daughters must be with that noble couple who had ridden to hunt with Nicholas. Surely they would ride south to the Earl of Sutherland's abode, perhaps even make a halt there. There had been no ship in the harbor, though they could have ridden north to the great abode of the Earl's kin at Girnigoe.

Between his own talents and those of Ruari, he should be able to discern their direction. His pace quickened with surety and determination to retrieve his daughters before it was too late.

"You wretch!" he heard Beatrice scream from behind him. The pewter cup struck the wall beside his head. Erik jumped at its impact, then glanced back.

Beatrice, her face contorted with fury, dove toward him, a blade held high in her hand. She was cursedly close. Erik realized he had scant time to pull his own blade when he heard a whistle beside his very ear.

A spinning blade flashed past him, the point embedding itself in Beatrice's chest. She gasped and took a step back, her own hand falling to the blood coursing from the wound.

Erik saw that it was his father's blade, the sapphire in the hilt glinting as if it winked at him.

Beatrice touched the hilt of the blade sunk into her flesh, coughed, and shook her head. "William always loathed me," she said, then coughed again. She slumped against the wall, then granted Erik a baleful glance. "Trust him to ensure my demise."

"It was not William who cast the blade," Ruari said with disapproval, "though it was doubtless his spirit that guided the blade home. My aim is not so good as that, upon that fact you can rely." He nodded once at Erik. "Your father could split a hair at forty paces with that blade, to be sure, and he never failed to astound a skeptic with his skill." Beatrice slumped to the floor, her eyes closing as she coughed more feebly. "I have never made such a good throw, though, to be sure, I never much liked Beatrice myself."

Erik made to step forward and ease Beatrice to a more comfortable position for her last moments. Ruari stayed him with a touch. "Do not venture near that viper," he counselled, then nodded at the knife yet in her hand. "She grips the hilt tightly for one so close to death. Leave her be, for she will be dead in truth by the time we return."

At that, Beatrice opened her eyes slightly and spat at the floor, showing his advice to be good with nary a word. Then her head drooped to her shoulder and Erik believed she knew no more.

He turned his back upon her, though, for his battle was not yet complete. He had to find his daughters, and he hoped that they were not departing too late.

For there was truth in Beatrice's claim. She had tried

to steal all of the promise Erik might find in reclaiming Blackleith, leaving him without affluence, without family, without his own children.

But Erik had witnessed the faith of Vivienne and he would never again be the same. His prospects might look to be dour in this moment, but he knew he would find his daughters.

And he would find Vivienne, whatever had happened to her. He would pursue her to the very ends of the earth, if need be, though he had little to offer her beyond himself.

He could only hope that might suffice.

# Chapter Eighteen

To VIVIENNE'S DISMAY, the Earl of Sutherland's gates were barred, and the gatekeeper was disinclined to wake his laird in the middle of the night to please a passing party of travellers. When Henry eloquently protested this miscarriage of Christian charity, the gatekeeper pointed him in the direction of an abandoned barn.

It had a hole in its roof and a rustling plethora of birds in its rafters. The occasional missile was launched from above, landing on the packed earth floor with a wet slap. Arabella chose to argue the matter, but Vivienne was too tired. She carried the girls to a corner less vigorously marked by the birds' droppings, folded her cloak over them all and went to sleep.

VIVIENNE AWAKENED to find a man's hand upon her breast and a sharp blade kissing her throat. Some hours had passed, she guessed, for it was lighter and the rain fell with less vigor. No thunder rumbled overhead any longer.

And Henry crouched beside her, his breeches loosed to free his prick. It was pale against the darkness and bobbed in anticipation.

"Lift your skirts and be quiet about the matter," he urged in a whisper.

Vivienne frowned at him, hoping to dissuade him with a bold manner. "Not in front of the children," she scolded indignantly, not troubling to lower her voice.

The blade dug more demandingly into her throat and Vivienne caught her breath. "You are to be quiet," Henry insisted. "Or I shall ensure that you are quiet forevermore."

"But the children . . ."

"Push them aside. They will never know the difference, and if they do, they will be well prepared for their futures."

Vivienne caught her breath, so intense was her dislike for this man. She was uncommonly glad that she had accompanied Erik's daughters, for she would ensure somehow that they were freed from the circle of his influence.

She eased Astrid from her lap, that child whimpering slightly as she was moved. Vivienne hushed her, tucking her more fully into her fur-lined cloak. She lifted Mairi then, who was a much greater burden. Henry let her move sufficiently to tuck the girls beneath the cloak and Vivienne saw the glimmer of Mairi's eyes as they opened.

She put her hand over the girl's brow, easing her eyes closed again, and to her relief Mairi followed her bidding.

"That is a fine pin," Henry said. "You must have pleased some laird well to have been granted a gift of such value."

"A man of merit surrendered it to me as a keepsake," Vivienne said.

Henry chuckled. "No doubt he granted a ripe wench like you more than that as a keepsake."

"He did indeed. He granted me his love and my memories of him. Those are keepsakes beyond price."

Henry sneered, uninterested in such details. "Aye, and you have stolen from your former mistress, as well, I would wager, by the look of your garb. Lift your skirts, wench. Please me well or you will surrender your keepsake, if not more, to my wife. She has a fondness for trinkets, and I have a fondness for granting them to her." His smile flashed. "They ensure that she asks fewer questions."

"You will take my life before you take this pin," Vivienne replied, her voice low with intent.

Henry struck her then, full across the face, then moved so that his weight was atop her. Vivienne cried out and he forced his hand between her teeth. He tasted of perspiration, the weight of him nearly crushing Vivienne, and she felt his prick seeking a harbor between her thighs. She struggled against him, to little avail, furious that she should be so abused.

Then Henry screamed with vigor, ignoring his own command for quiet.

Mairi, who had scampered to Vivienne's aid, gripped a fistful of his hair and bit his ear again.

"This child is no better than an animal!" Henry cried. He tried to strike the child, his move sufficient that Vivienne could push his weight from her chest. He swung his fist at Mairi and Vivienne slapped his face so hard for endeavoring to strike the child that he took a staggering step backward.

Little Astrid was immediately behind him. She bumped into the back of his knees apurpose and sent him sprawling backward. He fell on his back, his exposed prick dancing in the morning breeze.

The girls giggled and Vivienne could not help but smile. "I thank you for your aid," she said and they clustered by her side, valiant defenders in truth.

Henry propped himself up on his elbows, anger in his eyes, but Arabella interrupted whatever he might have said. "Henry? Henry! What are you doing out of our bed?" She appeared out of the shadows opposite, her hair askew and her chemise rumpled. "And what is all this noise? Do you not know how early in the day it is? Surely you know by now how desperately I need to have a good night's sleep?"

Henry's prick lost its enthusiasm at the sound of his wife's voice.

Arabella halted beside him, her indignation clear. "Henry!"

That man sat up, passed a hand over his brow, then glowered at Vivienne and the two girls as he fastened his chausses beneath his wife's cold eye.

He shook a finger, but Vivienne granted him no chance to threaten her.

"Your husband assaults me in the night, my lady, as any person with their wits about them can see," Vivienne said, certain that no maid had ever dared to utter the truth to Arabella before. The lady knew of her husband's deeds, though, for she caught her breath and paled. Her lips tightened as she looked down at him. "I am certain that you understand that I will not remain in a household in which I may be attacked in the night."

"But you cannot leave my service before I am prepared to be rid of you," Arabella argued, for surely she was one who preferred to have her own way.

"I have every right," Vivienne retorted. "Your husband has no right to attack me in the night. Further I will take these two children into my custody, for there is no guarantee that they will be spared similar abuse within your household."

"But they were granted to our custody," Arabella argued, clearly thinking of the benefit of that donation to the convent when Henry had sins for which to atone.

"And I have wits to know that you do not truly desire them." Vivienne took the girls by their hands, and they looked up at her. Their cautious optimism fairly broke her heart, for they had been poorly served by recent events. She smiled for each in turn and squeezed their hands, encouraged when they returned that squeeze. "It is my hope to return them to their rightful father."

"But he is dead, is he not, Henry? Beatrice said her first husband was dead, I am certain of it."

"Then she lied to you, for he was not dead just yesterday."

"The pin," Mairi said, a glow in her voice. She stretched to her toes and Vivienne bent so that the little girl could brush the silver pin with her fingertips. "I remember the pin."

"Yes, your father gave me his pin. Should Fortune smile upon us, we shall shortly see it back in his hands again."

"But you cannot do this," Arabella protested. "You cannot simply decree what shall be. You are merely a maid, albeit once recently come to my service. You should heed me!"

Vivienne stood straight and tall. "I am a noblewoman with as many rights as you hold. My name is Vivienne Lammergeier. If you have cause for complaint with my deeds, you are welcome to bring your plea to the court of my brother, Laird of Kinfairlie. Be warned, however, that he will see justice served."

With that, Vivienne gathered her cloak and led Erik's daughters into the first glimmer of morning's sunlight. She turned their steps toward Blackleith, not caring how long it took her to walk that far.

To make the distance pass more quickly, she began to tell the girls the tale of Thomas the Rhymer.

Thomas had barely met his fairy queen before they heard hoofbeats on the road behind them. Vivienne paused, uncertain who might ride before them, and then heard horses racing toward them from ahead as well.

She stood in the middle of the road, her hair unfurled, her boots wet, Erik's pin upon her cloak, and his daughters holding fast to her hands. She saw the distinctive black hue of Ravensmuir's stallions before she recognized her brother Alexander's colors, before she saw her brother Malcolm fast by his side. Elizabeth rode another stallion, and a trio of trusted men from Ravensmuir rode the last three. The black stallions fairly breathed fire as they raced down the road, their coats gleaming in the morning light.

Vivienne blinked back tears of joy at the sight of them. "It is my brother come to ensure my welfare," she said to the girls. "We have nothing to fear." Then she pivoted and knew she had spoken no less than the truth, for Erik Sinclair rode toward her on a chestnut destrier. Ruari Macleod was fast behind him, but Vivienne had eyes only for Erik.

Erik dismounted with a leap and ran the last increment toward her. Mairi shouted in recognition and he lifted her high, then swung her around while she laughed. Astrid was more cautious, her memory shorter, though she reached out and tugged at the ends of his hair.

Then he stood, his children at his knee, his eyes shining a brilliant sapphire. "I have reclaimed suzerainty of Blackleith," he said, evidently aware of Alexander's gaze fixed upon him. "And my wife Beatrice is dead. I have little to offer, Vivienne, for my abode is more humble than what you have known, but I love you with all the vigor of my heart." He stretched his hands out to her even as her heart soared. "Will you wed me in truth, Vivienne Lammergeier?"

There was such a lump in Vivienne's throat that she could not summon a word in reply. She shook her head in wonderment, her tears falling at the movement, and saw Erik's dismay. "I will," she said huskily. "I will, with pleasure."

And he laughed and caught her fast in his arms, kissing her with such ardor that she did not care who witnessed their embrace.

For against all odds, against even her own expectation, Vivienne's quest had led her precisely to where she most desired to be.

IT PROVED THAT ALEXANDER and Malcolm had left Ravensmuir in pursuit of Erik and Vivienne on the morning after the trio's escape. Tynan had declined to accompany the party, suggesting that it was time Malcolm assumed such responsibilities. Elizabeth had come in pursuit of Darg, as she was the only one who could see the fairy, and she was disappointed to announce that the spriggan was not in their company.

Erik had already guessed as much.

The group from Kinfairlie had lingered at the abode of the Earl of Sutherland, certain that Vivienne and Erik must pass that way or arrive there eventually. Alexander had also brought back the steeds that the Earl had lent to Erik and Ruari, which relieved Erik mightily. They all returned there, once reunited.

The Earl, it proved, was well pleased with Erik's return, for he had numerous concerns about Blackleith's administration. A party was dispatched to retrieve the bodies of Nicholas and Beatrice, to see them honorably buried, and to loose the two maids. Those women were delighted to have escaped the household of Henry and Arabella, and were quick to offer to serve at Blackleith.

And to the delight of all—and the particular approval of Alexander, Laird of Kinfairlie—the Earl of Sutherland saw fit to have Erik and Vivienne wed in his own chapel. The banns were waived by the priest and Erik overheard the Earl telling Vivienne that a son would be a welcome addition indeed.

ON THE MORNING AFTER the celebration of his second nuptial vows, Erik Sinclair arose early. He sat for a long moment and watched the first sunlight caress Vivienne's cheek, smiling at how deeply she slept.

They had loved long into the night before and he resolved to let her slumber late if she so desired. They need make no haste back to Blackleith.

He left their chamber, well content, and checked upon his daughters. They slept curled together, Astrid still sucking her thumb. Mairi's eyes opened as he watched them and she lifted her hands to him, as she had when she had been tiny. Erik picked her up, caring naught for her weight, and tucked her against his hip. She laid her head upon his shoulder, as trustingly as if he had never been gone, and the sweet smell of her nigh rent Erik's heart in two.

He broke his fast at the Earl's board, Mairi on his knee. There were few awake so early, and those who sat beside him said little. He accepted a few belated congratulations and shook the hands of a few men, both familiar and unknown to him.

Mairi was quick to steal his comb of honey, mischief dancing in her eyes at her own success, and Erik was content to let her have it.

When he rose from the board, the Earl's cook came to his side. "The Earl has said as I should offer you some food, sir, both for your journey home to Blackleith and a wee bit for the winter ahead."

Erik nodded, pleased to accept. "I have no inkling of the inventories we will find there, so your offer is most welcome."

The plump cook beamed and flicked a finger beneath Mairi's chin. "Winter will be at our doors soon enough, sir, and the bairns have need of a hot meal each day."

"I can aid you," Erik offered but the cook shook her head.

"I shall have it brought to you, sir, though you shall have to find a way to carry it. I have not a sack in this house that can be spared."

"My saddlebags have little of merit in them. I will clean them out."

The cook nodded and bustled away. Erik collected his saddlebags and sat in the corner of the hall. Mairi hunkered down beside him, examining each item that he removed, then waiting expectantly for the next.

The bag Ruari had taken on the ship had little enough in it, but the other, which had arrived with Fafnir, was still heavy. There were several wrinkled apples within it as well as a chunk of bread hard enough to be used as a weapon. The grappling hook was still there and might be of use in future. The ale in the leather bottle did not have a smell that invited a man to partake of it.

"What is this?" Mairi demanded, wrinkling her nose at the smell of some bundle. She turned it impatiently in her small hands, so persuaded was she that Erik must have brought her some treasure or trinket.

He wished he had done so but knew he had naught that might intrigue her.

Erik echoed her expression, hoping to make her smile at least. "Very old cheese, perhaps more aged than you."

"It smells."

"Indeed it does. I doubt that even the Earl's hounds will eat it," Erik said and she laughed. She scampered across the hall then, unfurling the piece of cheese as she went, and presented it to one of the Earl's hounds. That dog sniffed it but once, then glanced away with disdain.

Mairi returned undaunted and gave the piece of cheese back to Erik, who had no desire for it but accepted it anyway. "He does not like it," she said. She dug in the bag and pulled out the second of the two chemises the Earl had granted to him. They wrinkled their noses in unison when she shook out the garment.

"We shall never get the smell of cheese out of that!" Erik said and Mairi cast it aside.

"Whose is it?"

"It was mine. The Earl lent it to me."

"Shall I give it back to him?"

"I think not," Erik said and they shared a smile. "Let him think it lost."

"It will be our secret," his elder daughter informed him solemnly, unaware of how precious such secrets were to her father. She turned her attention back to the bag, but found little more of interest.

Indeed, everything in the bag was redolent of old cheese. Erik left it open for the moment, hoping the smell would diminish before the cook brought the food for him.

"But what of this one?" Mairi demanded, having turned her attention to the first bag.

"There is naught left in there," Erik said, and fanned the flap of the redolent saddlebag optimistically. It appeared to make no difference in the smell.

"Of course there is," Mairi insisted, then held out her hand. "What is this?" Something smooth and red gleamed against her palm, its resemblance to a drop of blood nigh stopping Erik's heart in fear.

But it was not blood. It was a gleaming droplet, to be sure, and one as red as fresh blood. But it was hard, like a jewel, and as cold as ice.

"What is it?" Mairi asked again when Erik turned it in his hands.

"It looks like a gem," he said. "Though I have never seen it before."

"Perhaps it was given to you while you were not looking," Mairi suggested, eyes alight. "Perhaps someone hid it in your bag so that you could give it to me." She smiled then, fully persuaded of her notion.

And Erik had an idea then of what his daughter had found. The gem was cold, after all, and of a red red hue.

He closed his hand over it while he thought and when he opened his hand to consider it again, the drop had grown.

It looked now like the bud of a flower, and Erik smiled. The fairy Darg must have granted him a boon in exchange for saving her life in the cavern, for she alone could have given him the red red rose wrought of ice that he needed to grant his new wife her every desire.

"What is it? I think you know," Mairi accused with childish conviction.

Erik smiled. "I think I do." He picked up his daughter, holding the fairy gem fast in his hand. "Let us get Astrid, and go to Vivienne, and she will tell us a tale."

"Is it the tale about Thomas the Rhymer?"

Erik smiled, for his daughters already pestered Vivienne to recount that tale again and again. "Nay, not that one."

"Is it a tale about the red drop?"

"It is that and more." He tapped Mairi's nose with a fingertip. "And if you are very good and listen very intently, it may well be that this magic stone—for that is what it is—will do something very special."

"As a gift for me?"

"As a gift for all of us, and a reminder that there is much we cannot see or explain."

In moments, they were all together in the chamber he and Vivienne had shared, the girls tucked into Vivienne's fur-lined cloak and their expressions expectant. Erik laid the gem upon the floor before them and pulled all three of them into his embrace. Vivienne laid her head upon his shoulder, her smile telling him that she too had guessed the import of the gem.

"Once upon a time, there was a distant keep known as Kinfairlie," she began. "And that keep was burned to the ground. It was rebuilt by the Laird of Ravensmuir, a tall and handsome man whose wife was the sole surviving descendant of Kinfairlie, and he had her legacy rebuilt, it is said, merely to see her smile."

"A nice man," Mairi said, nestling deeper into the cloak.

"A kindly man indeed," Vivienne agreed, sharing a smile with Erik. He watched his daughters, knowing that Vivienne already held them in thrall with her tales, and knowing that they would come to think of her as their true mother in little time. He leaned back and watched the red gem, which had already begun to sprout another petal.

"Kinfairlie had a castellan to mind its halls and store-rooms while the laird and lady were not there, a castellan who held the keys to every door in the keep," Vivienne continued. "And that castellan had both a wife and a daughter, a beautiful daughter, a daughter who loved to play in the castle. As it was newly built and it was as-sumed that she could find no trouble within its walls—and truly, it must be said, because she had more than a measure of persuasive charm—she was allowed to go wheresoever she would within Kinfairlie's walls."

The red gem already had a greater resemblance to a bud, though the bud was yet small. Erik saw that his daughters' eyes were closing, that Vivienne concentrated on the telling of her tale, and he savored the promise of their surprise.

The gem fattened, as a bud will before it opens.

"But what the castellan and his wife did not know was that there was an old tale about Kinfairlie, a rumor that Kinfairlie was a portal between the realms of fairy and that of men," Vivienne said and both girls opened their

eyes at that to regard her with awe. "Further, it had been
known to happen that a fairy suitor spied a mortal lass
through that portal and lost his heart utterly with a single
glance. It was said in the village that such fairy men
courted their mortal sweethearts for three nights, then
captured them forevermore, leaving a bride price of a
single red red rose wrought of ice."

SO THEY PASSED a good portion of the morning, the sunlight playing upon the hair of Erik's wife and his daughters, Vivienne's tale holding them ensnared within a
cocoon of myth.

And when the last word of the tale had crossed Vivienne's lips, Erik indicated the gem with a single gesture.
He savored the wonderment of his three companions, for
they had been so enthralled with the tale that they had not
noted its transformation.

The gem had become a red red rose, one so cold that
it might have been wrought of ice, and when Vivienne
lifted it in marvel, Erik saw the glimmering puddle it left
upon the floor.

"You brought me this," Vivienne said, her smile all the
thanks that he could ever need.

"Your bride price," Erik said, his words uncommonly
hoarse. "Though I am no fairy suitor, and I would offer
you more than three nights of courtship."

Vivienne laughed. "The rose tells no lie, all the same.
We are destined lovers . . ."

"And our paths entwine forevermore," Erik agreed,
just before he claimed Vivienne's lips with a kiss.

For that was a good portent indeed.

*Dear Reader,*

I loved giving Vivienne her happy ending, especially as she had to work for it in overcoming Erik's objections. I hope you enjoyed their story, too. Alexander's tale about the red red rose is one that just fell out of my fingertips—it intrigues me, though, so it will probably turn up in another book about the clan at Kinfairlie.

Next will be Alexander's book, in which Madeline and Vivienne have their vengeance upon him. THE SNOW WHITE BRIDE is a bit different for me: usually my heroes are the ones burdened with dark secrets and my heroines determinedly unravel those mysteries and heal those wounds. This time, it's the heroine who is mysterious. Did Eleanor really kill her last husband? What about her first husband? And what is her scheme for Alexander? As you may have guessed from the title, all it takes is a hero's kiss to make Eleanor question everything she thinks she knows about men.

Please be sure to drop by my virtual home, Chateau Delacroix, at http://www.delacroix.net. Have a cup of mead, warm your feet by the fire, and listen to the gossip in the great hall—and be sure to enter Chestwick's contest to win a free book.

Until next time, happy reading!

More
Claire Delacroix!

Please turn this page
for an exciting preview of

*The Snow White Bride*
and see how the trilogy began with

*The Beauty Bride*

# The Beauty Bride

## *Chapter One*

THE AUCTION OF RAVENSMUIR'S relics promised to be the event of the decade. Madeline and her sisters had spent the short interval between the announcement and the event ensuring that they would look their best. Uncle Tynan had declared it imperative that they appear to not need the coin, and his nieces did their best to comply.

It was beyond convenient that they could pass kirtles from one to the next, though inevitably there were alterations to be made. They might be sisters, but they were scarcely of the same shape! Hems had to be taken up or let down, seams gathered tighter or let out, and bits of embroidery were required to make each garment "new" for its latest recipient.

There were disagreements invariably between each one and her younger sibling, for their taste in ornamentation varied enormously. Madeline preferred her garments plain, while Vivienne savored lavish embroidery upon the hems, preferably of golden thread. These two did not argue any longer—though once they had done so heatedly, for Madeline sorely disliked to embroider and had been convinced as a young girl that it was unfair for her to endure a hateful task simply to please her sister.

Now, they bent their heads together to make Madeline's discarded kirtles better suit Vivienne, while Vivienne's quick needle made short work of any new garb destined for Madeline. Vivienne was also taller than Madeline, even though she was younger, so the hems had to be let out.

Annelise was shorter even than Madeline, so those hems had to be double-folded when a kirtle passed to her. This often meant that the finest embroidery was hidden from view, though this suited Annelise's more austere taste. Isabella, sadly, was nigh as tall as Vivienne, but could not abide golden embroidery. Her hair was the brightest hue of red of all the sisters and she was convinced that the gold of the thread made her hair appear unattractively fiery. When kirtles passed to her, the sisters would couch the gold with silver and other hues, and the kirtles would be resplendent indeed.

Finally, Elizabeth had the last wearing of each kirtle. This had never been an issue, for she seemed wrought to match the height of Isabella perfectly and was not overly particular of taste. Elizabeth was a girl inclined to dreaming, and was oft teased that she gave more merit to what she could not see than what was directly before her.

But there was a new challenge this year, for Elizabeth was twelve summers of age and her courses had begun. With her courses, her figure had changed radically. Suddenly, she had a much more generous bust than her elder sisters— which meant that she turned crimson when any male so much as glanced her way, as well as that Isabella's kirtles did not begin to fit her. There proved to be insufficient fabric even with the laces let out fully to grant Elizabeth an appearance of grace.

Tears ensued, until Madeline and Vivienne contrived an embroidered panel that could be added down each side of the kirtles in question. Isabella, who was the most clever with a needle, embroidered patterns along their length that so matched the embroidery already on the hem that the panel appeared to have been a part of the kirtle all along.

Shoes and stockings and girdles took their own time to be arranged, but by the time the sisters arrived at Ravensmuir and were summoned to the chamber of the auction, no one could have faulted their splendor. They had even wrought new tabards for their brothers, with Alexander's bearing the glowing orb of Kinfairlie's crest on its front, as was now his right.

SO THEY RODE beneath the gates of Ravensmuir, attired in their finest garb. A rider came fast behind them, a single man upon a dappled destrier. He was darkly garbed and his hood was drawn over his helm. Madeline noted him, because he rode a knight's horse but had no squire. He did not appear to be as rough as a mercenary.

Oddly, Rosamunde answered some summons sent by him into the hall. She cried a greeting to this mysterious arrival, then leaned close to hear whatsoever he murmured. Madeline was curious, for she could not imagine what messenger would seek her aunt here, no less what matter of messenger would ride a destrier instead of a horse more fleet of foot. He had but a dog as companion.

"The colors of Kinfairlie suit you well," Vivienne said, giving Alexander's tabard an affectionate tug.

"This work is a marvel!" Alexander declared, sparing his sisters a bright smile. "You all spoil me overmuch, by sharing the labors of your needles." He kissed each of them on both cheeks, behaving more like an elderly gentleman than the rogue they knew and loved. His fulsome manner left the sisters discomfited and suspicious.

"You were not so thrilled at Kinfairlie, when we granted it to you," Vivienne noted.

"But here there are many to appreciate the rare skills of my beauteous sisters."

Years of pranks played by this very brother made all five sisters look over their shoulders.

"I thought you would tickle us," Elizabeth complained.

"Or make faces," Isabella added.

"Or tell us that we had erred in some detail of the insignia," Annelise contributed.

"To grant compliments is most unlike you," Vivienne concluded.

Alexander smiled like an angel. "How could I complain when you have been so blessedly kind?" The sisters stepped back as one, all of them prepared for the worst.

"Do not trust him," Madeline counselled. The two elder sisters shared a nod.

"Alexander is only so merry at the expense of another," Vivienne agreed.

"Me?" Alexander asked, all false innocence and charm.

"Well, at least you are not garbed like a duchess," Malcolm complained. He gestured to the embroidery on his tabard. "This is too lavish for a man training to be a knight."

"At least you do not have to wear this horrendous green,"

Ross said, shaking his own tabard. "I would not venture to name this hue."

"It matches your eyes, fool," Annelise informed him archly.

"We spent days choosing the perfect cloth," Isabella added.

"I surrendered this length of wool for you, Ross," Vivienne said. "And I will not take kindly to any suggestion now that it would make a finer kirtle than a tabard."

Ross grimaced and tugged at the hem of his tabard, looking as if he itched to cast it aside. "The other squires at Inverfyre will mock me for garbing myself more prettily than any vain maiden." He tugged at the tabard in vexation. "What if the Hawk will not take me to his court?"

"You need fear nothing. Our uncle is most fair, and Tynan has sent him a missive already," Madeline said soothingly. Her gaze followed the stranger and Rosamunde as they entered the keep, her curiosity unsated by what she had seen.

"A maiden might take note of you, Ross, if you look your best," Elizabeth suggested shyly. Ross flushed scarlet, which did little to flatter the fiery hue of his hair.

"Our fingers are bleeding, our eyes are aching," Vivienne said with a toss of her tresses. "And this is the gratitude we receive! I expected a boon from my grateful brothers."

"A rose in winter," Annelise demanded.

"There is no such thing!" Malcolm scoffed.

"You should pledge to depart on a quest," Elizabeth suggested. "A pledge to seek a treasure for each of us."

"Sisters," Ross said with a roll of his eyes, then marched toward the nearest ostler.

Madeline had no further time to wonder about the stranger who had summoned Rosamunde. There was the usual bustle of arrival, of horses to be stabled and ostlers running, of squires and pages underfoot, of introductions being made and acquaintances being renewed. The stirrup cup had to be passed, sisters had to dress, and the company had to be gathered.

Soon, the moment would be upon them. The auction that all awaited, the auction that made the very air tingle at Ravensmuir!

"EVERY SOUL IN CHRISTENDOM must be here!" Vivienne whispered to Madeline as they entered the chamber behind Alexander. Dozens of men watched their entry, standing politely aside as the family proceeded to the front of the chamber.

"Not quite so many souls as that," Madeline said. She had felt awkward since their arrival, for men seemed to be taking an uncommon interest in her.

"Perhaps you will find a husband here," Vivienne said with a merry wink. "Alexander is most determined that you choose soon."

"I shall choose in my own time and not before," Madeline said mildly, then knew a way to distract her sister. "Perhaps Nicholas Sinclair will be here," she added, her tone teasing.

Vivienne tossed her hair at the mention of her former suitor. "*Him!* He has not the coin for this."

Alexander stood aside and gestured that Madeline and Vivienne should precede him. He seemed stiff, and uncommonly serious.

"Smile, brother," Madeline whispered to him as she passed. "You will never catch the eye of a merry maid with so sour a countenance."

"The Laird of Kinfairlie must have need of an heir!" Vivienne teased with a laugh.

Alexander only averted his gaze.

"He never remains somber for long," Vivienne said as they sat upon the bench. "Look! There is Reginald Neville."

Madeline spared no more than a glance to the vain boy who imagined himself to be besotted with her. As usual, his garb was not only very fine, but he labored overhard to ensure that all noticed it. Even as he waved to her, he held his cloak open with his other hand, the better that its embroidery might be admired.

"I have only rejected him a dozen times." Madeline's tone was wry. "There might yet be hope for his suit."

"What a nightmare his wife's life will be!"

"And what will he do once he has exhausted the treasury he has inherited?"

"You are always so practical, Madeline." Vivienne edged closer, her voice dropping to a conspiratorial whisper. "There is Gerald of York." The elder sisters exchanged a glance, for that somber and steady man's endless tales put them both to sleep without fail.

"His bride will be well-rested, that much is beyond doubt."

Vivienne giggled. "Oh, you are too wicked."

"Am I? Alexander will turn his gaze upon you next, and demand that you wed soon."

"Not before you, surely?"

"Whyever not? He seems determined to wed all of us in haste."

Vivienne nibbled her lip, her merry mood dispelled. "There is Andrew, that ally of our uncle."

"He is nigh as old as the Hawk of Inverfyre, as well."

"Ancient!" Vivienne agreed with horror. She jabbed her

elbow into Madeline's side. "You might be widowed soon, if you wed him though."

"That is hardly an attribute one should seek in a spouse. And I will wed none of them, at any rate."

The Red Douglas men and the Black Douglas men arrived and took to opposite sides of the hall, all the better to glower at each other from a distance. Madeline knew that Alexander preferred to ally with the Black Douglases, as their father had done, but she could not bear the sight of Alan Douglas, their sole remaining unwed get. He was so fair as to be unnatural. He fairly leered at her, the rogue, and she averted her gaze. Roger Douglas, on the other side of the hall, as swarthy as his cousin was fair, found this amusing and granted her a courtly bow.

Madeline glanced away from both of them. Her heart leapt when she found the steady gaze of a man in the corner fixed upon her. He was tall and tanned, quiet of manner and heavily armed. His hair was dark, as were his eyes. He stood so motionless that her eye could have easily danced past him.

But now that she had looked, Madeline could not readily tear her gaze away. He was the stranger from the bailey, she was certain of it.

And he was watching her. Madeline's mouth went dry.

His hair looked damp, for it curled against his brow, as if he had ridden hard to arrive here. He leaned against the wall, his garb so dark that she could not tell where his cloak ended and the shadows began. His gaze darted over the company at intervals, missing no detail and returning always to her. He stood and watched the proceedings, his stillness making Madeline think of a predator at hunt. The sole bright spot upon his garb was the red dragon rampant emblazoned across the chest of his tabard.

She felt his gaze upon her as surely as a touch and she knew her color rose.

"Look!" Elizabeth said, suddenly between Madeline and Vivienne. "There is a little person!"

"The chamber is full of persons of all size," Madeline said, glad of some diversion to make her look away from the dark stranger.

"No, a very small person." Elizabeth dropped her voice. "Like a fairy, almost."

Vivienne shook her head. "Elizabeth, you are too fanciful. There are fairies only in old tales."

"There is one in this chamber," Elizabeth insisted with rare vigor. "It is sitting on Madeline's shoulder."

Madeline glanced from one shoulder to the other, both of which were devoid of fairies, then smiled at her youngest sister. "Are you not becoming too old to believe in such tales?" she asked.

"It is there," Elizabeth said hotly. "It is there, and it is giggling, though not in a very nice way."

The elder sisters exchanged a glance. "What else is it doing?" Vivienne asked, evidently intent upon humoring Elizabeth.

"It is tying a ribbon." Elizabeth glanced across the chamber, as if she truly did see something that the others did not. "There is a golden ribbon, Madeline, one all unfurled around you, though I do not remember that we put it upon your kirtle."

"We did not," Vivienne whispered, dropping her voice as their Uncle Tynan raised his hand for silence. "Madeline does not like gold ribbons on her kirtle."

Elizabeth frowned. "It is twining the golden ribbon with a silver one," she said, her manner dreamy. "Spinning the two ribbons together so that they make a spiral, a spiral that is gold on one side and silver on the other."

"Ladies and gentlemen, knights and dukes, duchesses and maidens," Tynan began.

"A silver ribbon?" Madeline asked softly.

Elizabeth nodded and pointed across the chamber. "It comes from him."

Madeline followed her sister's gesture and found her gaze locking with that of the man in the shadows again. Her heart thumped in a most uncommon fashion, though she knew nothing of him.

"You should not speak nonsense, Elizabeth," she counselled quietly, then turned her attention to her uncle. Elizabeth made a sound of disgust and Madeline's heart pounded with the conviction that the stranger watched her even as she turned away.

"As all of you are aware, the majority of the treasures will be auctioned on the morrow," Tynan said after he had extended greetings and introduced the family. Rosamunde stood at his side, radiant in her rich garb. "You will have the opportunity in the morning to examine such items as are of interest to you, before the bidding begins at noon. Of course, there will be many more arrivals in the morning." The company stirred restlessly and the sisters exchanged a glance of confusion. "You gentlemen have been specifically invited this night for a special auction, an auction of the Jewel of Kinfairlie."

"I did not know there was Jewel of Kinfairlie," Vivienne whispered with a frown.

"Nor did I." Madeline looked at Alexander, who steadfastly ignored them both.

"I thank you, Uncle," he said, clearly uncomfortable with the weight of the company's attention upon him. "As you all have doubtless ascertained, the Jewel of Kinfairlie is flawless."

"Where is it?" Vivienne demanded and Madeline shrugged that she did not know. A few men leered and she began to have a foul feeling in the pit of her belly.

How could there be such a gem and the sisters know nothing of it?

Alexander turned to face Madeline, and gestured toward her. "A beauty beyond compromise, a character beyond complaint, a lineage impeccable, my sister Madeline will grace the hall of whichever nobleman is so fortunate as to claim her hand this night."

Vivienne gasped. Madeline felt the color drain from her face. The sisters clutched each other's hands.

Alexander turned to the company, and Madeline suspected he could not hold her gaze any longer. "I urge you gentlemen, selected with care and gathered this night, to consider the merits of the Jewel of Kinfairlie and bid accordingly."

"Surely this is but one of his pranks," Vivienne whispered.

Madeline felt cold beyond cold, however. If this was a prank, it required the complicity of many souls. If this was a mere jest, it was difficult to see how it would not compromise Alexander's repute with his neighbors.

But it was beyond belief that he would truly auction her.

To Madeline's dismay, Reginald made the first bid with undisguised enthusiasm.

"Alexander!" Madeline cried in horror.

But her brother granted her a glance so cool as to chill her blood, then nodded to the company that the bidding should continue. He stood so straight that Madeline knew he would not rescind his words.

But to sell her? Madeline's gaze flicked over the company in terror. What if one of these men actually bought her hand?

They seemed intent upon trying to do so. Reginald countered every bid, raising the price with such reckless abandon that his purse must be fat indeed.

The bidding was heated, so heated that it was not long before Gerald of York bowed to Madeline and stepped back into the assembly, flushed with his embarrassment that he could not continue. Madeline sat like a woman struck to stone, shocked at her brother's deed.

Reginald Neville bid again with gusto. Was there a man within this company who could match Neville's wealth? The older Andrew grimaced, bid again, then was swiftly countered by Reginald.

He glared at the boy and shook his head.

"Is that the sum of it?" Reginald cried, clearly savoring this moment. He spun in place, his embroidered cloak flaring out behind him. "Will none of you pay a penny more for this fair prize of a bride?"

The men shuffled their feet, but not a one raised his voice.

"Reginald Neville," Vivienne whispered, her tone incredulous. Her cold fingers gave Madeline's a tight squeeze of sympathy. Madeline still could not believe that this madness was occurring.

"Last chance to bid, gentlemen!" Alexander cried. "Or the Jewel will be wed to Reginald Neville."

Madeline had to do something! She rose to her feet and every man turned to face her. "This would be the moment in which you declare your jest to be what it is, Alexander." She spoke with a calm grace that did not come easily, for her heart was racing.

"It would have been," Alexander said, "had this been a mere jest. I assure you that it is not."

Madeline's heart sank to her very toes, then anger flooded through her with new vigor. She straightened, knowing her anger showed, and saw the dark stranger smile slightly. There was something secretive and alluring about his smile, something that made her pulse quicken and heat rise in her cheeks. "How dare you show me such dishonor! You will not shame our family like this for no good reason!"

Alexander met her gaze and she saw now the steel in his resolve. "I have good reason. You had the choice to wed of your own volition and you refused to take it. Your own caprice brings us to this deed."

"I asked only for time!"

"I do not have it to grant."

"This is beyond belief! This is an outrage!"

"You will learn to do as you must, just as I have learned to do as I must." Alexander lowered his voice. "It will not be so arduous a fate, Madeline, you will see."

But Madeline was not reassured. She would be wed to the highest bidder, like a milk cow at the Wednesday market. Worse, they all found it to be merry entertainment.

Worse again, the highest bidder was Reginald Neville. Madeline could not decide whether she would prefer to murder her brother or her ardent suitor.

She swore with inelegant vigor, thinking it might dissuade Reginald, but the men in the company only laughed. "You are all barbarians!" she cried.

"Oh, I like a woman with spirit," said Alan Douglas, fingering his coins. He offered another bid which was swiftly countered by Reginald.

"No marriage of merit will be wrought of this travesty!" Madeline declared, but not a one of them heeded her. The bidding rose higher even as she stood, trembling with anger. She could hear Vivienne praying softly beside her, for doubtless Vivienne feared that she would face a similar scene soon.

Could matters be worse?

Reginald bid again, to Madeline's dismay. She felt the weight of the stranger's gaze upon her and her very flesh seemed to prickle with that awareness.

No matter who bid, Reginald countered every offer. He urged the price higher with giddy abandon and as the company became slower to respond, he began to wink boldly at Madeline.

"You are worth every *denier* to me, Madeline," he cried. "Fear not, my beloved, I shall be stalwart to the end."

"So long as victory can be achieved with his father's coin," Vivienne said softly.

There were but five men bidding now, the counterbids coming more slowly each time. Madeline could scarce take a breath.

"Out of coin?" Reginald demanded cheerfully as one man reddened and bowed his head, leaving the fray.

Four men. Madeline's mouth was as dry as salted fish.

Roger Douglas thumbed his purse, then outbid Reginald.

Reginald pivoted and upped the bid, fairly daring Roger to counter. That man bowed his head in defeat.

Three men. Reginald's manner became effusive, his gestures more sweeping as he became persuaded of his certain victory. "Come now," he cried. "Is there not a one of you willing to pay such a paltry sum for the Jewel of Kinfairlie?"

Then two men were left, only Reginald and the uncommonly pale Alan Douglas. As much as she loathed Reginald, it was a sign of her desperation that Madeline began to wish that Reginald would triumph. At least Reginald did not frighten her, as Alan did.

Every bid Alan made, Reginald defeated with gusto. He did so quickly, flamboyantly, clearly not caring how much he paid.

But then, Vivienne had spoken aright. It was his father's coin and though there would be no more once it was spent, Reginald showed no restraint in ridding himself of its burden.

Alan frowned, stepped forward and bid again. The company held its collective breath.

Reginald laughed, then topped the bid, his tone triumphant.

There was a heavy pause. Alan glared at Reginald, then his shoulders dropped. He stepped away in defeat, his pose saying all that needed to be said.

"I win! I win, I win, I win!" Reginald shouted like a young boy who had won at draughts. He skipped around the floor, hugging himself with delight.

Madeline watched him with disgust. This was the man she would be compelled to wed.

There had to be some means of escape from Alexander's mad scheme.

Reginald chortled. "Me, me, *me!* I win!"

"You have not won yet," a man said, his voice low and filled with a seductive rhythm. "The winner can only claim his prize when the auction is complete."

Madeline's heart fairly stopped as the dark stranger stepped out of the shadows. Though he was not much older than Alexander, he seemed experienced in a way that Madeline's brother was not. She did not doubt that he would win any duel, that his blade had tasted blood. He moved with a warrior's confidence and the other men created a path for him, as if they could do nothing else.

"He is a fool to wear such an insignia openly," muttered one man.

"Who is he?" Madeline asked. She jumped when Rosamunde spoke from behind her. Her aunt had moved while Madeline had been distracted by the auction.

"The King of England has set a price upon his head for treason," Rosamunde said. "Every bounty hunter in England knows the name of Rhys FitzHenry."

"I daresay every man in Christendom knows of me, Rosamunde," the man in question said with confidence. "Grant credit where it is deserved, at least." He spared Madeline a glance, as if daring her to show fear of him. She held his gaze deliberately, though her heart fluttered like a caged bird.

Rhys then doubled Reginald's bid with an ease that indicated he had coin and to spare.

THE LADY MADELINE WAS PERFECT.

She was the proper age to be the surviving child of Rhys's cousin Madeline Arundel. She shared her mother's coloring and her mother's name. Her supposed family were so anxious to be rid of her without a dowry that they resorted to this vulgar practice of an auction, something no man would do to his blood sister.

And Rhys had to admit that he liked the fire in this Madeline's eyes. She was tall and slender, though not without womanly curves. Her hair was as dark as ebony and hung unbound over her shoulders, her eyes flashed with fury.

Rhys had seen many women, but he had never seen one as beguiling as this angry beauty.

A single glimpse of her had been all it had taken to persuade Rhys that buying Madeline's hand was the most effective solution to his woes.

After all, with Caerwyn beneath his authority, he would have need of a bride to have an heir. And wedding this woman, if she indeed proved to be Madeline's daughter and the sole competing heir for Caerwyn, would ensure that no one could challenge his claim to the holding. He did not fool himself that he had sufficient charm to win the hand of such a bride any other way. Rhys had no qualms about wedding his cousin's daughter, if Madeline proved to be that woman. In Wales, it was not uncommon for cousins to wed, so he barely spared the prospect of their common blood a thought.

Indeed, she would be compelled to wed some man this night, and Rhys doubted that any would grant her the even-handed wager that he was prepared to offer to his bride. Rhys had to believe he could grant a woman a better life than that offered by her family or this irksome boy, Reginald.

Marriage was a perfect solution for both of them.

And so he bid.

And so the chamber fell silent.

It was as simple as that. Madeline would be his.

Rhys strode forward to pay his due, well content with what he had wrought.

The young Laird of Kinfairlie responsible for this foolery spoke finally with vigor. "I protest your bid. You were not invited to this auction and I will not surrender my sister to your hand."

Before Rhys could argue, Tynan granted the younger

man a poisonous glance. "Did I not warn you that matters might not proceed as you had schemed, Alexander?"

Alexander flushed. "But still . . ."

"The matter has passed from your grasp," Tynan said with finality. Rhys knew that Tynan would indeed have cast him out if Rosamunde had not vouched for his character. The lady Madeline had some souls concerned for her future, at least.

"You cannot claim her!" Alexander cried. "I will not permit it."

Rhys smiled a chilly smile and let his gaze drift over the younger man. "You cannot stop me. And you cannot afford to exceed my bid."

The young laird flushed crimson and stepped back with a murmured apology to his sister, which Rhys thought long overdue.

Rhys then turned to the huffing Reginald Neville. "Have you no more coin?"

Reginald's face turned red and he threw his gloves onto the floor. "You cannot have that much coin!"

Rhys arched a brow. "Because you do not?"

Anger flashed in the boy's eyes. "Show your coin before we continue. I insist upon it!" Reginald flung out his hands and turned to the assembly. "Can we trust a man of such poor repute to honor his debts?"

A murmur passed through the company and Rhys shrugged. He sauntered to the high table, removing a chamois sack from within his leather jerkin. The lady caught her breath when he paused beside her and Rhys studied her for a heartbeat. Her eyes were wide, a glorious simmering blue, and though he sensed her uncertainty of him, she held her ground.

It was not all bad that she was as aware of him as this. He

liked the glitter of intelligence in her eyes, as well as the fact that she had tried to halt this folly. He was accustomed to women who spoke their minds and a bride who did as much would suit him well.

He smiled slightly at her, hoping to reassure her, and she swallowed visibly. His gaze lingered upon the ruddy fullness of her lips and he thought of tasting her, knowing then how he would seal their agreement.

But first, the agreement had to be confirmed.

"You need not fear, sir," Rhys said coolly. "I will owe no debt for the lady's hand." There were more than enough gold coins in his sack, but Rhys was not anxious to flaunt his wealth. He cautiously removed only the amount necessary, and stacked the coins upon the board with care. Tynan bent and bit each one of them to test their quality, then nodded approval.

"Then, have her!" Reginald spat in the rushes with poor grace and stormed from the room. His gallantry, in Rhys's opinion, was somewhat lacking.

There was utter silence in the chamber as Rhys reached out and laid claim to Madeline's hand, such silence that he heard her catch her breath. His hand was much larger than hers and her fingers trembled within his grasp.

But she did not pull her hand from his and she held his gaze steadily. Again, he admired that she was stalwart in standing by the terms of agreement. He bent and brushed his lips across her knuckles, feeling her shiver slightly.

Alexander placed a hand upon Rhys's arm. "I do not care for convention or broken agreements. You cannot wed my sister—you are charged with treason!"

Rhys spoke softly, not relinquishing the lady's hand. "Do not tell me that the Laird of Kinfairlie is not a man of his word?"

Alexander flushed scarlet. His gaze fell upon the stack of coins and Rhys knew that he had desperate need of those funds.

He leaned closer to the boy, the lady's hand yet firmly clasped in his own, and dared the new heir of Kinfairlie. He would show the lady, at least, what manner of man her brother was. "I will grant you a chance to rescind your offer, though it is more than you deserve. Reject my coin, but solely upon the condition that the lady shall not be sold to *any* man."

It was clear that the younger man struggled with this decision. He appealed to his sister with a glance. "Madeline, you must know that I would not do this without cause."

And he reached for the coin.

"Cur!" she cried, her scorn matching Rhys's own. Rhys turned to her, his breath catching at the fury that lit her expression. "Take it then, Alexander! Take it, for whatever debts you have, and reject whatsoever loyalty Papa might have thought you owed to your siblings."

Alexander's hand shook slightly as he claimed the coins. "Madeline, you do not understand. I must think of the others . . ."

"I understand as much as I need to understand," she said, her words as cold as ice. "God save my sisters if you think of them as you have thought of me."

"Madeline!"

But the lady turned her back upon her sibling, her bearing as regal as that of a queen, her gaze locking with Rhys's own. He saw the hurt that she fought to hide and felt a kinship with her, for he too had been betrayed by those he had believed held him in regard.

"I believe there is a meal laid to celebrate our pending

nuptials, sir," she said, her words carrying clearly over the hall.

Aye, this bride would suit him well. Rhys lifted her hand in his grip and bent to brush his lips across her knuckles in salute. She shivered and he smiled, knowing their nuptial night would be a lusty one.

"Well done, my lady," he murmured, liking that she was not readily daunted. "Perhaps our agreement should be sealed in a more fitting way."

A beguiling flush launched over the lady's face and her lips parted as if in invitation. Rhys gave her hand a minute tug as the company hooted, and she took a pace closer. He could fairly feel the heat of her breath upon his cheek and her cheeks flushed. Still she did not look away, though her breath came quickly in her uncertainty.

Rhys entwined their fingers, then lifted his other hand to her face. He moved slowly, so as not to alarm her, well aware of her uncertainty. She would be a maiden, without doubt. It would not do to make her fearful of his touch. Rhys tipped Madeline's chin upward with his fingertip. Her flesh was soft beyond belief, her valor admirable. He smiled slightly, saw a spark in her eyes that reassured him as little else might have done. This was no fragile maiden who would fear her own shadow.

Rhys bent and captured Madeline's sweet lips beneath his own. To his satisfaction, the lady did not flinch, nor did she pull away.

Aye, this was a wife who would suit him well.

# The Snow White Bride

## *Chapter One*

~

*Kinfairlie, Scotland—December 1421*

THE SNOW WAS FALLING fast and thick, the starless sky was darker than indigo, when she knew that she could flee no further. The small village that rose before her seemed heaven-sent: it was devoid of tall walls and barred gates. She was skeptical that it truly could be this peaceful anywhere in Christendom, but the town's tranquility soothed her with every successive step.

She saw the church and decided immediately that this sleeping town, with its quiet trust that the world was good, would be her sanctuary.

For one night, at least.

The church portal was unlocked, and she sighed as one last fear was proven groundless. She inhaled deeply of the scent of beeswax candles, the air of prayer and devotion, the silence of a holy place.

Sanctuary.

She slipped through the door and let it close behind her, then leaned her back against the cold wood. There was a single small glass pane over the altar, and the light cast by the snow illuminated it and the central aisle. It was a humble church, to be sure, for she could see its emptiness even in the shadows. The altar was devoid of chalice and monstrance, but perhaps even here, such treasures would be locked away.

She did not care. She found a bench at the front of the church, perhaps one used by the priests, and eased herself onto it. She did not really trust her circumstance until she sat down and stopped running for the first time in what seemed an eternity.

Then she listened.

There was no sound at all. No hoofbeats pounded in pursuit. No hounds bayed as they found her scent. No men shouted that they had spied her footprints in the snow.

The falling snow might prove a blessing, for it would quickly hide her path and disguise her scent. She sat, intending to wait the necessary interval until that point, until she knew that she was safe.

For the moment, at least.

She felt every ache in her exhausted body, and realized only now how cold she had become. She could not feel her fingertips, so she crossed her arms and folded her hands against herself. She supposed that her belly must be empty, but she was too numb to be certain.

She sat and marvelled that she could hear nothing except the faint echo of the sea. Was it possible that they had abandoned the hunt?

She waited and she listened and slowly, she began to be

warmer. She willed herself to wakefulness, but her body had endured too much of late to deny itself the chance to rest. It was not long before she gathered her booted feet beneath her, wrapped her ermine-lined cloak more tightly about herself, and dared to consider sleeping for the first time since Ewen had died.

Although she murmured a prayer, she did not pray for her husband's recently departed soul. She knew that Ewen was lost beyond redemption, she knew that he roasted in Hell. Worst of all, she knew that deep in her heart, she was glad.

On the morrow, she would begin to atone for her wickedness. On this night, she managed only to draw her hood over her fair hair before her eyes closed and she slept.

THERE WAS A STRANGER in Kinfairlie chapel on the first day of Christmas.

The first morning services were attended mostly by the women of Kinfairlie, both from the keep and from the village, for there would be several services this day. Madeline arrived with her sisters: Vivienne, Annelise, Isabella, and Elizabeth. Both Madeline and Vivienne were ripening with child, though the other sisters were yet maidens. They were a noisy party, for Madeline and Vivienne had not been home since their nuptials, and they chattered even as they arrived in the village chapel.

The woman kneeling at the altar started at the sound of their arrival. She caught her breath and glanced over her shoulder, fear etched on her features.

She was so beautiful that Madeline gaped in astonishment.

And she was a stranger.

There were few strangers in Kinfairlie, particularly at this time of the year. Madeline was intrigued, as was probably every other soul who had come to the service.

This woman was no maiden, for she wore a gossamer veil and circlet over her hair. What Madeline could spy of the woman's hair was more golden than flax. In that moment that she stared in terror at the sisters, Madeline noted skin so fair that the woman might have been carved of alabaster. Her eyes were a startlingly vivid hue of green and her lips as red as rubies. She might have been of an age with Madeline.

But the stranger's fear was almost palpable. She pivoted abruptly after scanning the arrivals. She drew the hood of her sapphire cloak over her hair to hide her features, and bent to her prayers once more. Madeline saw her shoulders tremble and wondered what horrors this woman had faced.

The cloak was remarkable in itself, of wool spun finer than fine, and trimmed with a king's ransom in ermine. The stranger was noble, then, for no common person could have afforded such a cloak. Yet she was unattended, and there was no fine horse outside the chapel. Such a woman would not travel on foot, or alone.

Not unless she was in dire peril.

The priest granted the praying woman a benign smile, then frowned at the boisterous sisters. Madeline and her sisters meekly genuflected and became silent as mice as they filed into the chapel. Madeline could fairly feel the questions of her sisters, and was not surprised to find herself edged closest to the stranger.

Who was this woman? What had brought her to Kinfairlie and why had she sought sanctuary in the chapel? Any other noblewoman would have rapped on the gates of the keep and demanded hospitality of a fellow Christian.

But she had no steed. Her boots were mired; there was

dirt on the hem of her cloak. She was trembling and there were circles beneath her eyes. She must have been afraid to ask for help, which said little good about her circumstance.

The service seemed impossibly long, and Madeline found herself thinking more about the stranger beside her than her prayers. Finally, the priest was done and the woman tried to leave the chapel after him.

The sisters had other ideas. They moved of one accord to surround the woman. The stranger jumped when Madeline touched her elbow, even with the barrier of the cloak between them.

"You are a stranger here," Madeline said.

The woman's eyes widened in her uncertainty, though she nodded at the truth of this. "I mean no harm to any soul. I halted only to pray." She tried to leave, but the sisters blocked her passage.

"Someone means harm to you, though," Vivienne said with conviction. "You would not have sought sanctuary in the house of God otherwise."

The woman stepped back. "Who are you, and with whom are you allied?"

"I am Madeline FitzHenry, once of Kinfairlie and now Lady of Caerwyn. These are my sisters. We are gathered to celebrate the Yule together in our ancestral home of Kinfairlie."

The woman's gaze flicked between them. "You must be kin with the Lammergeier."

"That is our family name," Vivienne agreed.

The woman took a deep breath as if to steady herself. "The Lammergeier are said to ally long with no man."

"That is somewhat of a harsh charge from one who does not know us . . ." Isabella began, but Madeline laid a hand upon her arm to silence her. The woman watched warily.

"Of what import is our alliance? Have you need of aid?" Madeline asked. "Do you fear someone who might have allies in these parts?"

"I have need of aid, but I dare not ask it of any soul. The price for assisting me could be too high." She gathered her skirts and made again to leave. "I thank you for your concern, but it would be safer for you to know no more of me."

"And what would be safer for you?" Madeline asked.

The woman halted and glanced back again, then shook her head ruefully. "I mean you no harm."

"Then tell us who you flee and why," Isabella said, always one unafraid of such details.

The woman studied each of them in turn. "How do I know that I can trust you?"

"Who else can you trust?" Madeline asked softly. "You have not so much as a steed, let alone a maid, to accompany you. I wager that you are in danger, and we would offer aid to you."

The woman's strength seemed to falter then, and she looked at the stone floor. Madeline had the sense that the woman fought her tears. She stretched a consoling hand toward her, but then the stranger straightened and tossed back her hair.

She spoke with a resolve though still her voice trembled. "My tale is not that uncommon. My father wed me to a man of his choice, a man far far older than myself. When I was widowed some years later, my father wed me to another such man."

"Who also died," Vivienne said, guessing the next part of the story as she was inclined to do.

"But not before my father himself died. I have no other kin than my husband's family: my mother died long ago and neither of my husbands granted me a child."

"Surely your dowry once again becomes your own?" Isabella asked.

The woman's smile was wry. "Surely not. My husband's kin would have me wed my husband's brother, though I tire of being wed against my will." Something flashed in her eyes then, a determination that was greater than her fear, and Madeline guessed that the woman did not like this brother.

She could not blame her for fleeing.

"It has long been said that a woman weds once for duty and once for love," Vivienne said. "To be wed twice for duty is beyond expectation."

"And against my every desire!" the woman said, her eyes flashing. "I have done all I can to avoid such a fate. I have left my old abode with only the garb upon my back, I have abandoned what should be my own, but it is not sufficient for them. They pursue me, like hounds at the hunt. Indeed, I dare not confess the name of that holding to any soul lest they find me again."

And she shuddered in a way that rent Madeline's heart. What had this unfortunate woman been compelled to endure?

"You have need of protection, not further flight," Madeline said.

"Who would be so fool as to protect me? My husband's kin are powerful."

"A new husband would defend you," Vivienne said.

The woman shook her head. "How could I wed a man in my circumstance? I have no doubt my husband's kin will stop at no evil to see me wed again to one of their own." She swallowed visibly and made to push past the sisters. "I am sorry. I should not have burdened you with my woes, not when you are gathered together in merriment and good health."

"But where will you go?" Elizabeth asked.

"As far as I must to be rid of them," she said, and gathered her cloak about herself as she hastened down the aisle. "I dare not linger here longer." And she stepped quickly away from the sisters.

"We cannot let her go," Madeline said and her sister nodded in agreement. "She will never flee further than they can follow."

"Surely her fears are overwrought," Vivienne said. "They might have threatened her, and they might even follow her, but only a madman would murder any new husband to keep her dowry."

"Doubtless she has fled too long and been alone too much to think clearly," Madeline mused, feeling sympathy for the woman. "I wonder when last she ate a meal."

"Or slept, without fearing that her avaricious kin would come upon her in the night." Vivienne shivered at the thought.

"She has need of a stalwart defender," Elizabeth said with gusto. "Like a valiant knight in an old tale, one who will vanquish all of her enemies."

"It will be a rare and honorable man who takes her cause," Annelise agreed.

"It will be a bold man, unafraid to face any foe to see his lady's safety assured," Elizabeth said, her love of tales evident. "He will slaughter dragons for her, and send evil flying from the gates!"

"There are no dragons to be bested," Isabella said wryly. "Only men with a taste for coin."

Madeline exchanged a smile with Vivienne as an idea apparently came to them both of one accord. "Hmmm," Madeline mused. "A brave knight, unwed and in possession of his inheritance."

"A man with a reputation for ensuring justice is served," Vivienne said as her smile broadened.

"Would it not be perfect if we knew such a man?" Madeline said.

Vivienne nodded. "Especially if the nuptial vows of such a man would ensure that a debt against his own sisters is paid in full?"

Elizabeth began to laugh although Isabella still appeared to be confused.

"Alexander found husbands for us when we had no desire of them," Madeline noted. "I say we return the favor, and aid this beleaguered noblewoman at the same time."

The sisters applauded this course, all delighted with the suggestion. "It would serve Alexander rightly to be compelled to wed," Isabella said as the others nodded.

"But the lady herself must agree," Vivienne said, and they hastened after her.

"Lady!" Madeline cried. "Stay your flight!"

The woman paused and glanced back, as if afraid to hope that any soul might assist her. She clutched the edge of the door, her knuckles white against the dark wood.

"My brother, Laird of Kinfairlie, has need of a bride," Madeline said.

"He is a man of honor," Vivienne said, "and one who will see you protected. He is not so hard upon the eyes, and can be charming."

"He is a bit mischievous," Isabella felt obliged to warn the woman.

"But he takes his responsibilities most seriously and serves Kinfairlie well as its laird," Annelise said.

"But I cannot expect such a man to wed me!"

"Perhaps you can," Vivienne said with a smile. She stepped forward and looped her arm through the other woman's elbow. "Come and look upon him. If he meets with your favor and wedding him seems to you a suitable scheme . . ."

Madeline took the woman's other arm. "Then you may rely upon us to arrange the details."

The hope that dawned in the woman's eyes was all the confirmation Madeline needed that their bold course was the right one. Alexander might try to evade his responsibility to wed, but once this beauty was in his bed, once he had a son to bounce upon his own knee, he would thank her and Vivienne for their aid in finding him such a bride.

Madeline was certain of it.